P9-CSG-381

# CRUEL AS THE GRAVE

Also by John Armistead

*A Legacy of Vengeance*
*A Homecoming for Murder*

# CRUEL
# AS THE
# GRAVE

## JOHN ARMISTEAD

CARROLL & GRAF PUBLISHERS, INC.
NEW YORK

First edition 1996

Carroll & Graf Publishers, Inc.
260 Fifth Avenue
New York, NY 10001

ISBN 0-7867-0303-2

Library of Congress Cataloging-in-Publication Data

Manufactured in the United States of America.

FOR AUDRA AND LAURA

*With special appreciation to Johnny
Finney, Dr. Ben Buchanan, Rudy Dossett,
Susan Callister, and Tommy Green
for special assistance along the way.*

*And again, many thanks to my literary
agent, Evelyn Singer, for encouragement
and wise counsel, and to Sandi, William,
and David for always being there.*

Set me as a seal upon thine heart, as a seal upon thine arm; for love is strong as death; jealousy is cruel as the grave: the coals thereof are coals of fire, which hath a most vehement flame.

—*Song of Solomon 8:6*

# CRUEL AS THE GRAVE

# 1

Narcssc Clouse rushed along the path. She hunched her shoulders and pulled her coat tighter together at the neck. The coat was too thin, but then, all she'd ever had was thin coats. Cheap. In fact, her whole life had been too thin, too cheap.

She bowed her head into a slashing gust of wind and couldn't imagine how cold it was. The ground was hard, the mud ruts of the road frozen, and she hurried, stumbled on. Would it snow today? Maybe it was too cold to snow.

Without looking up, Naresse turned off the road onto a trail leading toward a barn. She had walked to the barn so many times along so many years that she no doubt could have walked it blindfolded.

In fact, she might as well have been blindfolded those many nights with hardly a sliver of moon to guide her as she made her way to the barn. Going back how many years? Over thirty now, was it? Going back to when they were both children almost, only just beginning to feel the heat of love, just understanding the barn was not just a barn and would be for them the secret place of passion and love forever.

*Love is strong as death* he always said. And it was. Strong enough to hold them together on and on even though all reason said it was hopeless. There were others to think of. His wife, her husband. And the children.

She had five children, now all grown up, except for Hugh, but he was already twelve. That's almost grown. She was only a couple years older than that when they came together for the first time.

Five grown children. She smiled. It pleased her to think that out at the Log Cabin young men the age of her daughter Lizzie sometimes hit on her, wanted her. Just last week one young blood said to her, "Naresse, you're the prettiest woman of color in all of Mississippi. No, better'n that. You're the prettiest woman period in all of Mississippi."

She walked inside the barn and moved quickly away from the gaping front doorway, moved to the right side near the steep, narrow stairway that led to the loft. The wind whistled overhead through rafters. "Too thin and too cheap," she mumbled, now moving into a stall. She still held her coat at the neck.

There was a faint musty smell of manure and rotted, damp hay and sweat from years before. How long had it been since an animal had been here? Years. Twenty maybe? How long had it been since old John Farris had died?

No matter. It had been years—twenty or more—and now over thirty since she'd climbed into the loft a girl and an hour later climbed down a woman, and the smell lingered—like the promises, promises which she still clung to but knew would never be kept.

She smiled. She really didn't mind the smell. She never had. The smell floated through her brain mingling sweetly with the smell of sweat and love and a thousand dreams of sunny days to come.

Only those days never did come. It seemed like winter never ended, nor the fear nor the pain; nor could she stop being a mother to their child.

Was that a car? Was he coming? She leaned her face close to a crack between two boards and looked out.

The earth outside was washed with a pale wintry light. A red-tailed hawk soared beyond the gnarled and massive oak that stood near where the house had been. But she heard nothing.

The wind whined as it twisted and swirled through the cavernous room, and she folded her arms across her chest and stamped her feet. She could smell the dust rising from the dry earthen floor.

On that earthen floor they had slow-danced to silent tunes. And, she thought with bitterness, it was the only place we ever danced. Dancing, like just being together, was forbidden.

She looked at her watch. Four forty-two. She'd told him to

meet her at four-thirty. "I don't care what you've got scheduled," she'd told him. "You damn well better be there."

No one in this world could make her angrier than he could. And, at the same time, no one brought her more joy. Not even their child.

Yes, she still loved him, had loved him all these years. He was her Abraham, and she his Sarah. Their love child was always there to remind her of what could have been had things been different. *I am black, but comely, O ye daughters of Jerusalem* . . .

She smiled and moved out of the stall. He used to say that. *Rise up, my love, my fair one, and come away. For, Lo, the winter is past, the rain is over and gone.*

She drew a deep breath and slowly released it, clamping her jaw as she did. But the winter wasn't past. Not this one and not any other. She was suffering through this one like all the rest with cheap, thin coats.

She had always wanted a leather coat. A black leather coat. Long. And maybe she'd get one soon. Maybe with the new raise she'd just gotten at the restaurant she could do that.

Why should she suffer? Why should her child suffer? He needed to take better care of her now more than ever before. She smiled. Her birthday was a week away. She could tell him to get her a leather coat. What would he say to that?

Would she really make good her threats? She wasn't sure. Maybe.

Dammit. Why should another woman enjoy all the warmth and comfort that should have been hers all these years?

Maybe they should have just run off somewheres and said to hell with everyone else. Would he have done that? Would he have left his parents, left everything else he dreamed of? For her?

She glanced toward the loft, toward the back corner. Up there they had played hide and seek when they were children—and up there their child was conceived thirty-two years ago. She knew exactly when that night was. She knew. There was never any doubt in her mind.

It was somehow different that time . . . Always there was

the wildness, the passion, the desperate hunger for each other
. . . But something was different that time, and—

She jerked her head around, looking toward the rear of the
barn, toward the tool room. What was that? A cat? A possum?

She shivered, not from the cold but from a sudden chill that
seized her soul. She should have brought a flashlight. But,
then, she'd never brought a flashlight, neither of them had.
Since childhood, they—

A thud. Something had fallen. The noise definitely came
from the direction of the tool room. Or from the loft above it.

She stepped slowly in the direction of the tool room. "Who's
there?" she called, pausing for a moment.

Silence.

She moved closer. Could he have already come? But why
would he be back there? Her heart was racing, swelling, like it
was going to rip out of her chest.

She moved toward the tool-room door. It was a homemade
door of rough pine planks, unpainted. And halfway opened.

She stood before the door, staring into the darkness. "You
there?" she whispered, knowing as she did that no one else
could have heard even if she'd yelled.

She started. She thought she saw a movement in the darkness, or maybe it was a breath of a sound.

"Who's . . ." Then her eyes widened. "N-no . . ." she
gasped. "Please . . . no . . ."

# 2

On January ninth, the third anniversary of her mother's death, Lizzie Clouse parked her automobile in the graveled parking lot on the west side of the Mt. Carmel Missionary Baptist Church in the Hebron community. The day was cold but sunny, and a clear, wintry blue sky stretched overhead from horizon to horizon.

No one was at the church, of course, not even Reverend Doffey. It was, after all, Monday afternoon.

Lizzie thought again about how kind and good the pastor had been to her family in those horrible days following her mother's death. He didn't say much. He didn't have to. Just his strong presence helped shoulder them through it.

She knew he was grieving along with them. He'd been a friend of her mother's since childhood. Lizzie had often heard her mother laugh and say maybe she should have married James Doffey and been a preacher's wife. "Now wouldn't that be the damnedest mess you ever seen?" she'd ask.

Lizzie got out of the car. As she shut the door, she thought again how she wished her mother could have seen this car. Naresse Clouse loved nice things, but never had much.

But she would have loved this car. A turquoise Mitsubishi Eclipse. Only one year old. Lizzie had bought it from Wayne Carr just before Christmas.

Wayne Carr, like her mother and Reverend Doffey, had grown up in the Hebron community. He owned several businesses, and was one of the town's wealthiest black citizens. Folks said he had the Midas touch, that anything he got involved in made him money.

7

One of his concerns was a used car business. He told Lizzie he was giving her a special deal. "For Naresse's sake," he said.

She'd always dreamed of having a car like this. And of taking her mother for a ride. Sometimes when driving along she'd think about that and the hurt thrust in, quick, and the bitter anger would choke her again, anger at whoever it was that shot Naresse Clouse in the face three years ago and hung up her body inside an old barn on the Farris place.

She couldn't think of anyone she knew who was vile and vicious enough to do such a thing. But, whoever he was, she wished to God he could be tormented himself, that he could taste the pain she felt, be punished again and again as she had during these past three years.

The sheriff, for some idiotic reason, couldn't seem to get past suspecting her father of the murder. He wouldn't look in any other direction. And no one was ever arrested. No one.

She heard a crow. Otherwise, all was quiet. She had not looked at the barn as she'd driven past a few moments ago. She couldn't help thinking about it, of course, just like you couldn't help thinking about a dog snarling at you across the road as you walked past even though you didn't look at it.

But, even before that day three years ago, the barn frightened her. She had to pass it every time she came to church. And she always looked at the woods on the other side of the road as she went by, even as a child.

The barn belonged to a white family who'd been good friends of her family even before her mother was born. It hadn't been used in years. Matthew Farris and his wife Esther lived in town and never came out to the old place anymore.

Matthew was another longtime friend of her mother's who'd been there for them. His wife Esther, however, was cool and distant. Lizzie had heard her mother say several times that she couldn't understand why in the world Matthew married her. What could he have seen in her? Esther Farris might be a famous photographer but she had the personality of a salamander. Or maybe a mud snake.

For some reason Lizzie always thought of snakes when she thought of the barn, of snakes slivering around on the floor inside, crawling in the loft along the beams. She had nightmares about the barn for years, and always there were the snakes.

Snakes, and her mother's stern warning not only to her but to Cynthia and Shamona as well. "Stay away from that barn. Don't ever, ever go there. Something terrible will happen to you if you do."

But it wasn't any of them that something terrible happened to, but her mother. What in the world was her mother doing there anyway? It was something that had never been answered by the sheriff's people or anyone else.

Mama 'Dele, Lizzie's grandmother, silenced all questions with a stern, "Let it alone, child. Let the dead rest in peace. And, Lord knows, your mama got precious little of it in her life. Let it alone."

Lizzie buttoned two of the buttons on her long black leather coat as she walked across the rear parking lot of the church, the gravel scrunching beneath her feet, and into the cemetery. H. C. Curry had given her the coat Christmas before last. She'd mentioned to him several times how much she liked this kind of coat, not so much thinking maybe he'd buy her one, as remembering how much her mother had wanted one.

There were two days that Lizzie felt she needed to visit her mother's grave. One was the day her mother died, and the other was her mother's birthday. Her birthday was only a week after her death day. Lizzie still had the unopened bottle of perfume she'd gotten for her three years ago. She's bought it the Saturday before she was killed.

The cemetery was hilly, and the ground soft from the rains. Mt. Carmel was originally a plantation church. The property was given to the newly freed slaves who still worked on the place right after the Civil War. Some of the grave markers showed birthdates going back to the 1840's.

Lizzie made her way around a low, crumbling brick wall that enclosed a family plot, and stopped before a two-foot-high black granite marker. Her eyes traced each curve and angle of each symbol once again, almost feeling the hardness of the stone without having to touch it.

NARESSE WINTER CLOUSE
Born January 16, 1941
Died January 9, 1992
"Asleep in Jesus"

Lizzie kneeled at the side of the stone and repositioned the blue vase that the wind had knocked over. She gathered the plastic red and yellow zinnias and slipped them back into the vase.

She didn't like plastic flowers, but she knew her fifteen-year-old younger brother Hugh had placed them there. So they'd stay.

She stepped back, looked briefly at the cement block marker to the left of her mother's. It was the grave of an uncle of her mother's, Mama 'Dele's brother. His name, Evans Winter, had been etched with a nail into the still-wet cement fifty years ago.

She looked again at her mother's stone. "Oh, Mama," she said. "I miss you so much."

She was so pretty and so full of life. And Lizzie, as a girl, had always dreamed of being as pretty as her mother. Her older sister Cynthia was. Everybody said Cynthia looked just like Naresse.

But it was Lizzie who had the same intense drive as their mother. Naresse Clouse started out in the kitchen washing dishes at the Wisteria Inn and worked her way up to assistant manager. She knew as much about running the place as the manager, Keesa Hudnall, ever thought about knowing, Naresse often said.

Lizzie heard another crow with its warning cry, and lifted her eyes to look at the trees which pressed to the edge of the cemetery clearing. It was a thick, tangled forest in which a small creek twisted back and forth.

As children, they played at the edge of the forest, venturing through a tangled web of vines and stepping onto the fern-blanketed floor beneath a canopy of tree limbs and into a world of the imagination every bit as wonderful as Alice's. Sometimes, when the church family gathered for dinner-on-the-grounds, there was plenty of time to play hide-and-seek along the steep banks of the creek. Her older brother Isaac always found some way to torment her and her sisters.

She remembered a particular cave sucked up under the bank at a sharp bend of the creek. She'd found it years ago and hid out there time and time again. The opening was concealed by a cluster of huckleberry bushes. She wondered if it was still there.

The sound of a vehicle on the road drew her attention from the distant past and the woods in front of her. She turned toward the parking lot.

A yellow Mercedes pulled off the road, halted for a moment near the butane tank on the side of the church, then rolled slowly to the edge of the cemetery and stopped behind her car. The door swung open, and a white man got out.

Lizzie had never seen him before. What was he doing here? White people never stopped at the church. Was he lost?

The man was wearing a camel-hair top coat, and his balding head seemed especially pale. He was tall and paunchy, probably in his fifties, she guessed. He stood looking her way. He took out a cigarette, lit it, and nodded at her. Then he began walking in her direction.

She glanced back at her mother's grave, then back at the man. What could he want? He came quickly across the cemetery.

He grinned as he drew closer, coming forward until he was only a short distance away. "Cold, isn't it?" he asked.

She nodded. "Yes." He had an accent, like he was from someplace else. The North maybe.

He turned slightly back toward the parked cars. "I see you bought your car from Wayne Carr in Sheffield."

Lizzie nodded, but didn't speak. She really didn't care to get into a conversation with some strange white man out here at Hebron. Again, she reminded herself this was Monday and neither Reverend Doffey nor anyone else would be dropping by. She was all alone.

Almost as if he read her discomfort, the man said quickly, "I was just riding by and saw the church." He took a deep draw of his cigarette, blew the smoke away from her direction as if they were inside a room, then said, "Wayne's a friend of mine. I know his sister Addie, too."

Lizzie immediately felt a bit easier. The man would have seen Wayne Carr's name on the sticker on the trunk of her car. But he mentioned Wayne's sister Addie. How in the world would he know her?

He looked toward the dark grave marker in front of her. "Naresse Winter Clouse," he read. "Is she a relative of yours?"

"She was my mother."

"Then you must be Shamona's sister," he said, smiling at her.

Lizzie started at the mention of her sister's name.

"Shamona applied for a job with our company," he said. "I interviewed her." He paused and nodded. Then shrugged. "Something might work out. She seems like she wants to work." He took another draw on the cigarette, then spoke through the exhaling smoke. "And you are . . .?"

She ran her tongue over her dry lips. "Lizzie . . . Lizzie Clouse." She looked back at the tombstone, more to avoid having to continue looking at this man's probing, direct gaze.

"Are you Patterson's daughter?"

"Yes," she said. Maybe he's from the college. Her father worked at the college.

He looked toward the marker. "She was mighty young," he said, obviously reading the dates chiseled into the stone.

Lizzie nodded.

"How did she die?"

She swallowed, then said, "Someone killed her." She really didn't care to discuss her mother's tragedy with a strange white man.

"Who did it?"

Her jaw tightened. She didn't answer for a moment, then said, "We don't know."

"I see." He dropped his cigarette to the ground, stepped on it with his foot, and ground it out. "Where did it happen?"

She slowly shook her head. "At a barn near our home."

The man turned to glance over his shoulder back toward the cars. He asked, "And you have no idea why anyone would want to kill her?"

Lizzie drew a quick breath through her open mouth, and released it. She was becoming more and more aggravated with this man pushing his way into her private family matters. Nevertheless, she answered, "No." And, even as she said that, she fought back the thought that some people, including Sheriff Bramlett, had definite ideas about the murder, even though no one could prove anything.

"You said a barn?" He glanced over his shoulder again, almost as if he thought someone might be coming or that he heard something.

"It's a barn near our house on the Farris property," she said, again not knowing why she was offering so much information.

"And that's near here?"

She nodded, wondering now why in the world this white man was way out here in the middle of nowhere. There was not a white family on this road for several miles.

He nodded thoughtfully. "That would be the family of Matthew Farris?" he asked.

She nodded. "Are you from the college, too?"

He gave a crooked smile. "No, but I know Matthew."

Somehow the mention of Matthew's name made her a little more comfortable. The Farris family farm was on the other side of the road from her daddy's farm. Her father still did some Saturday work in town for Matthew. For Esther really. Yard work. It was a curious thing, but her father liked Esther, said she was good to him, a fine Christian woman. Lizzie sure couldn't see it. There was no doubt in her mind that Esther Farris despised them all.

The man had a curious look on his face as he stared at her. "You used to go to that barn as a child, didn't you?" he asked.

"What?" The question startled her.

He grinned and looked away. "Never mind," he said. "Just something I remembered."

She hunched her shoulders and looked up at the sky. Why was he asking all these questions?

He turned his head back to her, nodded as if reading her mind, looked back to the gravestone, and nodded again. "Well, Lizzie Clouse," he said. "I'm guessing that you saw something you shouldn't have." He gave a low laugh. "Yes, I bet you could really scare somebody to death." He chuckled as if he'd made a joke.

"What . . . ?" she asked.

The smile remained in place. "Maybe we'll talk later," he said.

He took out his cigarette package, shook free another cigarette and put it to his lips. Then, cupping a match in both hands, he lit it, inhaled deeply, smiled at her again and abruptly turned and walked away.

Lizzie watched him as he moved toward the two automobiles, puzzled at his last words, almost wanting to call after

13

him and ask him to explain what he meant; but, at the same time, she wasn't really sure she wanted to know.

She watched the yellow Mercedes back around and leave the church parking lot, and it occurred to her that the man hadn't said his name.

That evening after supper, Rory Hornsly mixed himself a second bourbon and water. He swirled the ice cubes around in the glass with his finger as he walked across the living room to his desk. The apartment was nice, comfortable, but just temporary. Hornsly was building a 3,200-square-foot French colonial house in Lakeside Villas, a newer, very upscale residential section of Sheffield.

To be sure, a four-bedroom house was a bit much for someone who lived alone, but he would enjoy the space. Fortunately, his carpenters had gotten the place blocked in before the winter rains began. If nothing went awry, he should occupy his new home in less than two months. The kitchen cabinets were scheduled to go in next week.

The house was expensive, but, then again, so was everything Rory Hornsly possessed. Nothing cheap appealed to him. Not cheap clothes or cars or women or houses.

And expensive meant money—and lots of money—had to come in. More money than he was making with the company.

It was a good outfit to work for. They'd treated him right. When a new plant was to be opened in northeast Mississippi, the company had given him first option of returning to his native state if he wanted. He took it.

After living in California some thirty years—getting married, having a family, getting a divorce, marrying again, another divorce—he'd never really thought much about returning home. After all, except for his butt-head brother living in Oxford, he had no relatives here anymore. And his son and family were in California.

That was the hardest part of leaving, not seeing his grandkids regularly. He'd just been back at Christmas to visit them, but it wasn't the same as being there all the time.

Nevertheless, the opportunity to move back had unexpectedly presented itself. And he grabbed it.

These last couple of years had been good. He not only had

his work for the company, but several other deals cooking here and there.

When running so many operations on the side, it's to be expected that one of them will occasionally go sour. After all, that's why they're called high risk.

High risk means the possibility of a quick return. But, and everyone understands this, it also means there's the possibility one can lose his ass. It's like gambling.

Well . . . not really as risky as gambling over on the river, but gambling nonetheless. That's what made it so exciting.

If Roach wanted something totally safe and secure, he should have just put his money in the bank. Of course, with interest rates as low as they are today, you might as well keep your money hidden in a sock somewhere.

Hornsly sat down at the desk, turned on the computer, and took a slow sip of his drink while he waited for it to come up. Then he placed his right hand on the mouse, moved and clicked it, entered a password, then watched as the review of his investors in the Union County operation came into view.

So what's this guy's problem? All of these people knew there was risk involved. They wanted a quick profit, wanted to pay no damn taxes on it, get in and get out quick. Bam, bam, thank you ma'am. That fast. Roach knew that before he gave him the money. What's all the crying about?

Would he go to the authorities? Who knows? Most people wouldn't want anyone to know they were dealing like this— but then again, stupid is as stupid does.

He took another sip of his drink, and thought about how fortunate he was to have stumbled onto this Narcsse Clouse thing. God almighty! This is dynamite. This was as good as money in the bank.

A couple of days ago, he was beginning to sweat all the threats. But suddenly, like a gift from heaven, this thing about her death falls into his lap.

And today . . . how lucky can you get? He wanted to see the barn he's heard so much about for himself and check the grave so he could confirm the dates . . . and then he runs into her other daughter at the cemetery. What was her name? Lizzie, was it? He couldn't be sure, of course, that the barn where she was killed was *the* barn, but maybe . . .

Everything comes to him who waits. This might not just get

them off his back but even be good for a few thou more. Who knows? That barrel ain't empty by no means.

He laughed out loud, picked up the telephone, and punched in the numbers. The call was answered on the third ring.

"It's me," Hornsly said, purposely trying to let the heavy confidence of his voice be felt. "Do you think it will *snow*. After all, it is *winter*, isn't it." He paused and chuckled.

There was silence on the other end of the line.

"You listen to me and listen real good," Hornsly continued. "I know all about dear, sweet Naresse. You and I need to talk again real soon. I've met both Shamona and Lizzie." He paused to let this sink in, then said, "It was Lizzie, wasn't it? She's the one who saw you. I know it was." He made a clicking sound with his tongue. "What if I'm just speculating now, but what if she remembers suddenly after all these years? What if some-one *helps* her remember?"

He chuckled again. "The fact is, anything that's covered up, no matter how snug, can get uncovered. You think about it. If we want to suddenly get down and dirty, then by all means let's get down and dirty."

The line buzzed dead. No matter. He'd been hung up on plenty of times before. You don't go far in sales without learn-ing to handle rejection.

He replaced the receiver. But this wasn't really rejection. This was terror that he'd just stabbed into somebody's heart. Absolute terror. He chuckled and lifted his glass again. And absolute terror is worth no telling how much money in the bank or sock or wherever. It was a good feeling.

# 3

Sheriff Grover Bramlett pushed open the heavy glass front door of Still Waters Nursing Home, stepped outside and took a deep breath of the cold, fresh night air. His appetite suddenly came out of hiding, and he wondered what Valeria was fixing for supper.

He'd lost his appetite once again when he'd gone inside the nursing home. There were precious few times when Bramlett's body couldn't use some food, any kind of food (one of his fondest philosophies was that there was no bad food, only bad cooks), but as soon as the smell of urine and helplessness slapped him in the face, his stomach did a half roll. Each time.

No doubt the fact that his eighty-five-year-old mother Regina Bramlett was Still Waters's newest resident had a lot to do with his feeling. In forty years of law enforcement, he'd seen plenty enough to make a stomach do flip flops, things the average citizen hadn't begun to see in the most horrible movie on TV, but all those things he'd seen didn't involve his mother.

It's a terrible thing to have to put your own mother in a nursing home. Taking her from the farmhouse in which she'd been born, and in which she herself had given birth to six children, was undoubtedly the hardest thing Bramlett had ever done in his life. But she'd gotten so much worse in the last few months.

She'd left the stove on one day and if his sister hadn't come in from Meridian when she did, no telling what might have happened. She reluctantly consented, then, to leave the house.

Regina Bramlett immediately regretted her decision. She hated everything about Still Waters. "The food is from tin cans," she told him each day when he came to see her.

"There's nothing but crazy people here. Who's watching out for my cows? What about my chickens?"

The only thing she found halfway acceptable was a black preacher named James Doffey who had visited with her yesterday afternoon. "He's the only one with a heart I've met in this hellhole," she told Bramlett.

He half turned his back to the stabbing wind coming out of the northwest and hurried across the parking lot to his Corvette. The Corvette had been seized from a dope pusher, converted into a departmental vehicle, and taken by Bramlett to use himself, perhaps, if the truth be known, because every deputy lusted after it.

How was he to know it was a butt-cramper, definitely not designed for larger people? He needed to swap back for a car like his old one, but he hadn't quite figured out what he'd tell the department's administrator, Robert Whitehead, was the reason he didn't want it anymore.

In less than four minutes he drove from the nursing home across town to his own house, parked in the carport, and walked into the kitchen. He patted his wife Valeria on the rump and kissed her on top of the head.

Valeria was taking flatware out of the drawer to set the table. "How is she?" she asked.

He shrugged his shoulders as he slipped his revolver from his belt and placed it on top of the refrigerator. "She hates it. She thinks I'm a terrible son."

"She said that?"

"No, but she thinks it. I know."

"There's supposed to be a hard freeze tonight and sleet. If she was still at home, she'd be up in the morning trying to check on those cows and probably fall and break a hip."

He sighed. "I know, I know," he said, walking into the den. Knowing that, however, did nothing to make him feel any better.

He eased himself down into his recliner, picked up the TV remote control and turned on the weather channel. Someday the girls would be trying to make him stay in some piss-smelling hellhole, he reckoned. He'd rather be shot by a bootlegger.

The picture came into view on the screen. A bad snowstorm in New England. Then the local weather. A hard freeze. The high for tomorrow wouldn't climb to forty.

Damn, damn, damn. It's only January. Spring is a lifetime away.

He looked up at the framed and matted photograph hanging on the paneled wall above the television set. It was a scene of early springtime in the woods, woods like he'd strolled through hundreds of times.

The focal point of the picture was a dogwood tree in full bloom. Sunlight bathed the white petals and made them dance with life. Old hardwoods, not yet in full leaf, stood around the dogwood. And at the base of the dogwood, peeking out from the blanket of winter's fallen leaves, was an old rusting tin can of some sort, perhaps more like a small bucket.

Probably from a couple of decades ago when a farmer's small cabin stood nearby before the land and strength were sucked dry.

Bramlett leaned back in the recliner and sighed. He longed for the blooming of dogwoods, the end of the freezing nights, and days of continual sunshine. He longed to take his new French easel and tramp out into the woods, set up his water-colors and paint for hours, one sheet after another.

Winter was a bummer. It seemed every bone in his high-mileage body ached more than usual. Maybe it was more than just the cold. Maybe—

Valeria stepped to the doorway. "Supper's almost ready," she said. She was frowning.

"What?" he asked. He hoped she wasn't going to start in on him again about why he didn't have any female deputies. He told her it was just a matter of no woman ever having applied; he didn't have anything against hiring women.

"I'm worried about Sylvia," she said, referring to Sylvia Mapp, her sister who lived down in Grant County. Sylvia was already a widow and continued to run her farm. "I think she's seeing some man."

Bramlett smiled. "Good," he said. "She's barely sixty. The fire ain't out yet."

"Watch yourself, Grover Bramlett."

He chuckled. "I only meant—"

"I know what you meant," she said, her face immediately flushing. He delighted in teasing her.

"You never listen," she said, turning back to the kitchen.

19

Good for Sylvia, he thought. Good for anyone who can find some warmth as life spins on into its wintertime.

He looked at the photograph of the dogwood in full flower once again. Everybody needs a little warmth. Because it just gets colder and colder the more into winter you go . . .

Rory Hornsly groaned and squinted his eyes open, looking into the blackness of the room. What the hell . . .?

It was the telephone. Ringing.

He reached to the night table, fumbled with the receiver, dropped it to the floor, groaned again, pulled it up to his hand by the cord, put it to his ear and mouth, then said, "What?"

"Mr. Hornsly?"

He tried to focus his mind, tried to push back the webs of sleep. His body ached with stiffness. "Who is this?" he asked. His mouth was chalky.

"Mr. Hornsly, someone is fooling with your car. I think they're trying to steal it. I've already called the police."

"What?" He sat upright in the bed, reaching for the lamp switch. "Who is . . ." The line disconnected.

He threw off the covers and rose to his feet. "Dammit to hell," he said with a snarl. He had a nice apartment, but he, like all the other residents, had to park in a unprotected lot. Last month somebody had keyed the left side of his car. Someone told him it might be gang related.

The apartment complex didn't even have a security man. Dammit. He would be so glad to get his house finished and move out of here.

He snatched open the bottom drawer of the chest of drawers, felt around under his sweaters till he touched the pistol, then quickly checked the clip. Fully loaded.

He shoved the clip back in place, pushed his feet into his slippers and hurried out the front door of his apartment.

The freezing air ripped right through his pajamas when he stepped out of the building.

God almighty! Why hadn't he at least put on a robe. The pavement was wet. Rain drizzled down through the reddish glow of the security light near where he'd parked his car.

Hornsly hurried forward. He could see his car. They hadn't gotten it yet.

He didn't see anyone. Maybe they were already inside the car trying to get it started.

He held the pistol in front of him, the fingers of his left hand clutching around his right hand holding the weapon, his finger already slightly depressing the trigger. He walked more slowly now, nearing the car.

He stopped about ten feet from the Mercedes, noticing, of all things, he said to himself, how the rainwater beaded on the roof, giving evidence of a good wax job. Damn. Why would he even think to notice something like that when some bastard was inside his car tearing out the wiring?

He couldn't see anyone inside the car. The parking lot streetlight reflected on the tops of the car seats. Were they bending over by the floorboard?

He took a couple steps closer, then quickly looked around to the left and then to the right. He didn't see anyone. Maybe they had just tried to steal his radio and left. Damn. Why didn't he have an alarm on his car? If you pay forty thousand dollars for a car, you damn well ought to buy an alarm.

Hornsly was sweating in spite of the cold. In fact, he'd forgotten the cold for a moment. He swallowed the thickness in his throat, and, pointing the pistol at the window of the vehicle, moved even closer.

He saw no indication that anyone was near the car. The doors were locked. He didn't think to grab the keys when he rushed out.

The headlights of a vehicle not far away came on. The car eased forward, toward him. It was a late-model Buick, light gray. Hornsly tensed for a moment. Was this someone just coming in? Or leaving? Had they seen somebody messing with his car?

The car stopped beside him, and the rain-slicked driver's window slid down.

Hornsly leaned forward. Was this someone he knew? "What the—"

A flash of light and a thudding sound pierced into Hornsly's brain. He gasped and thought someone had punched him in the chest. Then, bam bam bam, and he reeled backward trying to keep his balance. His pistol slipped from his fingers.

He spun around toward his car, trying to lift his hands to

grab the fender, but his arms wouldn't move. He sank to his knees, then plunged head first to the pavement.

He could hear the vehicle driving away, and he was aware that his face and teeth were pressing into the wet, rough asphalt.

He felt like he was floating, spinning, falling softly on and on. He could hear voices, shouting, then someone screaming.

He felt hands pulling at him, turning him over. Floating. A siren. Then he was drifting, farther and farther away . . .

# 4

When the telephone rang, Sheriff Grover Bramlett groaned, opened one eye and looked at the illuminated dial on the bedside clock. Four twenty-eight.

Valeria got up with him, made coffee while he shaved, then, after he was dressed and had put on his hat, she stood at the door to the carport with his coffee in one hand and a glass of Slimfast in the other. For several weeks, ever since Dr. Bill Jourdan said he ought to lose twenty-five to fifty pounds, she'd given him Slimfast for breakfast.

He took the coffee and Slimfast from her, set both on the small table beside the door, and put his arms around her and squeezed and lifted her up off the floor at the same time. He growled and said, "Maybe they could get along without me for another half hour."

She laughed and hit him on the shoulder with her fist. "Put me down, you dirty old man," she said. "Go to work."

She opened the door as he picked up the cup and the glass, and closed it after him. She, of course, thought he was joking. The fact was, however, that even after thirty-seven years of living with that woman, just touching her hand or looking at her excited him.

He shuddered at the outside cold, yet felt warm inside as he walked beside the car. He glanced over his shoulder at the closed rear door, then poured the glass of Slimfast into the planting bed beside the carport before getting into the car with his coffee.

Bramlett pulled into the parking lot of the Vers la Maison, Sheffield's most upscale apartment complex, and parked behind a Chakchiuma County patrol car with blue and white

23

lights flashing. Two other patrol cars were also on the scene, as well as an ambulance from County General. A crowd of curious onlookers stood near the building's entryway.

He glanced at his watch. Just after five. He grunted as he pulled himself up out of the Corvette. Maybe the next crack dealer would be driving a full-size car and—

" 'Morning," Deputy H. C. Curry greeted him with a half-yawn. Curry had a crime scene sketchbook in his hand.

The sheriff knew it was very early for his young associate. Curry was single, and, even though he still lived at home with his parents, tended to get together with buddies in the evenings and drink a few beers.

In fact, the sheriff worried about his young friend's drinking. He worried because Curry was one of the three deputies he depended on most. The other two were Johnny Baillie and Jacob Robertson.

"What do we have?" Bramlett asked. He hadn't even had a chew yet, and wouldn't until he'd had a decent breakfast at the Eagle Café.

"White male. Shot several times, apparently. Other residents report hearing four or five shots. His name is Hornsly. Worked in Tupelo. No one seems to know much about him. Kept to himself."

"Any witnesses?"

Curry shook his head. "No, sir. Only a few people who report hearing the gunfire. There was a weapon beside the body. Doesn't seem to have been fired. A Beretta twenty-five caliber auto. We'll check it out."

"Let's have a look," Bramlett said, moving toward a cluster of deputies.

Curry led the sheriff to the side of a Mercedes where a pajama-clad body sprawled on the pavement. Dr. Greg Thompson, medical examiner-investigator for Chakchiuma County, was bending over the man. Deputies Johnny Baillie and Jacob Robertson held flashlight beams on the victim's face.

Both young men nodded in greeting at the sheriff.

"I assume he lived here?" Bramlett asked.

"Yes, sir. The apartment manager is standing over there," Curry said, nodding toward a group of people on the other side of the Mercedes. "He says the guy lived alone. He moved here from California, he thinks. At any rate, he said, he gets a lot of mail from California."

"Oh?" Bramlett said with a chuckle. "And how would he know that?"

Dr. Thompson stood up and smiled at Bramlett. "Well, Grover. Are we interfering with your morning jog?"

Bramlett grunted and didn't bother to reply.

"Zip him up," Dr. Thompson said. He peeled the latex gloves off his hands. "Multiple wounds. Close range. I'll get to him later this afternoon."

"This afternoon?" Bramlett asked. The irritation in his voice was obvious.

The doctor shrugged. "Got plenty of living sick folks to take care of first, Grover. He ain't gonna get any sicker." He laughed at his own joke and walked away. Two paramedics stepped forward to take care of the body.

"This is his vehicle," Deputy Baillie said. "We've already run a check on the tag. It's registered to Rory C. Hornsly of this address."

Bramlett felt the chilly morning air tingling on his face. "Jacob, get some men ready to search the whole area as soon as there's a little more light. Might have a weapon in the weeds off the side of the street somewheres. I assume we've already got the names of the folks who heard shots?"

"Drumwright is working on it," Curry said, indicating Steve Drumwright, another investigative deputy. "You want to take a look in his place?" He jerked his head toward the apartment building.

"Sure," Bramlett said, turning to Curry. "Where's that manager?"

Timothy Worley, manager of the Vers la Maison apartments, let them into Unit 28 on the second floor. Worley looked to Bramlett to be in his early thirties, was thin with blond, receding hair, and wore a brown aviator-style leather jacket with his shirttail hanging out below it.

"I can't believe this is happening," he said as he pushed open the door and stood to one side so the lawmen could enter the apartment. "We've never had any problems. This is a nice, quiet neighborhood. Our tenants pay good money to live in a safe place." He shook his head. "I can't believe it."

They stepped into a large room with off-white walls and beige wall-to-wall carpet and large, comfortable-looking furniture. The abstract paintings on the wall in metal frames, the heavy curtains on the windows, and the tall Oriental vase on a small table to one side testified to good taste and money.

Bramlett turned to H. C. Curry and grinned. "Since you're looking for an apartment, maybe this one will do," he said.

Curry snorted. "Maybe if you can get the county supervisors to raise my salary, I can afford it."

"Ask the man what it costs," Bramlett said.

Curry ignored him.

"It's a two-bedroom apartment," Worley said, following Bramlett into the middle of the room. "In fact, all of our apartments are the same size. We allow pets but no children."

Johnny Baillie went into one bedroom and H. C. Curry into another. Both had slipped transparent latex gloves on their hands.

"He lived alone, you said?" Bramlett asked.

Worley nodded. "Yes. He worked in Tupelo, which I found strange. I mean, why didn't he just get a place to live there?"

"Where did he work?"

"One of those furniture factories. I can't remember which one. I'll have to check my records in the office. We have all that kind of information."

"What about friends? Visitors?"

Worley shook his head. "Not many. Occasionally, a woman stopped by."

"Can you give us a name?"

He slowly shook his head. "She came at night. She'd stay a while. Then she'd be gone. She drove a Blazer."

"What about anybody here at the building? Anybody seem especially friendly with Hornsly?"

"John Packard. He's in number fifteen. I saw them together occasionally."

"Anybody else?"

"Not that I can think of."

Johnny Baillie came out of a doorway. "Looks like he used this room for an office," he said. "Desk, filing cabinet, papers."

"And this is the bedroom," H. C. Curry said, emerging from the other doorway. "Covers tossed back. Lamp on."

"And he went outside in his pajamas and slippers when it's almost freezing," said Bramlett.

Neither deputy commented. Bramlett turned to the manager. "We appreciate your help, Mr. Worley. I'm sure we'll need to talk with you some more."

The man made no motion to leave; rather stood looking at the deputies now opening drawers of the small tables in the living area.

"I'll let you know when we're through," Bramlett said, motioning with his hand toward the front door.

Deputy Steve Drumwright entered the apartment. Drumwright was an eager young man in his early thirties with, as Valeria once described him to Bramlett, dark good looks. "Five people say they heard the shots," he said to Bramlett. "One says she looked out her window and saw a car speeding out of the parking lot right afterward. She said it was too far away for her to see the license tag, and she wasn't sure what kind of car it was. Not too small and not too big was all she could say."

Baillie went back into the bedroom office. Curry walked over to the kitchenette and opened the refrigerator.

"At least we won't have to look at trucks," Bramlett said to Drumwright. "There's a John Packard in number fifteen. Why don't you bring him up here for me."

Drumwright nodded and left.

"He wasn't much into cooking," Curry said, closing the refrigerator door. "Just the basics. Orange juice, ice cream, grape jelly, beer, steak."

"We'll need to check the local eateries," Bramlett said. "Probably had a regular place for his supper, maybe breakfast, too. See any photos of him?"

"There's a framed one on the chest of drawers in the bedroom. Him and a couple of kids. Grandchildren, I suppose."

"Let's pull it." Bramlett opened a drawer beside the sink. Dish towels, and not many. Nothing else. "What's in the bedroom?"

"Nice clothes in the closet. Expensive shoes. A few books. Novels, looks like."

Bramlett moved into the other bedroom. Johnny Baillie was going through one of the desk drawers.

"Anything exciting?" Bramlett asked.

"Checkbook," Baillie replied, holding up a wallet-style bank account register. He set the checkbook on the corner of the desk and picked up a small notebook. "Address book." He placed the address book beside the bank book. "Plenty of file folders, envelopes. Paycheck stubs. He worked at Adamstown Furniture in Tupelo. Judging from the amount he was paid, I'd definitely say he didn't work on the line."

Baillie touched the top of the computer. "We'll probably need to find passwords for whatever he's got in here."

Bramlett grunted. He turned and went back into the living room. There was a small photo on top of the television set of a young couple with three children. The man in the photo was blond-headed, much like the man who had died in the parking lot outside. The woman looked to be Oriental, small. The children were beautiful—a boy possibly the age of Bramlett's twelve-year-old grandson Marcellus, and two girls, both younger.

The picture was taken in bright sunlight in what appeared to be a backyard. They were standing in front of some tall, sprawling shrubbery. Smiling.

Bramlett put on his reading glasses and picked up the framed photo and looked at it close. Yes, a lovely little family. They were probably just now waking up. The whole family. And, as soon as Johnny Baillie could find something with an "In case of emergency, notify so-and-so" on it, they would get a phone call.

Whether this family was the one to be notified or not didn't make any difference. In a very short time they would receive a call if not from the sheriff's department then from another relative telling them that Rory Hornsly was dead. Shot to death. Bramlett wondered about their reaction.

Drumwright escorted a short, chunky man wearing a black and gold Saints sweatshirt into the room. The man glanced around the living room, shuddered, closed his eyes and pressed his fingers to his forehead.

"This is John Packard," the deputy said to Bramlett.

The sheriff extended his hand. "I'm Sheriff Bramlett," he said.

Packard gave him a weak handshake.

"Please, have a seat," Bramlett said with a wave of his hand toward the couch. "I'm sure you can help us a great deal."

He looked at Drumwright and nodded at an armchair. The deputy gave a short bob of the head, indicating he understood the sheriff was directing him to sit down and take notes of Bramlett's interview.

The sheriff sat down in another chair.

"We understand you were a friend of Rory Hornsly," he said.

Packard swallowed. He was rubbing his hands together. "Yes."

"When was the last time you saw him?"

"Last night. About eight-thirty, I guess." Packard made a moaning sound without opening his lips. Then he said again, "This is awful."

"How long have you known him?" Bramlett asked.

"I moved in here in November. What's that? Two months?"

"Did you know him before that?"

"No. I came here from Jackson with the phone company. Lots of the people in this complex go someplace on weekends. Most of them are young. It's almost like a college dormitory. They go home or to Memphis or wherever. Rory and I would get together for a drink. Occasionally, we'd go out to eat or to a movie."

"What about family?"

"He was divorced. Like me. His son lives in California. He flew back there for Christmas. Wanted them to come here for a visit, but . . ." He didn't finish.

"Is that his family in the photo on the TV?"

Packard nodded. "That's Bill. Rory was very proud of him. He's an engineer. The wife is Niki. She's Japanese."

"Did Rory indicate anyone he was having problems with?"

"No . . . Well, he did say something about some people who didn't know anything about business. I think that's how he put it. Sometimes investments go bad, he said. Everybody knows that. I think he'd been in business with somebody and things had gone sour and they were upset."

"Do you know who these people were?"

"He never said."

"Would they have been local?"

Packard shrugged. "I think so. But I'm not sure. He never mentioned any names. Once he got a phone call. I was here—

sitting right where you are—and somebody phoned. I didn't really understand what was being said. But Rory told the guy he'd have to be patient. Everything was going to work out, that he'd soon have more money than he would know what to do with. The guy said some other things, I guess. Finally, Rory told him to go to hell and hung up the phone."

"Did the person call back?"

"Rory took the phone off the hook."

"Did he mention a name while he was talking?"

Packard shook his head. "No. And when he was through talking, he laughed and said something about the fact the guy had never been out of Mississippi long enough to know the world was round. Then he made us another drink and said he was planning to fly back to California this summer to see his family."

"Where is his former wife?"

Packard rubbed his forehead again, then said, "Wives. He'd been married at least three times. I remember him saying that. But, he never called any of them anything but 'bitch.' He'd say, 'The bitch did this' or 'The bitch did that.' You know."

"I see," Bramlett said, studying the man. Packard's face was flaccid, colorless. He no doubt piloted some desk. His fingers had that short, stubby look.

Bramlett continued. "What about lady friends?"

Packard cleared his throat. "He was seeing someone from work. Elsie something. He had been dating a teacher, but that played out."

Bramlett cut his eyes at Drumwright. The deputy was scribbling in the notebook on his knee. He looked at Packard again. "You know Elsie's last name?"

"I can't remember right now. Maybe it'll come to me."

"And the name of the teacher?"

"Alice Fielder. She's from Etowah. Nice-looking. I don't know why he quit seeing her. He just said she wanted more out of their relationship than he could give."

"Which one drove the Blazer?"

"Alice."

"Did Hornsly have other friends?"

Packard pressed his lips together and shook his head. His eyes darted around the room. Then he replied, "I . . . I really can't think of anyone else. He talked at times as if he wanted to return to California. Then sometimes he said he'd like to go back to Oregon. He used to live there, too."

Bramlett wondered if he was lying . . . not just not telling the whole truth. Then he thought of the small supply of groceries in the kitchen. "Where did he take his meals?"

"He usually ate someplace in Tupelo before coming home. Different places. Sometimes he'd get something at the Eagle Café here in Sheffield. Occasionally, he'd holler at me, and we'd go to the Wisteria Inn."

Bramlett was a regular customer at the Eagle Café, but didn't remember ever seeing this man or anyone who resembled Hornsly. But then, Bramlett never went there in the evenings. Probably there was an entirely different set of customers from the ones he saw often during the week. He'd see what Floyd Clements, the owner of the restaurant, could tell him about Rory Hornsly.

Bramlett placed his hands on his knees and pushed himself up. "Thank you, Mr. Packard. You've been very helpful." He nodded at Drumwright, letting the deputy know he could now escort the man out of the apartment.

Bramlett stepped to the doorway of the bedroom. H. C. Curry was searching the closet. "Anything interesting?" the sheriff asked.

"Nice rags," Curry replied. "The best of everything. Shoes, ties, suits. He was definitely into clothes. Cool dresser. Gold chains on the dresser."

Bramlett grunted. He wondered how Curry would describe the way he dressed. What did he think about the Dickies trousers he wore every day?

Of course, Bramlett didn't give a damn what anyone thought about his clothes. He dressed for practical wear and comfort. Dickies wore like iron. Dickies for the job, Levi's when off duty. Dress slacks for church on Sunday. Keep things plain and simple was his philosophy about clothes.

He moved into the other room. Johnny Baillie had pulled out all of the desk drawers and positioned them on the carpet. He was bending under the desk, looking up at the underside.

In a moment, he moved his head carefully out from under the desk and stood up. "There was a lot of cash under the file folders," he said. "Hundreds. Probably several thousand dollars."

31

Bramlett picked up the checkbook from the corner of the desk and thumbed through it. In addition to the routine payments to utility companies and other household costs, there were many recent checks made out to Johnny Lee, a local contractor. The amounts were sizable. Apparently, Hornsly had a very nice construction project in the works.

Also, there was a check to Patterson Clouse for fifty dollars. Bramlett remembered Clouse. He was a black man, and a janitor at the college. His wife had been killed a couple years back. The body was found in a barn. She'd been shot, stabbed, and hanged. Brutal.

They never got anywhere with that investigation. Bramlett felt there was a good chance Clouse himself had killed his wife, but there was absolutely nothing to build a case on.

Bramlett had questioned the man for hours on several occasions. But he never broke. In the sheriff's mind, the man was as hard and cold as they came.

Ironically, during that investigation, Deputy H. C. Curry and Clouse's daughter Lizzie started dating. Bramlett wasn't sure how serious they were. Lizzie was a teacher at the high school. Smart, vivacious, a leader in the Chakchiuma County chapter of the NAACP.

He set the checkbook back onto the desk.

"You might want to see what's written on this," Baillie said to the sheriff, handing him a notepad.

"I didn't come up with much," H. C. Curry said, stepping into the room. "His suits came from a couple of stores in Tupelo. We can check with them."

Bramlett took the notepad. There were three names at the top with phone numbers beside the names. The first was Keesa Hudnall. Hudnall was the manager of the Wisteria Inn. The second was James Doffey. Was this the same as the black preacher who was good to visit his mother? The third was Wayne Carr.

Carr was a local black businessman. He was into several endeavors: funeral home, pool hall, dry cleaners, a used car lot, a good number of rental properties. Probably a lot of stuff Bramlett didn't know about.

There was also a notation in the middle of the pad. It simply said, "Call Roach." Bramlett didn't know anyone named

Roach. In the margin beside the word Roach was written "Black Snow."

Then there were two names at the bottom of the page. Each name was printed out with a pencil, very carefully, as if done slowly and thoughtfully. And each letter had been retraced several times. A rectangle had been drawn freehand around the two names.

Bramlett handed the notepad to Curry. "What do you make of this?"

The young man took the notepad and read silently. Then he stiffened and his eyes jumped up at Bramlett. "What the hell is this supposed to mean?"

Bramlett shrugged. "Maybe they can tell us," he said.

The two names on the notepad were the daughters of Patterson and the late Naresse Clouse—Shamona and Lizzie Clouse. Out beside Lizzie's name was written: "She is the one who saw them together."

# 5

H. C. Curry snatched up the telephone on the left side of Hornsly's desk and started jabbing at the dial buttons.

Sheriff Bramlett scowled. "Don't phone her right now," he said, knowing the deputy was trying to reach Lizzie Clouse.

Curry looked at him, his hand paused above the buttons.

"We'll talk to her in person," Bramlett continued. "Later." He knew the young man was concerned about his girlfriend. But he also knew, whatever the personal involvements were, the case must proceed along the same orderly rules of investigation as any other case. You didn't conduct telephone interviews when a person was readily available, no matter how slight the interview.

Curry placed the receiver back into the cradle.

"Here," Baillie said, handing the sheriff a small card he'd just found in Hornsly's billfold.

Bramlett looked down at the card. It gave Hornsly's name, address, and phone number. At the bottom, in the blank beside "In Case of Emergency, Notify" was handwritten the name William F. Hornsly, with a Lafayette, California, address and phone number.

Deputy Jacob Robertson entered the apartment. "No other weapon found so far," he said to the sheriff, referring to the search being conducted in the parking lot and surrounding area for any physical evidence.

"Help Johnny finish up here," Bramlett said to the tall deputy. "H.C. and I will start checking into his background. You can begin by searching that bedroom." He nodded toward the doorway of the room H. C. Curry had just searched.

Curry made a face.

34

Bramlett chuckled. "Jacob is just going to confirm what a good job you did," he said. He knew Curry didn't like having Robertson, or anyone else for that matter, go over an area he'd already worked, but, at the same time, none of the sheriff's deputies knew houses like Robertson.

Robertson had worked in construction during the summers when he was in high school and junior college. He understood houses, and where something could be hidden. If Hornsly had squirreled away something in that bedroom, Robertson would find it.

"Come on," Bramlett said to Curry. "Let's go to the house." By house, he meant the headquarters of the sheriff's department which was located on the bottom floor of the Chakchiuma County courthouse.

He glanced at his watch. It still wasn't time to get up.

At headquarters, Bramlett picked up a new file folder and wrote "Rory Hornsly" on the tab. His secretary, Ella Mae, wouldn't be in till eight. Curry was checking the computer for anything on the victim.

Bramlett held the card from the billfold in one hand and dialed the listed telephone number with his other hand. He then leaned back in his swivel chair.

What time was it in California anyway? And he wondered how one of his daughters would react if they got a wake-up call early one morning telling them their father was dead. Especially, that their father had been shot dead in a parking lot wearing only his pajamas on a cold winter's night.

The phone was answered on the third ring. The voice on the other end of the line was obviously sleep-grogged. "Hello?" It was a woman.

"This is Sheriff Grover Bramlett in Sheffield, Mississippi. I'd like to speak to William Hornsly."

"Who?"

"William Hornsly."

"No, I mean, who did you say you were?"

"Sheriff Bramlett here in Mississippi. Are you Mrs. Hornsly?"

There was a muffled sound as if she were holding the

mouthpiece against her chest or cupping her hand over it. Then, a man's voice. "Hello?" There was an edge to the voice.

"Mr. Hornsly?"

"Yes? What's wrong?"

"I'm calling in regard to Rory Hornsly," Bramlett said slowly. In the many times he'd had to tell a loved one of a death, it never seemed to get easier. "He listed you to be notified in case of an emergency."

The voice became choked. "What is it? Is something wrong with Dad?"

"I'm very sorry," Bramlett said. "Rory Hornsly was killed this morning. Murdered."

There was a gasp, then a long silence on the other end of the line.

Then Bramlett said, "I take it you are his son?"

"Yes . . . How, for god's sake?"

"He was shot. We don't know why or who did it. We're just beginning our investigation. Are there any other relatives close by?"

"Well . . . Thatcher lives near there. That's Dad's brother. Just a minute. Let me look up the address." There was a muffling noise again. Then, "No, I thought we had his address in our address book, but we don't. We did, but someone gave us a new address book at Christmas and we haven't put in the names we don't talk to. I mean . . . well, Thatcher is my father's brother. Damn! I can't think. What town is that?"

Bramlett assumed he was either asking his wife or himself.

"Oxford," he said a moment later. "He lives in Oxford. He teaches chemistry at the college there."

"Okay," Bramlett said. "Any other relatives?"

"No. Dad lived here in California most of his adult life. Hell. I tried to talk him out of moving back there. All his friends are here. Who ever moves to Mississippi? I asked him that over and over."

"When was the last time you talked with him?"

"Let's see? Dammit. When, honey? When did Dad call? Wasn't it just last Saturday?" A silence. Then, "I think he called Saturday. He was just out here Christmas."

"Did he give any indication anything was wrong?"

"No. Not at all. I need to come there. You are at Sheffield, aren't you?"

"Yes."

"Is there an airport? Or do I fly to Memphis or what?"

"The nearest airport is Tupelo," Bramlett answered. "Did he mention anyone he was having difficulty with?"

"No. What is your name again? Honey, get me something to write with. And your phone number? God, this can't be happening."

Bramlett gave Hornsly his name and phone number, then asked, "Do you know a woman named Elsie? Someone said your father was seeing her."

"I don't know anything about that. Look, I'm leaving as soon as I can get a flight out."

Bramlett thanked him and said for him to check with him as soon as he arrived. Then he hung up the phone and looked at the doorway. H. C. Curry stood waiting.

"And?" asked Bramlett.

"No warrants. Nothing unusual on Rory Hornsly. I looked through his address book. Not many listings. There is another Hornsly, though. In Oxford. Thatcher Hornsly. Maybe a son?"

"Brother," Bramlett said. "Phone him and see if he can get over here this morning."

Bramlett looked down at the legal pad on his desk. He'd written ten names: Wayne Carr, James Doffey, Keesa Hudnall, Shamona Clouse, Lizzie Clouse, Patterson Clouse, Alice Fielder, Elsie Doe, Johnny Lee, Thatcher Hornsly. And Adamstown Furniture. He looked up at Curry.

"You think Lizzie is awake yet?"

The deputy shrugged.

"Phone her," Bramlett said. "Just tell her we need to come talk with her."

Bramlett's eyes followed the sweep of the headlights as Curry drove them through the still-dark streets of Sheffield toward the quiet neighborhood of older houses where Lizzie Clouse lived. The image of her mother's body hanging in the barn out in the Hebron community kept flickering in his mind.

Naresse Clouse was about fifty, a black woman who worked at the Wisteria Inn, the finest restaurant in Chakchiuma County. He remembered her as a small, energetic woman with eyes that danced with excitement or joy or both. She was the assistant manager of the place, and worked her way around the tables in the dining room checking to see if everything was okay, if the food was satisfactory, did anyone need anything else. She remembered each person's name, and made you feel like you belonged there.

The manager of the restaurant was a red-faced man named Keesa Hudnall. Folks commented that he pretty much let Naresse run the whole show, that she was the reason behind the remarkable quality of the food and service.

Bramlett was surprised to discover the woman was as old as she was. When he'd seen her flitting around at the restaurant, carrying laughter like sunshine from table to table, he'd taken her to be in her thirties. But she had children in their thirties.

She'd been shot in the head, brutalized, probably after being shot, and hung up from an inside edge of the loft with a length of rope. Bramlett gave his head a quick shake, wanting to shake away before it could focus the image of the protruding tongue and bulging eyes.

There were no real suspects in the case. He'd talked to all of her children. In addition to Lizzie and her sister Shamona, there was an older brother, another sister, and a teenage son.

Keesa Hudnall was so distraught he could hardly talk. Bramlett wasn't sure exactly why the man was so upset, whether it was the loss to the restaurant or to himself that compelled such remorse.

The husband, Patterson, wasn't leveling with him. Bramlett knew that. Clouse was grieved enough at the death of his wife, but so were many men who killed their wives. Yet, he never broke. Never.

And then only a few months ago, Lizzie's roommate, another young schoolteacher, was murdered. Jo Ann Scales. Bramlett made a slow, weary shake of his head thinking what all Lizzie Clouse had been through.

Curry parked at the curb in front of a small board and batten cottage set back from the street. Two large magnolias in front shielded most of the house from view.

"Lizzie lives here?" Bramlett asked, looking at the house and recognizing it.

"Uh-huh. She gave up her apartment in November and moved in with Nena Carmack."

As Bramlett got out of the car, he remembered Nena Carmack, a pretty redhead Deputy Jacob Robertson was dating. "What about her and Jacob?" he asked. "They serious or what?"

"I think he'd like to ask her, but he's still working up the courage part. Then there's his mother."

"What?"

Curry looked toward the house. His cheek was taut. "It's a long story," he said with a shrug.

Bramlett nodded and turned his shoulders against a surge of cold wind.

Lizzie Clouse opened the door. She looked to Bramlett so much like her mother Naresse. Petite and wired. At least wired was the word that came to the sheriff's mind. Energy. Movement. Life. And, like her mother, she was quite pretty.

"What is it?" she asked, still holding the door open. "What's wrong?" She was dressed, apparently all ready for school.

"Everything's fine," Curry said, reaching out and taking her arm, and, at the same time, steering her back into the living room.

Bramlett closed the door as he followed them inside.

Nena Carmack was standing at the doorway to the kitchen. Her eyes met Bramlett's eyes. Her look was hard, not hiding the dislike she had for the sheriff.

He nodded, but she made no response. Instead, she turned away from the doorway and moved out of sight. Bramlett remembered her temper was as hot as her hair was red. He'd only been doing his job. And now, especially in that she might end up marrying Jacob Robertson, he wished he could establish some sort of cordial relationship with her.

"We need to ask you a few questions," Bramlett said to Lizzie.

"Is something wrong with Daddy?" she asked.

Curry backed her to the couch and they sat down together. "He's fine," he said, putting his arm around her shoulders.

Bramlett lowered himself into an armchair. "A man was killed during the night. Rory Hornsly. Do you know him?"

Lizzie's eyes narrowed. "No. I've never heard that name. Why?"

"He lived over in the Vers la Maison apartments. Worked for Adamstown Furniture in Tupelo." As Bramlett made these statements, he watched her face closely, watched for a flicker of recognition. Her eyes remained narrowed, confused. "We found this in his apartment," he continued, handing her a photocopy of the notepad.

Lizzie took the sheet of paper and read the list of names. When she finished, she looked up quickly. "What?" she asked. "What is this supposed to mean? Who am I supposed to have seen?"

Bramlett shook his head. "I'm hoping you can tell us. This man certainly seems to have known you."

She gave a quick headshake. "I never heard of him."

"We don't know much about him yet," Bramlett said, half-standing and taking from his inside coat pocket the photograph of Hornsly with his son Bill's family. He handed the photograph to Lizzie and sat again. "He look familiar?"

She held the edges of the photograph with both hands, staring down at it. She wrinkled her nose and shook her head. "No . . . wait. He does look a little familiar." She looked up at Curry as if asking for help in remembering. The deputy merely returned her stare. She looked back at the picture.

Suddenly, her eyes brightened in recognition. "Yes," she said. "At least . . . I think it's the same one."

"What?" Bramlett asked.

"I went out to Hebron after school yesterday to visit Mama's grave. It was three years ago yesterday that . . . that . . ." She paused for a moment, then continued. "And then this man came up." She tapped a finger on the photograph of the smiling Rory Hornsly with his son's family. "He was driving a Mercedes. A yellow Mercedes." She frowned and shook her head. "I don't ever remember seeing him before that."

"He was at the cemetery?" Bramlett asked.

She nodded. "The cemetery at the church. Anyway, I thought it was real strange for this man to be coming to the church. At least, that's why I thought he was there. Of course, nobody was at the church. Reverend Doffey was still at work, I'm sure."

"Reverend Doffey?" Bramlett asked.

The deputy immediately removed his arm from around Lizzie's shoulders and withdrew a small notebook from his shirt pocket. He knew the sheriff meant for him to record the information his girlfriend was giving them.

"He's our pastor," she said.

"James Doffey?" he asked.

"Yes. He's from Hebron. In fact, he and Mama were good friends growing up."

"What about Wayne Carr?" Bramlett asked, remembering the name of the black businessman also written on Hornsly's notepad.

She tilted her head and looked at him questioningly. "What?" she asked.

"Was he a friend of your mother's also?"

"Why . . . yes. Very old and very good friends. Why? What has all this got to do with this man you're talking about?"

Bramlett shrugged one shoulder. "We don't know, just trying to fit a lot of odd pieces together. And, this Hornsly. When he came to the cemetery, did you talk with him?"

"Yes. And he did say he knew Mr. Carr. In fact, he said he was a friend of his." She looked questioning at Curry, then back to the sheriff. "Who is this man?"

Bramlett didn't answer. "Tell me. What else did he say?"

"He said he had interviewed Shamona for a job at his company."

"I see," said Bramlett. "What about the name Roach? Does that mean anything to you?"

"That's someone's name?"

Bramlett gave a half smile. "A nickname, I presume."

"No."

"What about the phrase Black Snow?"

Lizzie gave a hard shake of her head. "No." There was an immediate look of weariness in her eyes.

"Now listen, Lizzie," Bramlett continued. "Did this man say anything else? Ask anything else?"

She drew a deep breath, held it for a moment, then released it, and said, "He said he knew Matthew Farris."

"What?" Out of the corner of his eye, Bramlett could see Curry writing down the name.

"He asked about her death, and I mentioned the Farris barn. He said he knew Matthew. He also said he knew Addie Carr. Wayne's sister."

"Anything else?"

She was slow to answer, then said, "He said . . . he said I saw something I shouldn't have. I think that's the way he put it. And that I could scare somebody to death."

41

"What did he mean?"

"I have no idea."

"What else did he say?"

She shook her head slowly. "I think he mentioned something about how cold it was. I can't remember anything else. I was just thinking he shouldn't be there."

"Shouldn't be there?"

She gave the sheriff a look as if he should understand what she meant. She didn't explain, and he wasn't sure whether she meant Hornsly, as a white man, shouldn't be in black folks' cemetery or if Hornsly shouldn't have intruded on Lizzie's private grief. Whatever.

"One more thing," he said. "This man Hornsly seems to have known your father. Perhaps Patterson did some work for him?"

Her eyes seemed to harden at the mention of her father, probably, Bramlett knew, because the sheriff had virtually accused the man of killing her mother.

"I don't know anything about that."

He nodded at her, then rose to his feet. "Thank you, Lizzie," he said. "If anything else comes to mind, give us a holler, okay?"

She made no response.

Curry slipped his notepad into his pocket and gave her a hard, long hug.

Bramlett turned his back to them to give them a bit of privacy, and, at the same time, he felt a bitter apprehensiveness flitting around at the very top of his stomach. According to this dead man, Lizzie had seen something or someone she shouldn't have. And, the man said, what she saw could scare somebody to death.

Bramlett walked slowly to the front door. His mouth was very dry.

# 6

Forty-five minutes later in a booth in the Eagle Café on Front Street, Sheriff Grover Bramlett waved the salt shaker over his Planter's Special: two fried eggs, four sausage patties, grits, and biscuits. Now this was what God meant breakfast to be all about.

H. C. Curry sipped his orange juice. He wasn't a breakfast person, he'd said to the sheriff, and every morning his mother still asked him if he wanted something to eat before he went to work.

Curry lived with his mother and father on a farm at the edge of town. His father Witt worked for the lumberyard and his mother Chancy at the hospital. They were good, salt-of-the-earth type people in the sheriff's estimation. Solid.

"You wanted to see me?" Floyd Clements asked. Floyd was the Miami native who'd lived in Sheffield for years and, in the wintertime, always talked about selling out and moving home. But he never did. His white T-shirt was so soiled already that Bramlett wondered if the man had changed it since yesterday.

"Sit down," Bramlett said, motioning with his fork to the place beside Curry.

Clements closed his eyes for a moment in a gesture of I'm-very-busy-right-now, then sat down.

"You heard about the man who was killed?"

Clements nodded.

"I understand he used to eat here occasionally."

Clements shook his head. "Yeah. Sometimes. We never talked."

"What can you tell me about him?"

"Nothing. Like I said, we never really talked much. He complained once about us not having hash brown potatoes. He wanted that for breakfast instead of grits. I told him they had potatoes at the Holiday Inn and maybe he'd like to have breakfast there from now on."

Bramlett wiped his mouth on the paper napkin. "You ever hear that the customer is always right?"

"What?"

"Never mind," said Bramlett. He couldn't imagine anyone not liking grits. "He ever come in here with anyone?"

"Another guy came with him sometimes."

"John Packard?"

He shrugged. "Yeah. And the other night he was with some guy I'd never seen. They were looking at photographs."

"Photographs of what?"

"I don't know. Whenever I came over, he turned them facedown. I never saw who they was of."

"Anything else?"

He shook his head. "Naw."

"Thanks," said Bramlett. "I appreciate your time, Floyd."

"Sure," Clements said, slipping quickly out of the booth and disappearing into the kitchen.

Before leaving for Tupelo to go to the place where Rory Hornsly had worked, Bramlett wanted to see Keesa Hudnall. They found Hudnall in his office at the Wisteria Inn. The Wisteria Inn was a motel on the highway near the hospital. Hudnall managed the motel's restaurant, which was considered by many, including Valeria, to be the best place to eat in Sheffield. Bramlett, however, preferred the Eagle Café.

"It's awful," Hudnall said, shaking his head after they were seated in his cramped office. "He used to come in here occasionally, usually in the evenings. He loved our ribs." He paused and put a cigarette to his lips, lit it with a wooden match, inhaled deeply, and continued speaking as he exhaled. "He wanted me to invest in a business venture. I hadn't decided whether to do it or not."

Bramlett gave Curry a sidelong glance, then asked, "Did he say what kind of a venture?"

Hudnall shrugged and tapped his cigarette on the large blue ceramic ashtray on his desk. "Something to do with clay in

Union County. I own some property over there. I was thinking about it. I hadn't decided."

"Did he mention anyone else who was investing?"

"No." Hudnall made another long draw, then nervously tapped the cigarette on the ashtray again. "It's not safe anywhere anymore."

Bramlett remembered interviewing Hudnall three years before when Naresse Clouse was killed. She was his assistant at the restaurant. "It seems this man knew Naresse Clouse," he said. "Would you happen to know anything about that?"

Hudnall frowned. "Knew Naresse?" He shook his head. "I hardly think so." He paused and slowly shook his head and closed his eyes. "Yesterday was the third anniversary of her death, you know."

Bramlett cocked his head. He remembered how distressed this man was at the time of Naresse's death. "If I recall, you had known each other for years."

Hudnall nodded. "My family ran the store at Hebron." He took another draw on the cigarette, exhaled, then continued. "Naresse and I played together as children. We were always close." Then he shook his head. "God, you can't imagine how much I miss her. She was closer to me than my sister." He paused, staring into space as if remembering, then gave a slight smile. "In fact, we worked together back when I was in college. I had to come home from Ole Miss every weekend to run the store on Saturday. My father insisted on it. So he hired Naresse to help me. She was still in high school. So, you see, we go way back."

"Yes," said Bramlett, "and then she was with you at the restaurant also."

Hudnall drew a long breath and seemed to sink down into his desk chair. "Oh, how I miss that woman. She was so good with customers. She couldn't be replaced. Everybody loved her."

A quick image of Naresse Clouse moving with happiness around the tables darted across Bramlett's mind, then, following it at once was the sight of her bulging eyes in death. And the barn on the old Farris place. "Matthew Farris also grew up out at Hebron," he said, thinking how all of these folks, like himself, had moved to town.

Hudnall's face darkened. "Never could stand the man," he said, "and don't care who knows it."

"Oh?" said Bramlett, surprised. Farris was a close friend of the Clouse family.

"I told him and that wife of his they weren't welcome at the Wisteria Inn anymore. We had an incident." He paused, shrugged one shoulder, then continued. "It was a long time ago. They didn't act very nice."

"Go on," said Bramlett.

"Well, I'm not sure exactly what happened. They were at one of the tables and suddenly she started yelling at him. She smashed a glass on the floor. Then she ran outside and he ran after her. Like I said, it upset everybody in the restaurant."

"And you don't know what they were fighting about?"

Hudnall shook his head. "She swore at him. I remember that. And, of course, Naresse was quite upset. She and Matthew were friends, as I'm sure you know. Their families lived by each other for years. Anyway, she said she didn't know what was going on. She'd been over to their table to check on things, but they didn't say anything in front of her. The woman was nuts anyway, she said. Matthew could have done better for himself."

Bramlett always thought about the dogwood photograph hanging in his den whenever Esther Farris was mentioned. The woman was a real artist. Maybe that had something to do with her temperament.

"About Rory Hornsly," Bramlett asked. "When he came here to eat, was he alone or with anyone?"

"There was a man named Packard he came in with sometimes. Once or twice he brought a woman."

"What was her name?"

"I never knew."

"Is there anything else that you can think of about Hornsly?"

"No," Hudnall said slowly, his brow knit as if thinking. Then, "No, I really can't."

"Thank you," said Bramlett, rising and nodding at Curry. "We may need to get back to you."

Hudnall stood also, snubbed out the cigarette in the ashtray, and followed them out of the office.

As the patrol car sped down the state highway with Curry driving, Bramlett stared at the slate-gray sky. The sky menaced either more rain or rain mixed with snow. Bramlett didn't care much for winter anymore. When he was younger, wintertime meant deer season and he looked forward to it, but now he hunted less and less. One of the only things he really liked about winter was the occasional clear blue sky when the light bounced off the sides of the old wood of barns and the ragged dead grasses of the fields. The colors were a painter's feast.

However, this day wasn't like that. It was as dreary as death. And Bramlett wondered about the strange man whose son was even now trying to arrange a flight to Mississippi where his father had just been murdered.

He wondered why that murdered man had written the names of Lizzie and Shamona Clouse on a notepad. Was sweet Lizzie lying to him? No, he doubted that.

He turned his head to look at the side of Curry's face. "You and Miss Lizzie got any plans?" he asked.

Curry blinked his eyes rapidly a couple of times and cocked his head slightly. "Plans?" he asked as if he hadn't quite understood.

The sheriff grinned. "You ain't getting any younger."

Curry shook his head. "I'm not thirty yet," he said.

Curry turned onto the industrial road north of Tupelo where several factories were located. The Adamstown Furniture facility was a sprawling, one-story metal building whose side was as long as a football field.

The deputy pulled open the glass front door for Bramlett to enter. A woman rushed out, brushed him as she hurried past and half-ran toward the parking lot.

Both men looked after her for a moment, then went into the building.

They were shown into a small waiting room furnished with two identical couches and two matching armchairs. The walls were wood-paneled, and a stack of glossy magazines fanned out over a coffee table. It looked to Bramlett like a doctor's waiting room.

They didn't have to wait long. Daniel Koph, a tall, square-shouldered, athletic-looking man with graying temples, came

into the room, introduced himself as president of Adamstown
Furniture, and led them to his office next door. As soon as the
three of them were seated, Koph said, "We're all in a state of
shock. Absolute shock. We might not be surprised to hear
about something like this happening in Memphis or Jackson.
But in Sheffield? Good Lord, what's this world coming to?"
The man's accent was Carolinian. North, Bramlett suspected.

"The world has already come to Sheffield and Tupelo and
every other town around here," Bramlett said. "What was Rory
Hornsly's position?"

"He was in charge of personnel," Koph said.

"Does that mean he took care of disgruntled employees and
things like that?"

"Yes. He was the officer to go to if someone had a problem.
We have over a hundred employees here at Adamstown. It was
his responsibility to hire and, at the same time, act upon rec-
ommendations from department heads that certain individuals
be dismissed."

"Could we have a list of people he's dismissed lately? Maybe
for the last year?"

Koph shrugged. "I suppose so. But I can't imagine it could
have been one of our people."

Bramlett gave a low grunt. "If it was someone who'd been
fired, he wouldn't be one of your people anymore, would he?"

Koph stiffened slightly. "I guess not. However, we have definite criteria for termination of service. No one should think he
or she had been unfairly treated."

"You'd be surprised," the sheriff said. "Now, did he also interview all prospective employees?"

"Yes."

"He recently interviewed a young woman named Shamona
Clouse. Could we see the record of that?"

"Shamona Clouse? I'm not familiar with that name."

"Like I say. He interviewed her for a position. She hadn't
been hired."

"Perhaps I should check with our attorney. We don't have
anything to hide, of course, but, with litigation these days
from people who feel their privacy has been invaded . . ." He
paused and gave Bramlett a look as if expecting him to understand his position.

Bramlett's jaw tightened, then he asked, "What if the woman grants you permission to show us the file?"

Koph picked up the telephone receiver and pushed three buttons. "Clarice, please check the employment applications in Rory's office and bring me one for a Shamona Clouse. Thank you."

Bramlett crossed his legs. "What can you tell me about Hornsly's personal life?"

"He was a good golfer."

Bramlett raised an eyebrow. "Really?" He had not expected a person newly dead to be simply described by someone who knew him in terms of a game.

"Whenever we had customers in from out of town, Rory would take them out to the country club for a round."

"Go on."

"He came from our California operation a couple of years back. He was originally from this area, I believe."

Bramlett nodded, studying Koph. The man obviously wasn't distressed about the death of his fellow worker. Was he just indifferent, or was he somehow pleased? The sheriff asked, "Did you see him much outside the office? Socially, I mean?"

"Company stuff. You know. The Christmas party. We'd be together at market, of course. Dallas or High Point. He liked to have a good time, if you know what I mean."

"Party type?"

Koph gave a slight nod. "Yes. He wasn't married, you know. Divorced."

"Who were his close friends here at Adamstown Furniture?"

"I don't know for sure." He paused, cleared his throat. "A lot of people knew him, of course. Perhaps Dave Sartoman, one of our sales reps. He's in Florida right now. Won't be back till tomorrow. I know he and Rory played golf together a lot."

"Anyone else?"

Koph thought for a moment, then said, "I really don't know of anyone else."

"What about anybody here he had problems with?"

"Problems?"

"Conflicts. You know, anybody he seemed to get crossways with."

Koph cleared his throat, then said, "Tilmond Moss."

"Who's he?"

Koph pressed his lips together and looked away, swallowed, then said hesitantly, his voice dropping lower, "He works in the business office. I never really knew why, but Rory and he didn't seem to get along. I really never pressed it. Just a personality conflict thing, I think."

"We'd like to see him," Bramlett said.

Koph nodded. "You can talk with him in the conference room," he said, rising from his chair. "I'll send for him."

Tilmond Moss was a stout man in his late fifties with squinty eyes, short black hair, and a double chin that folded over his collar. He frowned at the two lawmen when he stepped into the conference room. There was a look of suspicion in his eyes. Bramlett introduced Curry and himself and asked him to have a seat at the table.

"You heard about Rory Hornsly?" he asked.

Immediately, the look of suspicion evaporated and his eyes seemed to sparkle. The corners of his mouth played with a smile. He answered. "Yes, it was just announced a while ago."

Bramlett thought he detected a note of pleasure in the tone of his voice. "I see," he said. "You don't seem to be very distressed."

He stiffened a bit and his lips drew into a thin line. He didn't bother to reply.

"I understand you and Hornsly didn't get along," Bramlett continued. "What was that about?"

His eyes narrowed. "He may have fooled a lot of people, but he didn't fool me. I knew what kind of a person he was."

Bramlett raised an eyebrow. "And what kind of person would that be exactly."

"He thought he could turn in unsubstantiated expense accounts and get reimbursed," he said. "I told him he'd have to abide by the rules. He didn't like that."

"Oh? What happened then?"

"He thought he could get me in trouble with Mr. Richards. That's the office manager. But Mr. Richards told him he'd have to supply complete receipts. Then he said things about me."

"What kind of things."

He glared at Bramlett. "Things. Not nice things. And he was one to talk. I knew about what was going on."

"And what was that exactly?"

He smiled in a self-satisfied manner. "I saw him at lunch

one day with someone. I watched them here at work. I knew what they were doing. I went and told Mr. Koph, but he didn't do anything about it."

"Someone who works here?"

"She's married. Her husband is a nurse at the hospital."

"Her name?"

"Elsie Kimble."

"Is there anything else you can tell us about Hornsly?" asked Bramlett.

His eyes widened. "Isn't that enough?"

After thanking Tilmond Moss and letting him go, Bramlett, with Curry right behind him, returned to Koph's office. "We'd like to talk with Elsie Kimble now," Bramlett said.

Koph sighed and nodded. "I thought you would," he said, lifting his telephone receiver. "I'll call her supervisor." He punched three buttons, then said, "Carl, this is Dan. I have a couple of folks here who would like to see Elsie." A pause, then, "I see. Okay, thanks."

He hung up the phone and looked at Bramlett. "He said she left a few minutes ago. Suddenly just ran out. That was shortly after word went around the department about Rory."

"We'd like her home address then," Bramlett said, rising to his feet and looking at Curry.

The deputy closed his notebook and rose also, nodding to the sheriff as he did, a nod that indicated he, too, figured the woman who almost ran over them as they came in was no doubt Elsie Kimble.

Koph's intercom buzzed. He lifted the receiver to his ear, listened, then said, "Thank you," and hung it up. "My secretary says there's no application form for a Shamona Clouse in the file. Maybe Rory put it someplace else. If so, we'll find it. All his files will be gone through today anyway. We have to clear out his office."

Bramlett frowned. "I'd appreciate it if you'd hold up on that," he said.

"What?"

Bramlett shrugged. "I know you wouldn't want any legal problems later on. I'm sure everything is okay, but you understand how some prosecutors can make obstruction of justice charges and all that." He gave a wan smile, watching the man for a reaction.

There was a scowl on Koph's face. "For how long?"

"Just a few days."

Koph sighed. "Okay. Anything else?"

Bramlett smiled. "Let me know when you find that list of people who've been terminated." He rose to his feet and said, "Thank you."

# 7

Elsie Kimble lived in south Tupelo in a middle-class residential area of mostly frame houses built in the early 1950's. The address Daniel Koph, president of Adamstown Furniture, had given Bramlett and Curry was a pale blue house trimmed in white with a single-vehicle carport beside which stood a huge pine tree. There was a dark green Honda Accord in the carport. Curry parked directly behind it.

They stood on the small front stoop and rang the doorbell. A grapevine wreath hung on the door. There was no immediate answer. Curry pushed the button again, then gave several sharp raps with his knuckles on the door.

Finally, the door opened partway, and before them was a thin, dark-headed woman Bramlett figured to be in her early thirties. It was the same woman who'd rushed past them at the doorway to the furniture factory.

"I'm Sheriff Bramlett of Chakchiuma County," Bramlett said, "and this is Deputy Curry. We'd like to talk with you about Rory Hornsly."

Her eyes closed for a moment, as if his words stabbed her, then, with a sigh of resignation, she stepped back and pushed open the door.

Once the three of them were seated in the small living room, Curry took out his notepad, and Bramlett studied her face for a moment. She was pretty, but her face was clouded with an intense, almost fretful look.

"We've come about Rory Hornsly," he said again. "You've heard, I believe, about what's happened to him."

Elsie Kimble made no reaction other than a slight tightening of her jaw. She held her hands together in her lap. In one was a

53

piece of tissue. Her makeup was smeared. She stared down at the floor.

Bramlett continued. "I'm told you were seeing him."

She waited before answering, then said, "We were friends. That's all."

Bramlett watched her face, her neck and ears, for any changes, any signs she was lying. He saw nothing. Of course, he knew if she were involved with the man, she could be so used to lying about it, that lies and truths would cause no separate reactions.

Bramlett pressed. "You understand that we'll be digging very deeply into his background. There's not much of anything that was a part of his private life that we won't be bringing to the surface."

Again she closed her eyes for a moment, then opened them and looked at the sheriff. "What does it matter now? He's dead." Her lower lip trembled as she spoke the word *dead*.

"Does your husband know about you and Hornsly?"

She was silent so long at first Bramlett thought she wasn't going to answer. Then she said very softly, "I told him we'd quit seeing each other. He's handled it, dealt with it."

"And your husband's name?"

"Buddy. Anthony, but everyone calls him Buddy."

"We were told he works at the hospital. Is that right?"

Her eyes blinked rapidly. "Oh, God. Don't tell me you're going to talk to him about all this? He can't tell you anything."

Bramlett spread his hands in a gesture of helplessness. "We have to talk to a lot of people, Mrs. Kimble. I'm really sorry."

"Damn!" she said. "Damn damn damn." She glared at Bramlett. "I might as well pack up now. No telling what he'll do after y'all see him."

Bramlett looked at her, wondering if she really would be in danger. He asked, "Has he ever abused you?"

She sighed. "Never mind."

"But he does work at the hospital?"

She nodded.

"How long has it been since you've seen Hornsly?"

"Yesterday. At work."

"What about outside of work?"

"I don't know. Maybe two weeks ago. I'm not really sure."
She closed her eyes, then said, "It was ending. It had to."

"Did he give any indication of special problems he was having with anyone?"

"No," she said opening her eyes again and looking around the room.

"Did he seem apprehensive about anything?"

She shook her head and pulled at the tissue in her hands.
"No."

"You know someone named Roach?"

"Roach? What kind of a name is that?" She shook her head again. "No."

"Does Black Snow mean anything to you?"

"No." She swallowed, then said, "Listen. My husband really can't tell you anything about Rory. They only met once or twice. At company parties. Damn, damn." Her eyes teared. "I just found out last week I'm pregnant." She paused, gnawed at the side of her lower lip, then continued. "This . . . this will be our first child . . ."

Bramlett tried not to think of her being in the same age category as his daughters. He wanted to will himself to be totally detached, completely objective. Yet, he couldn't help but notice the fierce anxiety that had gripped her. She had become very pale. He wished he could tell her he wouldn't have to talk to her husband. But, at the same time, he knew there was no way he could avoid checking out a man whose wife was having an affair with the victim. Just on paper without having ever met the man, Bramlett would have to set this man at the top of his suspect list.

Then, thinking to press a previous question harder, he asked, "Do you know of anyone Hornsly had problems with? Anyone who especially didn't like him?"

"No. No one."

"Can you tell me anything about his family?"

"He has a son in California. Three grandchildren. And a brother here in Mississippi. He teaches at Ole Miss. They don't get along."

"Why not?"

"I don't know."

"Is your husband at work now?"

"No," she answered softly. "He's off today. He and a friend went hunting. They won't be back till late."

Bramlett looked at Curry and nodded. Then he said, "Thank you, Mrs. Kimble," and stood up. "That will be all for now. We'll probably have to get back to you."

Bramlett directed Curry to drive them back to Sheffield. Inside his office at headquarters, Bramlett leaned back in his swivel chair, propped his feet on the corner of his desk, and unfolded the foil pouch of Red Man tobacco on his stomach. In front of the desk in captain's chairs sat his three investigative deputies, H. C. Curry, Johnny Baillie, and Jacob Robertson.

Johnny Baillie told him Thatcher Hornsly, the victim's brother in Oxford, said he couldn't come over, that he had too much to do, and that he was sure that Rory's son could handle everything when he arrived. Baillie had also checked out the handgun found at the scene. It belonged to the victim himself.

Robertson reported on his search of Hornsly's apartment. "We found nothing stronger than Jack Daniel's whiskey," the redheaded deputy said. "But we did find over fifty thousand dollars in cash, mostly in hundred dollar bills."

The sheriff considered this as his fingers kneaded the stringy, moist tobacco into a tight wad. "What else?"

"The man's closet was filled with nice clothes," Robertson said. "Hart Shaffner and Marx suits, Coogi sweaters, Polo shirts, Cole Haan shoes. And all kinds of ties. He must have had a hundred ties."

"Any clip-ons?" asked Bramlett as he pushed the wad into his cheek and held his hand for a moment at his mouth to hide a smile should it involuntarily twist his lips. Ever since Robertson had started going out with Nena Carmack a few months ago, he'd become keenly conscious about clothes.

Before, the country-bred deputy was interested in no apparel except hunting or fishing stuff, and possessed, according to Curry, only one neck tie, a clip-on.

H. C. Curry's eyes widened instantly in surprise, then immediately hardened into a glare. Bramlett knew he shouldn't have mentioned the clip-on, that what Curry had told the sheriff about trying to teach Robertson to tie a necktie was not to be repeated.

"Sir?" asked Robertson, flushing a bit.

Bramlett lifted the empty Styrofoam cup from the desk blotter, spat, then said, "Nothing." He looked at Curry. "What names do we have?'

H. C. Curry shifted in his chair, held the legal pad closer to his eyes and read, "Names listed on the notepad found in the victim's apartment: Lizzie Clouse, Shamona Clouse, James Doffey, and Wayne Carr. His checkbook register has checks made out to Johnny Lee and Patterson Clouse."

"Johnny Lee's a building contractor," Bramlett said, watching Curry carefully, knowing the tension the deputy must feel. This was personal. Patterson Clouse was the father of Shamona and Lizzie. Curry had been seeing Lizzie for some time, and, Bramlett suspected, was planning to marry her.

He saw a stiffening of the deputy's neck muscles, but nothing more. "Go on," he said.

Curry cleared his throat, then said as he kept his eyes on the legal pad, "Then we were given the name of a woman named Alice Fielder, a woman he used to see. Then there is Elsie Kimble, a woman he'd been seeing, and her husband, Buddy Kimble, who we haven't talked to yet. And Dave Sartoman, a man Hornsly worked with at Adamstown Furniture. And Daniel Koph, his boss at Adamstown."

"Wayne Carr, I think we all know," Bramlett said. Carr lived in Sheffield, was a businessman. Bramlett saw him each week at the noon Rotary luncheon at the Holiday Inn. He was a big man with a big laugh, about the same age as the sheriff. While the sheriff didn't know him well, he thought of him as friendly, competent, and very civic-minded.

"Reverend James Doffey is pastor of Mt. Carmel Baptist Church in the Hebron community," Curry said. "He's fifty-two, works as a mechanic at Fred's Auto here in Sheffield."

"What?" Bramlett said, suddenly quite interested. "That's where I have my cars worked on. What does he look like?"

"Medium height, dark, real strong-looking," Curry said.

"James?" Bramlett said, trying to picture each of the men at Fred's in his mind. There was only one black mechanic that he could remember, a barrel-chested man whose name patch on his shirt read *Jim*. "Is that Jim?"

Curry nodded. "That's him. But he goes by James. Jim is just what his boss put on the shirt."

"I sure didn't know he was a preacher," Bramlett said, lowering his feet to the floor. "Go on."

"On the notepad were also the words Roach and Black Snow. They could be nicknames."

"What else?"

"Lizzie mentioned that Hornsly said he knew Addie Carr, Wayne Carr's sister."

Bramlett nodded and reached for the Styrofoam cup again. "And this Hornsly interviewed Shamona Clouse for a job at Adamstown Furniture in Tupelo and showed up at a cemetery out at the Hebron community where he talked to Lizzie Clouse."

"She's never seen or heard of him before then," Curry said curtly, almost as if defending his friend from any guilt by mere association with this murdered man.

Bramlett gave a low grunt, wondering what possible reason the man had in writing down her name and the name of her sister on that notepad.

Bramlett and Curry found Johnny Lee at a building site in east Sheffield. "Let's step outside," Lee yelled in the sheriff's ear above the sharp whine of a nearby power saw.

The two lawmen followed the contractor outside and onto the front porch. "Cold weather always makes me think I ought to go back to coaching," Lee said, shoving his hands into his pockets. "At least in basketball season you was indoors all the time." He was a solidly built man, and with his smashed nose looked more like a former football player than the college basketball star Bramlett knew he'd been.

At one time Lee had been a coach at Sheffield High, but that was years ago, as Bramlett remembered it, probably right after the man finished college. He was never a head coach, just an assistant, and now had been a contractor for more than twenty years.

"I understand you were building a house for Rory Hornsly," Bramlett said, reaching to his back pocket for his foil pouch.

Lee looked toward the street as a van marked Taggert's Plumbing parked. He waved at the man behind the wheel, then looked back at the sheriff. "Still am building it. It's over in Chartes Acres. Nice place. Why?"

"Someone killed him this morning."

"What?" Lee flinched. "Damn. Why? How?"

Bramlett slowly opened the pouch, keeping his eyes on Lee. "We don't know much about it yet. Tell me about him."

Lee reached inside his jacket and pulled out a cigar with his thumb and forefinger. "I don't really know what I can tell you . . ." He paused and began unwrapping the cigar. "Murdered? Shit out of luck. That's sure screws things up, don't it? What am I supposed to do about his house?"

"You know of any problems he was having?"

"I didn't see him all that much. He trusted me to do things the way they should be done. I think he just wanted a house for tax purposes, you know. I guess he could have bought one, but maybe it was an investment." He licked the cigar, then said, "This day is not working out well. I was hoping to get slabs poured on two other job sites but the weather didn't cooperate. And now, this." He put the cigar into his mouth and struck a match to it.

"I noticed in Hornsly's checkbook register 'house' was written out by checks made out to Patterson Clouse," said Bramlett.

Lee puffed, then said with the cigar clamped in his teeth, "Mr. Hornsly was handling the cleanup on his own. Patterson worked for him on Saturdays to keep the site cleaned up."

"He doesn't do any work for you then?"

"Naw. He works out at the college during the week."

Bramlett nodded. He knew all about Patterson Clouse. "Did you know of any problems Hornsly was having?"

Johnny Lee tapped his finger on the cigar to clean the ash, then said, "Like I said. I never knew him well. One of the guys said he'd seen him out at Club Hawaii." He grinned. "I'm too married to do the honky-tonk thing myself."

Bramlett looked toward the front doorway of the house. "I'd like to talk to whoever saw him out there."

Lee nodded and said, "Sure. It was Tony Sloan. Wait here. I'll get him." He placed the cigar in his mouth again and went back inside the house. Curry wrote down the name mentioned in his notebook.

A moment later, a wiry young man with blond hair pulled back into a ponytail stepped out onto the porch. His eyes were a dull blue-green. He looked at Bramlett, then at Curry, then back to Bramlett. "You wanted to ask me about Mr. Hornsly?"

Curry asked the man how to spell his name, and for his phone number and street address, and wrote down the information as the man responded.

"Did you know Rory Hornsly?" Bramlett asked.

Sloan shook his head. "Not really. Sometimes he'd nod at me when we'd see each other at Club Hawaii. That was just a few times. Most of the time he didn't seem to recognize me. He'd just seen me here on the job whenever he stopped by. I been working for Johnny eight years."

"When was the last time you saw Hornsly?"

"Couple of weeks ago. He was there with the same woman he always come with. I don't know who she is. Johnny said somebody killed him?"

"That's right," Bramlett said. "You ever see this woman anyplace else?"

"Naw."

"Did you ever see him with anyone else?"

"No, sir. They'd come in, sit at a corner table, have a few beers, dance some. I never saw them talk with anybody else."

"And you don't have any idea who this woman was?"

He shook his head. "No, sir. She was a lot younger than him, though. Maybe young enough to be his daughter, if you know what I mean. Dark-headed. Pretty. I figured rich guys like him can always get young, good-looking women, you know."

"Thank you, Tony," the sheriff said. "We'll probably be getting back to you."

Curry backed the patrol car into the street, shifted into drive, and asked, "Elsie Kimble?"

"I don't know," Bramlett said. "She wasn't separated from her husband. Going out to a public place with another man would have been very risky, I would think. Maybe we're dealing with someone else. Maybe he's talking about the woman from Etowah. What was her name?"

Curry glanced at his notebook. "Alice Fielder." Then the deputy whistled through his teeth. "Hornsly really got around for an old guy."

Bramlett looked at him. "Old? You think of him as old?"

Curry smiled. "Well, he was over fifty, wasn't he?"

Bramlett grunted at the young man's playful jab, then looked out the window at the high-priced real estate they were passing. Chartes Acres was one of Sheffield's most exclusive areas. And it did seem a bit strange to him that Rory Hornsly would be building a house thirty miles from the place where he worked. "Let's go back to headquarters," he said. "Let's see if we can get an address on Alice Fielder."

Chicken crap is thick and heavy on the man's shoes, Bramlett thought. Running around with other men's wives. Running around with more than one woman at a time. It was getting thick and heavy.

# 8

Since his wife Valeria had a Woman's Missionary Union luncheon at the church, Sheriff Grover Bramlett ate fries and two cheeseburgers at the Eagle Café. These days most fast food hamburgers tasted more and more like cardboard to Bramlett, whereas Floyd Clement's still had a delicious amount of juicy grease. Nothing, as far as Bramlett was concerned, was quite as satisfying as fat.

Returning from lunch, Bramlett stopped at his secretary's desk. Ella Mae Shackleford, a widow in her late fifties with two grown sons, smiled up at him and wiped her mouth with a paper napkin. She was eating an apple and drinking a diet drink.

Bramlett frowned. "No wonder you're so skinny," he said. "That all you eating?"

She finished chewing with her mouth closed, still smiling, then swallowed and said, "I prefer to think of myself as trim."

He grunted. "Whatever. Pull the file on the homicide of Naresse Clouse," he said. "It was three years ago. Please."

"Yes, sir," she said, swiveling around in her chair and reaching toward a nearby filing cabinet. "Deputy Deise said to tell you he's gone to Tupelo to check out the clothing stores where Rory Hornsly might have shopped. He didn't come up with anything here in Sheffield." Ella Mae was the only one, as far as Bramlett knew, who didn't call Begard Deise by the nickname Beggarlice.

Bramlett grunted and then went on into his office without waiting for her to find the file, placed his hat on the halltree, and sank down in the desk chair. This was Tuesday, his favorite day of the week. It was his favorite because his watercolor class met on Tuesday nights at Etowah Community College. It was the one night of the week he was not to be disturbed. This week he'd gotten a nice barn done.

The barn was located down in Itawamba County. He'd passed it once, and stopped and taken a whole roll of film. He'd also made a few quick sketches.

Ella Mae brought him the Naresse Clouse file. "Have fun," she said with a smile as she turned and left the office.

He opened the thick file folder. On the first page was a five-by-seven photo of a smiling black woman. Naresse Clouse. Lizzie did favor her—same eyes and mouth—but the other sister looked more like her.

Bramlett had not known Naresse Clouse outside of the restaurant at the Wisteria Inn where she worked. He remembered her laugh. She had a good, unrestrained laugh. Few people could let go a laugh like that.

He turned the page and read. She was killed January ninth, three years ago. Bramlett looked at his watch. Today's the tenth. Yesterday was the anniversary of her death.

She only lacked a week being fifty-one when she died. Five children: Isaac, Cynthia, Lizzie , Shamona, and Hugh. Isaac, the oldest, had told Bramlett he knew his own father had killed her, although he couldn't offer anything the sheriff could use as evidence or even point Bramlett in a viable direction for discovering something a court might consider.

Bramlett turned the sheets on which were attached color photographs of the crime scene. Several shots of the exterior of the barn. Closeups of the footprints in the barn. Prints that were definitely from Naresse's shoes. And prints of a set of rubber boots. About a size ten. Photos of another set of prints that matched Patterson Clouse's shoes.

Then there was a photo of Naresse Clouse hanging from a beam by the neck on a rope. There were closeup photos of her face from several angles after the body had been stretched out on the barn floor. She'd been shot in the face, the bullet entering to the left of her nose. The autopsy report stated she was definitely dead before she was stabbed and hung up. The weapon used to stab the body was never recovered. The savagery of people toward other people never ceased to amaze Bramlett.

He reread the interview with Isaac Clouse, her son. H. C.

Curry had taken the notes. Curry later told Bramlett Isaac Clouse had been a premier athlete at the old black high school in the last few years before desegregation. Football, basketball, baseball. And he had gone on to Jackson State and played football and baseball for a couple of years, then dropped out of school.

Now he was known mostly as someone who spent a lot of time hanging around the Log Cabin, a black juke joint west of town, and doing who knows what all the rest of the time. Bramlett didn't like or trust the man.

Why, then, had he believed his accusation of his own father? Probably because of the interview sessions with Patterson Clouse himself.

Isaac accused his father of beating his mother. He said they fought violently, that Patterson accused her of seeing another man, although, Bramlett noticed, Isaac didn't seem to care much one way or the other if this was true. In fact, at one point in the interview, he denied Patterson Clouse was really his father, saying his father was a man, and Patterson was a nothing.

When pressed about this denial of paternity, Isaac backed off. Bramlett suspected the man wanted someone else to be his father to justify the brawling he did with Patterson. Bramlett recalled that, during the investigation, the two of them got into a fight, and the son hit his father with a baseball bat, gave him a brain concussion and a nasty cut on the brow. The father refused to press charges, saying, in fact, that he'd accidentally hit himself with the bat.

There were interviews with the other children. Each of the daughters talked about how much they loved their mother, and, yes, Naresse and her husband Patterson fought, but not so much more than other folks, and they strongly denied that Patterson had ever abused her physically.

None of the three felt there was any substance to their elder brother's accusation against their father. Bramlett read from Lizzie's interview: "Daddy loved Mama. He loved her desperately. He wouldn't have harmed her for anything in the world."

The youngest of the five children was Hugh, twelve at the time of his mother's death. He was big for his age, and quiet. He would never answer anything but a direct question, and then with a simple yes, sir or no, sir. When Bramlett asked questions that required another answer, the boy merely sat with his mouth shut tight.

Bramlett even had H. C. Curry interview the boy without Bramlett present, thinking perhaps he could make headway with him. But still nothing.

There was an interview with Keesa Hudnall, the fifty-eight-year-old manager of the Wisteria Inn. He couldn't imagine going to work each day at the Wisteria Inn and not having her there with him, he said. He knew she and her husband Patterson didn't get along, but he couldn't imagine him killing her.

There was an interview with another white man, Dr. Matthew Farris. Bramlett picked up the file page in his hand. Lizzie had mentioned that Rory Hornsly said he knew Farris. Coincidence? He adjusted his glasses and reread the interview.

Farris was a professor at Sheffield College and had also known Naresse's family all his life. He and Naresse were the same age, he said, and were constant playmates when they were small children.

The Farris family lived not far away, the very next farm, in fact, from the house Naresse had grown up in on land her father farmed. Naresse's father, he said, sharecropped Farris land until Naresse's father was able to buy the land for himself.

Matthew Farris still owned his own family land, but lived in town now. The old farmhouse had burned down years ago. The barn, however, was still standing. It was the barn on the old Farris place where the body of Naresse was found.

Farris, who taught history at the college and preached occasionally in churches throughout the county, was also very shaken by Naresse's death. "You have to understand," he said in the interview. "I was an only child. She was as much like a sister to me as anyone could have been."

He expressed sympathy for Patterson, said he'd heard they fought a lot, but couldn't imagine the man could have done this horrible thing.

He really didn't know Patterson all that well, he said, although once in a while he stopped by to see Adele Winter, Naresse's mother who still lived at the house. The farm actually belonged to her, he explained. It was her husband, Frazier Winter, Naresse's father, who had purchased the land from his father. When Farris was a child, he said, he'd eaten about as many meals at Aunt Adele's table as at his own.

Bramlett turned the page and scanned the interviews with Naresse's husband, Patterson. He didn't have to reread the lines word for word. The memory was still fresh.

Patterson Clouse, fifty-six, had worked as a janitor at Sheffield College for over thirty years. He'd never been arrested, was tall, lanky, hard-muscled, and balding.

During the interviews, Bramlett remembered, he had a habit of rubbing his large hand over his forehead, as if he were wiping away the sweat, or fear. He was quiet, and, on several occasions, broke down and cried. Bramlett thought it was probably more guilt than grief.

The man admitted, and never denied, that he'd gone to the barn looking for Naresse. He didn't know why he'd gone there, but he did, and after seeing her hanging there, he had run away. He hadn't looked closely at the body, didn't realize she'd been shot, but rather thought she'd hung herself, he said.

The murder weapon was never recovered. Clouse owned a shotgun and a deer rifle, but no pistol. The bullet had exited through the rear of the skull, tearing a large chunk out of the back of the woman's head. A 9 mm slug had been recovered from a feed sack on the other side of the barn.

Patterson Clouse couldn't say specifically where he was on that Thursday afternoon when the murder took place. He seemed to have left the campus of Sheffield College and gone back to Hebron. But, he claimed, everything was a big blank in his mind. Then the following morning, he went to the barn and saw her hanging there, then ran away.

The body was discovered in the late afternoon on Friday by a man hunting deer, Amos Putt, who went into the old, abandoned barn out of curiosity. Putt was a bootlegger and snake-catcher.

There was a stairway leading up to the loft. The killer seemed to have carried the body up the stairway, looped the rope around a large beam and dropped it over the side.

The barn was old and weathered, musty, Bramlett recalled. He'd seen it before, once when driving through those backroads down in the southwestern corner of Chakchiuma County, and returned early one Saturday morning, made sketches and photographs, and later done a couple of half-sheet watercolors of it.

That was a year or so before the murder. Bramlett tried to remember . . . had he ever gone back to paint it again? It seemed he had. Yes, because as he painted, he became more and more depressed thinking about the body of Naresse Clouse hanging up inside and that he'd never arrested anyone and that the killer was still free. He left without finishing the painting.

Bramlett closed the folder and leaned back in his chair. At the time he'd been so convinced Naresse Clouse had been killed by a jealous husband, Patterson Clouse. And Patterson Clouse, a janitor at Sheffield College, worked part-time for Rory Hornsly, a businessman building an expensive house in one of Sheffield's most affluent neighborhoods. And this businessman seemed interested in the death of Clouse's wife. Why?

The sheriff moved forward, reached for the telephone receiver and punched Deputy Curry's intercom number. Then, in a moment, he said, "H.C., let's take a run down to the Hebron community."

Leaving the paved road not far from the Old Hebron Baptist Church, the white church, H. C. Curry drove slowly on the rut-scarred road winding south toward the Clouse farm. The snarled limbs of small leafless trees pressed close to the open ditch on either side of the road.

As Curry wheeled the patrol car over the plank bridge and into the front yard of Patterson Clouse's house, Bramlett glanced at his watch. Almost two o'clock.

He looked up at the roof line of the paintless house. It sagged in the middle like a swayback horse. A thin stream of gray smoke twisted up out of the single chimney on one end of the roof. On the other end was a bent and rusting television antenna.

Adele Winter, Naresse's mother, answered Bramlett's knock at the door. She was almost as old as Bramlett's own mother, frail-looking and stoop-shouldered with coarse, straight gray hair. Draped over her shoulders was a pink shawl.

"Mrs. Winter," the sheriff said, "I don't know if you remember me, but I'm Sheriff Bramlett and this is Deputy Curry. We talked with you—"

"I remember," she interrupted. The look in her eye was not inviting, and not exactly suspicious, but rather more one of impatience.

"We're looking for Shamona," Bramlett said, conscious that the old woman was standing there with the door half open, letting the heat out and the cold in.

She studied him as if considering whether to let him in or not, then, finally, she stepped to one side so they could enter, and then closed the door behind them.

"She's in back," she said in a raspy voice, walking toward a hallway. "I'll get her."

The room was stuffy, with a scent of smoke from the woodburning stove. Bramlett had been in this very room, talking with Naresse Clouse's mother, husband, and each of her children.

Mrs. Winter returned. "She's coming," she said gruffly. Then she went through another doorway into the kitchen and shut the door behind her, letting the sheriff know that she had no interest in whatever he might want to talk with her granddaughter about. He also understood that she probably blamed him, as did her granddaughter Lizzie, that her daughter's killer had never been brought to justice.

Shamona Clouse entered the room. She was wearing a light-green warm-up suit and a baseball cap with her hair pushed up under it. With her broad face and small nose, she didn't resemble her sister Lizzie at all. Bramlett had forgotten how different they looked. He did remember that this woman was younger than Lizzie yet already had three school-age children.

She looked at Bramlett, then at Curry, then back to Bramlett, obviously waiting for him to explain why they were there.

"May we sit down?" the sheriff asked.

She nodded and sat down in the middle of the couch. Bramlett sat down in an armchair while Curry took a ladder-back chair next to him.

"Miss Clouse, we wanted to talk with you about Rory Hornsly," Bramlett said. He watched her face for some glimmer of name-recognition. There was none. "He was the personnel manager of Adamstown Furniture."

She nodded slowly, then said, "I applied there for a job, but I don't remember anybody by that name."

He handed her a photograph of Hornsly. "He was the man who interviewed you. A white man in his fifties."

She gave a slight nod, staring down at the photograph. "He do something wrong?"

"He's dead. Somebody killed him this morning."

Her eyes shot up at Bramlett. "Killed?"

"That's right. Do you recognize him?"

She made a face, still looking at the photograph, and nodded her head. "This is the man who talked to me. I remember him asking me if I'd ever used a computer and could I type." She paused and shook her head in a gesture of disgust. "What I was wanting was a job on the line. Who needs to type on the line?" Bramlett didn't respond. She continued. "I'd heard they got good benefits there. Hospital insurance and all. But I ain't never heard from them since he talked with me. He's dead, you say?" She looked back to the picture. "You reckon I'll have to fill out another application?"

"I wouldn't think so," Bramlett said, at the same time wondering why her original application wasn't in the file in Hornsly's office. "Can you remember what y'all talked about?"

She shook her head. "Like I said, I was wanting to get on the line and he kept talking about computers. I got three childrens to feed."

"He wrote down your name at his apartment on a notepad. And he visited the cemetery over at the church where your mother is buried."

"What?" Her eyes had a puzzled look in them.

"Lizzie says he asked her about y'all's mother."

She looked away, thinking, pursing her lips. Finally, she looked back at Bramlett. "Yes, that's right. He did ask about Mama. But I can't remember why. He sure sounded like he thought I'd get the job. I came home expecting to get a call from them at anytime. I gave Auntie Birdie's number, since we ain't got a phone here. She just lives over the bottom."

Bramlett nodded. Out of the corner of his eye he could see Curry was jotting down the name of the aunt. "And Birdie's last name?" he asked.

"Birdie Hunt. But she don't know nothing about this man. I

69

just go back there once a day to see if I got any calls. She stays home most of the time. I do worry some that they gonna call while she's out."

"Did Hornsly ask about your father?"

"No."

"Hornsly was building a house, and apparently your father did some Saturday cleanup work for him."

"I know Daddy was doing some odd work on Saturdays, but I didn't know it was for him." She handed the photograph back to Bramlett.

"Do you remember what Hornsly asked about your mother?"

"He ask her name. And I told him. I almost got the impression he knowed her. But he didn't know she was dead. He seem surprised when I told him."

"What else did he say?"

She shook her head. "I don't remember anything else." She paused, then said, "Oh. He asked me where she was buried, and if there any barns near the house. I told him where the church was, and that there was lots of barns around. We got a barn, I told him, and she was killed in a barn. He seem real interested in that and want to know how to find the barn where she died." She paused, then said, "I just wanted a good job, you know?"

Bramlett nodded and thought on all this for a moment, then asked, "You remember anything else he said?"

She shook her head.

Bramlett smiled in what he hoped as a bridge-building, I'm-grateful smile, then pushed himself to his feet.

They left the house and got back into the patrol car. "Where next?" Curry asked as he turned the car to the left.

"Let's visit Matthew Farris," the sheriff said. "Maybe he can tell us about his buddy Hornsly."

Curry looked at him. "Buddy?"

Bramlett smiled and said, "Maybe. Let's find out."

Matthew and Esther Farris lived in a modest brick house a block from the campus of Sheffield College. With its hip roof and deep front porch, the house resembled the turn-of-the-century-style architecture used on so many of the older homes near the college.

"We checked at your office and were told you'd already gone for the day," Bramlett said as Matthew Farris opened the door.

Matthew Farris waved his hand for them to enter and gave a smug smile but made no reply, as if someone like Bramlett wouldn't be able to understand a college professor's schedule. Bramlett had never cared much for the man. In his opinion, Farris wore his religion stitched too brightly on his sleeve.

Esther Farris joined them. As they took their seat in the den, Bramlett noticed on the coffee table the same large book of glossy photographs that was on his own coffee table at home. It was a book of photographs taken by Esther Farris of dilapidated barns and abandoned tenant shacks in Chakchiuma County.

The woman took beautiful pictures that moved the soul, he reflected. Yet, in person Esther Farris was a cold one, a woman who he'd rarely heard say two words, whose dark eyes had a look of perpetual pain, as if she carried in her heart some deep agony of years past that would not let her go.

She had a slightly hooked nose, was probably in her early fifties, the sheriff guessed, and was too thin. Her hair was dark like her eyes, too dark, in fact, for a person of her years.

It was Bramlett's understanding that she'd met Matthew in Texas, in Dallas, when he was in school there. He'd come to speak at her church. At that time she worked as a photographer for a small community newspaper. This he got from Valeria.

Bramlett did love the photographs this woman took, and one of his favorites hung in his den. It was the dogwood in full bloom in early spring. She obviously felt intensely about her subjects. That, he reflected, is what talent is all about.

With his Ph.D. in history, Matthew Farris had returned to teach at the college many years before. During the last ten years or so, his reputation as a speaker had been growing. Now he flew all over the country preaching at Bible conferences and assemblies. Whenever he was scheduled to speak at their church, Bramlett quickly found an ox or two in a ditch and stayed away.

"We're investigating the death of Rory Hornsly," Bramlett

said, looking at Matthew, "and we're told you two were friends."

Farris held the smug smile. "We weren't friends. We just happened to go to Sheffield College together. That was a long time ago, of course."

"But you haven't seen him in years," Esther Farris said, her eyes intense on her husband.

Her look to the sheriff and her tone seemed almost as if she were instructing him. "How long exactly?" Bramlett asked.

Farris spread out his hands in a gesture of not remembering. "His death is a terrible thing. But I can't be of any help to you, Grover. Outside of the school, I really don't have any associations other than church. And, of course, as you must know, Rory Hornsly was not much of a church person."

Bramlett raised an eyebrow. "How did you know that?"

Farris cleared his throat. "Well, I'm just guessing, of course."

"When was the last time you saw him?" Bramlett asked again, cutting his eyes at Curry to double-check that the deputy had his notepad open and ready. He did.

"I really don't know."

Bramlett noticed a slight whitening of Farris's left ear. "Years? Months? Days?"

"Months. I don't know. He may have come to one of the alumni functions we have here at the college. It seems that may have been it. Maybe it was last year."

"I see." Bramlett said. "It seems odd to me, but apparently Hornsly had some interest in Naresse Clouse." He paused, noticing a slight parting of Farris's lips and a startled look which seemed to flicker for a moment in his eyes. Otherwise, the man made no response. Bramlett asked, "I know you were close to the Clouse family. Would you have any idea what that interest was?"

"No, I wouldn't," Farris said. His voice seemed a bit more strained. "I didn't even know he knew her."

"Matthew really doesn't have anything to do with those people anymore," Esther said, looking at Bramlett with her eyes seeming to challenge him. "They just worked for Matthew's people years ago. That's all."

"Oh?" Bramlett said. He'd heard a faint note of contempt in the way she'd said *those people*. He looked at Farris. "Somehow I had the impression you were still close to the family."

Farris seemed suddenly quite uncomfortable. "Not really," he said. "Of course, I've known them all all my life. And occasionally I have to run out and check on the property and run into one of them, but . . ." He didn't finish.

"Were you close to Patterson?"

"He married into the Winter family. It was really the Winters that were associated with my folks. Adele and her people."

"Patterson is the only decent one in the whole family," Esther said flatly. "Bar none."

Bramlett couldn't help but feel uncomfortable that Curry was hearing this. *Bar none* would, of course, include Lizzie. Then he asked, "When was the last time you saw Patterson?" The question was directed at Matthew.

"I can't really say. Of course, at the college I see him once in a while, but no more than just to speak to."

"Do you have any idea why Rory Hornsly might be interested in Naresse Clouse?"

"No," said Matthew Farris. His voice had suddenly become very faint.

Bramlett thanked them both. Then he and Curry left the house.

As they walked back to the car, the sheriff said to Curry, "Never could stand either one of them myself."

Curry said nothing. He opened the car door, eased himself onto the seat, and slammed the door hard enough to shake the whole car.

# 9

When school was over, Lizzie Clouse drove out to Hebron. All day and in every class, in front of her mind, no matter where she turned, was the image of the white man who'd come to the cemetery yesterday. She tried to focus on her students, tried to listen to what they were saying, yet the image of this man now dead kept bleeding through.

The features weren't clear. His face was a blurred white blank, unrecognizable. Did she actually look at him when they talked? She wasn't sure. Would she even have been able to recognize him again afterward? Again, she wasn't sure. Had this man really known her mother? And he'd talked with Shamona.

Lizzie worried about Shamona. They were only a year apart and had been constant companions growing up, yet had taken such different roads in high school.

Whereas Lizzie determined early she wasn't going to live in a house with a wood-burning stove and took college prep courses, Shamona was pregnant at fourteen with her first child, Kasan. By the time she had her seventeenth birthday, she'd had three children: Kasan, Annie, and Sue. All were now in elementary school.

Shamona dropped out of school when she was pregnant with Kasan, and had never gone back. She worked off and on at the Wisteria Inn until Naresse died. Since then, she'd had a series of jobs at other restaurants and fast food places, but she wanted something that paid more and offered benefits.

A few miles before Lizzie reached Hebron, she noticed a light-gray car behind her. She didn't recognize it, but it looked a little like her brother's car.

The car made the turn as she did onto the dirt road leading to her father's place. It seemed to be getting closer to her, almost tailgating. She slowed then, to make the turn up to the house. The other car then went on. She didn't get a look at the driver.

As she parked in the front yard, she noticed her brother Isaac's Buick was at the edge of the house. She frowned. What was he doing here? She was pleased and displeased at the same time.

Isaac was six years older than Lizzie. They'd never been close. The whole time she was growing up, he either ignored her and her sisters completely or tormented them or embarrassed them.

Maybe he'd come to see if Mama 'Dele would give him more money. Isaac was always needing money. Gambling debts, a smack of crack here and there. He never stayed with a job longer than a month or two. Now he hadn't worked in months. His last job had been at the Wisteria Inn. Lizzie was surprised the manager, a white man named Keesa Hudnall, had put up with Isaac as long as he had. She assumed it was because Keesa and Naresse had not only worked together but had been friends for years. Finally, however, Keesa had to fire him. Even so, Lizzie herself occasionally yielded to his persuasiveness and gave him twenty dollars.

No matter how much he distressed her, Lizzie loved him and knew he loved her. There was no doubt in her mind that if she was ever in desperate trouble, she could yell for her big brother. At the same time, she could not envision any possible situation she could get into where he would be of any help whatsoever.

Furthermore, he had been her mother's favorite, although for whatever reason, Lizzie could never understand. Maybe it was nothing more than the fact he was a boy child and the firstborn at that.

Isaac and their father had never gotten along well. In fact, not long after her mother's death, they got into a horrible fight and her father was put into the hospital. Isaac had hit him with a baseball bat. It was Isaac, Lizzie was sure, who'd put it into the sheriff's fat brain that Patterson Clouse was the most likely person to have killed Naresse.

Frequently she told Isaac that he ought to stop by and see

Mama 'Dele. Adele Winter was seventy-eight now, and looking more and more frail. Lizzie knew she had never stopped grieving for her daughter. In fact, none of them had. The wound was still too green. Lizzie also worried about her grandmother. More and more, she did less and less.

At one time she could be counted on fully to look after the kids while Shamona worked. But not anymore, in Lizzie's opinion, although Shamona thought Lizzie was overreacting, and that their grandmother was still quite capable of running after three energetic children. Lizzie knew different.

In spite of her chiding, Isaac rarely came to the house, saying he didn't care to be around his father, Patterson. This was just an excuse, Lizzie knew, because Patterson was working at the college till six every evening whereas Isaac rarely worked at all. Lizzie suspected it was because their grandmother would get on him again about living with the woman he lived with.

At least he's here now, she thought as she stepped up onto the front porch.

Isaac looked up at her as she came through the door and gave a quick smile. "Hey, little sister," he said.

She nodded and looked at Mama 'Dele sitting in her chair. She had the fingers of one hand pushing against her forehead. Distress was pressed into her face.

"What is it?" asked Lizzie, closing the door behind her.

"Mama 'Dele say that idiot sheriff was just here," Isaac said. The smile he gave her was gone now, and in his eyes was growing that furious look Lizzie had seen all too often, usually as a forewarning that he was getting ready to strike out, to hit something or someone.

Mama 'Dele looked up at Lizzie as if pleading or hurting or both. Protruding from her mouth was a smooth-shaven black gum stick.

"Why?" Lizzie asked.

Isaac lifted his hands and spread them in a gesture of confusion. "How the hell should I know? I get word he's asking for me."

"What?"

"You should know. That punk you go with is right with him all the time."

Lizzie bristled. "What's that supposed to mean? H.C.'s not a punk."

A mocking smile twisted Isaac's lips. "Oh? And do you know that from firsthand experience, Miss Sunday School?"

"Stop it!" snapped Adele Winter. "You leave your sister alone."

"It's all right," she said to Adele. Then, glancing around, she asked, "Where's Shamona?"

"In her room," she answered. "Ironing."

"What does the man want with me?" Isaac asked.

"A white man was killed this morning," Lizzie said. "He seems to have known Mama."

Adele looked up sharply. "What? He knowed Naresse? Who?"

Lizzie shrugged. "I didn't know him. But yesterday when I was at the graveyard, he drove up and came over to talk to me." She paused and shook her head, then continued. "He worked for a furniture place in Tupelo. It seems he'd interviewed Shamona about a job."

Isaac frowned. "What was a white man doing there?" he asked. "Why would he talk with you?"

Lizzie shrugged and shook her head.

Adele grunted and took the stick out of her mouth and stuck the chewed-into-a-brush end into a jar of Garrett snuff on the floor beside her chair, then slipped the stick back into her mouth, positioning the brush now filled with powdered tobacco between her cheek and gum, and said, "H.C. was with him. They come to talk to Shamona about the white man."

Lizzie nodded. "And?"

"She recognized his picture, she said, but she had no idea who he was."

Isaac gave a cynical laugh. "That idiot won't find whoever killed anybody. He sure didn't do nothing about Mama, and the killer was right under his fat nose."

Lizzie stiffened. "Shut up," she said. "Daddy ain't never hurt Mama."

He laughed again. "There was somebody else she loved. That's why he done it."

"Stop it," said Adele.

Isaac's eyes were fixed on Lizzie. "Ask Cynthia," he said.

"Stop it!" the old woman said louder. "Let your poor dead mama rest in her sweet peace."

Lizzie looked at Adele. She was crying.

Isaac nodded his head in resignation and backed up toward the stove, holding his hands behind him, his eyes still locked on his sister. He continued to nod. "I know what I'm talking about."

"You don't know anything."

He gave a cynical snort, then said, "Talk to Lydia Gressete. She'll tell you."

"Lydia Gressete's a drunk," said Adele. "She don't know nothing."

Isaac smiled at Lizzie with a mocking smile. "Ask Lydia," he said. "She'll tell you."

Lizzie started to speak, but, now looking again at the tears in her grandmother's eyes, she held her tongue. "I'm going to check on Shamona," she said. Then she left the room.

Shamona related to Lizzie what the sheriff had asked her about the man. It was, she said, the man who'd interviewed her for the job at Adamstown Furniture, and he had asked about their mother, acted like he knew her. That was all she knew, she said.

When Lizzie returned to the front room, she found Isaac had gone already. She leaned down and kissed her grandmother on the cheek. "I've got to run," she said. "I'll talk to you later."

The old woman looked up. Lizzie could see the worry in her eyes.

She gave her a hug and said, "It's going to be all right. Everything's going to be fine."

Within twenty minutes Lizzie was back in town. She parked her car in front of a small clapboard duplex house on Howser Street. The windows of the apartment on the right were boarded up. The blackened streaks running out from under the plyboard covering the windows testified of a fire. A red sign with letters in white warning Keep Out was tacked to the front wall. The fire, Lizzie recalled, had happened over a year ago.

On the left was the apartment of Lydia Gressete. Lydia had been one of Naresse Clouse's closest friends all her life. Lizzie wanted to believe her mother had never been interested in anyone but her father, but . . . after all, her mother was human. Things like that happen. It's not the end of the world.

Anyway, Lizzie wanted to know one way or the other. It seemed important right now. While part of her would just as soon not know, another part demanded surer knowledge, yes or no. Somehow, something like that could have had to do with her mother's death.

Lydia lived alone. She'd been married and divorced three times. Naresse frequently told Lizzie that her friend had no sense when it came to men. She always picked the worst of the litter, feeling sorry for him, it seemed, and then would allow him to kick her around.

Naresse would then tell Lizzie, "If any man was to ever lay a hand on me, I'd cut him quick. I means he would be singing soprano in church from then on." Lizzie smiled as she remembered her mother's words, and got out of the car.

Lydia Gressete was long coming to open the front door to answer Lizzie's knock. When she did, she stood for a moment, blinking at the outside light with a look of confusion on her face as if trying to figure out who the young woman was. She had a bandanna tied around her head and was wearing a quilted bathrobe.

"What?" she said in a choked voice.

"Lydia, it's me. Lizzie Clouse."

The woman smiled. She was missing one of her front teeth and the other teeth were cigarette-stained. Her skin was as dark as any person of color Lizzie had ever seen. "Come in, child," she said. "Come in out of the cold."

Lizzie had never been inside Lydia's house before and was unprepared for the heavy, pungent smell of mingled odors—cooking, human, cigarette smoke, dampness—all floating in and out of each other. The front room could not be more than ten feet square, she guessed, with a low ceiling. They sat down together on the couch.

Lydia coughed long and hard, holding her hand to her mouth. When she finished, she ran her fingers lightly across her forehead as if wiping sweat from her face. Indeed, Lizzie could see a sheen on her skin, no doubt from the exertion of the coughing fit.

"I been sick," Lydia said. "I just set here in the house all day and hurt. I ain't got nobody to take care of me."

"What about your children?" Lizzie asked, remembering

that the woman did have children, but how many and who they were she didn't know.

She shook her head. "They don't care. They up there in Chicago, and they don't even call half the time. My baby boy he stay in a nice place, and he all the time want me to come be with him." She frowned. "No, no, I done told him over and over. I ain't living up there where they kills peoples all the time." She shook her head hard. "Hell, no, I told him. Double hell, no."

"I'm so sorry, Lydia," Lizzie said. "I didn't know."

She coughed, gagged, then coughed again. "I ain't got nobody to help me. My brother gone now. There ain't nobody."

Lizzie remembered that Lydia's brother was in the state prison at Parchman for dealing drugs. She then said, "I know you were close to Mama. Since y'all were girls."

Lydia smiled and said, "Yes. That's right. Child, there ain't a day goes by that I don't miss your mama. She used to bring me good stuff from the restaurant." She closed her eyes and tilted her head back. "What you talking about? Roast beef and fruit. Extras, she say. Umm-hum. So good." She opened her eyes again. "Where you now?"

"I'm still here in Sheffield. I teach at the high school."

"Your mama was sure proud of you. You all right, girl." She put her hand to her mouth as if beginning another coughing spell, then closed her mouth tightly and swallowed, forcing it under control.

"Lydia, a man was killed. A white man. He seems to have known Mama."

"White man? What white man?"

"His name was Rory Hornsly."

The woman turned one ear a bit toward Lizzie, then said, "I don't know that name."

Lizzie nodded. "I see," she said. She swallowed. "Lydia, I need to know some things . . . about Mama."

The woman's brow wrinkled. "What? What kind of things?"

Lizzie took a deep breath, then continued, talking faster, "My brother Isaac always claimed Mama had a gentleman friend all these years. He's even claimed that man was his father, instead of Daddy."

Lydia looked away and ran her tongue around the inside of

her mouth. Then, still looking away, she said, "Why you want to go asking questions like that for? Your mama is dead and buried in the cold earth. Let her sleep in peace, child."

"No. I need to know. It's not that I would think less of her if it was so. It's not that. But somehow I'm wondering if this can be related to what happened to her."

Lydia's face snapped back to look at Lizzie. Her eyes narrowed. "What? What you talking about?"

"Right now nothing makes any sense. I'm trying to sort things out. Please, Lydia. Tell me what you know."

The woman was silent for a long time, looking closely at Lizzie's eyes as if trying to read them, trying to ascertain the depth of her concern about the matter and whether that concern was deep enough.

Finally, she said, "Your mama loved your daddy. That's a fact. But there *was* somebody else, someone she had on the side." She paused and shrugged. "So what? She deserved to have some pleasures in life. Don't we all? It goes by too damn quick. And then it's over. You just get sick and waste away day by day until your time. Maybe your mama was the lucky one." She jerked with a sudden cough which seemed to seize her unaware. Then she swallowed, licked her lips, and continued. "Your mama was a very beautiful woman. She could have had all the mens she wanted. And, maybe there was a couple. But there was really just one man. One very special man." She paused and nodded slowly at Lizzie as if waiting for her to acknowledge she was following.

"Go on."

"This wasn't some one-night stand thing, you know. It went on for a long time. She loved him very much, and, he loved her, so she say."

"Who was he?"

Lydia smiled. There was a faraway look in her eyes, a look of recalling happier days. "She used to call him her Abraham. She said one day they was going to be together, that they'd have plenty of money because . . ." Her voice trailed away, and the smile faded. Her eyes quickly hardened. Then she looked down at her hands.

Her hands had begun to fidget and she seemed to pant.

"What?" Lizzie asked. "What is it?"

The woman looked away. "All that was a long time ago," she said. "We needs to leave your mama alone now."

"Tell me the man's name."

She shook her head. Her eyes seemed to cloud over, like she was drifting away from contact with Lizzie. "I don't know who he was," she said. She coughed, then added, "Maybe it was just talk. You know. Maybe just a game your mama was playing with me."

"What do you mean?"

Lydia shrugged. "Maybe she just made it all up." She turned her face to Lizzie and smiled. "We used to lie to each other . . ." She smiled. "What you talking about, child?"

"But—"

"I have to take my medicine now," Lydia said, standing up, "and then lie down a while. That's all I can tell you."

"But who would know this Abraham?" Lizzie pressed, not believing he didn't exist.

"If he ever was real, he probably dead now, too. Let it be, child. Let it be." She stood there, waiting for Lizzie to stand up.

Lizzie rose to her feet, thanked her and told her she hoped she'd feel better. Then she walked out onto the front porch. Lydia quickly closed the front door behind her.

Lydia Gressete moved to the front window and held the curtain aside so she could have a clearer look. She watched Lizzie get into her car and drive away. Then she let the curtain fall back. She shuffled across the room to the telephone table.

She opened the Chakchiuma County directory and turned the pages until she found the place. She said the telephone number to herself out loud, then dialed the digits on the rotary phone.

The phone was answered on the third ring. She talked hurriedly, nervously. "This is Lydia Gressete," she said. "You remember me?" She continued without waiting for a reply. "I was a friend—a very *good* friend of Naresse Clouse. She told me everything. I means, *everything*. Her daughter Lizzie was just here, and I started to tell her what I knows, but I didn't. I just told her a little. Anyways, we needs to talk."

She listened a moment to the confused, stammering voice

on the other end of the line, then said again. "Lydia Gressete. You think about it. I'll call you later on."

She placed the phone carefully back onto the cradle, and grinned and chuckled. "They gonna pay for my medicine. I means, they gonna pay for it all."

# 10

As Sheriff Grover Bramlett approached his secretary's desk on his way to his office, he noticed the concerned look on Ella Mae's face. "The nursing home called," she said. "It seems there some trouble with your mother. They want you to call right away."

Bramlett hurried into his office and stood beside his desk while he dialed the number of the Still Waters Nursing Home.

"This is Sheriff Bramlett," he said to the woman who answered with a cheery voice—too cheery, thought Bramlett for such an unpleasant place. "I had a call something was wrong with my mother." His speech was choked.

"Nothing serious, Mr. Bramlett," she responded. "It's just that Mrs. Bramlett has decided not to eat anymore."

"Do what?"

"Eat. She says she's going to starve herself to death. This just started this morning, so it's not a major deal yet. She wouldn't eat breakfast and wouldn't eat lunch. Perhaps she'll eat supper. They usually come around by then. But Mr. Shaw wanted you to know just in case . . ."

"In case what?" Bramlett said.

"Nothing. They always start eating again. They don't ever mean what they say."

"My mama always means what she says," said Bramlett with a slight moan. "Always."

"Maybe if you could drop by before suppertime. We serve at five-thirty."

"I'll come right now."

"No, no. That's not necessary. Any time before supper would be good."

Bramlett hung up the receiver, and sat down in his desk chair. He wiped his palm across his mouth and chin. His mother was determined not to like it. She'd told him from the beginning she wasn't staying at no damn old folks home and why didn't he go ahead and blow her head off with a shotgun just like he would have a suffering coon dog. She told him he was a damn sight kinder to dogs than he was to her.

Johnny Baillie stepped into his office. "We haven't got anywhere with Rory Hornsly's computer," he said. "All his files are locked with passwords. We'll keep trying."

When he left, Bramlett glanced at his watch. Almost four o'clock. He still had plenty of time to go to the nursing home before she ate.

Tonight was Tuesday night and he'd planned to be home for supper no later than six, then leave at once for Etowah Community College and class with his maestro Gloria Fisher. He couldn't wait for her to see the painting he'd done. It was another barn, abandoned, and year by year, board by board, collapsing to the earth and dying.

He reached for the telephone intercom to buzz H. C. Curry. There was only one more interview he wanted to make before breaking off for tonight.

In less than ten minutes Sheriff Bramlett and Deputy Curry arrived at Carr's Funeral Home, which was located in north Sheffield across the street from Douglass Junior High. Douglass Junior High had been the black high school until the late sixties and total integration. Now, all seventh, eighth, and ninth graders in Sheffield attended Douglass. Several leaders of the local black community still seethed at the demotion, as they saw it, of their school.

A tall, thin woman with light skin and thick glasses showed the sheriff and deputy into Wayne Carr's well-appointed office. Wayne rose from behind his desk to greet them.

"Hello, Grover," he said, shaking Bramlett's hand enthusiastically. Then, taking H.C.'s hand, he laughed and said good-naturedly to the sheriff, "You gonna ruin your reputation running around with the likes of this fellow." He laughed again and pounded the young man on the back. "Sit down, sit down," he said, sweeping his hand toward the several arm-chairs facing his desk.

Carr was as tall as Bramlett, and possibly heavier. His hands were huge and his shoulders broad and bulky, testifying to the athletic prowess of his younger days.

In fact, the sheriff had been told by several people that, had his knee not gone out, Wayne Carr could have played pro foot-ball. Now, however, his girth had increased manifold times, and his face was fleshy.

Once the three of them were seated, Bramlett said, "We're investigating the death of Rory Hornsly."

Carr's smile slowly faded. He looked steadily into Bramlett's eyes. His eyes, the sheriff noticed, had faint red-blue lines twisting through them and a look of great weariness, as if either the weight of the world or of business or long-ago locked-up secrets were crushing down upon him.

He nodded slowly, then responded, "Yes, I heard he'd died." He shook his head and cleared his throat. "Such a tragedy."

"Did you know him?" Bramlett asked.

Carr cleared his throat again. "No, no. I didn't, actually," he said, shifting in his chair.

The deputy was writing in the small pad opened on his knee.

"That's interesting," said Bramlett. "He seemed to have known you."

Carr swallowed, then opened his mouth slightly and, the sheriff thought, was going to lick his lips. Then he closed his mouth and swallowed again. He glanced at Curry's hand with the ball-point pen resting on the notebook, then said, "Well, I meant I didn't really know him, if you know what I mean."

"What was your relationship with him exactly?" asked Bramlett.

He cleared his throat again. "Actually, we did some business together, a land deal." He paused and waved his hand as if dismissing the dealing as a trifle, as nothing important.

"When was this?"

"A year ago or so. It wasn't really a big thing, and it wasn't mutually satisfactory, so I got out of it. I really haven't seen him since."

"When was the last time you talked with him?"

Carr looked away, his eyes gazing at something on the wall

above Bramlett's head, thinking, then he answered, "I really can't say for sure. Several weeks, I suppose."

"I understand he knew your sister Addie, also."

Carr sucked in his lower lip for a moment, moistened it, while, Bramlett noticed, his eyes seemed to harden.

Then he said, "Yes, I suppose he did."

"What was their relationship?"

"Addie and I have some mutual business arrangements. The interests Hornsly and I had together . . . well, Addie was involved also. But, like I said, it wasn't really that big a thing, and I doubt she's talked with the man in months."

Bramlett leaned back more in his chair, nodding thoughtfully, wondering if the man was lying, or how much of the truth he wasn't letting out. Probably a lot. He didn't seem to care one way or the other that a former business partner was dead. And Bramlett also knew enough about the small interlocking business community of Chakchiuma County to know any mutual partnership between a black man and a white man was unusual.

"Do you have any idea what Hornsly's relationship with Naresse Clouse might have been?"

There was a sudden, involuntary jerk of Wayne Carr's head, almost as if Bramlett had physically reached out with his hand and slapped him across the mouth. "What?" he asked. "Naresse . . .?" He closed his mouth tight, then, as if forcing himself to regain his composure, a composure momentarily lost by the mention of the woman killed three years before in an abandoned barn.

"You did know Naresse, didn't you?"

Carr looked down at the top of his desk, wincing slightly as if hit by a moment of pain, and he said, his voice dropping, "Yes, of course."

"Now," Bramlett said, now leaning slightly forward and turning his good ear a bit more toward Carr. "And what about her and Hornsly?"

Carr looked up at the sheriff and drew a long, uneven breath, exhaled and said, "I had no idea they knew each other. He never said anything to me about her. I can't imagine."

Bramlett felt for the first time that the man was talking absolute truth, nothing hidden, no coyness. "Did you know Naresse well?"

Carr nodded sadly. "Yes, we even dated some in high school. That was a long time ago." There was something of a faraway look in his eyes.

"What about her husband, Patterson? Is he a friend of yours as well?"

Carr's jaw clamped hard for a moment and his eyes jumped to look at the sheriff. The look was cold and hard. "Hell, no."

Bramlett cocked his head. "Oh? What's the problem?"

Carr seemed to shudder, then shook his head hard a couple of times. "Why in the hell she married somebody as stupid and . . ." He paused, shuddered again, then said, "Naresse Winter could have done a damn sight better." He shook his head again.

"Sounds like you thought a lot of her," Bramlett said gently, fishing, wondering if maybe the relationship between Wayne Carr and Naresse Winter Clouse could have been a lot fresher than just since they were in high school.

Carr sat silent for a while. Finally, he gave a wan smile and said, "Yes, I did think a lot of her. She was my first love, I guess you could say."

"And you have no idea why Rory Hornsly would have been interested in her?"

"No," he said, no longer smiling. "She didn't have any money or . . ." He stopped suddenly as if he'd said more than he intended, as if his guard had fallen for a moment.

Bramlett crossed one leg over the other in a deliberate manner, almost as if letting Carr's final remark hang out there in the air between them so they could all three observe it and consider it more carefully. "Why would he have been interested in her if she'd had money?" he asked.

Carr looked away toward the wall on which hung half a dozen framed certificates of recognition from various civic groups in Sheffield. Finally, after a long moment, he looked back at Bramlett. "Hornsly was a greedy bastard. He had no sense of honor or decency or any concept of anything that didn't have a price tag on it. Things and people, to him, were objects to be bought and sold. Naresse and Hornsly . . .?" He paused, then said, "No way."

He dropped his eyes to his hands on the desk blotter. A sudden heaviness seemed to have collapsed upon him.

"Thank you, Wayne," said Bramlett, rising. Curry put away his notebook, stood also.

Wayne Carr slowly rose, unsteadily. He seemed distracted now.

Bramlett left the room and Curry followed. Once outside and into the chilly afternoon daylight, Bramlett asked, "Well? What do you think?"

Curry glanced back at the double glass doors to the funeral home. "I think the man loved Lizzie's mama very much."

"No doubt about it," Bramlett said, reaching for the door handle of the patrol car. "No doubt about it at all."

"Where now?"

Bramlett cleared his throat, then said, "I'm going to check on my mother now. I'll get back with you later."

Still Waters Nursing Home was on Anderson Road at the western edge of Sheffield. Bramlett drove slowly, almost as if delaying seeing his mother and feeling her disappointment once again.

Regina Bramlett had now been at Still Waters two weeks. And Bramlett had visited her every day, usually in the evening. Valeria also came every day, usually in the morning, and sat with her a while.

Eddie Shaw, the nursing home's young administrator, told him not to worry, many patients were like this, it would take a little time, but she'd accept it after a while.

As Bramlett stopped in the visitors' parking lot in front of Still Waters, he wondered not only how long it would take his mother to accept her new life, but how long it would take him to get over the guilt he felt for putting her here.

He entered her room. She was lying on her back in bed, staring at the ceiling. At least in her room he didn't smell urine. In the hallway, the odor was strong, and intensified his guilt.

"How are you?" he asked, pulling a straight back chair near to the side of the bed as he sat down.

She closed her eyes as if going to sleep, made him wait a long time before she answered. Finally, she said, "How the hell am I supposed to be, all cooped up in here like a chicken. There're a lot of insane people in here, you know." She opened her eyes and turned her head to look at him. "Some old bat out in the hall this afternoon told me the Russians got spies in here. Can you imagine that? How am I supposed to even talk with somebody like that?"

"They tell me you won't eat," he said.

She looked at the ceiling again and shook her head. "I'm in too much pain to eat. Pain, I tell you. I'll be dead soon and then you all can be happy."

"Stop it, Mama. You know we only want what is best for you."

She snapped her head back to look at him. "Then get me out of this damn place. Take me home, for God's sake."

"Just give it some time, Mama. You have to adjust."

"What if somebody gets sick or something and needs me . . .?"

He shook his head and said, "There's nobody there to get sick, Mama. Everybody's gone."

She sighed wearily and closed her eyes. "How long does it take a body to starve to death?"

"You aren't gonna starve to death."

"It's not just me, but my cows and chickens."

"Mama, you know I've got a man taking care of the place. Now, why don't you stop all this foolishness and eat something." He started to remind her the cows and chickens were gone, but he didn't. It would just upset her all the more.

"All you think about is that damn job of yours. Why couldn't you have farmed instead. Are you ashamed of farming?"

"You know better than that."

She didn't speak for a long time. Finally, she asked, "What are you working on now that you didn't have time to come as soon as they called to tell you your mother was starving to death?"

"Another killing."

"Anybody I know?"

"No, ma'am. A man named Hornsly."

"And what's so interesting about a killing that you don't have time to check on your mother?" She had a way of pounding an idea, like you'd pound a nail with a hammer, again and again.

He didn't know whether she really wanted to know about

the case or not. Then again, it was something else to talk about, something maybe for her to get her mind on. He leaned back, a bit more relaxed, and said, "Hornsly seemed to have been interested in a woman who was murdered a while back. Naresse Clouse."

Regina Bramlett nodded. "Yes. I remember. She was killed out on the old Farris place." She knew Matthew and Esther Farris, of course. In fact, Matthew's mother and she had been good friends. She closed her eyes again, then added, "I remember when Matthew's mother got old and sick and how good he was to her. He's such a fine man."

Bramlett shook his head in resignation and glanced at his watch. "I got to go now," he said, rising. "I want you to eat tonight, okay?"

She didn't respond.

He moved to the side of the bed, leaned down and kissed her on the forehead, then turned to leave.

"Grover," she said. "I'm just now thinking . . . Don't go pushing too hard on this Naresse thing."

He froze, then looked at her. "What?"

"Leave the dead alone. That's all I got to say. Leave all that buried. Go now, and let me rest."

He stared down at her for a moment, wondering what she was remembering, what she was thinking. Then, he simply said, "Yes, ma'am," and left the room.

# 11

It was full dark Tuesday evening by the time Deputies Johnny Baillie and Jacob Robertson arrived in Oxford, sixty-three miles west of Sheffield. Sheriff Bramlett had assigned them the task of interviewing Dr. Thatcher Hornsly, a chemistry professor at the University of Mississippi and brother of the late Rory Hornsly. Baillie had phoned in advance to set a time for the interview.

They found the professor's house easily. It was a two-story, double-verandah Victorian house two blocks south of the square, probably built, like many of the surrounding houses, around the turn of the century.

Hornsly himself answered their knock at the front door and led them into a high-ceilinged room where sofas and several armchairs crowded against each other and paintings and photographs in frames of assorted sizes and styles covered the walls.

"I hope this won't take long," he said, as soon as they were seated. "My son plays for the high school basketball team and the game starts in just a bit. My wife has already gone." He shifted uneasily in his chair.

Robertson nodded as if he understood, but he didn't. How could being at a basketball game, even one in which your child was playing, take precedence over trying to find out who killed your brother? The man did resemble the victim in a vague sense, but his graying hair had receded more, and his face was not as full.

Baillie took out his notebook to take notes on Robertson's interview.

"I know this is a hard time for you and your family . . ."

92

Robertson began, pausing for a moment and, at the same time, noticing Thatcher Hornsly twist his mouth in an expression that seemed to indicate impatience with the deputy's implied sympathy.

Robertson exchanged a quick look with Baillie, who seemed as taken aback as Robertson.

"Thank you," Hornsly said. "Will this take long?"

"No, sir," Robertson replied. "We'd just like as much information about your brother as you can give us. We're trying to build a list of his associates, friends, and family, and anyone he may have had business dealings with."

"To be blunt about it, Rory and I didn't see each other," he said hurriedly. "It's sad, I suppose, but that's the way it is in our family. Our parents are deceased, there are no other children, I'm five years older than he—so we hardly associated growing up—and he didn't even bother to send a graduation gift to my daughter when she finished high school last year. We weren't even planning to send him an announcement about Tyrone's graduation. He graduates this coming May. So I don't know if I can help you much or not."

"I'm sure anything at all you can tell us will be helpful," Robertson said.

Hornsly sighed and eased forward in his chair as if preparing to get up. "We grew up in Bruce, I came here to Ole Miss, and had graduated and gone to L.S.U. for grad work before he was out of high school. We really didn't keep in touch, as I said." He shifted around in his chair, then continued.

"Anyway, he went to Sheffield College, then was in the military for a couple of years, went over to Vietnam, but I don't believe he saw any action. Then he moved to California, Lafayette, married some woman from out there." He paused and looked up, then continued. "Damn, I almost couldn't remember her name. Barbara. Anyway, they had one child. Bill. I haven't seen him since he was an infant, I don't suppose. Rory and his wife got divorced, he married a couple more times, divorced again each time, and he decided to leave California. I was quite surprised when he moved back to Mississippi. Why, I haven't the slightest idea."

"When was the last time you talked with him?"

He made a wry smile, then said, "Believe it or not, he phoned a couple of weeks ago. That took me aback, of course. I couldn't think of anything more unpleasant than for us to get together. He'd just returned from visiting his son in California. I put him off, told him right now everything was so chaotic around here—and it was—I mean, with my daughter still home for Christmas break. She goes to the University of Virginia, by the way. So, I put him off. Said maybe something could be worked out after the first of the year."

Robertson tried to maintain a pleasant expression on his face. He didn't want to alienate someone he was trying to coax information out of. He himself, however, couldn't imagine not wanting to be with family.

"And that's all he wanted?" Robertson asked. "To visit you all?"

Hornsly gave a low laugh. "Of course not. You obviously didn't know my brother. He wanted me to invest in some scheme. Rory always had a scheme. He was an operator, you see. Somewhere out there was a way to strike it rich quick. He would really have liked for me to have stumbled across some formula in the lab—maybe something to grow hair . . ." He paused and chuckled at the idea, then continued. "After he'd said how wonderful he thought it would be for us to get together, and I told him, in effect, no, he then said he was on to something big, an investment, and several guys were getting into it, and, naturally, he knew teaching college couldn't be all that lucrative, and with one kid in college and another soon to be. Naturally, he thought I might like to get in on a vehicle guaranteeing a quick return."

"What kind of an investment?"

Hornsly shook his head, smiled cynically, and answered, "I wouldn't let him tell me. I knew damn well he couldn't even remember the names of my children, and he wouldn't have known Joanie was home from Virginia—or even old enough to be in college, for that matter—if I hadn't have mentioned it first. So I told him I wasn't interested. He said maybe just a thousand or two. I told him no. I didn't even want to hear about it." Professor Hornsly held up his hands and spread them apart in a gesture of resignation, Robertson supposed, to mean that was the only way to handle a brother like Rory Hornsly.

"And that was the last time you talked with him?"

"Yes. Definitely. I'm sorry he's dead. I truly am. I plan to attend the funeral—that is, if it's here in Mississippi. Now, if they're taking him back to California—well, I don't think I could go that far, but . . ." He didn't finish.

"Did he mention who else was investing with him?"

"No. Like I said, I cut him off. He would have. Whether they were real people or not, who knows?" He glanced at his watch.

"Did you ever invest any money with him?" Baillie asked.

Hornsly shifted uncomfortably in his chair. "Yes, yes, dammit." He looked toward the doorway as if making sure no one else was around and could hear his confession. "Right after he moved back from California—and God only knows why he came back—he told me about a deal up in Union County. Apparently, they mine clay up there. I looked into it. They do mine clay up there, a high quality clay for industrial use. And he was putting together a lease of land from some fellow who owned the property. He told me I could expect a fifty percent profit within a year. Naturally, with interest rates on savings as low as they are, it was tempting." He pressed his lips together as if having to say what he was going to say next was so unpleasant he'd rather not. Finally, he opened his mouth and said, "Like a fool, I gave him four thousand dollars. It was money I'd earmarked for Joanie's education." He shook his head. "When the time came to pay me, he said there were complications, that the money was all tied up. When I finally pressed him just to return my money, he said he couldn't do that."

"Did you ask him about it when you talked to him on the phone?"

Hornsly nodded. "I told him he was welcome to come to my house to see me anytime he came with four thousand dollars cash in his hand. Until that time, I told him, I didn't want to see his face."

He gave an exasperated sigh, looked hard at his watch as if reminding the two deputies he had a basketball game to get to, then said, "That's really all I can tell you." He rose to his feet, indicating the interview was over.

Robertson stood also, as did Baillie, thanked Thatcher Hornsly, and then, at the front door, Robertson looked the man in the eye and said as pointedly as he could, "Please, believe me,

Mr. Hornsly, we know how difficult all this must be for you right now.''

The man glared at him for a second, then shut the door firmly.

# 12

Lizzie Clouse stood holding the refrigerator door open, glancing from shelf to shelf to see if anything looked appealing. Plastic containers of leftovers. Eggs. Raw vegetables in the crisper. Nothing looked good. In fact, she almost felt like anything she swallowed would come right back up.

She took a can of Diet Coke out from the lowest rack on the door, then closed the door and turned to the table where her roommate, Nena Carmack, sat eating a turkey-and-dressing TV dinner.

Lizzie set the can on the counter, took down a glass, opened the refrigerator again, scooped up a handful of ice cubes from the tray in the freezer, and dropped them into the glass.

The doorbell rang.

Lizzie and Nena looked at each other. Nena made a face, indicating she had no idea who it could be. "I'll get it," Lizzie said, leaving the room.

She opened the door. Keesa Hudnall stood on the porch with his hands shoved down into his pockets. "I started to come by yesterday," he said, and she could smell the alcohol on his breath. His face was flushed.

Lizzie didn't want to invite him in, especially since he'd been drinking. But this white man had been a friend—a good friend at that—of her mother's. "Come in," she said, not knowing what else to say.

"Oh, no," Keesa said, holding up his hands. "I know you're right in the middle of supper. I . . . I just wanted you to know that . . ." He paused and his shoulders sagged a bit. Then he said hurriedly, "All day yesterday, I kept thinking about her. I just wanted you to know I was thinking about you all. I miss her, too, you know."

Then, he turned around and hurried down the steps and up the walk back to the street where he'd parked his car.

Lizzie watched him, and an image flashed in her mind of the days when she'd stop by the restaurant and Keesa, the manager, and her mother, his assistant only in name since in actuality she ran the place, would be laughing together and teasing each other.

She closed the door against the cold, not waiting to see him drive off, then returned to the kitchen.

"It was Keesa Hudnall," she said to Nena. "He worked with Mama at the Wisteria Inn." She smiled. It did make her feel better to know that at least one other person outside the family realized that yesterday had been the anniversary of Naresse's death.

She picked up the glass and the Diet Coke can and sat down at the table. She opened the can and filled her glass, then stared at it. She really didn't want anything to drink, either.

"I can't eat," she said, "and the sheriff . . ." She didn't finish.

Nena wiped her mouth with a paper napkin, then said, "The sheriff's an idiot. You know that."

The phone rang. Lizzie rose, stepped to the counter and answered it. It was H. C. Curry.

"Hey," he said. "You okay?"

"No," she said sharply, feeling emotion swell that single small word, emotion suddenly beginning to slip out from under the lid. "Why don't you come over."

"I'm on my way," he said, and the line went dead.

Lizzie returned the receiver to the cradle and stood with her hand still touching it for a moment, as if contact with the receiver somehow kept her in contact with H.C. Then she slipped on her long black leather coat and walked to the window to watch for his arrival.

A light mist was falling through the glow of the streetlamp. There was a car parked in front of the neighbor's house across the street. Someone visiting, she supposed. The car wasn't directly under the streetlamp, but she could see well enough to recognize that it was quite similar to the car she saw behind her going out to Hebron. It was light-colored, a Buick like her brother's. Must be a popular model.

Curry's car pulled up in front. She called to Nena to say she was leaving, then hurried down the front steps and up the walk. The wind whipped at the bottom of her coat. She thought again how much her mother had admired such a coat, how she'd talked of getting one but never had. There were so many things her mother never had a chance to do—like go to college, or be manager of the restaurant, instead of remaining assistant manager year after year.

Three times during her tenure as assistant manager at the Wisteria Inn the position of manager had come open, and all three times her mother got all excited, thinking maybe this time she'd get the job, and all three time Mrs. Caldson hired somebody else. And each time it was a white person. The thought goaded Lizzie.

H.C. was already out of the car, waiting for her by the curb. He turned to look at the gray car. It was leaving now. Then he looked back at her.

"Let's go," she said, hurrying around him to the car.

She had opened the passenger door, was seated, and had pulled the door closed just as he opened his own door.

"What's going on?" he asked as he slid behind the wheel.

"Just drive," she said. "I need some air."

He turned the ignition switch and shifted into gear. "Something wrong with you and Nena?"

She shook her head and looked out the window at the houses they were passing. It was one of Sheffield's older neighborhoods. At one time, the town's wealthiest white citizens lived here, sixty or seventy years ago. Now, many of the larger homes were divided into apartments. Some smaller ones, like the cottage she and Nena rented, remained single-family dwellings.

She groaned. "Everything seems to be closing in on me," she said.

He turned onto Gordon Hills Road. The mist became heavier, and he flipped the windshield wipers to a higher speed.

"I guess that man coming to the cemetery and asking about Mama . . ." she began, then paused. They were passing Wal-

Mart and her eyes were already moving up ahead to the bright lights of the sign announcing CARR'S CARS.

"He was just some dude," H.C. said. He increased the speed of the car as they neared the city limits. "No telling why he got shot. It didn't have anything to do with you."

They rode in silence, the lights of Sheffield far behind them now, a foggy darkness blanketing everything broken only every once in a while by the light of a farmhouse. And, she remembered, it was cold like this that Thursday . . .

"Mama had gotten off work early for some reason," she said softly. "I don't know why. I'd been out to Hebron myself that afternoon, went out straight from school to pick up something at the house. I can't even remember what now. And when I left the house, I stopped at Hudnall's to get something. Then I went back to my apartment. I hadn't seen her at the house. Mama 'Dele was there, but no one else. Daddy was out at the college. I guess, for whatever reason, she had gone to that old barn."

She paused. When the sheriff had talked with her and her sisters, he said it looked like she'd gone to the barn to meet someone. He wanted to know if they had any idea who that might be. He asked if she was seeing another man.

That was when Lizzie told him to go to hell.

H.C. drove without speaking. He seemed to sense she needed someone to just be there, not someone to tell her she ought to be getting over it now, that it was, after all, three years ago and people do have to get on with their lives.

"Then you phoned," she said. "You just said there was a problem and I needed to come home right away. Actually, I thought it was Daddy. I thought he'd had a heart attack or something. The sheriff's cars were all parked in the road and in the front yard. And Shamona was screaming."

She ran her fingers across her cheek, smearing the tears on her face. She couldn't stand to think about her mother, her strong, laughing, smiling, joyous, beautiful mother, to think about this one being hung up and . . .

Lizzie pounded her head back against the headrest and moaned. "Damn damn damn! Why does God let things like this happen?"

H.C. continued to drive. Neither spoke for several minutes.

100

They were nearing the Scooba County line now. "Why did you go out there that day?" he asked.

"What?" She startled by him speaking.

"You said you went out to Hebron that day for something after school."

She wiped the other side of her face. "I can't remember. It's all a blur. I was at the house—just ran in and out—Mama wasn't there. Mama 'Dele was watching television. And then I stopped at the store. I don't even know why I stopped. Gas, I guess. Yes, I think it was for gas." She shook her head. "I can't remember."

She leaned her head back on the headrest and closed her eyes. "I still have nightmares about that barn," she said.

"You never did go there, did you?"

She shook her head. "No, of course not."

"Sometimes, something like that helps, you know. Puts it all to rest."

She jerked her head to look at him. "Are you serious? I think it would make me physically ill to go there."

He reached out and patted her leg. "Okay," he said. "But if you ever change your mind and decide to go, call me. We'll walk in there arm in arm." He smiled at her.

She reached out her hand and squeezed his shoulder. "You're a good man, H. C. Curry. Did I ever tell you that?"

He smiled. "Yeah. You told me. But I want you to tell me something else."

She squeezed his shoulder again. "I can't now. Not yet. It wouldn't be fair to you."

She withdrew her hand. No, right now marriage was even further out of the question than she realized.

"I guess we'd better go back," she said. "You working tonight?"

"I'm on call. This is Tuesday night. Sheriff Bramlett is at his watercolor class."

A yellow road sign on the right indicated a crossroads was just ahead. Curry removed his foot from the accelerator and began to slow down so he could turn around.

After H. C. Curry dropped her off at the house, Lizzie got in her car and drove out to Hebron. It was shortly after seven when she arrived at the house and parked beside her father's pickup.

Mama 'Dele and the children were sitting in the front room watching television. Sue, aged nine, jumped up immediately and ran to give her a hug. Annie, one year older, gave a wave. Kasan, twelve, didn't even look around.

"Where's Shamona?" Lizzie asked her grandmother, dropping her keys on a chair. Sue returned to the front of the TV and sat down again.

The old woman jutted her jaw in disapproval and shook her head. Lizzie knew that she didn't want to say what she thought in front of the children. Shamona was out. That's all that could be said.

Each of the three children were fathered by a different man, and Shamona hadn't wanted to marry any of them. Their great-grandmother, Adele Winter, had always been in most ways more of a mother to the three than Shamona.

"Where's Daddy?" Lizzie asked.

Adele turned her face to look at her, and Lizzie could see the disgust. She understood.

Lizzie found him in the kitchen. Had the weather been milder, he would have been out on the back porch, but now he was in the kitchen.

He was sitting at the table with a glass of pale-amber whiskey and water in front of him, his hands cupped protectively around the sides of the glass. He looked up and smiled when he saw her.

"Hey, baby girl," he said, holding out an arm. "Come give your old daddy some sugar."

She gave him a kiss and a hug, then sat down at the table. It was early yet. She knew this was probably his first drink. According to Mama 'Dele he'd been drinking more lately, how much more, she had no idea, only he stayed longer in the kitchen than usual. Then, she said, about eight-thirty he would go to bed.

Patterson Clouse always referred to his mother-in-law as "Mrs. Winter." Their relationship had always had something of an old-fashioned formality about it. Lizzie had never heard her father offer an opinion one way or the other about his wife's mother.

And, Lizzie had never heard Adele Winter criticize her father. At the same time, Isaac had told her things he'd heard her say, things she'd said to Naresse in years past, things about how Naresse was lucky he was available when he was, and she could have done much better if she hadn't been so stupid, if she'd only listened to what her mother was trying to tell her all these years.

None of this made a lot of sense to Lizzie at the time. She only knew her father loved her mother, that her mother loved him in her own way, although she wouldn't admit it. And—of this one fact Lizzie was convinced and would allow no contradiction by Isaac or anyone else—her father loved his wife with all his heart, and there was no way on God's good earth that he could have ever killed her. No way.

"How's school?" Patterson asked, smiling at her. She knew he loved her, too, just like he loved all of his children, probably even the son who acted like he despised his father, who, as long as Lizzie could remember, had treated the man with contempt, verbally and even physically abusing him. And, baffling as it was, Patterson took it, like he was absorbing it, like he cared too much for his son to fight back and hurt him.

"A man was murdered this morning," Lizzie said. "A white man."

Patterson's smile sank into a scowl. He lifted his glass, took a swallow, then set down the glass. "I heard."

"Who was he?"

Patterson turned his glass around in his hands. "Just a man. I been doing some work for him. He's building a new house. It was good Saturday work."

"I saw him yesterday afternoon at the graveyard."

His brow wrinkled. "What?"

She nodded. "I was paying respects to Mama, and he drove up and came over to talk with me. He seemed interested in Mama."

Lizzie detected an instant hardening of her father's eyes. "He didn't know your mama," he said flatly, firmly, as if not only stating a truth but making a truth out of an untruth should it exist.

"Did he ever talk to you about Mama?"

He took another drink, wiped at the corner of his mouth with his thumb, then said, "Naw. He didn't know her." He lifted the glass and drank, then set the glass down hard.

"He had my name written down in his apartment," Lizzie said. "And Shamona's."

Patterson's hand tightened on the glass. "What you mean?"

"I don't know. He told me I'd seen something I shouldn't have, that what I'd seen could scare somebody real bad." She paused and shook her head. "I don't have any idea what he was talking about."

"What about Shamona? How come he know her?"

"She applied for work at the furniture place where he works. He also asked about Wayne Carr."

Patterson's jaw muscle tightened. He said nothing.

Lizzie continued. "And Addie. He mentioned her, too."

"What?" Clouse said. "What about Addie?"

She shook her head. "Nothing. He just said he knew her."

He ground his teeth for a moment, then said, "He didn't know her neither." He took a long swallow from his glass, draining it. Then he pushed back his chair and took his glass to the counter. "You want something to drink?" he asked. He opened a lower cabinet for the bottle.

"No. Daddy, I've been upset about this all day. If there's any way this man had anything to do with Mama's death—"

"He didn't," he interrupted. He stood for a moment with one hand on the glass and the other hand touching the bottle, staring down at the countertop. He said, "Listen, about Addie . . ." He didn't finish. Instead, he turned, gave her an apologetic smile, and said, "Excuse me." He walked out of the room toward the bathroom in the hallway.

She sat there for a moment, then left the table and returned to the front room. Mama 'Dele and the children were watching some program she'd never even seen.

None of them looked in her direction. The volume was too loud. Mama 'Dele didn't admit that her hearing was slipping, but Lizzie knew it was.

She looked at each of the children in turn. They were so beautiful, so full of life and wonder. She worried about them sometimes. In many ways times were harder now than when she and her sisters were growing up, especially with so much drugs and crime around. She never heard of drugs when she was their age. Now it was everywhere.

She heard the toilet flush, stood looking down at the children and her grandmother a bit longer, silently praying God would take care of them each one. Then she returned to the kitchen.

Her father wasn't there. She glanced at the counter. His empty glass was still there, but the bottle was missing. He'd gone outside.

She pulled the door closed behind her as she stepped onto the porch. She felt the cold air on her flushed face and reached to her neck and turned up the collar of her coat. It only took a moment for her eyes to adjust to the darkness, and in that moment she realized Patterson wasn't on the porch.

"What . . .?" she said aloud, looking out into the backyard. She could see only darkened shapes she knew to be outbuildings, fences, a tractor. There was not enough light to have seen a man had he been there.

She placed her hand on the railing as she reached down with her foot to feel the top step.

As if she'd been slapped in the face, the sharp loud unmistakable crack of a firearm struck her ears, and she instantly reeled, and grabbed the railing with both hands.

It was so loud she wondered for an instant if indeed she'd been shot or, if not actually hit, then shot at.

"Daddy!" she cried out. "Where are you?"

There was no answer.

# 13

Lizzie stumbled down the steps, managed to keep her balance and stand upright. "Daddy!" she screamed.

The only sound was of a dog somewhere. She tried to focus, tried to consider where the sound of the shot had come from.

She looked in the direction of the barn, a dark silhouette rising up against the starlit sky. That was the direction of the sound.

She hurried along the muddy path leading toward the barn. Her father kept no stock right now, the barn was unused, and had been since not long after Naresse died.

She half ran, her eyes more accustomed to the darkness now, and passed the fence post only a few paces from the front of the gaping door. She stopped.

Leaning back against the doorjamb was her father. His arms dangled at his sides. In one hand he loosely held the neck of the whiskey bottle. In the other hand he held a pistol.

"Daddy. . . ," she said, her voice suddenly hoarse. "What . . .?" She moved closer to him.

He smiled. "Hello, baby girl," he said.

"What . . . what was that shot?"

He turned his head to look back into the barn. "I saw a rat," he said with a sneer. He lifted the bottle and took a drink.

"A rat?" she asked, looking toward the door of the barn. "How can you see in the dark?"

He shrugged. "Never mind. Just talking. I ain't drunk."

She moved closer. Now she could reach out and touch him. She held out her hand, palm up. "Let me have the gun, Daddy."

He gave a smile and handed her the whiskey bottle. "Take this for me. I don't need no more."

She took the bottle and said, "Come inside. It's cold out here."

"Cold? Baby girl, you don't know what cold is."

"Please, Daddy. Come inside."

He shook his head, then said, "Go on. I'll follow you."

"Take my hand, Daddy."

"No. Go on now, like I told you. I'm coming on my own."

She took a step backward, then turned around and started walking in the direction of the house. She looked back. He smiled and moved away from the barn, following her. He waved at her to go on. She did.

She stepped up onto the porch and turned. She held the bottle in both hands pulled against her coat and watched him slowly move toward her. He wasn't holding the gun now. He'd put it either in his pocket or belt. She couldn't see well enough to make out which. She could only see he wasn't holding it. In fact, it occurred to her, he must have had it on him while he was sitting at the table with her earlier, talking.

Patterson stopped at the foot of the steps and looked up at her. He smiled. "Baby girl, you go on into the house. I wants to sit out here by myself a while."

"Daddy, it's cold. Please come into the house."

He smiled. "I'm all right. I just wants to sit a while, baby girl. You can understand that, can't you?"

She gave a sigh of exasperation and resignation, then turned, opened the door, wiped her feet on the mat, then went back into the kitchen. As she closed the door, she wondered if she should insist on him giving her the pistol.

But maybe that would just emphasize to him that she didn't trust him, that she didn't think he could handle all this himself. She opened the lower cabinet and returned the bottle to its accustomed place.

She heard the unmistakable sound of her father's pickup truck starting, the high whining of the engine spinning to life.

Lizzie snatched open the back door and stepped onto the porch. The roar of the truck was loud, and even before she could turn to look around the side of the house, she knew he was leaving, driving fast, the tires of the truck spinning on the slick road.

She stood on the porch and listened as the sound of the truck grew fainter, at the same time wondering where could he be going—and why?

She hurried back into the house, grabbed up her keys and looked at Mama 'Dele and the children still watching TV. None looked in her direction. Without a word she left the house.

As she drove hard back toward Hudnall's Grocery and the paved road, she stared at the tracks of vehicles slicing through the mud and now rushing under the front of her headlight beams. She had no idea which belonged to her father's truck.

In minutes she turned left onto the paved road. Was this the way he went? There was no way to tell. Tracks of wet mud on the asphalt led in both directions. She swung into the graveled parking lot in front of Hudnall's and stopped beside the pay telephone booth.

She phoned the sheriff's department, was put on hold for what seemed like five minutes, then H.C. answered.

"I . . . I don't know what's going on," she told him. "Daddy's been drinking and he's got a gun."

"What? A gun?"

"It's just the way he left. I mean, racing off in his truck like he was going someplace." She was trying not to cry.

"Listen," he said. "Everything is going to be all right. I'll ride around. I mean, where could he go? The Log Cabin maybe?"

"I don't know. Maybe."

"Where will you be, at your place or out there?"

"Here," she said. "I'm going back to the house in case he comes back."

She replaced the receiver and turned around and looked toward the beauty shop across the street. Her face felt very hot.

Deputy H. C. Curry stood and walked over to Begard Deise's desk. Deise was hunt-and-peck typing on his computer keyboard. "Just a minute," he replied to Curry's invitation to accompany him on a drive. He typed a couple more characters, then said, "There." He smiled with satisfaction at having finished a difficult task.

Moments later, the two deputies left the parking lot with Curry driving.

"Why the Log Cabin?" Deise asked.

"Lizzie said he'd been drinking," Curry answered. "And I figure he'll want to continue. And, he's been there often enough."

"You really think he's dangerous?"

Curry gave a low snort. "Anybody who's been drinking and is carrying a weapon is dangerous. To himself or to whoever he gets upset with."

"Who's he upset with?"

"I'm not sure."

Neither of them said anything the rest of the five-mile ride out the twisting county road until they reached the Log Cabin. The Log Cabin was a juke joint. On Friday and Saturday nights it was jammed with customers and jumping with live music and dancing and the parking lot was full. But on weeknights it was fairly tame, just a few folks enjoying a beer or two.

Curry made a quick count of the vehicles parked in front. Six. Four autos. Two pickups. He didn't recognize either of the pickups as Patterson Clouse's.

Inside there was the thick smell of cigarette smoke and stale beer. The men sitting at the tables turned to look at the two deputies as they made their way to the bar. Their eyes, Curry noticed, were fastened on Deise, the white deputy.

Three of the men nodded at Curry. Patterson Clouse wasn't there. Curry recognized two of the men from the lumberyard where his father worked. In fact, Witt Curry had spent a lot of time here himself over the years.

Big Red Dye, standing behind the bar with his arms folded across his chest, had immediately looked away when he saw who was coming through the front doors. Dye was tall, taller even than the six-three Deise, and pot-bellied. His hair was graying now, but had been red when he was younger. His skin was a dull yellow, and his face sploshed with large brown freckles.

As Curry and Deise moved against the bar itself, Dye's face was still turned toward a black-and-white television screen flickering at the end of the bar. The volume was turned down. From the Peavey speakers anchored in the corners of the ceiling came the mournful sounds of John Lee Hooker.

" 'Evening, Red," Curry said, placing both hands on the bar top.

Only then did the owner of the Log Cabin turn and look at Curry. He gave a thin smile, and, Curry noticed, didn't look at Deise at all, but kept his eyes on Curry, waiting for an explanation for this intrusion.

Curry gave a tilt of his head for the man to follow him further down the bar and move out of any possible hearing range of the men sitting at the tables.

Dye unfolded his arms and moved with Curry. Deise stayed at the elbow of his fellow deputy. Both leaned over the bar toward Dye, who placed his forearms on the bar top and moved closer toward them.

"Has Patterson Clouse been here?" Curry asked.

Dye shook his head, then asked, "Why you looking for him?" There was a sharpness to his tone. His dislike of law-enforcement people, even one of his own race like Curry, was apparent.

"Nothing big," Curry said. He looked toward the cluster of tables and the beer-drinkers. None was looking in their direction. He turned his face back to Dye. "When was the last time he was here?"

Dye shrugged one shoulder. "I don't know. Not for a while. He ain't all that welcome, you know."

"How come?"

"You remember," Dye said, keeping his eyes fixed on Curry, ignoring Deise. "He and that whacko son of his got into a brawl. I had to call you folks out here. I told Isaac he ain't ever to come back, and he ain't been. He like to have killed Patterson."

Curry nodded. He did remember. Isaac Clouse had taken a baseball bat to Patterson.

Dye continued. "It took four or five men to pull him off. I mean, he beat his father with that thing. We had to get an ambulance. Awful." He shook his head as if still not believing, or at least, understanding what had happened.

"What was all that about?" Curry asked.

"They both drunk. 'Course, they been drinking before they come here, 'cause I don't serve nobody what's already drunk." He paused and looked at the deputy as if waiting for some acknowledgment of this important fact.

Curry nodded, not so much in belief of the juke joint owner's close observance of the law as to maintain a certain level of trust and goodwill with the man he was interviewing.

"Anyways," Dye continued, "they got into an argument, and I told them to take it outside."

"Argument about what?"

Dye shrugged and said, "Don't know. But they'd got crossways with each other in here once before. But that time Patterson just turned around and left. He should have left this last time, too. 'Cause, then his son went outside and came back in a minute with a bat he'd gotten out of his car."

"What was the argument about?" Curry asked again.

Big Red glanced again toward the customers at the tables and then looked back to Curry. He smiled his proprietor smile and spread his hands incongruously with his conversation, a gesture, it seemed to the deputy, designed to communicate to whoever might be watching that he wasn't cooperating with the law officers.

He said, however, "Isaac was the most drunk. In fact, I'm not sure Patterson was really drunk. May not have been at all, now that I think about it." He paused, looked down at the bar top for an instant, then made a sweeping look which took in the white deputy Deise again, and finally back to Curry. "Naw, he may not have been all that drunk. Maybe a bit high. I'm saying that 'cause he was trying to get Isaac's keys away from him. He didn't want his son to drive in his condition. Drunks don't usually consider that about other drunks, you know. And, that's when all the pushing and shoving started."

He paused and turned to gaze in the direction of his customers, not so much focusing on them now, aware of what they might think, as remembering what had happened. He continued. "I remember Isaac saying he knew something. He get right down in his face and yelled it. 'I know!' he screamed at him. Whatever that was supposed to mean."

Dye then looked back at Curry. "Patterson looked like he'd been slapped. Then he shoved Isaac hard—I means real hard, almost knocking him down —and everybody standing around laughed. Patterson just walked away and sat down at a table, and that looked like it was the end. Next thing I knows, that fool Isaac done gone out to his car and got a bat and is in here trying to beat his daddy to death." He paused and shrugged. "That's about it, I s'pose."

Curry nodded. "And that was the last time you saw them?"

Dye gave a little smile. "Last time I saw Isaac. Patterson he come back some. Not much, like I told you, but some."

"You know a white man named Rory Hornsly?"

Dye slowly shook his head. "Unh-uh."

"Appreciate it," Curry said.

Curry and Deise were almost back to the Sheffield city limits when a transmission came over the radio that a pickup truck had run off the road into a ditch on north Fargo Street. No injuries reported. Curry snatched up the radio and said to the dispatcher, "This is unit three. We're responding." Fargo Street was in the oldest black section of town.

In less than four minutes, Curry rounded a hard curve on Fargo Street and parked the patrol car behind a cluster of several men standing in the middle of the street. Sticking up from the ditch on the right side of the road was the rear end of the truck.

"Ain't nobody hurt," said one of the men, with a smile to Curry. He tilted his head indicating a direction beyond the truck. "That's him over there. He missed the curve."

Patterson Clouse was sitting on the edge of the road, his arms wrapped around his knees. He was staring straight ahead, oblivious to the crowd gathering in the street behind his truck.

Curry walked up beside him and squatted down on his haunches. "You okay. Mr. Clouse?" he asked.

Clouse turned his head to look at Curry. His eyes gave no sign of recognition. He didn't respond.

Curry leaned close to his ear and said softly, "Where's the gun?"

Clouse dropped his eyes for a moment, then looked toward the truck. He still didn't speak.

Curry stood up, returned to the patrol car and got a flashlight, and then carefully stepped down beside truck. He opened the driver's door and shined the beam of light inside the cab, first slowly over the seat, then on the floorboard. On the passenger side of the floorboard was a revolver.

He slid across the seat, reached down and picked up the

weapon and shoved it into his front pocket. Then he got out of the truck, slammed the door, and, keeping the butt of the pistol hidden by covering it with his right hand, he walked back to Clouse.

"Let's go home, Mr. Clouse," Curry said, reaching down to take the man's arm. "You can figure out what to do with your truck tomorrow."

As he helped the man to his feet, Curry wondered who in this neighborhood Clouse was on his way to see before he ran off the road . . . and what exactly he was planning to do once he got there.

# 14

After his class, Grover Bramlett left the fine arts building on the campus of Etowah Community College and returned to his car. He placed his fishing tackle box of watercolor supplies and his block of paper on the seat beside him, then withdrew from his pocket a small notebook.

He turned on the dome light and opened the notebook and read again the address of Alice Fielder. He'd planned to stop by and talk with her after class. Ella Mae had found her address for him. The street was not far away.

A minute or so later he parked in front of a small older house and walked up onto the porch. He noticed a red Blazer parked in the driveway as he rang the doorbell and took off his hat.

The porch light came on. "Who is it?" a woman's voice asked through the closed door.

Bramlett identified himself, and the door opened.

"I've been expecting you," she said.

Bramlett stepped inside and closed the door behind him. Alice Fielder was attractive, in her late thirties, blonde, and wearing jeans and a tan sweatshirt with a cluster of blue and yellow flowers embroidered on the front. They sat down in the front room in two easy chairs.

"I understand you were a friend of Rory Hornsly," he said.

She nodded. "We saw each other some," she said. "I can't believe it."

Bramlett couldn't help but notice this woman didn't seem grief-stricken. "I was told you two had been dating," he said.

"I haven't seen him in a while. We probably weren't going to go out anymore. There just wasn't any chemistry there, if you know what I mean."

Bramlett nodded. He could understand that. Somehow he couldn't picture this woman and Hornsly together. He especially couldn't picture her going to a honky-tonk. He said, "Someone told us they'd seen Hornsly with a woman at Club Hawaii. Would that woman have been you?"

Her mouth twisted into a smile. "What is Club Hawaii?"

Bramlett shrugged. "I didn't really think so," he said. "Do you know of anyone he might have had problems with?"

She shook her head. "No," she said. "I met him at an alumni function a few months ago. I teach here at the college. History. We only went out a few times."

"Do you know of anyone else he was seeing?"

"Someone mentioned to me about a woman he works with. I don't know her name."

Bramlett figured she was talking about Elsie Kimble. "Was there anyone else at the college who knew him well?" Bramlett was thinking that Hornsly had told Lizzie Clouse that he knew Matthew Farris. Farris, like this woman, taught at the college.

"No. Not really."

"I'm told he knew Matthew Farris."

She gave a faint smile. "Rory couldn't stand the man. Do you know Matthew?"

Bramlett nodded. "Yes."

"Well, then. Perhaps you can understand why he and Rory didn't get along."

Bramlett raised a questioning eyebrow.

She shrugged and smiled. "They're a bit strange. The Farrises, I mean. Once . . ." She paused, gave a shake of her head as if it weren't important.

"Yes?" said Bramlett.

"Once Matthew and I had lunch together to discuss a committee matter. Later, I saw Esther at the store and she acted huffy." She gave a little laugh, and smiled again. "I couldn't believe it. As far as Rory is concerned, though, I don't know of anything else I can tell you."

Bramlett thanked her and stood up. "If something comes to mind," he said, "please give me a call." He handed her one of his business cards.

115

She took the card, then rose from her chair and walked to the front door with him.

Bramlett arrived home just after ten o'clock, entered the house through the door which connected the carport with the kitchen, and set his fishing tackle box filled with watercolor supplies on top of the small set of free-standing shelves against the back wall.

Valeria was lying on the couch in the den watching television.

"The barn came in second," he said, referring to one of the two watercolors he'd taken to his class at Etowah Community College. Each Tuesday night each member of the class brought two paintings done during the week. At the beginning of class, the students studied each other's paintings and, with a show of hands, selected the top three for the week. Second was as high as Bramlett had ever gotten.

"Gloria said I'd done a good job with the foreground grasses," he said. Gloria Fisher was the teacher, a forty-year-old woman who looked to Bramlett like she'd just stepped out of the 1960's. She wore her gray-streaked dark hair almost to her waist and Indian beads of some sort around her wrists.

"Margaret called," Valeria said, referring to their oldest daughter who lived in Memphis. "She's coming down with the flu. I may have to run back up there."

"Oh?" he asked, turning toward her. "Kids sick, too?"

Valeria was still looking at the television screen, but not, he could tell, focused on it. "Just Margaret," she said. "But they'll probably get it too." She shifted her position. "Some man called. He wanted you to phone him when you got in. Said it was important. The name and number are on the pad by the phone."

Back in the kitchen, Bramlett looked down at the note Valeria had written. Bill Hornsly, son of Rory. It was a local number. He lifted the receiver and dialed.

A clerk at the Wisteria Inn answered the phone and buzzed Hornsly's room.

"I got in about an hour ago," he said. "Have you found out anything yet?" He spoke rapidly.

"We're working," said Bramlett.

"Was it a robbery or something?"

"It doesn't look like it."

There was a long silence on the other end of the line, then Hornsly said, "I'd like to see him."

"Of course," said Bramlett. "The body is at the hospital. Would you like someone to go with you?"

"No," he replied softly.

"There had to be an autopsy," Bramlett explained. "It's the law."

"I understand." There was a short pause, then, "Are you saying you think it was somebody he knew?"

"We don't know at this point. Possibly."

"When can I see you?"

"What about first thing in the morning? My office is in the basement of the courthouse."

"I'll find it," he said, and hung up without saying good-bye.

Bramlett replaced the receiver and stood looking down at it, wondering if indeed the killer was not only someone Hornsly may have known, but someone his son may have known as well.

# 15

Wednesday morning Sheriff Grover Bramlett leaned back in his swivel chair and adjusted his reading glasses, then looked over the typed notes Jacob Robertson had given him describing the crime scene. No ammo casings were found at the site. That could point to the weapon being a revolver—although shooters had been known to pick up after themselves when they used automatics.

There was another note from Robertson, this one about preliminary autopsy report. Hornsly had been killed by a 9 mm projectile. The weapon recovered at the scene was a twenty-five caliber, Robertson said. Hadn't been fired. The witnesses described hearing rapid fire. That meant it was probably an automatic. One witness saw a car speeding away right after the shots. The shooter wouldn't have had time to find and pick up spent casings in the dark. Probably fired from inside another vehicle.

He picked up a computer printout of calls units responded to last night. Mostly routine. The name Patterson Clouse jumped out at him. Drove his truck into a ditch. Curry and Deise checked it out.

Clouse did some odd job-type work for Rory Hornsly. Bramlett wondered if he could tell them anything about the man or about—

The intercom on his telephone buzzed. His secretary Ella Mae said, "Mr. Bill Hornsly is here to see you."

Bill Hornsly was tall, lean. His face looked haggard and his eyes were puffy as if he'd had little sleep. He sat in one of the captain's chairs facing Bramlett's desk and looked at the sheriff, as if awaiting an explanation.

Bramlett spread his hands and said, "Mr. Hornsly, this is what we know . . ." He related the facts involving the shooting in the parking lot. Then, "When did you last talk with him?"

He swallowed and drew a jerky breath as if steadying himself, then answered, "Last Saturday. He usually phoned once a month or so."

"Did he indicate any problems he was having?"

Hornsly shook his head. "No. Not at all. He didn't care much for his job. I think he and the president of the company didn't get along. But he said he was working on some deals and had a lot of money due to come in soon. He was thinking about moving someplace else. Memphis, I think he said. I told him to come back home."

"Did he say where this money was going to come from?"

"No. Dad always had several irons in the fire. He was always on the lookout for a new wrinkle, an investment that was just cropping up." He paused for a moment, then continued with a softer tone. "He never did anything to hurt anyone."

"When was the last time you saw him?"

"He came home just last month, for Christmas." He paused, bit gently at his lip, then continued. "He was in California for so long. It was really home. I never could understand why he came back here after all these years. He didn't have any real ties here anymore." He made a face, then said, "He and his brother didn't even exchange Christmas cards."

"Did he ever say exactly why he moved back?"

"No. Everyone tried to talk him out of it." He made a slow shake of his head. "He just said he had some connections that were worth something."

"What did he mean by that?"

"I assumed he meant some ways he could make money."

"Did he mention any friends he had back here?"

"No. Not that I remember anyway. Of course, Dad was never without friends. He never met a stranger."

"Did he ever mention someone named Roach?"

A shake of the head indicating no.

"Does the phrase black snow mean anything to you?"

Another head shake.

"We are looking into your father's papers as best we can.

Would you happen to have the passwords for his computer files?"

"No," Hornsly said. "I need to go to his apartment and take care of his stuff."

"I'm afraid I'll have to ask you to wait on that a little longer," Bramlett said apologetically. "We're still working there."

Hornsly nodded slowly. Then he said, "I guess I need to go to the funeral home and see what I need to do."

Bramlett put his hands on the arms of his chair and pushed himself up. "Please let us know if we can help you with any of this," he said, rising.

Hornsly nodded again. His eyes stared fixedly across the room as if a wave of pain had just passed over him.

After showing Bill Hornsly to the front door, Sheriff Bramlett stopped at Deputy Curry's desk. "Anything unusual about the Clouse deal last night?" he asked.

The deputy cleared his throat. He didn't look up at the sheriff. He said, "There was a weapon in the vehicle."

Bramlett raised his eyebrows, waiting a further explanation.

"It was on the floorboard," the deputy said, "not concealed. I gave it to Lizzie when we took him home."

Bramlett nodded. Lots of folks in Chakchiuma County had weapons in their vehicles. Nothing was ever made of it unless there were also drugs or the driver was a DUI. "I want to talk to him," he said. "He still work out at the college?"

Curry nodded and mumbled, "Yessir."

Minutes later, they left headquarters driving out of town to the northeast with Curry at the wheel. Only three miles from the city limits was Sheffield College, a small liberal arts school with an enrollment of less than three hundred. The college was founded in 1878 by a Presbyterian minister named Claystone Lee who was originally from Sheffield but had spent the war years at his post teaching Greek and Latin at Yale, then returned to help rebuild his devasted homeland.

The narrow road entered the campus through a gateway formed by two massive brick pillars standing on either side of the road and connected by an arched wrought-iron sign from the top of one pillar to the other which read "Sheffield College," then under in smaller letters, "Class of 1922."

Most of the buildings on the campus were old, none constructed more recently than the late forties, and all of the main facilities finished before World War I. Curry stopped in a visitor's parking space in front of Grant Hall, a three-story building with columns in front. Air-conditioning window units identified those rooms on the second and third floors which were faculty offices and also were a reminder that central air could not yet be afforded at an always-financially-strapped small college like Sheffield.

The lawmen identified themselves at the office and told the curious secretary that they wished to speak with Patterson Clouse. She offered to have him paged, but Bramlett assured her that wouldn't be necessary, if she could just tell him where he would be working, they could locate him.

She directed them to Garrison Hall, the science and math building. On the first floor, a pleasant-faced woman in the hallway (Bramlett took her to be a professor) said she hadn't seen Clouse, but he could be in his workshop, and showed them the stairway to the basement. "You can't miss it," she said. "It's the last door on the left."

Bramlett heard a woman's voice when he reached the bottom of the steps. It wasn't distinct, but excited. Curry was right behind him.

"Use your head, dammit," the woman said. The voice came from the other end of the short hallway where daylight from a half-basement window flowed into the otherwise darkened hallway.

Bramlett moved to the doorway. Inside was the workshop, and standing between two workbenches, were a man and woman, both black. The man was Patterson Clouse.

He flinched when he looked up and saw Bramlett and Curry. The woman, dressed in a short red dress, didn't look familiar to the sheriff. She was probably in her late forties, he guessed, trim and very dark-skinned.

She turned to look at them, and her face instantly hardened. She glared at the sheriff as if to show her disdain for him.

Her chest expanded slightly, and she held her head up. "What you want?" she asked, now placing her fists on her hips.

121

Bramlett ignored her, but said to Clouse, "We need to talk with you, Patterson," wondering as he spoke, who this woman was.

The woman crossed her arms in a defiant gesture.

"Haven't you bothered him enough?" she asked, her eyes still hard on Bramlett.

"It's okay," Clouse said to her. He was holding a screwdriver and had a small part of an electric motor in his hand. "I'll talk to you later. Go on, now. I'm okay."

She looked at him as if trying to decide whether or not to leave. Then she sighed, turned and picked up a red purse from the workbench beside her.

"And may I ask who you are?" Bramlett said to her.

She cocked her head slightly, then said, "You may. Which doesn't mean I have to tell you a damn thing. But I will, and that is only because I have nothing to hide any more than Mr. Clouse does. My name is Addie Carr."

Bramlett immediately recognized the name of Wayne Carr's sister.

"Go on," Clouse said to her again.

She reached out, squeezed his hand, shot a final look of contempt at the sheriff, and left the room.

Bramlett stood looking toward the windows, waiting until the clicking of the woman's high-heeled shoes on the hallway floor stopped, indicating that she'd reached the stairway and was ascending to the floor above.

He then surveyed the room. There were two half windows with frosted glass and motor belts, coils of electrical extension cords, and various tools hanging on nails in the walls. Both workbenches were cluttered with tools and electric motors. It looked like Clouse was in the midst of tearing down a vacuum cleaner.

Bramlett also glanced at his deputy, who he knew was extremely uneasy at the moment. Curry had hardly spoken on the short drive from headquarters.

Bramlett cleared his throat and said, "Patterson, we wanted to talk with you about Rory Hornsly." He paused, watching for some reaction on the man's face. Clouse laid the screwdriver and part on the workbench. He crossed his arms and stared vacantly down toward the space between the sheriff and the deputy.

Bramlett continued. "You knew he was dead?"

Clouse nodded, and said, "I heard."

"We understand you worked for him."

Clouse nodded again. "That's right."

"What exactly did you do for him?"

The man shifted his weight to his other leg, then answered, "I worked at the house he's building. Just on Saturdays."

"I see. And when was the last time you saw him?"

Clouse now was looking at H. C. Curry, and Bramlett wondered for a instant what the man thought about the deputy as a possible son-in-law. Then Clouse said, "I worked out there Saturday. He come by for a little while. Didn't stay long."

"Did you know he had the names of your daughters Lizzie and Shamona written down in his apartment?"

"I heard."

"Why do you reckon he did that?"

Clouse shrugged. "I ain't got no idea. I didn't even know he knowed either one of them."

"He also came out to the cemetery at y'all's church and seemed interested in your wife's grave. You have any idea why?"

Clouse lifted his eyes to look at Bramlett. "That man never knew Naresse. I think he just saw Lizzie standing there by the grave and came over. He didn't have no interest in Naresse."

"What is your relationship with Addie Carr?"

Clouse turned his head. Bramlett could see the man's neck muscles tighten. "She's a friend," he said. "An old friend." He looked up at Curry as if looking for some question or response. The deputy had his eyes focused on the notebook he was writing in.

"Do you know of anyone Hornsly was having a problem with?" Bramlett asked.

"Naw. He seemed like a nice man. He was never late paying me."

"And you have no idea what his interest in Naresse was?"

Clouse's eyes flashed as they bored into Bramlett's eyes. "I done told you he didn't even know Naresse. Now if you ain't got nothing else to ask me, I need to get back to work."

Bramlett held the man's look, wondering why he was so insistent that there was no connection between Hornsly and his late wife. Then he said, "Tell me about the gun."

Clouse drew a long breath and looked away. He didn't respond.

"It was on the floorboard of your pickup," Bramlett continued. "Perhaps it had been under the seat and just came out when you ran into the ditch. Was that how it was?"

Clouse looked back at the sheriff with confusion in his eyes as if he wasn't sure what the sheriff was saying.

"Was it under the seat?" Bramlett pressed.

The man blinked as if his brain had suddenly clicked on understanding. "Naw," he said, now looking evenly into Bramlett's eyes. "It was on the seat beside me."

"Why were you riding around with a gun? Who were you going to see?"

"I was just riding. I wasn't going to see nobody."

Bramlett didn't say anything for a moment, then he smiled. "We'll find out, Patterson," he said. "Don't you worry. We'll find out."

Then he turned and left the room. Curry hurried after him, slipping his notebook back into his pocket as he walked.

"Well?" Bramlett said once they were in the car and leaving the campus. "You make any sense out of this?"

"Why didn't you ask him where he was early yesterday morning," Curry asked. There was a sharpness to his voice.

Bramlett turned his face to look at the young man. "What's wrong with you?"

"You don't really think he had anything to do with the murder of this Hornsly guy, do you?"

"He did work for Hornsly."

Curry shook his head in exasperation. "Was that it? He *worked* for him? What about all the construction workers at his house? What about all the people who worked with him at that furniture place? Are you going to talk to them as well?"

"Maybe this is too personal for you," Bramlett said. He turned to look out the window. They were passing an old cabin with smoke swirling out the chimney. The place was so ramshackle that if it hadn't been for the smoke, Bramlett would have thought it abandoned.

"What about this Addie Carr," Bramlett said. "Is Patterson seeing her or what?"

124

Curry made a face. "Lizzie never said anything about it."

"What do you know about her?"

"Nothing really. Wayne Carr's sister. I've seen her here and there. But never with Mr. Clouse."

They were passing another cabin. The front porch had caved in. There was no smoke from the chimney.

At headquarters, Lizzie Clouse was sitting in a chair outside Bramlett's office. She popped to her feet when she saw Bramlett and Curry approaching. Her hands were clenched into fists.

Curry mumbled a hello.

"I want to talk to the sheriff," she said tersely, her eyes not on Curry but on Bramlett.

Curry stood for a moment looking at her, then slowly turned and walked toward his desk.

Bramlett smiled. He genuinely liked Lizzie. He'd first come to know who she was not long after she finished at Ole Miss and came to Sheffield to teach at the high school. She'd written him a letter wanting to know how many "persons of color" were employed on the force.

Then he'd gotten to know her better three years ago when her mother was killed. And, more recently, last fall when her roommate Jo Ann Scales was murdered. It bothered Bramlett that she seemed to dislike him so much.

He smiled pleasantly without trying and extended his hand toward the opened doorway of his office. Then he followed her inside.

"Please sit," he said, nodding at the chairs in front of the desk. "Can I get you a cup of coffee?"

"No," she said curtly, sitting down on the edge of a chair.

Bramlett sat down at his desk, placed his hands on the arms of the chair and said, "Now, Miss Lizzie. What can I do for you?"

"You can tell me why you are harassing my father," she said. Her speech was clipped, sharp.

He didn't expect this. He asked, "What are you talking about?"

"You've just been out to the college to see him." Her eyes were fixed on him, challenging him.

He nodded. "We just went out to ask him about Rory Hornsly. He did work for the man. You did know that, didn't you?"

She didn't answer immediately, as if thinking how to frame what she was going to say. Then she said, "I knew Daddy was doing clean-up work for some man on Saturdays. But he never even mentioned the man's name to me. That's how little he was thinking about the man when he wasn't working for him."

"And this same man came to the cemetery asking about your mother," he said. "Have you figured out why yet?"

Lizzie's gaze at him was unblinking. She didn't answer for a moment, then said, "No."

"He obviously thought you saw something, or, as he wrote on the notepad, you saw someone with someone else. You figured that out yet?"

"No," she said again. There was irritation in her tone.

"I see," said Bramlett slowly, keeping his eyes on her. She had always reminded him a lot of his youngest daughter Elizabeth. Elizabeth was single, lived in Atlanta, was stridently independent, thirty years old—about the same as Lizzie, he figured. And, like Lizzie Clouse, stubborn and hard-headed. Elizabeth never listened to a thing he said.

"By the way," he said. "Is Lizzie short for Elizabeth?"

She looked back at him. "What?" she asked, more as if wondering why he'd asked the question than not understanding what he'd said.

"Just curious."

"No," she said, a confused look on her face. "Why?"

"Nothing. It's not important." He started to mention sometimes Lizzie was short for Elizabeth, but didn't.

Lizzie eyed him appraisingly. Then she said, "Why were you talking with my father?"

The sheriff slowly shook his head. "We are talking with anybody who had any dealings with Hornsly. Everybody." He rubbed his finger along the side of his cheekbone. "But tell me. How did you know we'd been out there?"

"I have ways."

"I see. And would one of those ways be Addie Carr?"

Lizzie stiffened a bit. "Addie is a longtime family friend."

"Is your father seeing her?"

Lizzie looked at him again, her eyes narrowing. "What of it?" she snapped.

"Then that's okay with you?" he asked.

She looked down for a moment, seemed to relax a bit, not much, but a bit, then met his look again. "Of course."

He nodded, wondering for a moment how his own three daughters would respond if he dropped dead and their mother started seeing someone else. Then he asked, "What can you tell me about her?"

"Why? Is Addie suspected of something?"

"No. I just . . ." He paused, then said, "Listen to me, Lizzie. I think you need to be careful . . ." He didn't finish.

She stared at him for a moment longer, then abruptly stood and left the room.

Sheriff Bramlett stared at the doorway through which she'd gone. Why don't they ever listen, he said to himself, thinking as much about his own daughter as Lizzie.

# 16

After leaving the sheriff's office, Lizzie Clouse drove out to Sheffield College. Last night she'd put her father to bed after H.C. brought him home. She'd taken the gun with her back to her place. She didn't say anything to Nena, just hid it in her own closet. She knew Nena would be upset about a gun being in the house. Lizzie didn't like the idea, either, but she couldn't have left it with her father.

Why did he have the gun with him anyway? And what is this about Addie Carr? It had never occurred to her that there could be anything between her father and Addie Carr.

Both Addie and her brother Wayne were longtime friends of her parents. Both had been with the family constantly in those horrible days right after her mother was killed, and, when afterward the days turned into weeks and everyone else stopped checking on them, both Wayne and Addie continued coming by.

But Addie and her father? Had something started to bloom recently without her knowing about it? And if it had, how did she feel about that?

Now that she thought on it, her mother and Wayne Carr did seem to have been close. Yet Wayne and her father really didn't have much to do with each other. Rather, it was Addie who kept coming to the house, bringing sugar cookies she'd made and sitting in the kitchen talking with her father. Most of the time, as Lizzie now remembered it, they weren't so much talking about Mama, as about their growing up together. Both had lived on farms near each other.

Lizzie tried to remember what she'd ever heard Addie say about her mother. She couldn't think of a thing.

She parked in front of Garrison Hall, and entered the building. Usually, in the wintertime when the weather was bad, she didn't bother to look outside for her father. Wintertime kept him busy working on the steam heating pipes and repairing minor things in various buildings. Patterson Clouse was one of twelve full-time maintenance employees at Sheffield College.

He wasn't in his workshop. She didn't see him in any of the hallways.

It was lunchtime. She went to the maintenance office thinking he might be there eating with his friends.

Jimmie Maxwell, who'd worked at the college even longer than her father, told her he'd seen Patterson driving off in his pickup not a half hour ago. He didn't have any idea where he'd gone.

The sky was overcast as if it might rain again. She shoved her hands into her coat pockets as she hurried back to her car.

"Lizzie!" a voice called.

She turned. Matthew Farris was walking toward her, grinning. She waited.

"You looking for Patterson?" he asked, stepping beside her.

"It seems he's left the campus," she said, then added, "For lunch, I suppose."

"I was just going over to the grill myself for a bite. I would certainly be thrilled if a beautiful young woman like you would join me."

Lizzie smiled. Matthew Farris was the only white man who'd ever called her beautiful. "I'm really not hungry," she said.

He took her arm. "Come on. You need to slow down a bit." The grill was located in the student union building, which was close by.

The grill was crowded with students. No booths were empty. "Are you in a hurry?" he asked.

She shook her head. "Not really," she said, thinking she would wait for her father to return.

"Why don't we get it to go and then eat in my office? That way we can talk."

She nodded in assent, and Farris placed an order at the counter for two hamburgers with fries and Cokes to go.

In his office on the second floor of Grant Hall, Farris swept several stacks of papers and books from the middle of his desk with one hand while holding the bag with the other. Then he took the meal out of the bag and set it on the blotter as Lizzie pulled up a chair to the other side of the desk.

They ate, neither speaking for a few minutes. Then Farris set his hamburger down, wiped his mouth with a paper napkin and took a sip of his Coke. He smiled. "You know," he said, "you look so much like your mother." There was a look of grief in his eyes, and Lizzie remembered again her mother telling her once that when she was a little girl she and Matthew played together constantly.

"This man who was killed . . ." she said. "He said he knew you . . ."

He frowned. "Yes, I knew him." He took another sip of his Coke and shook his head as he swallowed. "He is not a very pleasant person. I mean, I'm sorry he's dead—something like this is always terrible—but I certainly didn't know the man well enough to be very upset by it."

"He came to the cemetery when I was at Mama's grave."

Farris raised his eyes to look at her. His eyes had a confused look. "What?" he asked.

Lizzie nodded. "He acted like he knew her."

Farris stared at her for a long moment as if wondering if he'd heard her correctly. Then he said, "I don't see any way in the world he could have known Naresse."

"Maybe at the restaurant."

Again, Farris shook his head. "No, if I recall, he wasn't even here when Naresse died." He took another bite of his hamburger, chewed deliberately and swallowed.

"He'd interviewed Shamona for a job," she said. "He asked her about Mama, and she told him where she was buried. I can't figure out why he came to the cemetery."

Farris put his hamburger down, and with the backs of his fingers slowly pushed it away. "Probably he was just riding by," he said.

Lizzie considered this, then said, "But where could he have been going? There's no one for him to have seen out there."

"Just sightseeing, probably."

"You think there's any way this man could have been connected with Mama's death?"

Farris's eyes widened slightly. "What?" he asked softly. "Why . . . how could that be?"

She thought for a moment, then said, "I'm just always grasping at this and that. It's just something that won't go away."

Farris reached out his hands and placed them on hers. "Listen," he said. "We all loved Naresse." He drew his hands away and dropped his eyes. "I miss her, too." He paused, then looked back up at her and gave a slight smile. "I also miss the old place, you know. Sometimes I go back there."

Lizzie looked surprised. "To Hebron?"

He nodded. "To the farm. Of course, there's nothing left but the barn. But I enjoy just walking around the land. Sometimes when I want to get away, I drive back out there. A lot of memories. Beautiful memories."

Lizzie shuddered. "Maybe for you," she said, "but not for me. It's the place my mother died. There're no good memories there for me, only one horrid nightmare."

His eyes stayed on her, studying her face. Then he said, "Maybe you should just let it all go, Lizzie. Your fretting and my fretting won't bring her back."

Lizzie's eyes met his eyes. "I'll never let it go," she said firmly, "not until whoever killed her is punished." She paused and nodded slowly, her eyes still on his eyes. "Never," she said again.

He smiled and reached out and patted her hand again. "I've got another class to run to," he said.

Lizzie stood up. "Thank you for the lunch."

"I'm always here if you need me," he said, walking her to the door.

As Lizzie left the building she thought about what he'd said about letting it go. How could he have said that? How could anyone who really loved Naresse Clouse just let it go? Certainly not Lizzie. No, she'd never stop until her mother's killer was found, caught, and punished.

At Adamstown Furniture in Tupelo, Sheriff Bramlett and Deputy Curry sat in front of the desk of Dave Sartoman, who, according to the company's president Daniel Koph, was a golfing buddy of Rory Hornsly. Sartoman looked to be in his mid-thirties, had sandy-colored hair, blue-green eyes, and a deep bronze tan, the kind of tan in the dead of winter one could only attain at a tanning booth.

"We understand you were a close friend of Rory Hornsly," Bramlett said, noticing on the desk there were no little framed pictures of a wife and children which the sheriff often saw in the offices of businessmen.

Sartoman lifted one side of his mouth slightly as if surprised at the statement. "I don't think I would have described us as *close* friends, but we had had a few drinks together. I mean, almost everyone else in management here has a family. Both of us were single."

"When was the last time you saw him?"

"It would have had to have been before I went to Florida. Business trip. I just got back this morning. I can't remember when." He looked up at the ceiling, as if thinking, then his eyes met Bramlett's once again. "We went out to get a drink together after work one evening, but I can't remember how long ago that's been."

"Do you know anything about some kind of investment venture Hornsly was working on?"

Sartoman grinned. "Sure. Rory was trying to get me to invest in a deal he had working. I told him I liked him too much to get involved in anything he was doing like that."

"Like what?"

"Something about mining clay in Union County. He was putting together a group of investors. He already had several, but he needed more." He shook his head. "I don't put my money into anything I know nothing about. And I don't know squat about clay."

"Did he mention any other investors?"

"Yes. He said a pastor was involved—as if that was supposed to assure me there was nothing funny about the deal—and a few other guys. Oh, one was a professor at the college in Sheffield."

"Did he mention any names?"

Sartoman shook his head. "He may have. I can't recall. He mainly was stressing to me how much money would be returned on the investment. He wanted ten thou from me." He laughed. "Rory was always wheeling and dealing."

"Exactly how was this deal supposed to work?"

"I never really understood why there was so much money in it. Something about buying clay and selling it to industry.

That's about all I know. I can't imagine there being that much quick money in clay."

"Did he have any other friends here at the office?"

"Not really. Of course, Rory was a friendly guy. You know. He had a good word for everybody. I can't imagine anyone killing him. Was it robbery?"

"We don't know. Did he carry large amounts of money?"

"He never went anywhere without at least a thou in his money clip. He did like to show the hundreds. He'd always ask a bartender, 'Got change of a hundred?' Rory had his warts just like all of us. But he was really a decent guy. I liked him."

"What about girlfriends?"

He shrugged. "Nothing that special, I don't think."

"I understand he used to see one of the women who works here. Elsie Kimble."

Sartoman grinned. "You don't miss much, do you, Sheriff? I really wasn't going to say anything about that."

"Why not?"

"Well, it's over, for one thing. And, more importantly, she's still wearing a wedding ring. As for myself, I don't mess around with married women. You can get shot doing that." He paused and had a funny look on his face, as if suddenly realizing the import of his words.

"Can you think of anything else to tell us?"

He was silent for a long moment, moving his fingers over to touch the silver letter opener laying on the desk blotter in front of him. He tapped the letter opener, then said softly, "The last time I saw Rory—I'm pretty sure it was the last time—he was agitated. I think it had to do with this clay deal. I don't know if something was wrong or not. Anyway, he needed more capital. He asked me if I was sure I didn't want to come in on it. I told him I was positive. Then he gave a weird grin and said something about him being able to squeeze blood out of a turnip. It was as if he'd just remembered something."

"What was it?"

"He didn't say exactly. I was probably thinking about something else. I don't know. Wait. He said something about pulling the legs off bugs to make them get in line a bit."

"Bugs?" Bramlett asked, exchanging looks with Curry.

Sartoman shrugged. "It didn't make any sense to me."

"Are you sure he said 'bug'?" Bramlett asked. "I mean, it wouldn't have been *roach*, would it?"

The man blinked his eyes rapidly, looking at the sheriff. Then he said, "Roach? Why . . . It *was* roach. That's what he said. I remember now because at the time he said it, I thought who in the world would even touch a roach, much less pull their legs off?"

"Did you ever hear him say anything about black snow?"

"Black snow? No. Not that I recall."

Sartoman leaned back in his chair and looked past the sheriff toward the door. On his face was an expression of quick contemplation, as if, it seemed to Bramlett, there was something more the man was wondering if he should say. Then he looked back into Bramlett's eyes. "Rory always dismissed it as something of no concern," he said, "but if it had been me, *I* would have been concerned."

"And what was that?"

"Elsie Kimble's husband. He came by here one day, here to the plant, and went straight into Rory's office. According to Rory—and he was laughing about this, mind you—the man threatened him."

"How threatened him."

"He told him he was going to kill him if he didn't stop seeing his wife."

# 17

At the hospital in Tupelo, a woman at the nursing station on the third floor told Sheriff Bramlett and Deputy Curry that Buddy Kimble had gone down to Jackson that morning to attend a seminar and wouldn't be back till late. The sheriff directed Curry to drive to Sheffield. The fields they passed along the way were half filled with standing water. It would be a long time before spring plowing.

"Let's stop by Sheffield College," Bramlett said as they neared town.

In minutes, they were on the campus and in the registrar's office.

Mrs. Clarese Tonniton had been registrar of Sheffield College thirty-two years, she said. She and her assistant were trying to put all the records of former students into the new computer system, but were starting in the present and moving back. "It will be a long time before we get to the sixties," she said.

"As best as I can figure from Hornsly's age," Bramlett said, "he should have graduated around sixty-three or -four or -five."

She was a heavy woman and seemed to be breathing hard as she stood at the filing cabinet pulling out and opening file folders. She looked at one for a moment, leaning slightly on the opened drawer, ran her fingers down a list of names, then snapped the file closed and slipped it back into the drawer. "Not in sixty-five," she said. She whipped out another file.

Rory Hornsly didn't graduate in 1964, either. She opened the 1963 file folder, then immediately said, "Aha. Here he is.

Majored in business. No honors." She handed the file to Bramlett.

He looked at the sheet. There were two columns of names, and Bramlett read each name. Rory Hornsly's name was in the first column.

Then he started at the beginning. His eye tarried on the name Matthew John Farris. "Matthew Farris finished this year also," he said to the deputy, who immediately wrote down the name in his notebook. He handed the sheet back to Mrs. Tonniton, and said, "Could we have a photocopy of this. And maybe the three years before and afterward. That would give us the names of everyone he was in school with."

Mrs. Tonniton shook her head. "I can't imagine someone from our college getting murdered," she said.

Bramlett gave her a smile. "Murder happens in the best of families sometime. Even to Baptists and Methodists."

It was after four-thirty by the time they got back to headquarters. The sheriff told Curry he needed to go to the nursing home. It was almost time for supper there and he wanted to look in on his mother. Then he left.

Curry checked the phone messages on his desk. Nothing.

He wondered if Lizzie might want to run get a pizza. He phoned.

The call was answered on the first ring. Lizzie sounded upset. "I'm worried about Daddy," she said. "I was just fixing to go out there. Aunt Birdie called and said he'd been by there this afternoon and told her he needed money. She loaned him four hundred dollars. She said he wouldn't say where he was going."

"Where would he go?"

"I don't know. I went out to the college at lunch to see him, but he was already gone. Jimmy Maxwell said he'd gone off in his truck. I just phoned Addie Carr. She hasn't seen him since this morning. She'd called me about y'all being out there, by the way. What was that all about?"

"Where's the gun?"

"It's at my place. I took it home last night after you gave it to me." She paused a moment, then continued. "So? You didn't answer me."

"Sheriff Bramlett read the report from last night. I had to mention the weapon."

"Did Daddy seem upset when y'all talked with him?"

"Not particularly. Addie was there when we arrived, by the way."

"I know," she said. "She's going to meet me out at the house."

"You going now?"

"Yes."

"I'll come pick you up," he said.

In less than twenty minutes they were at the house in Hebron. Patterson hadn't returned. "He all right," Mama 'Dele assured her.

Lizzie paced back and forth across the room. She glanced at her watch. "I thought he might have gone by to see Addie," she said.

"Who?" asked Mama 'Dele.

"Addie," Lizzie answered, turning near the front door and walking back. "Wayne's sister."

"Why?"

"She's a friend . . ." She paused. She had almost said *of Daddy's*, but that might not sound right to her grandmother.

"What has Addie Carr got to do with Patterson?" Adele Winter persisted.

Lizzie stopped and sat down quickly on the couch beside Curry. She sighed, then said, "Apparently they've been seeing each other some."

The old woman gave a snort. "Poor, poor Naresse. Her poor body ain't even cold yet."

"Mama's been dead three years now."

"Still ain't right. Not with that woman anyways."

"Why? What's wrong with Addie?"

Adele slowly shook her head. "Your mama right now rolling over in her grave that we all should be talking about her husband and that woman in the same breaths."

Lizzie stared at her, waiting for some further explanation, but none was forthcoming. She looked back at Curry. "I couldn't find Daddy, but I did see Matthew Farris. We had lunch together."

Adele pouted her lower lip as if in disgust. She said nothing.

"What is it?" Lizzie asked her.

"I don't know what he ever saw in her anyways," Adele blurted out.

Both Lizzie and Curry looked at her in bewilderment. "What?" asked Lizzie, not following the old woman's line of thinking.

"That woman he married," she said.

Lizzie smiled and shook her head. She then reached out her hand and placed it on Curry's hand. She read the perplexed look on his face, then said, "Mama 'Dele and Mama never cared much for Matthew's wife."

"I see," he said.

"No," continued Lizzie. There was a sudden twinkle in her eye. "You have to understand, Matthew's family and our family have been close for years. I think Mama 'Dele thought she should have had the right to approve of whoever Matthew married. Isn't that right, Mama 'Dele?"

Adele scowled but didn't answer.

"So," continued Lizzie, "Mama and Mama 'Dele never thought Esther was good enough for Matthew." A slight smile played along her lips and she waited to see if Curry caught the irony of that statement. He nodded, and she said, "Esther is a well-known photographer, you know. She's had exhibits all over the county, published books of photographs."

Curry nodded. He had seen the framed photograph of the dogwood in bloom that hung in the Bramlett's den.

"I remember seeing Esther at Hudnall's one day." Hudnall's Grocery was the only store of any kind in the rural community of Hebron. "She was all rushing around, obviously in a hurry, and, I thought, upset about something. She's the kind of woman who is always rushing someplace. Anyway, she dropped the gas nozzle and swore. That surprised me." She glanced at Adele. "You know how Matthew is about cursing," she said to Adele. Then, to Curry, "Matthew is very religious, you know."

The old woman made some other grunt.

Lizzie cut her eyes at her again, then went on. "Esther snatched up the hose and shoved it back into the pump, then ran right past me going inside to pay. She looked right into my eyes and didn't even speak. I mean, she acted like she didn't even know who I was."

"She knowed who you was," Adele said.

Lizzie shrugged. "I guess. Yes, I know she knows me. But that's how she is."

They heard the *clomp, clomp* of a car crossing the plank bridge from the road to the front yard. "That will be Addie now," said Lizzie.

"What!" said Adele. "You mean she's coming over here?"

"She's concerned about Daddy," Lizzie said defensively.

The old woman began to shake all over, grabbed the arms of her chair and squeezed and struggled to her feet. "Maybe I be dead by the time she gets here," she said, glowering at her granddaughter. "May your mama forgive your stupid self." Then she left the room.

Lizzie and Curry stared at each other in confusion as they heard the slam of Adele Winter's bedroom door.

# 18

Lizzie pulled open the front door at the first knock. Addie Carr hurried into the room. "Burrr," she said. "It's freezing out there."

She took off her dark-blue wool coat and handed it to Lizzie. She was shorter even than Lizzie, in her mid-fifties, and petite with fine facial features. Her skin was dark and smooth. She smelled of a sweet perfume mingled with cigarettes.

Lizzie introduced H.C. Addie ignored him, didn't even respond to his mumbled "How do you do?"

She gave a quick smile at Lizzie as she sat down on the couch. Lizzie sat down beside her, looking at her, feeling slightly awkward knowing this was a woman who had developed some sort of relationship with her widower father. Curry sat down in a chair beside the couch.

The idea of her father with Addie Carr was something she wasn't at all used to. It was still too new, too improbable, too unlike anything she could ever have expected. This woman was known as someone who had been places and done things, who'd spent most of her adult life in the North. That was probably why her grandmother was so upset at the idea of her being here.

What Lizzie knew was this: Addie Carr was the sister of Wayne Carr, Sheffield's wealthiest black person. She herself drove a new Cadillac Fleetwood, lived in an expensive apartment at Vers la Maison, the same apartment complex where Rory Hornsly had lived and died.

Addie Carr had returned to Sheffield from Chicago during Lizzie's last year in high school. She remembered there was quite a stir. Even her mother was upset. No one knew exactly what she'd done in Chicago. Some said she worked in a night club, some said she was a dancer. Naresse, Lizzie's mother, used to say the woman had been whoring all these years up there and that's why she had so much money.

Addie glanced around the room, then asked, "Where's Mrs. Winter?"

Lizzie swallowed, then said, "She's in her room. She's not . . . feeling well."

Addie gave a slight smile. "I understand," she said. She sat up straight and looked hard at Lizzie. "Tell me when you saw him last."

"Last night I was over here," she said. She started to say something about putting him to bed after H.C. brought him home, but didn't.

Addie cleared her throat and lowered her eyelids slightly, still looking at Lizzie. "Patterson phoned me this morning. Early. He was using the phone down at the Armstrongs'. He told me he needed to get his truck. It was stuck, he said. I phoned my brother, then came to pick up Patterson. One of Wayne's men met us at the truck and helped Patterson get it out." She paused and put one hand on Lizzie's hand. "Wayne is a lot better friend of Patterson's than he realizes, by the way," she said. She squeezed Lizzie's hand, and looked at her as if awaiting a response. Lizzie had no idea what the woman was implying. Then she continued. "Later I went out to the college to check on him." She looked at Curry. "That's when you and Sheriff Bramlett came."

Curry made no response except to look away from her.

She continued. "He's wrong about Patterson," she said.

Curry nodded but still didn't reply.

"This has all got something to do with that man Daddy did Saturday work for," Lizzie said. "That's what all this is about now. Isn't that right, H.C.?"

H.C. nodded. "Yes," he said.

Addie's face twisted in displeasure. "The man was scum. I'm glad he's dead."

Lizzie's eyes widened in surprise. "You knew him?"

"I knew him to be a crook. I'm not surprised somebody shot him." She closed her eyes for a moment, then opened them. "But forget him. Let's think about finding Patterson."

141

"He stopped by his sister's place. She stays out of town a ways."

"I know Birdie," Addie said with a smile. "Listen. I really don't think he's gone far. I can't see him leaving without telling me something." She glanced at her watch. "In fact, he may try to get in touch with me. Does he have any money?"

"Birdie loaned him four hundred dollars."

She nodded, her eyes narrowed in thought. Then she said, "He'll probably call me before he actually leaves." She smiled at Lizzie. "Your father and I go back a long way, girl. I care for him a lot." She leaned over and hugged Lizzie. "Don't worry," she said. "He's okay. I know Patterson. He's okay."

Curry dropped Lizzie off at her place. He had to get back to work he said.

She didn't even go into the house. Instead, she jumped into her car and drove. In minutes she parked in the driveway of Wayne Carr's columned planter-style house in a predominately white neighborhood of Sheffield. She remembered when she bought her car from him how he'd written down on a slip of paper how much her monthly payments would be and then said to her, "For Naresse's sake."

Her mother had liked the man, she knew that. Whenever his name was mentioned she got a little sparkle in her eye. And Addie had said he was a friend of her father's even if Patterson didn't realize it—whatever that was supposed to mean.

She wasn't sure even as she rang the doorbell exactly what she wanted to ask Carr, but suddenly she felt she needed to reach out to people who cared about her mother, and who might know something about what was going on with her father.

Wayne Carr's wife Lucille answered the door. Lizzie had seen her before, knew who she was even though the woman didn't know her. "Yes?" she asked, and Lizzie at once smelled alcohol on her breath.

Lucille Carr was Wayne's second wife, at least ten years younger than he, slightly taller than Lizzie and was wearing a blond wig. She eyed Lizzie suspiciously.

"Is Wayne home?" Lizzie asked. "I'm Lizzie Clouse."

The woman's look of suspicion turned instantly to a look of

scorn. Lucille Carr tilted her head back slightly. She didn't say anything and didn't move.

Lizzie swallowed and stammered, "I . . . I'm a friend of Addie . . ." This just popped into her brain.

Lucille Carr turned away from the door and Lizzie stepped into the foyer. The woman left then, and Lizzie stood second guessing herself. Was this a good thing to do? She felt flushed.

She heard raised voices, not quite distinct enough to understand all of what was being said, but enough to know Lucille Carr was upset and Wayne Carr was upset that she had yelled. A moment later, Wayne, smiling broadly, walked into the foyer.

"Lizzie," he said, reaching out his hand to her. "What a nice surprise." He took her hand in both of his and led her into a finely furnished living room.

As soon as they were seated, Lizzie said, "My father has gone off."

Carr leaned back in his chair. His smile faded. "Gone off?"

Lizzie nodded. "I'm not sure why I came to see you. I hope I'm not causing a problem . . ."

Carr made a gesture with his hand dismissing the thought of a problem, then said, "You could never cause me a problem. You know that."

"Addie came by the house. I . . . I think she and Daddy are . . . good friends."

Carr grinned. "They were good friends before your daddy and Naresse ever got together." His grin widened slightly. "I'm his friend, too. I understand he got the truck up and running this morning. By the way, you can tell him I said he needs more than new tires. He needs to let me put him in a decent machine."

Lizzie nodded. Apparently Addie had told her brother Patterson slipped off the road because of his tires. "I appreciated you helping out," she said.

"Anytime," he said, a slight smile playing at the corners of his mouth again.

Lizzie felt uncomfortable. She cleared her throat, then said, "You said when you sold me my car that you were giving me the deal you did for Mama's sake." She paused and waited for him to explain.

He nodded. "You know Naresse and I grew up together. We

143

all grew up out there at Hebron. Addie and Patterson—well, to tell you the truth if you ain't figured it out already—they were sweethearts all through school. I mean, since before they was in high school, they was sweet on each other. Addie was planning to marry him. No doubt. Then your mama came along."

Lizzie had never known this. She swallowed, then said, "You mean Daddy and Addie . . .?"

Carr nodded. "To put it bluntly, when your mama moved in on Patterson, he never knew exactly what hit him. They got married right away." He smiled, and added, "Poor Addie. I don't think she ever got over it. Even all those years up in Chicago, I think she was in love with Patterson."

Lizzie shifted in her chair. This was not what she expected to hear. "I never knew that," she said softly.

Carr glanced toward the doorway as if checking to see where his wife was, then said, "Narcsse and I were good, good friends." He nodded and gave a wan smile. He didn't speak for a long moment, then turned his eyes back on Lizzie. "That's why, anytime I can do something for one of you kids, I'll do it. Like your brother . . ." He stopped, his mouth clamped shut as if the words had slipped out too quick, slipped out before he'd thought about them.

"My brother? Isaac?"

Carr looked down at his hands and nodded. "He needed some help. Not long ago." He shrugged. "It wasn't all that much."

"You loaned him money?" Lizzie asked. She knew her brother well enough to know he had no shame, that he'd ask anyone to give him money, and that he was constantly getting into trouble with his gambling. She shook her head. "He'll be back to see you."

"I can handle it," Carr said, beginning to smile again. "It's just that . . ." He paused and gave a little laugh. "Now, you came to tell me Patterson has gone off."

Lizzie nodded. "Addie says not to worry, but . . . I'm really not sure why I came . . ."

Carr smiled. "That's all right. You—" He looked up at the doorway. Lucille Carr was standing there now.

"We'll be through shortly," Carr said curtly.

Lucille didn't look at Lizzie. Her eyes were fixed on her husband, and her mouth twisted into a sneer. "I can't believe you."

"I said we'll be done shortly," Carr said. His neck muscles tightened.

"You bastard!" Lucille said, suddenly stepping forward and grabbing at Carr's hair. "Bringing the woman's own daughter right under my roof. What are you doing now? Sleeping with the slut's own daughter? God, what a bastard."

Carr was instantly on his feet, backing away from her, holding up his hands to ward her off.

She lunged at him, and, as quick as the strike of a snake, he shoved her aside, hard.

She gave a sharp cry and fell sideways, crashing into a small table and knocking a lamp to the floor. The lamp shattered.

Lizzie was on her feet, wanting to dash to the front door and get away.

Carr spun back to look at her. Both fists were clenched. His face was distorted with fury. "You'd better go," he said, his voice shaking.

She hurried past him, looking down at Lucille sitting beside the shattered lamp with her face in her hands. Her shoulders were shaking and she was sobbing. "I'm sorry," she wailed. "I'm sorry . . ."

# 19

Bramlett was standing at the kitchen table watching the mixture of burnt umber and ultramarine blue flow down the glistening sheet of watercolor paper. Running a sky wash was, for him, the most critical moment in a painting. The success or failure of the entire effort rested, to a great extent, on this brief procedure of controlled spontaneity.

He watched the edge where the paper and masking tape securing it to the drawing board met for any developing backwashes. He watched the dry, white outline where the roof of the dogtrot house would go, ready to sponge up any errant trickles of water.

*There's nothing but crazy people here*, his mother had told him when he stopped by the nursing home. *I feel like I've been put into a jail to die.*

He tried to coax her into eating the English peas. She'd always liked English peas. *I told you those peas come from tin cans*, she'd said. *You want your only mother to die from tin poisoning?*

Maybe convincing her to move off the old place was a mistake. Maybe—

The telephone rang.

"Damn," he muttered under his breath, not wanting to leave the drying wash in case a problem developed. "Can you get that?"

Valeria was in the den watching an old Montgomery Clift movie on television. She loved Montgomery Clift. She walked into the kitchen and answered the wall phone.

"Hello?" She listened, then said, "Just a minute." She held out the receiver to him.

He sighed and rose from his chair and took the phone. Valeria patted him on the shoulder and returned to the den.

"This is Sheriff Bramlett," he said.

"Grover, this is Ellsworth Daniels," a croakish voice said.

Daniels was probably in his late seventies and operated a gun shop north of town a few miles. He sold hunting supplies, both gun and archery, ammunition, and was an excellent gunsmith. Every time Bramlett dropped by to trade with him, he grumbled about federal regulations and forms he had to fill out and how this was his last year in the business. Bramlett knew, however, that Daniels would probably drop dead at his workbench some day in the process of hand-tooling a firing pin.

"Everything all right, Ellsworth?" asked Bramlett.

"It probably ain't nothing," he said. "But it's been bothering me and it pretty much ruint my supper, I mean, just the fretting about it, you know."

"Oh? And what seems to be the problem?"

"I had a colored fellow in this evening, about four o'clock, I think. His name is Patterson Clouse. You know him?"

Bramlett's grip on the receiver tightened. "Yes, I know him," he said into the mouthpiece. "Why?"

"Well, I mean is he okay?"

"He's not a hoodlum, if that's what you mean. Why?"

"He came in wanting to buy a revolver. A secondhand Smith & Wesson revolver. Model 32. And I told him there was a five-day waiting period. He said he couldn't wait that long. Then he left. I wouldn't have thought much about it except he seemed so jumpy. And he'd been drinking besides."

Bramlett sighed, then asked, "Did he say anything about why he wanted a gun?"

"He said he was having trouble with a rat. I told him I could sell him a twenty-two rifle for a lot less money and he wouldn't have to wait. But he said he had a rifle."

"Don't worry about it, Ellsworth. We'll look into it," Bramlett said. He couldn't hide the weariness in his voice.

He hung up the phone, and turned back to the table and looked down at the drying wash. The paper buckled a bit and the sky looked muddy. "Crap," he murmured. "Crap crap crap."

He snatched the masking tape off the drawing board and took the still damp sheet in his hands and crumpled it into a ball. He was damn tired of burnt umber-ultramarine blue skies and guns.

He sat down in the chair, still crushing the paper ball in his hand.

It was just after eleven o'clock when Sheriff Bramlett's telephone rang again. He'd gone to bed at ten but couldn't sleep. He couldn't get the frustrated, anxious look in his mother's eyes out of his mind. And jumping in and out were concerns about Patterson Clouse and a weapon.

He'd phoned Curry and told him about the call from Ellsworth Daniels. Curry said he'd have units keeping an eye out for Clouse's truck, and that they'd bring him in for more questioning if they saw him. Bramlett knew Clouse would probably find somebody who'd sell him a handgun if he kept at it.

When the phone rang, Bramlett thought it was probably Curry calling to say they'd picked up Clouse. He hoped it was that, and not a call telling him the man had shot somebody.

"What?" he blurted into the mouthpiece.

It was the night dispatcher, Todd Falkner. "Somebody just phoned saying he saw somebody dump the body of a black woman out in the woods off Costa Road. At first he wasn't going to identify himself. Then I told him there was probably a big reward in this somewhere," Falkner said with a low laugh. "He couldn't give me his name and address fast enough."

"Where is he now?" Bramlett asked.

"He's on his way down here. He said he'd have to lead us there. There was no way he could tell us how to find it."

"Call in Baillie, Curry, and Robertson," Bramlett said. "I'll be right in."

He climbed out of bed without turning on the light and looked down at the darkened form which was Valeria's back. "Sorry to wake you," he said.

"It's okay," she replied. "I wasn't asleep anyway."

He stood there for a moment, looking down at her back. He felt a tightness running across his chest.

# 20

Forty minutes later, four sheriff's department patrol cars turned off the paved county highway onto a logging road which was nothing more than two ruts twisting back and forth through the thick brambles and trees. Deputy H. C. Curry drove the lead car. Sheriff Bramlett rode shotgun while Gale Lonsdale sat in the backseat directing them. A dark mass of pine needles slapped at Bramlett's side of the windshield as they eased into the woods.

"The road's not really all that bad," Lonsdale said. "At least up to where it is. You can't go much beyond that, though. It's pretty muddy up beyond where we found it."

"Who's we?" Bramlett asked.

"Now, Sheriff. You already asked me that, and I told you I'm not one to talk about delicate things."

Until he arrived at headquarters after the call from the dispatcher, Bramlett had never seen Lonsdale. He was probably in his mid-thirties, had a dark mustache and a rugged-looking face. His light-brown hair was pulled back and tied behind his head with a leather thong. The first thing he asked Bramlett was about the reward. The sheriff said he wanted to see this body first.

Bramlett had assumed the man was coon hunting, or maybe even night-hunting deer. He immediately dismissed the latter, knowing Lonsdale would never have phoned if he was doing that. Lonsdale acted quite flustered when questioned harder about why he was out on a logging road in the middle of the night.

Then the sheriff understood. The man was with a woman. And, at Lonsdale's age, there would be no good reason for not

149

simply going to his place or hers or even a motel—unless they were very afraid of detection.

"Tell me again what you saw," said Bramlett.

The man gave a low laugh. "Like I done told you. I was parked out here and this other car came up and a man got out and pulled out a body and left."

"And he didn't see you?"

"Naw. We was sitting in the dark, of course."

"Did you recognize him?"

"No, sir. Not at all."

The car thudded across a deep hole, and Bramlett grabbed the dashboard. Then he said, "Can you describe him?"

"He was big. Mean-looking, if you know what I mean."

The car made a hard, almost right angle, turn to the right, and bare limbs of saplings scraped across the windshield. "You could see that in the dark?" Bramlett asked.

"There was light from his car. You know, the inside light was on."

"I see," said the sheriff. "Are you married?"

"Married? Naw."

"Then she is," Bramlett said.

"Now, Sheriff, I already told you I ain't one to talk about such things." He chuckled. "It's not far now," he said. Then, a moment later, "There."

Curry stopped. In the harsh light beams Bramlett saw the dark, twisted shapes of oak branches, and, for a split second, thought of how he'd recently learned to use a palette knife to pull paint along the rough texture of watercolor paper and render nicely twisted limbs like the ones in the headlights.

"See," Lonsdale said. "There it is."

Bramlett could barely make out something in the road. He opened his door and got out.

Deputies moved from the cars to the body now stretched out on the edge of one of the twin ruts. "I had to move it," Lonsdale said. "That was the only way I could get my car by."

A half dozen flashlight beams focused on the face as Curry dropped down beside her and felt under the side of the jaw for a pulse. There was a dark-red hole in the side of her head. Curry shook his head and stood up.

"Know her?" Bramlett asked him.

"I've seen her before," he answered. "But I don't know her name."

Bramlett turned to look at Lonsdale. "And you don't know her?"

"Naw. Hell, naw." The young man's eyes were fixed on the face of the dead woman.

Bramlett moved around a small tree, holding up his hand in front of his face to make sure he didn't get poked in the eye by the end of a branch, and then stepped on something that rolled. "Damn!" he said as his feet went out from under him and he crashed to the ground, landing on his rump. "Dammit to hell," he said, his palms pressing on the rain-soggy leaves.

Several hands helped him to his feet at once. He moved his light around on the ground until it revealed a rusty half-gallon lard can. The reddish side of the can was peppered with holes of what was probably squirrel shot.

"You okay, Sheriff?" someone asked.

"Yeah," he said. "These old ankles of mine have been turned every which way but loose over the years. Doesn't take much to throw me on the ground."

He brushed the bottom of his trousers, feeling the wetness and the grit from the ground. He'd have Robertson work this whole area in the morning. He was out when the dispatcher phoned his house. He could make up the time tomorrow.

He turned to Lonsdale. "What about the woman with you?" he asked. "Did she know her?"

"What?" he asked, blinking his eyes and looking back to the sheriff.

"Did she recognize her?"

Lonsdale looked at Curry, then at the other deputies, and chewed at the side of his lower lip. He said, "Sheriff, I'd rather talk to you in private."

Bramlett looked at Curry. The deputy gave a slight roll of his eyes, indicating he had no idea what Lonsdale was getting at.

"Okay," Bramlett said. "Come with me."

Playing the oval of light from his flashlight on the road in front of him, Bramlett led Lonsdale beside the row of parked cars until the two of them were out of earshot of the others.

"What?" Bramlett said, turning to him.

"Well, I just didn't want to say it back there, you know." He paused and nodded in the direction of the deputies still clustered around the body. "But the man I saw dump out the body was a black man."

"A black man?"

Lonsdale nodded. "Yes, sir. He was black."

"You sure?"

"Yes, sir. I'm sure."

Bramlett's eyes were fixed on the man. "And you think you'd recognize him if you saw him again?"

Lonsdale nodded. "I think so. Yes, I'm sure I could."

Bramlett reached to his back pocket and pulled out his foil pouch. It was going to be a long night indeed.

Lizzie Clouse got out of bed, pulled on her bathrobe and went into the kitchen. She'd been lying in bed over an hour and couldn't fall asleep.

She glanced at the clock on the stove. Twelve-thirty. Nena was out with Jacob. He was off tonight. She didn't remember if Nena had said where they were going.

She wished Nena would realize Jacob Robertson was the best thing that had ever happened to her.

Lizzie took the bottle of white wine out of the refrigerator and poured herself a glass. Then she put the bottle away and went into the living room, sat down on the couch and curled her legs up under her.

She sipped the wine. Where could Nena and Jacob be so late? Maybe they went to Tupelo. Still, they should be in by now.

There was a sound, slightly muffled, but clear enough to catch her attention. She turned her head. Sounded like back beyond the kitchen. She sat very still. She heard nothing else.

She set the wineglass on the end table beside the portable phone and, as she stood, she thought she heard the sound again. Like something banged against the side of the house. In back.

She grabbed the phone and punched in H.C.'s home number.

He answered on the second ring. "I just got in," he said. "Homicide. This wo—"

"I think there's a prowler in my backyard," she interrupted.

"I'm on my way," he said, and the line buzzed dead.

Lizzie tried to think. What was along the back wall of the house? The kitchen door opened onto the right side. Then there were concrete steps, three, down to ground level. Hydrangeas. Several hydrangeas grew along that wall. A window opened into the utility room.

She went into the bathroom and locked the door. She looked around for something heavy, something that could be used for a weapon. Oh, God, she stood and prayed. Please, please! She saw nothing that would do.

She waited. It seemed like an hour. Where was H.C.?

Then, she heard a pounding. *Oh, God—*

"Lizzie! Lizzie!"

It was H.C.'s voice.

She unlocked the bathroom door and hurried through the front room to the door.

She looked out the window beside the door. H. C. Curry stood in the full glare of the porch light.

She jerked open the door and he stepped inside. He was wearing a leather bomber jacket and jeans. In one hand he held a heavy flashlight and in the other his handgun.

"You okay?" he asked hurriedly.

"Yes. I know it's probably nothing. Maybe a cat or something. It's just that it . . ." She didn't finish.

"I'll check," he said, moving quickly through the house and into the kitchen.

"Nena and Jacob are out," she said, following him, feeling safe now that he was here and, at the same time, a little foolish at having called him.

Curry opened the back door, pushed back the screen with his forearm as he carefully descended the steps. He swept his light quickly across the entire yard, then more slowly, going back over the yard again. Unclipped man-high clumps of privet bushes massed around the three sides of the shallow yard, defining the property line. A single, large sweetgum tree rose in one corner.

Curry moved out away from the house a few steps, still holding his weapon at the ready and, with his left hand, moving the light beam along the roof. Then slowly across the upswept, leafless shoots of the hydrangeas.

"I'm sorry," Lizzie said. "One of the neighbors does have a big dog. I think it's a lab. I've seen it out here before."

Curry stepped closer to the side of the house and focused his light on the window to the storage room. He moved closer, running the light along the windowsill. He leaned forward a bit, trying to see better. "There are some chipped places there," he said. "Of course, they could be old."

He dropped the light beam to the ground in front of the window directly between two of the hydrangeas. On the ground in the rain-softened earth was the unmistakable print of a boot.

# 21

H. C. Curry took Lizzie with him down to headquarters where he got the kit for making a plaster cast of the bootprint. Then they returned to the house. He made the print quickly, in case more rain came before morning. The print was crisp at the edges, obviously made since the last rain. When had that been? About suppertime. About six hours ago.

Curry put the cast and kit in the trunk of his car, then went into the house with Lizzie. She poured him a glass of wine, and they sat down on the couch.

He told her about the woman's body on the logging road, that she looked familiar, was older, but he didn't know her. He took a long sip of his wine, then said, "The sheriff told me someone phoned to tell him your father tried to buy another gun today."

Lizzie put her hand to her throat. "What?" she gasped.

Curry nodded and took another sip. "We're looking for his truck," he said. "We'll find him."

She poured them each another glass of wine. Lizzie looked down into the wineglass and said, "I can remember crawling up into Daddy's lap when he was watching football on television," she said. Then she talked of good memories from long ago.

Jacob Robertson and Nena arrived about one-thirty. They seemed surprised to see Lizzie still up and H.C. at the house. Robertson mumbled something about having to go, and left.

H.C. stretched out on the couch with his head in Lizzie's lap. After he started snoring, she slipped up, covered him with an afghan and went on to bed.

She got up at six. He was already gone. What day was it? she asked herself. Thursday.

Everything was so muddled together. She phoned Lynwood Wilson, the principal at the high school, and told him she would be out again today. Personal day, she said. He wasn't happy at all, but she didn't have time to worry about her often-times strained relationship with him right now.

Half an hour later she buttoned the top button of her coat as she left the house and hurried to her car. The temperature was in the mid-thirties.

She drove steadily through the going-to-school traffic, headed out of town and toward the Hebron community. Maybe her father had gone back home? Why did he feel he needed a gun? Was he afraid of someone? Or . . .

She shook her head. She couldn't believe, didn't want to believe, he was looking for someone. Should she tell Shamona about the gun? No, for now she'd keep that to herself.

At Hebron, the school bus was just leaving the house with Shamona's three kids on it. Her father's pickup wasn't there.

Inside the house, she found Mama 'Dele sitting in her easy chair and Shamona on the floor in the middle of the room. Two shoe boxes, the corners repaired with tape, were beside her, and spread out over the rug were old yellowing photographs and papers.

"I found these," Shamona said to Lizzie as she unbuttoned her coat. "It's Mama's stuff. I couldn't sleep last night and decided to clean out the closet in our room and these two boxes were on the top shelf back in the corner."

"I keep telling her to throw all that old stuff away," grumbled Adele Winter. She was scowling, obviously quite displeased about something.

Lizzie folded her coat across the end of the couch and sat down on the floor. She picked up a snapshot and stared at it and smiled. "Look at Mama," she said. "She must have been in high school. Isn't she pretty?"

The picture showed Naresse and a young man, both dressed up. She handed the photo to Shamona. "Looks like they going to a dance," Shamona said. "Who is this man, Mama 'Dele?" She stretched out and held up the photograph so the old woman could see it.

Adele made a face and gave a slight jerk of her head. "That's that Doffey boy," she said. "Y'all needs to take all this stuff outside the house and toss it in the fire pit. Ain't nobody bothered to look at it for thirty years and more."

"Doffey?" Shamona asked. "You mean Reverend Doffey?"

"Let me see," Lizzie said, holding out her hand and taking the picture again. Yes, she could see the resemblance, but the man was quite a bit heavier now. "It must have been a prom or something."

"Look," Shamona said, handing Lizzie another photograph. "Here's the gang."

It was an Easter photograph, probably taken twenty-five years ago, of Isaac, Cynthia, Lizzie, and Shamona, the four of them like a step ladder. Hugh wasn't born yet. The sun was shining and each was dressed in new clothes. Even Isaac was smiling. He did have a nice smile. And, she had to admit, he'd made a handsome man.

Shamona opened a manila envelope and let several papers slide out. She unfolded one. "It's my birth certificate," she said. "I want this." She set it off to the side.

Lizzie sat up. "Are they all there?"

"Here's yours," Shamona said, and handed her a small original copy of the document. Lizzie stared down at it. Here was the information about her birth, Naresse and Patterson Clouse being her parents, that she was born in County General in Sheffield.

"And here's Isaac's," Shamona said.

"Let me see that," said Lizzie. She took the certificate and at once ran her eye to the line for the father's name. Patterson Clouse was typed into the space with what appeared to be a manual typewriter.

Shamona opened another certificate and immediately grinned. "Look," she said, holding it up for Lizzie to see. "It's Mama and Daddy's marriage certificate." She handed it to Lizzie.

Lizzie dropped Isaac's birth certificate and took the marriage certificate. The minister had signed it. Reverend Bernie Armstrong. And in his own hand he had dated it. February eleventh. She wasn't sure she had actually ever known when her parents' anniversary was. She didn't recall them even mentioning it or celebrating it and—

Her eye suddenly jumped back to the date. Then she snatched up Isaac's birth certificate again.

"What is it?" Shamona asked.

Lizzie held the two certificates side by side, studying them. Then she said softly, "Isaac was born August fourth . . . and Mama and Daddy were married February eleventh . . ."

Shamona stared blankly at her, as if she had no idea what her sister was trying to point out.

Then Lizzie said, "The same year. Isaac was born six months after they were—"

Adele gave a low moan. Lizzie looked up at her. The old woman was sagging to one side in her chair. Her mouth gaped open with her tongue protruding and there was a terrified look in her eyes.

"Mama 'Dele?" Lizzie asked, pushing herself to her feet. "Mama 'Dele!"

"What is it?" Shamona asked, jumping up.

"Mama 'Dele!" Lizzie yelled, taking the old woman by the shoulders.

There was no response from the old woman.

Sheriff Bramlett slowed when he saw the ambulance with flashing red lights speeding toward him as he drove south on the state highway winding to the Hebron community. Behind the ambulance came a speeding Mitsubishi with warning lights flashing. The car was by him too quick to clearly recognize the people in it, but he thought it was two black women.

He'd gone into the office early. Bill Hornsly phoned, wondering where things were. Bramlett tried to assure him they were doing all they could.

Then he turned the pages of the Hornsly file, and wondered if this new victim tied in with him. He reread the interviews with Shamona and Lizzie.

Then he closed the file and knew he needed to mull on all this, to see if something would suddenly pop to the surface of his subconscious where all kinds of strange things were prone to lurk. Maybe some linkage between two important pieces of the crime puzzle would float up.

He decided to retrace Rory Hornly's known steps the day he was killed. Apparently he left work Monday and drove out to

Hebron. Why? Bramlett had absolutely no idea. Hornsly had asked Shamona about where Naresse was buried, and about a barn. And at the graveyard he'd talked with Lizzie. What was he interested in? Maybe the graveyard held an answer, or maybe something out there would shake the murky bottom of his subconscious.

Bramlett left headquarters in the Corvette alone. There was hardly any traffic, and the only thing unusual along the way was the ambulance that had just passed him.

When he reached Hudnall's Grocery, he took the dirt road just beyond it and drove carefully down a curving hill. Winter rains and traffic had formed a single pair of ruts in the middle of the road. Bramlett hated meeting other vehicles on roads like this. There was hardly enough room to cross each other without riding dangerously close to the bordering ditches.

It was nothing but hardwoods until he rolled slowly over a plank bridge, then pasture for an eighth mile or so until he passed the Clouse house. Was there some possible connection between the murder of Naresse Clouse and Hornsly?

Bramlett drove around another curve and looked to the left. The barn came into view. He slowed as he passed it. It looked the same as it had three years before.

He came to the church and parked near the edge of the cemetery. This would have been the same place Hornsly parked. Lizzie's car had been here also.

He left the car and walked across the cemetery. The ground was mushy from the rains. His eyes fell on a small statue of an angel lying on its side in the brown grass. One arm was broken off.

He had no trouble finding the grave of Naresse Clouse. He had attended the funeral. He remembered studying the mourners clustered about the grave as the minister read Scripture, wondering as he focused on each person if he or she could be the murderer. There were a lot of mourners.

He reached the grave. There was nothing unusual about the marker. Granite. Name and dates. Plastic flowers. He looked at the woods close by. A fox squirrel was chattering. He remembered Shamona had mentioned that Hornsly asked her about a barn. Why? Did he know something about Naresse's death?

Bramlett returned to his car. In minutes he was nearing the

barn again. He turned off the road onto what had been the drive to the house. The house, he'd been told, burned down several years back.

He parked the car and sat for a moment looking toward the barn. It was in rather good condition, considering it hadn't been used in all these years. It was constructed in the typical manner of barns raised in the twenties and thirties. The siding was weathered, unpainted, the loft and front doors opened.

Bramlett had first noticed this barn about four years ago. He came out on a Saturday and made some sketches and did a watercolor.

He opened the door of the Corvette and strained as he pulled himself out. He hated the thought of having to decide who should get the car when he turned it in. It was a headache he'd rather avoid for now. He closed the door and walked toward the barn.

He remembered that day three years ago as if it had been yesterday. The call came in that a black woman was dead and her body hanging in a barn out in the Hebron community.

It was freezing cold, sleeting. Even now, he could still see the face. It was so distorted and twisted that he couldn't believe it was the same pretty, lively woman who worked at the restaurant. Her husband Patterson was missing. He'd run away.

They found him a few days later. All attention had been focused on him in that he'd left. Bramlett spent hours and hours interrogating the man, but he never broke. He denied knowing anything about the killing of his wife, said he was looking for her and found her in the barn. He thought she'd killed herself, and he was so upset that he ran away.

Why did he look in the barn? He wasn't sure. It's just where he looked.

Bramlett talked with a string of people—family members mostly, like Isaac Clouse, the eldest child who was convinced his father Patterson killed her, the daughters Lizzie, Shamona, and Cynthia, who were convinced there was no way on God's green earth that their father could have done it. Others who had known the family, like Matthew Farris and Brent Payne.

The only possible motive Patterson could have, as far as Bramlett could see, was jealousy. Isaac indicated there was another man. The girls denied it. No one else seemed to know anything about it.

Bramlett walked around to the west side of the barn. The ground was very soft, much worse than at the cemetery. He didn't want to get down to his ankles in muck. He turned to go back to the front of the barn.

He noticed the roof. It was in good shape. In fact, now that he looked more closely at it, the tin on the roof didn't look all that old, not like a structure that had been left to the elements for years. The rusting process that turned the tin to a burnt sienna color had hardly begun. This roof, now that he studied it, could hardly be two years old.

He stood in the very front of the building, looking up at the loft. Probably an owl, a bunch of bats and swallows all nesting up there. In the dark. Darkness hides many things.

Did Rory Hornsly go inside?

He stepped through the doorway. Light flowed in narrow streams through the cracks between the warped planks. There was a musty smell. Everything was very still. His eye fixed for a moment where her body had hung. Then he shook his head and turned away.

He returned to his car then, trying to remember as he opened the door, the last time he set up his easel here to paint this barn.

Bramlett drove back to town and to his house. When he'd left early that morning Valeria told him to come home by ten because her sister Sylvia Mapp and Sylvia's *person*, as Valeria referred to her widowed sister's beau, were coming by the house to pick up Valeria. The three of them were going to Memphis for the day to visit a museum and have lunch someplace nice, then stop by and check on Margaret and the kids. Margaret still wasn't feeling well.

Bramlett tried to explain to Valeria that he couldn't possibly go, even though he would love to see the traveling exhibit of pre-South Seas paintings by Gauguin. He especially would love seeing his grandchildren, Marcellus and April.

He could at least come on to the house and meet Carl, she said.

Carl Ward, according to Valeria, was a life insurance salesman who lived in Tupelo. His wife had died of cancer several years ago, and Sylvia had met him at the Lee County library in the genealogy section. You meet the nicest people in the genealogy section, she told Valeria.

Bramlett parked beside a dark-blue Cadillac Sedan DeVille in his driveway. Carl Ward, Sylvia, and Valeria were in the den. The man rose to meet Bramlett, and gave him a firm handshake. "Sorry you can't go with us," he said as he sat down again on the couch beside Sylvia. Ward was in his sixties, bald, of medium height, and quite thick through the middle. He nodded at Bramlett and said, "I've admired your watercolors at Sylvia's place. You're quite good. I'll have to commission you to do something for my office."

Bramlett leaned back in his recliner. He liked this man at once. Anyone who liked paintings couldn't be bad. "I wish I could go with you all," he said. "But we're up to our eyeballs in work."

"A man was murdered right outside his apartment the other night," Valeria explained.

Sylvia Mapp, who looked enough like Valeria to be her twin, nodded and said, "Carl knew that man, didn't you, Carl?"

Ward cleared his throat. "Yes. He had a policy with one of the companies I represent, and when he moved here I was contacted. I checked with him to see if he needed anything else. We talked. Then later, he called me. Wanted to know if I wanted a piece of something he was putting together." Ward paused and shook his head. "It wasn't my kind of thing. I begged out."

Bramlett sat up straighter in his chair. "What kind of a deal was it, exactly?"

"Something about clay. I don't know anything about clay. I know timber, now, and livestock, but not clay. Besides . . ." Ward paused and grinned. "He used a phrase that means an automatic no to me. He said, 'This deal sounds too good to be true.' Whenever somebody tells me that, I know it probably is too good to be true, and you can lose big time. He told me some of the people he had going in on it. I really was only familiar with a couple of them anyway."

"Do you remember their names?" Bramlett asked.

"One was Wayne Carr. The other was James Doffey. They both have policies with another company I represent—not the same one Hornsly was with, by the way, but a good company. I only represent good companies."

"You know them?" asked Bramlett, surprise in his tone.

He shrugged. "Not well. They ordered their policies through the mail, and I followed up on them." He smiled. "I'm good with names. That's my business. People. I talked with them on the phone. I haven't actually met either of them. But when Hornsly mentioned their names, I remembered."

"Carl is a very careful person," Sylvia said, looking at him with obvious pride. Then she looked quickly at Bramlett and said, "Besides, Carl is as honest as the day is long. And he would never get involved in something that might not be completely on the up-and-up."

"Oh? And this deal wasn't?" Bramlett asked.

Carl Ward raised his eyebrows in an I'm-not-sure gesture, then said, "Anytime someone wants me to put up the money in straight cash—no checks accepted—all kinds of flags go up for me. Hornsly said he was buying the property where this rich deposit of premium clay was real cheap from a guy who would only take cash. So he was putting up cash himself and asking all the investors to do the same. The profit—which was to be big and quick—would also be paid in cash." He paused and raised his eyebrows again. "You know what that means."

Valeria looked confused. "I don't. What does it mean?"

Ward looked at her. "Hornsly wasn't subtle about it at all. What he said to me was: 'Whether you want to report it is strictly up to you.'" Ward shook his head. "That's exactly the kind of thing I give a wide path to. Anytime people are dealing straight cash, it's for one reason only, and that's to evade taxes. Now, I don't like paying taxes any more than the next man, but I'm not getting myself into any deal like that."

A few minutes later, Bramlett stood in the driveway and waved good-bye as Carl Ward drove off in the Cadillac with Sylvia Mapp sitting beside him and Valeria in the backseat headed for Memphis. He would need to get back with Wayne Carr and the Reverend James Doffey. They'd both stepped in something. He could smell it.

In Tupelo at the North Mississippi Medical Center, Buddy Kimble led Deputies Jacob Robertson and Johnny Baillie to a small nurses' break room on the third floor south. Once inside, he closed the door, and the three men sat down at the table.

Kimble glared at the two lawmen. He was a thin man with a long neck, and wore a white uniform. His face was heavily pockmarked. He waited for them to speak.

"Mr. Kimble, we're investigating the murder of Rory Hornsly," Baillie said. "He worked at Adamstown Furniture here in Tupelo with your wife."

"So?" he snapped. "There're hundreds of people who work there."

"Yes," continued Baillie, "but . . . we've heard that you once had some hard words with him."

Kimble's lips curled in a sneer. "Listen, dammit," he said tersely. "I didn't kill the son of a bitch, if that's what you're asking. If I had, I would tell you. I'd be proud to have done it, to have rid this world of one of the sorriest . . ." He paused as if words failed him in describing his disdain for the man. "Anyway," he continued, "I can't tell you how happy I am he's dead."

"I see," said Baillie. "And would you mind telling us where you were Tuesday morning between midnight and five A.M.?"

"Right here. I had to do the graveyard shift. You can check with my supervisor. I went hunting when I got off at six."

Robertson made a notation in his notebook and looked up at Baillie. Baillie nodded at him, then looked back at Kimble. "I'm sorry we have to ask you these questions," the deputy said.

The man shook his head and gave a twisted smile. "It doesn't matter," he said. "Last night I packed up and moved out."

"I'm sorry."

"Don't be. I should have done it years ago."

Baillie and Robertson rose to their feet. "Thank you, Mr. Kimble," said Robertson, slipping his notebook into his shirt pocket. "Perhaps if you could point us in the direction of your supervisor?"

"Gladly."

After seeing off Valeria, Sylvia, and Sylvia's *person*, Bramlett went back into the house. He couldn't get that barn out at the old Farris place out of his mind. He sat down on the couch and opened the large photo book on the table. Beautiful pictures, all in color, a heavy, glossy paper, high quality. Barns and abandoned shacks of Chakchiuma County. The book itself cost over fifty dollars. All the pictures were taken by Esther Farris.

He turned the oversize leaves one by one. Many of these barns he'd painted in watercolor himself. He continued turning the pages. In particular, he was looking for a photograph of the barn at the Farrises' old farm.

The telephone rang. Bramlett turned one more page, then stood and walked to the kitchen.

"Hello?" he answered, knowing at this time of day it was probably one of Valeria's friends calling to chat for half an hour or so. He could never understand how women could talk so—

"Mr. Bramlett? This is Still Waters Nursing Home. We've been trying to reach you at your office. That's the number you gave us."

He gripped the receiver tighter. "Yes? What's wrong?"

"It's your mother," the woman's voice said. "She's disappeared."

# 22

The sky was overcast with low, dull yellow-gray clouds as Sheriff Grover Bramlett raced over the hills down Highway 45. How in the world could the attendants at Still Waters not notice an old woman leaving? After all, she is eighty-five. It's not like she sprinted away or scooted behind a hedge and duck-walked her way to freedom.

He swung into the left-hand lane and overtook a logging truck. The speedometer swept past eighty, then dropped back as he pulled into the right lane again. Freedom? Was that what he was doing, keeping his mother, like she said, in a jail?

Bramlett slowed as the Corvette rose over the next hill. County Road 110, the road to the Ettawe community, was on the left. He pulled down the left-turn signal, then wheeled the car onto the dirt road, glancing as he did so at the cinder block building painted white which faced the highway but was accessed by a drive from the county road. Club Hawaii, a honky-tonk. In the daylight you could clearly see the faded freestanding tin-faced marquee and the general seediness of the building's facade. There was a harsh loneliness about the empty parking lot with clumps of weeds sprouting around the timbers marking parking spaces.

How in the world would his mother have gotten out here? Who could she have persuaded to take her back to the old place?

He forced himself not to speed through the curves of the road. The tacky mud flung against the insides of the fenders as he fought to stay in the dual ruts centered on the road.

In ten minutes he bounced across the plank bridge connecting the road with the narrow drive winding up to the small

166

white farmhouse on the hill. Chimney smoke. His mother was home.

"Don't you know you like to have given me a heart attack?" he said to her as soon as he walked into the front room.

Regina Bramlett was sitting in her easy chair near the open fireplace with a satisfied smile on her face. "I don't see why you was worried," she said. "Where did you think I'd gone? Las Vegas? Sit down. You make me nervous jumping around like that."

"I haven't begun to jump. You haven't seen me jump. How did you get here anyway?"

She gave a sly smile. "I flew through the air like Mary Poppins." She cocked her head and looked up at him. "How come you don't ever take me to the motion picture show anymore?"

Bramlett sighed and sat down on the couch. "Mama, I just don't have time to come all the way out here to check on you. Sometimes my work schedule is so heavy . . ." He paused. He closed his eyes and leaned back .

"You working on the colored woman thing, aren't you?"

He flinched. "What?"

"That woman who got killed out at Marie Farris's place." Marie Farris, dead ten years or better, was Matthew Farris's mother.

Bramlett nodded. "Yes and no."

"What's that supposed to mean?"

"Actually I'm dealing with a couple other deaths. And somehow . . ." He started to say they all may be related, but didn't. He knew she really wasn't all that interested.

She shook her head and stared into the fire. "Marie used to worry all the time about that boy of hers. She told me once to pray for him, to pray God would jerk him up right and keep his feet from straying to the house of death."

Bramlett blinked and said, "What's that?"

"That's what she called it. 'The house of death.' That's from Proverbs, you know." She turned her face to look at him. "You do listen to the preaching, don't you, Son? I don't want you going down to the house of death."

"Are you talking about Matthew?"

She gave an exasperated sigh. "Of course I'm talking about Matthew. Marie and John only got the one child. You know that."

"I don't understand . . ."

"Marie said he'd been seeing some white-trash girl. She didn't know who it was. Some honky-tonk hussy, she said."

She paused and had an enigmatic smile on her face. Bramlett knew she was thinking of the irony, of how this son of her friend was now a Bible-thumping lay preacher of Phariseeisms of every kind. His mother couldn't stand such self-righteous religiosity.

She looked at him, awaiting a response.

He nodded. "Yes, it's funny. Now, did Mrs. Farris say what this woman's name was?"

Regina Bramlett shook her head. The smile faded, and a look of distress folded across her face. She squinted her eyes at him and said, "Listen to me, Grover. I know y'all are worried about me setting the house on fire or something and killing myself. But, you have to understand, I'm *dying* at that damn nursing home. I want to die here in my own house. Don't you understand that?"

Bramlett nodded his head and reached out his hand, taking her hand, and squeezed. "Yes, Mama," he said. "If this is what you want, we'll find a way to work it out."

"And, besides," she added. "If a twenty-year-old forgot she'd left a pot of water on the stove, would everybody suddenly think she was addled? Of course not. Now, get a life."

Lizzie Clouse left the hospital shortly after ten-thirty that morning. Her grandmother was sleeping. The doctor thought it was a stroke, but they didn't know how bad it was yet. They'd run tests this afternoon, he said. Shamona said she could stay till noon. That gave Lizzie a little time.

She saw Keesa Hudnall in the lobby as she was leaving. He was coming by to see a friend. He blanched when Lizzie told him about Adele. "Is she conscious?" he asked. "I mean, is she lucid?"

Lizzie told him right at the moment, she was struggling to stay alive. She thought his questions odd.

She drove to the house of her aunt, Birdie Hunt. Birdie was her father's older sister. There were nine children in the family, and Birdie and Patterson, only ten months apart, had been close all their lives. Birdie lived alone in a shotgun house on the outskirts of Sheffield. Her husband disappeared years ago. He just went to work at the sawmill one morning and never showed up for work or ever came home. She had no children.

Lizzie had never seen a black person with eyes as pale a gray as the eyes of her aunt Birdie, and now those eyes reflected a deep anxiety and pain. "I don't know where he be," she said. "He come by here all out of breath, saying he need some money, saying that fool sheriff was after him again." She paused and shook her head. "Child, you got a friend that works for the sheriff. Can't you get him to talk some sense to that man?"

"Did you give Daddy money?"

She closed her eyes for a moment, then said, "Some."

"Enough to buy a gun?"

The woman blinked her eyes rapidly, and turned one ear more toward Lizzie. "Gun? What gun?"

"I've got his pistol at my place. Now he's trying to buy another one."

"I gave him four hundred dollars."

"Did he act like he was afraid?"

She nodded. "Yes. I'd say so. He ain't no fool."

"Like how?"

"Like he know ain't no black man ever gonna get a fair trial in this country. That's just the way it is."

Lizzie thought on this for a moment, then said, "This whole thing is tearing me up, Aunt Birdie. This white man getting killed . . . well, now suddenly all this stuff about Mama coming back. And Daddy's out there somewhere maybe with a gun."

"Now you know your daddy didn't have nothing to do with your mother's death. Don't you know that?"

"I do. But other things are suddenly jumping up. Like . . . and I don't know what this is supposed to have to do with anything . . . but Shamona and I were looking at some old stuff of Mama's, and . . . well, we found out Mama was pregnant with Isaac before she married Daddy. That's what we were talking about when Mama 'Dele . . ." Her throat became thick and she couldn't continue. She put her hands to her forehead.

Birdie looked away. Then she said, "That was all a long time ago, child. Your mama is dead now. What difference does all this have to do with anything?"

"Nothing, I guess. But . . . well, I just didn't expect it."

Birdie Hunt didn't say anything for a long time. She looked at the child of her favorite brother as if trying to decide what to say or if to say it. Finally, she said, "There ain't nobody in this world I love more than your daddy. You know that, don't you?"

Lizzie nodded.

"So I'm gonna tell you this even though I ain't sure I should or what all it means. Maybe I'm the only what who knows besides your daddy now, and, I guess, Mrs. Winter." Mrs. Winter was the same address of respect that Patterson had always used for his mother-in-law, Adele Winter.

Lizzie focused her eyes on Birdie and waited.

Birdie cleared her throat, then continued. "I never understood it all. But the fact is, your mama and daddy never really had all that much to do with each other before they married. Oh, they knowed each other, but Naresse was always dating other boys, the ones with the flash cars and all. Your daddy never had nothing to offer anyone but a strong back and the willingness to kill himself with hard work to make a good life for a woman and their children." Again, she shook her chin. "Actually, your daddy was seeing Addie Carr at that time. Everybody thought they was going to marry. It looked that serious. I means, they be seeing each other for a couple of years." She paused, and the muscles in her cheek twitched. "Then he sudden like marry Naresse. It just didn't make sense to any of us." She gave a long shake of her head. "Didn't make no sense at all. And, of course, Addie Carr and your mama never got along. Then, here six months after Naresse and Patterson marry, a baby born." She raised a hand and touched her mouth with her fingers, touched her lips as if the words she'd just uttered pained her deeply.

"I questioned him about it," she said. "I means, I loved him and I wanted to know what was going on. He just say, 'Maybe we fudged a bit.' 'Course that was a lie. I talked to him just before their wedding day and he was as scared as a rabbit with the hounds snapping at his feets."

Lizzie took a sharp breath. "Are you saying what I think you're saying?"

Birdie Hunt shook her head. "Child, I shouldn't be telling you all this. I don't know why I am. But I do know your daddy never been with no woman when he married your mama."

"Who then? Who was it?"

"Isaac's father? I don't know. I don't think your father ever knowed. In fact, I think Adele and Naresse and them somehow convinced him he be Isaac's father. She shrugged one shoulder. "But what difference do it all make now?"

Lizzie rose unsteadily to her feet. "I . . . I've got to go. Got to check on Mama 'Dele . . ."

"I'm sorry, child," Birdie said, following her to the front door. "I'm sorry."

# 23

Sheriff Bramlett made a tent of his fingertips with his elbows on the desktop as he listened to Deputy H. C. Curry tell him that there were no reports on Patterson Clouse's pickup, and, no, Curry really didn't have any idea who, if anyone, Clouse was looking for.

Bramlett grunted. "I'm sure we'll know one way or the other soon enough." He leaned forward in his chair and tapped a sheet of paper on the desk with his fingers. They were notes based on his conversation with Sylvia's man, Carl Ward. "Right now I want to drop in on Wayne Carr again."

Ten minutes later Bramlett and Curry were once again sitting in Wayne Carr's office at the funeral home. Carr leaned forward in his chair, smiling at the sheriff, but his eyes betrayed a certain apprehensiveness. "Like I said, Grover," he said, "I have a lunch meeting at noon."

Bramlett nodded with understanding. "This won't take long. I just wanted to be sure I'm clear about some of the details you told us."

Carr gave a slight nod. "Sure. I understand."

"You said you and your sister Addie were involved in some sort of land investment with Rory Hornsly, I believe."

"Yes. That's right."

"Would that have had something to do with a clay mining operation in Union County?"

Carr's Adam's apple bobbed as he swallowed. He replied, "Yes. That's what it was." His jaw became set as if the whole matter was very distasteful to talk about.

"How was this supposed to work?"

"Hornsly was putting together money to obtain a tract of

172

land from a man. I'm not sure what the status of the deal is right now."

"And you gave him cash?"

Carr's left eye gave a twitch. He was obviously surprised that Bramlett knew about the money transaction. He nodded. "That's right."

"How much?"

Carr was slow to answer, and Bramlett knew the man was probably considering whether Bramlett already knew the answer and was testing his veracity. Finally, apparently deciding the sheriff already knew anyway, he replied, "Ten thousand. That was from Addie and me."

"And?"

"What?"

"What happened to your money?"

Carr's hands on his desk tightened into fists. "Hornsly said the deal was still in the works. He wasn't sure how long it would be before everything was set up."

"And you believed him?"

Carr's eyes narrowed and he tilted his head back. "I don't know what he did with my money. But I wanted it back."

"How did your sister feel about all this?"

"You've met my sister. How do you think she felt?"

Bramlett didn't bother to answer. He could well imagine the fiery Addie Carr's response. He said, "Hornsly was apparently known for fast deals. Did you think you'd been had?"

Carr breathed a bit quicker, then said, "Listen. I couldn't stand the guy. I've talked to him no telling how many times about getting my money back. He kept giving me a song and dance. Addie, too. She was more upset about it than I was, I think. But ain't neither one of us *killed* the guy over it, if that's what you're driving at."

"Do you know anyone else who 'invested' in this deal?"

Carr sighed. "James Doffey asked me about it. He put in some. I'm not sure how much."

"Anyone else?"

"I'm sure there were others. But I don't have any idea who."

Bramlett smiled and crossed one leg over the other. "We're just trying to flesh out the whole thing," he said. "And you wouldn't have any idea how Naresse Clouse might be connected with Hornsly?"

Carr gave a sigh of exasperation. "No. I don't have any idea."

"And when we talked Tuesday, you indicated you and her husband Patterson are not the best of friends."

Carr glared at the sheriff. He didn't bother to respond.

Bramlett continued. "What, exactly, was your relationship with Naresse Clouse?"

"We were friends."

"Just friends?"

Carr spoke through his teeth. "What are you trying to say?"

"We've been looking into all of this quite thoroughly," Bramlett said slowly, deliberately. "Things aren't all that hard to dig up, as I'm sure you can imagine." He was bluffing, of course, making the man think either he already knew or was close to finding out whatever there was to find out. Bramlett thought he detected a bit of sweat beginning to form on the man's forehead.

"Listen," Carr continued. "I don't know what you've heard, but it's a lie."

Bramlett smiled. It was so nice to get a subject like this. The man was denying things no one had yet accused him of. "Why is it a lie?" he asked.

Carr shook his head. "This is private business. It has nothing to do with any of this."

Bramlett smiled. "As I said, these things aren't hard to check out."

Carr's hands relaxed and his shoulders suddenly stooped. He looked very tired all of a sudden. Then he nodded slowly. "It was a long time ago," he said. His eyes seemed to glaze over slightly with a faraway look. "She and Patterson weren't getting along. She wanted to leave him. We'd known each other since we was children, of course." He paused and his head drooped a bit. "I was married, too. My first marriage. It wasn't working out. It didn't last long." He looked back at Bramlett, his eyes at once focused again. "But that was *after* she was married. Isaac was already four or five, I think. Cynthia was about two."

Bramlett nodded, then asked, "What about your sister and Patterson?"

"God, I have no idea what Addie saw in him, but she wanted to marry him. Then Naresse came along, and, just like that, they was married. I mean, Addie didn't even know she and

Patterson was broke up, and suddenly everybody is saying Naresse and Patterson are getting married. I was afraid Addie was going to commit suicide or something. I mean, she'd been planning on marrying Patterson since they were children. She tried to talk to him, and he didn't sound to her, she said, like he even *wanted* to marry Naresse. It was something his father was making him do. Damnedest thing. Then Addie left. She left and went to Chicago." He shook his head. "You would think she'd hate Patterson for what he did to her, but somehow as time went by, it was Naresse she blamed. She blamed her for stealing Patterson." He shook his head again. "It was the damnedest mess you ever saw."

Bramlett considered this for a moment, then said, "You knew Addie and Patterson been seeing each other now?"

Carr nodded. "Yes. I've never seen her happier than she's been lately. I think she wants to reclaim whatever lost time and love she can."

Bramlett looked at his watch. "Well, Wayne," he said, "I guess we'd better run on and let you keep that important business luncheon." He smiled at Carr, then turned to Curry and nodded. They stood up at the same time. Carr didn't move.

During the noon hour Bramlett drove back out to Ettawe to check on his mother. Valeria wouldn't be back from Memphis until late.

He took two vegetable plates in Styrofoam boxes from the Eagle Café, and he and his mother sat at the table and ate. When he kissed her good-bye, he told himself he was just going to have to leave her in God's hands.

He met H. C. Curry at headquarters, and the two of them went to the Vers la Maison apartments. It was only two days since Rory Hornsly, wearing his pajamas and carrying a pistol, had been gunned down in the parking lot of the exclusive complex.

Addie Carr's apartment was on the opposite side of the building from Hornsly's. Her front door faced the central courtyard and the kidney-shaped swimming pool.

"What?" she snapped at Bramlett as she opened the door to his knock. He hadn't yet said anything.

"We'd like to talk with you," Bramlett said, trying to smile pleasantly.

She admitted them into the living room and stood for a moment with her arms tensed at her sides and her body rising up and down on the balls of her feet like a bantamweight fighter awaiting the opening bell. Then she sat down stiffly on the edge of an armless chair.

Bramlett made a quick survey of the room as he and Curry sat down on the sofa. A large painting with a geometric design hung over the fireplace. The furniture was modern, leather, and only in black and white.

Addie Carr looked at the sheriff with obvious contempt and said, "Your harassment of good, innocent people like Patterson Clouse is despicable."

Bramlett held his smile. "We aren't trying to harass him, Miss Carr. We only want to ask him a few questions. Do you know where he is?"

"I wouldn't tell you if I knew."

"You need to understand," Bramlett said, "we're not accusing him of anything."

"That's damned good of you, since he's done nothing wrong." The tone of her voice challenged either of the lawmen to say anything to the contrary.

"We are investigating the death of a man named Rory Hornsly, and it seems there may be a connection between him and Naresse Clouse. So far the only thing we've come up with is that Patterson worked part-time for Hornsly."

"That man was a crook," she said.

Bramlett nodded. "I understand you and your brother invested a good deal of money in a business venture of his."

She bristled. "He stole our money. I felt like killing him myself. He was scum."

"Did Patterson invest any money with him?"

"Are you kidding?" she asked with a incredulous laugh.

"I thought perhaps he'd been putting some aside. Some people—"

"Putting some aside? Sure. With raising five children and a wife like Naresse who spent whatever she could as fast as she could." The distaste she had for Patterson's deceased wife was obvious in her tone.

Bramlett considered this for a moment, then asked, "Do you

know of anyone else besides your brother and yourself who invested money with Hornsly?"

She made a wearied sigh, then said, "I think James Doffey did. I don't know who else."

"Do you know anyone named Roach?"

"No."

"Do you know anyone who Hornsly was having problems with?"

"Listen. I didn't know the man. I personally never even had any dealings with him. My brother made all the arrangements. I gave my money to Wayne. I had my reservations about it then, and I still can't believe Wayne was so taken in. What I knew about Hornsly was only this: He stole my money. I didn't even like Patterson working for him on weekends."

"I understand you and Patterson were friends before Naresse came along."

Her eyes squinted and she said slowly, "She was a bitch. I don't have any idea who killed her, but I'm sure she had it coming. She was a slut."

"Your brother seemed to think pretty highly of her."

"Men are fools."

Bramlett raised his hand and gently rubbed the side of his neck. An acute frustration was pulling at him from all sides. He was getting nowhere. He could smell nothing.

He cleared his throat. "You've used a rather strong word to describe Naresse," he said carefully. "Are you implying she may not have been the most faithful of wives?"

She sneered. "She was as faithful as a bitch in heat."

Bramlett nodded slightly, then said, "Someone once inferred that Patterson may not be the father of all his children." The someone, of course, was Isaac himself.

"There always has been some talk."

"And who might the father be?"

She gave a wry smile. "Who knows? Who cares?"

Bramlett kept his eyes on her. He didn't respond at first. Finally, he said, "We've been doing some checking. The names of certain men seem to be associated in people's minds with Naresse Clouse."

Her eyes flashed at him. "Listen to me," she said tersely. "I don't have to hear this trash in my own house."

"What are you talking about?" Bramlett asked, purposely giving her a taunting smile.

"You're accusing my brother, and I don't have to hear it. What about the Reverend Doffey? Have you checked into him?"

"We're a long way from finishing," Bramlett said. "Are you saying Reverend Doffey may have had something to do with Naresse?"

Addie Carr looked exasperated. "No, not really. Why don't you ask him? I'm not accusing anybody of anything."

He nodded thoughtfully, then asked, "And you're quite sure you don't know where Patterson is?"

"Are you accusing me of lying?"

"No. And I'm not accusing Patterson of anything, either. It's just that he did know Hornsly, and maybe there is something he knows that could help us."

"I really don't have any idea where he is," she said.

"Did you know he is shopping for a handgun?"

Her cheek gave a twitch. "What?" she asked.

"You have any idea who he's looking for?"

Her chin trembled slightly. Then she answered softly, "No. I don't."

"We appreciate your time, Miss Carr," Bramlett said, standing up.

"Well?" Bramlett asked as soon as they were in the car. "What's your estimation of what Miss Addie Carr had to tell us?"

"Where to?" asked Curry, driving slowly out of the Vers la Maison's parking lot.

"Fred's Auto," Bramlett replied. James Doffey worked as a mechanic at Fred's Auto.

Curry nodded, then made a left turn and said, "I think Addie Carr didn't like Hornsly or Naresse Clouse very much. And I don't have any idea why she said what she said about Reverend Doffey. I think that's a lie."

"I'm sure it is," Bramlett said, not having any idea why it would or wouldn't be so. His eyes were on the sky in the west. The sun seemed to be trying to burn its way through the yellowish haze.

Fred's Auto was one block over from the courthouse on Gunter Street. Bramlett and Curry entered the office. A woman with blond hair pulled back into a ponytail and wearing jeans and a T-shirt asked if she could help them, then spoke into an intercom mike, asking "Jim" to please come to the office.

Fred Thomas owned the shop, worked there as a mechanic himself, and employed three other mechanics. James Doffey was the only black employee. He was wiping his hands with a red shop towel as he came into the office.

"Where can we talk?" Bramlett asked pleasantly after shaking the man's hand.

Doffey was about the same height as Curry and barrel-chested. His dark face was twisted with concern. "What is it?" he asked. "What's happened? Is it Lucy?" Lucy was his wife.

Bramlett smiled. "No. Everything's fine. We understand you knew somebody we're checking on."

The sheriff noticed the young woman looking at them from her desk with intense curiosity. He said to Doffey, "Let's go out into the shop."

Doffey led them to the bay where he had a late-model Ford raised on the rack. He was obviously in the process of draining the oil when he was paged.

A tall, gaunt-faced man in the next bay stared at Curry and Bramlett, his eyes also reflecting curiosity. Bramlett nodded at him and then spoke in a lowered voice to Doffey. "Reverend, we found your name and the names of several others in the apartment of Rory Hornsly."

Doffey's eyes were red-rimmed as if he were losing sleep. He glanced at Curry, then looked back to the sheriff, waiting for a question.

"I understand you invested money with him," Bramlett continued.

Doffey nodded. "Yes. I heard about his death. Tragic. How can I go about getting my money back?"

"I don't know about that," Bramlett said. "I would suggest you talk to an attorney. When was the last time you spoke with Hornsly?"

Doffey continued to wipe his fingers with the towel. "About two weeks ago. Since then, I left messages on his answering machine, but he didn't return my calls."

"I suppose this was about the money you invested with him?"

Doffey nodded and glanced at the other mechanic. The man was standing in his bay as near to them as possible without being more obvious in his eavesdropping.

"Let's step outside," suggested the sheriff.

Doffey led them through the rear of the shop and through a metal door into the enclosed lot where about ten vehicles were parked. Doffey turned to face them and said, "I had a little money after my father died. The interest is so low at the bank I talked with a businessman about investing it. He said he'd just put some money with Mr. Hornsly. It seemed like a good deal. I talked with Mr. Hornsly and he said I could double my money in six months. It sounded too good to be true."

"I'm afraid most things that sound too good to be true usually aren't true," Bramlett said sympathetically.

"Mr. Hornsly said it was just a matter of time before we'd get a return on our money. He said I just needed to be patient."

Bramlett nodded. "And your businessman friend was Wayne Carr?"

"Yes. He said he and his sister were investing in it, too."

"How much did you give him?"

"Five thousand dollars."

Bramlett couldn't suppress a grimace. Then he said, "I understand you were a friend of Naresse Clouse."

Doffey's face showed confusion at the change of subject. He looked again at Curry. "Yes," he said slowly, cocking his head slightly and turning his eyes back to Bramlett. "I was her pastor."

"But I'm told you knew her a long time back, even when y'all were children."

He nodded and said, "Naresse and I grew up together out at Hebron. We were in Sunday school together at Mt. Carmel since before I can remember."

"Do you know any way Naresse and Rory Hornsly were connected?"

"What? Naresse and Hornsly?" He shook his head. "Not that I ever knew of. I was a good friend of hers and she never said nothing about him. In fact, I don't even think he was here yet when she passed."

Bramlett rubbed his fingers across his chin slowly and

looked toward the sky. He felt quite uncomfortable now, but cleared his throat again and said, "Reverend, I don't really like to have to ask you anything like this, you being a man of God and all." He paused and shoved his hands into his pockets, at the same time moistening his dry lips with his tongue. There was a sour taste in his mouth. "But someone has suggested that you and Naresse may have been more than just friends."

The lines around his eyes deepened. "What do you mean?" he asked.

Bramlett shrugged and glanced at Curry as if asking for help. He saw the tautness of the young man's jaw. He was looking away and held his notepad at his side as if to say he knew Doffey's answer would be nothing to write down. "Well," continued the sheriff, "I'm not exactly sure. I think some folks obviously think Naresse Clouse went with other men sometimes . . . and you have been suggested as one of those."

Doffey swallowed hard, then asked, "Why would anyone say something like that? I mean, we were friends and used to talk a lot. In fact, she would come talk to me about a lot of problems she was having." He gritted his teeth, then said, "I don't know why people talk like they do."

"Can you tell me what problems she was having?"

Doffey drew a long breath, then slowly released it. "Like I said, I was her pastor. She come to talk to me about things."

"Like what?"

"Mostly about her children."

"Which ones?"

"Mostly just Isaac. She was worried about Shamona, too, but mostly Isaac."

"Why was she worried about him?"

"His drinking. Fighting. The fact that he couldn't hold down a job."

"Did she talk about her husband, Patterson?"

The man slowly shook his head. "I don't know if I should repeat any of that or not. What she told me was all in confidence."

"I can appreciate that, Reverend," said Bramlett, "but we're trying to find out who killed her. At least, we think there may be some connection between her and this Hornsly man."

"I can't see a connection. Like I said, I don't think Mr. Hornsly was here when she died."

"Does the word Roach mean anything special to you?"

"No."

Bramlett's shoulders were beginning to ache a bit, and he realized that he'd had them tensed up against the cold. This questioning seemed dead-end. Then he said bluntly, "Do you have any suspicions as to who Naresse Clouse's lover was?"

Doffey started. "What?"

Bramlett rolled his shoulders. "Can you give me the name of a man who may have been her son's father or who Patterson would have cause to be jealous of, or whatever? I mean, it's only a matter of time till we turn it up ourselves. Those kinds of things can never be completely hidden, you know. We always find out."

Bramlett noticed the tightening of Doffey's facial muscles, and how his eyes seemed to widen slightly. He cleared his throat and said, "No . . . I . . . I don't have . . ." He paused and swallowed hard and looked away.

Bramlett turned to look at Curry. "Ready?" he asked. Then he turned around and walked back toward the shop.

Curry got into the car and slammed his door. Bramlett pulled his own door closed and looked back toward the glass front door. The woman with the pony tail was standing behind the door staring at them.

The deputy put his hands on the steering wheel and squeezed the wheel tightly. Then he said, "What the hell was that all about?"

Bramlett sighed. "Just pushing a little. Seeing what would happen."

"You might as well have accused him to his face of having an affair with her." His voice was shaking.

Bramlett wasn't sure whether it was because James Doffey was a pastor or because Naresse Clouse was Lizzie's mother, or what. But he knew he'd touched a nerve ending with his deputy. And he also knew that the Reverend James Doffey was not telling them everything. And not telling them something very important.

# 24

Before leaving the office at five o'clock, Grover Bramlett read over a report by Deputy Begard Deise on clothing stores in Tupelo. Two stores, MLM and Reed's, carried the brands of clothing found in Rory Hornsly's closet. The salesclerks at both stores knew Hornsly, but no one knew him outside of the store.

Bramlett arrived at his house and parked in the carport beside Valeria's Plymouth. Valeria wasn't home from the trip to Memphis with her sister and her sister's beau, the man who'd known the late Rory Hornsly. Carl Ward is pretty sharp, thought Bramlett as he placed his holstered revolver on top of the refrigerator. After all, he hadn't jumped in on Hornsly's get-rich-quick scheme.

Bramlett glanced at his watch. They'd be at Margaret's now. He wished he was there with them.

Bramlett made his own supper. Two cans of sardines in water, crackers, Oreos, and a Diet Coke. When he was done, he sealed the sardine cans in a plastic bag and took them out to the garbage dumpster. The smell of sardines, Valeria said, made her ill. So he didn't want to leave the exposed cans in the kitchen garbage can.

After he ate, he poked an extra large chew of Red Man into his jaw and took a plastic cup out of the cabinet. He'd have to rinse it out before Valeria got home. But it was nice, for a change, to be able to enjoy a chew in the house—especially on a night like this when the winds were coming from the north, and cold. Every old football injury he'd ever had hurt worse standing outside in the cold taking an after-supper chew.

Then he cleared the table and spread out his watercolor gear:

butcher tray palette, two jars (one to rinse out brushes, the other for clean water), his D'Arches block of paper, and fishing-tackle box of paint tubes. Next he opened the brown plastic recipe box in which he filed three-by-five photos, put on his reading glasses, and began thumbing through the barns section.

One by one he looked at them. Some he'd painted several times, yet no two paintings were close to being alike, some he'd sketched out but had not yet painted. Some he'd done nothing with.

He paused at the photo of the barn on the old Farris place, then pulled it out and tilted it to get full light. Was the photograph made before or after the body of Naresse Clouse was found? He wasn't sure. The picture had no date on the back like some did. The slant of the sun indicated he'd taken the shot in the early morning. A piece of corrugated tin roof was twisted up on the left side of the barn down near the eaves. The result no doubt of a wind storm.

The telephone rang. It was deputy Adam Martin from headquarters.

"Sheriff, we've just got a call that someone with a weapon is trying to break into a house on Walkerson Drive. Two units are on the way. I thought you'd like to know. The caller was Wayne Carr. He says Patterson Clouse is trying to kill him."

Walkerson Drive wound through a cluster of expensive homes in east Sheffield. Three Chakchiuma County patrol cars with blue and white warning lights flashing were parked at the house when Bramlett arrived.

Deputy Begard Deise stood at the edge of the front lawn with his narrow shoulders hunched against the cold. Deise, who seemed to enjoy people calling him by the nickname Beggarlice, was the son of a Pentecostal preacher and belonged to a gospel singing group known as the Hallelujah Harmonizers. Bramlett walked up to him.

"Where are we?" the sheriff asked.

Deise took a draw on his cigarette, then said, "We've got deputies in the house with the family. Everyone is okay. We're spread out around the house searching the bushes."

"What happened?" asked Bramlett.

184

"The dog started barking. It was in the house. And Mr. Carr switched on the outside lights in the backyard and looked out, and this guy was standing there with a weapon in his hand. He ran out of the light, and Mr. Carr called us. He says the guy was Patterson Clouse."

Bramlett nodded. Patterson Clouse had always been so cool, reserved. He'd hardly said anything in his own defense during the intense questioning periods three years ago. He had the appearance as if none of this really mattered to him. At the same time, he would neither admit to killing his wife nor accept the suspicions that another man might be involved. Now he had apparently changed his mind, about another man, at any rate.

There was shouting from behind the house.

Deise said, "Looks like they've got something." He started up the driveway at a half run, holding his hand on his holstered weapon. Bramlett followed.

"On the ground!" someone shouted, "Now! Facedown!"

Several deputies stood at the back section of the yard, flashlights beamed on the ground. Bramlett hurried forward. One deputy was kneeling down. He yanked Patterson Clouse's hands behind his back and clicked handcuffs on him.

The same deputy patted down Clouse, then said as he stood up, "No weapon."

"He's flung it somewhere," Deise said. "Find it."

The deputy grabbed Clouse's shirt behind his neck and jerked him to his feet. Lights glared in his face. He looked like a man in the sharpest pain, his mouth twisted and his eyes shut tight.

"Take him down and lock him up," Bramlett said with a sigh.

He turned back to his car. His guts ached. Seeing Clouse's face like that was nothing like what he'd seen on the man before. And, for the first time, Bramlett was very unsure that he'd killed his wife and strung her in that barn three years ago. However, he must know something. Bramlett had to find out what he knew as soon as possible.

Back at the office, he phoned home to see if Valeria was back. She answered. She'd gone on the bed, she said, but hadn't fallen asleep yet. "We had a good time," she said. "I really do wish you'd plan to take off Saturday and let's all go back up there. Marcellus has a basketball game in the morning and a soccer game in the afternoon. Then we could all go out to eat at this new place we found today. They had ribs on the menu. I bet you'd like it."

"Maybe," he said. "How's Margaret?"

"About the same."

"The kids?"

"April may be coming down with it."

He made a little grunt, then said, "Don't wait up for me. I don't know how long I'll be."

He hung up the phone and looked at his watch. They should have him in the conference room by now.

# 25

Sheriff Grover Bramlett didn't stay at headquarters as late as he'd thought he would. He got nowhere trying to talk to Patterson Clouse. Clouse wouldn't say a word. He sat in the chair at the table in the conference room and moaned and wept. Finally, Bramlett had told the deputies to take him over to the cells and lock him up. Maybe in the morning the man would talk. A Ruger thirty-eight-caliber revolver was recovered under some shrubbery in the backyard.

The next day, Friday, dawned clear and cold. Bramlett's head ached from lack of sleep. By eight A.M., he sat at his desk and listened to Deputy H. C. Curry tell him about the bootprint outside the window at Lizzie's house. The revolver and a black snap purse lay on the desk blotter.

Then the sheriff said, "Baillie got some casts from that logging road. Tires, footprints. Check it out." He tapped the purse. It was a woman's purse, vinyl. "Somebody just brought this in. It was found not far from the woman's body. Apparently tossed out into the trees by whoever dumped the body. The driver's license says she's Lydia Gressete, Sheffield address, fifty-three year-old female, a hundred twenty pounds." He paused, then said, "The weight doesn't seem to have been updated in a while. I think my own license is about fifty pounds or so off."

"Who is she?" Curry asked.

Bramlett spread his hands in a don't-know gesture. "We haven't found family yet. We're checking some of the neighbors right now."

The intercom buzzed. It was Bramlett's secretary, Ella Mae. "Sheriff, Mr. Wayne Carr is here to see you."

"All right," he said. "Send him in."

Carr was dressed in a white suit with a flaming red tie. Bramlett and Curry stood as Carr entered the office.

Curry excused himself, leaving Carr alone in the room with the sheriff. "Listen, Grover," he said. "I won't even sit down. I'm in a hurry. But I just want you to know, I'm not pressing charges against Patterson Clouse."

Bramlett frowned. "What?"

Carr shook his head, his smile held steady. "No, he was drunk. No problem." The smile dropped a bit, and he asked, "I mean, you did get the gun, didn't you?"

"We got it."

He shrugged his shoulders and smiled broader. "Then, no sweat, okay? Let's just forget the whole thing." He shook hands again with Bramlett, nodded and said, "I've got to go." Then he was gone.

Bramlett sank back into his chair. What was that all about? he asked himself. Why would Wayne Carr be so eager to tell him this?

Curry walked back into the office. "I just phoned Lizzie," he said. "She says Lydia Gressete was one of her mother's best friends. In fact, Lizzie just saw her. Naturally, she's all upset."

Bramlett stroked his chin, then scratched the side of his neck. "Have somebody go over to the jail and bring up Clouse. Maybe he knows this woman."

Within fifteen minutes, Patterson Clouse was sitting at the table in the conference room. His shoulders sagged and his eyes had a look of deep sadness. Curry sat at the end of the table with a notebook in front of him, while Bramlett sat across the table from Clouse.

"You were out of your mind with drink last night, Patterson," Bramlett said. "Any man could have done what you were doing. The good thing is, we got there before you hurt anybody or yourself." He paused, watching the man's face carefully for any reaction. He saw nothing change. "So," he continued, "I thought maybe now after a good night's sleep, you might want to tell us what exactly you were trying to do."

Clouse held his hands together loosely in his lap. His eyes

were looking toward the middle of the table, gazing, not focused. He said nothing.

Bramlett hovered his hand over the pistol. "We found this in the bushes at Carr's house," he said. "Is it yours?"

Clouse didn't respond.

Bramlett continued. "Where did you buy it?"

Clouse looked up at the sheriff, as if weighing his words before he spoke them. Then he said softly, "Tupelo. On Ida Street."

"Who were you going to shoot, Patterson?"

He drew a deep breath, released it, then half closed his eyes. He obviously wasn't going to answer.

Bramlett leaned back in his chair. "Tell me about you and Wayne Carr. What has he done to you?"

Clouse gave a slight shake of his head. "Nothing," he said.

"Nothing? Nothing? And for nothing you were trying to kill him?"

Clouse pressed his lips tightly together. He didn't reply.

"Was it about Naresse?" Bramlett asked. "I mean, I can understand how a man would feel if, as the Good Book says, another man was plowing with his heifer."

Still no response.

Bramlett waited a few moments, then asked, "Did you know Lydia Gressete?"

Clouse slowly lifted his eyes again to look at the sheriff. "What?" There was a look of confusion in his eyes.

"She's dead. We found her body last night dumped out in the woods."

Clouse's hands jerked. "Dead? Wha—" He stopped and closed his eyes. In a moment he opened his eyes and said, "She was a fool."

"Why do you say that?"

"She was supposed to be Naresse's friend, but one time she tried to tell me trash about her."

"What trash?" He spoke softly, fully aware that this was probably the longest sentence Patterson Clouse had ever said to him, and he didn't want to spook him.

"About Naresse and Reverend Doffey," Clouse said. He shook his head hard. "That was a lie and I knowed it."

"Why would she say that?"

"She claimed they went out together one night after work."

189

"After whose work?"

"Naresse did some catering on the side. Sometimes Reverend Doffey helped her."

Bramlett nodded that he understood, then asked, "Do you know why anybody would kill Lydia Gressete?"

"No." His voice was very low.

Bramlett stood up and turned to Curry. "Let him go. We can find him if we need him." Then he left the room.

Gale Lonsdale was sitting in one of the chairs against the wall outside Bramlett's office talking with a pinched-faced woman Bramlett recognized as a newspaper reporter from Tupelo. Lonsdale stood quickly when he saw the sheriff approaching. The reporter stood also. She held a notepad in front of her.

"Sheriff, I understand you already have someone in custody in regard to this murder," she said, stepping close to him. She wore thick glasses and had close-cut dark hair.

"No," Bramlett snapped. "That's incorrect. I don't have anything for you yet."

He gave a jerk of his head at Lonsdale, indicating he wanted the man to follow him into his office. Once they were inside, Bramlett closed the door, and took a seat behind his desk, at the same time, with a wave of his hand instructing the man to sit down in one of the chairs before the desk.

The sheriff took a legal pad out of a side desk drawer, placed it on the blotter, and picked up a newly sharpened pencil. "Now tell me in as much detail as you can what happened, what you saw," Bramlett said, his eyes fixed on Lonsdale's eyes.

The man held the sheriff's gaze and placed a hand on each arm of the chair, shifted his weight, then said, "Like I told you last night, this car came up the road, and a man got out and dumped this woman's body."

Bramlett pressed the pencil eraser gently against his lower lip. "Let's go back before that," he said. "How long had you been parked up in there?"

"Not long. Maybe fifteen minutes."

"Have you been there much?"

"Naw. Just hunting. In the daytime." He winked at Bramlett and gave a knowing smile. "I wasn't expecting nobody else to be coming up there at night, of course. 'Else I wouldn't have gone there."

"Who were you with?"

Lonsdale grinned. "Now, Sheriff, I told you already I can't tell you that."

"Was she underage?"

Lonsdale frowned. "I ain't no fool, Sheriff."

"Then she's married."

Lonsdale, smiling again, gave a slight shrug. "I guess you might say that. But she's thinking of leaving him."

"Our investigators at the scene this morning tell me the tracks of your car indicate you were about thirty yards from where the other vehicle stopped. Did the driver of the other vehicle see you?"

"Naw. He just pulled up, got out and took the body out, then turned around and left."

"You saw this?"

"Sure."

"Then what did you do?"

"We left. It's hard to stay in the mood after something like that, if you know what I mean."

"When did you see the body?"

"When we was leaving. It was laying directly across the road. That's why I had to get out and move it. I didn't want to just run over it. I might have knocked off my muffler or something."

Bramlett winced. Then he cleared his throat and said, "You said you could see him clearly enough to recognize him?"

"That's right."

"In the dark?"

"The inside light was on when he had the door open. That's how I could see him."

"Did you know him?"

Lonsdale gave a slight snort. "I didn't know him. I told you that already. But I'm good with faces. I'd know him if I ever saw him again. You don't forget a face like that."

"Like what?"

"You know. All twisted up with meanness."

"Can you describe him?" Bramlett placed the point of his pencil on the legal pad.

191

"Let's see . . ." Lonsdale said, leaning back slightly in his chair. "He was a big black guy."

"You're sure he was black?"

Lonsdale nodded. "Yes, sir."

"How old would you say he was?"

Lonsdale shrugged. "Maybe forty. Yeah, I guess about forty."

"What was he wearing?"

"Wearing? A jacket. I think it was leather. And one of those caps, you know, the knit kind."

Bramlett shifted in his chair. "What about facial hair?"

Lonsdale scratched the side of his head. "I guess so. Maybe a mustache. I mean, it wasn't all that much light, you know."

Bramlett studied the man carefully. He thought how he would really hate to have to rely on this man's identification of a suspect in a lineup. He said, "Is there anything else you can tell us?"

"Not right now, I don't think."

"What did that reporter ask you?"

He shrugged a shoulder. "My name and stuff like that."

"Did you tell her what you saw?"

"I told her I saw the man pull out the body."

"Did you tell her the man was black?"

"Naw."

Bramlett gave Lonsdale a knowing wink. "Let's just hold that for a while, okay? And maybe it would be best if you didn't talk to reporters anymore. Or else what you have to say might hinder us from doing in court what we need to do. Understand?"

"Sure. No problem."

Bramlett pushed himself to his feet. "I appreciate you coming in, Mr. Lonsdale," he said, indicating the interview was over.

Bramlett walked over to Deputy Curry's desk. "I want to have another talk with the Reverend James Doffey," he said.

Curry scowled and pushed back his chair.

As soon as Bramlett and Curry walked into the office at Fred's Auto, before they could say anything, the woman behind the desk leaned over a microphone, pushed the On button, and said, "Jim, come to the office."

Bramlett scowled at her. "Maybe it's Fred we want to see," he said.

She raised an eyebrow. "Fred?"

"Never mind."

James Doffey's face showed concern when he stepped into the office and found the two lawmen waiting for him again, and, once again, he led them into the shop area and to an empty bay away from the other mechanics.

"A woman has been killed," Bramlett said, his eyes on the eyes of the Reverend James Doffey. Doffey stood in front of a tall tool chest.

He looked at Curry, then back to the sheriff. He said nothing and his lips were pressed together.

"Her name was Lydia Gressete," Bramlett said.

Doffey swallowed and put his hands on his hips. "She wasn't a member of my church."

"Did you know her?"

"Only slightly."

"I see," said Bramlett. "I understand you helped Naresse Clouse occasionally with her catering."

"A couple of times. That was all. Just when it was something big and she needed a couple of extra people. I got four children to feed and send to college. I do all the extra I can."

Bramlett nodded. "Tell me, what kind of things did she cater?"

"Weddings. A few funerals. The last time I helped her was at one of those college things."

"Sheffield College?"

Doffey nodded and wiped his forehead with the back of his hand. Bramlett noticed he was beginning to perspire. Suddenly, he looked up at the sheriff as if something had just occurred to him. "This man who got shot. Hornsly. . ." he said.

"Yes?"

"I remember seeing him at one of those faculty things. I thought it was strange at the time, since he didn't teach at the college. In fact, he made quite a fool of himself that night."

"Like how?"

"He'd had too much to drink and he got into a thing with Dr. Farris."

"Matthew Farris?"

193

Doffey nodded. "Yes, sir. And it was something about Dr. Farris's wife. Dr. Farris told him to keep his hands off of her. I saw them sitting on the couch earlier, in fact, and Hornsly did act pretty familiar, hugging her and all. Then, after Dr. Farris got in his face, Hornsly just started laughing and walked away."

"What else?"

Doffey shook his head slowly and said, "That's about it."

"I see," Bramlett said. He noticed one of the other mechanics had a wide broom and was sweeping the floor, moving closer and closer to them, obviously, thought the sheriff, in order to eavesdrop. "And the fellow with the broom," asked Bramlett. "Who is he?"

Doffey looked confused. "What?"

The other mechanic picked up the broom and hurried away.

Bramlett took one step closer to Doffey and said, "Think hard now, Preacher. Why would Lydia Gressete make up a lie about you and Naresse?"

"I don't know. Except, of course, Lydia didn't like me. I don't think she really liked Naresse that much, either. I mean, they was supposed to be good friends and all that, but sometimes I think she was jealous of her."

"Jealous? Why?"

"Lydia was also a friend of Addie Carr. And, of course, Addie and Naresse couldn't stand each other."

"Why?" Bramlett asked, even though he already thought he knew the answer.

"Because of Patterson. Addie was all set to marry him herself before Naresse took him away."

"I see. And what about Wayne Carr and Naresse. We've also heard things . . ." He didn't finish.

Doffey seemed to be perspiring more. "I don't know nothing about any of that," he said. He looked toward Fred Thomas, owner and chief mechanic of the shop, who stood with his hands on his hips and an unlit cigar clamped in his mouth. He glared at his mechanic talking to the sheriff and deputy on company time.

Bramlett glanced at Fred, waved his hand in greeting, then said to Doffey, "Okay. We'll let you get back to work. Thank you."

Bramlett stopped for a moment and spoke to Thomas, asked

about his son who was playing basketball down at Mississippi College, then walked back to the car with Curry following. In less than five minutes they had returned to headquarters and were walking in the door.

Johnny Baillie saw them entering the office suite and called to them. They stopped and waited for him to walk over.

"The folks from the crime lab in Jackson just arrived a little while ago and are out at the scene," he said. "But I had one of them look at the cast of the bootprint you made last night at Lizzie's, H.C. He did a quick eyeball comparison with the casts we'd made ourselves at the crime scene." He paused as if making sure both Bramlett and Curry were following him in thought, then continued. "Anyways, they look the same. Even I can tell that. I mean, it's the same size and brand. Exactly."

# 26

Esther Farris opened the door. She looked from Bramlett to Curry, then back to Bramlett. Her dark eyes flashed, and she drew a deep breath and squared her shoulders.

"Matthew isn't here," she said quickly and firmly before Bramlett could even ask.

He tried to smile pleasantly. "Actually, we wanted to talk with you," he said.

Her eyes widened slightly, and she didn't move, as if deciding whether to stand on the door stoop in the cold to talk with them or invite them inside. Bramlett stepped forward and she moved away from the doorway. Curry followed, closing the door behind him. Then she led them to the den.

As soon as they were seated, Bramlett looked around at the framed photographs on the wall. There were at least twenty of varying sizes: broken-down cabins, barns, and outbuildings. The skeleton of a dog, he supposed, lying amid a tangle of brown grasses. "I do love your work, Mrs. Farris," he said. "I have one of your pictures hanging in my den."

She sat perfectly motionless and made no response, waiting for him to state his business. She obviously cared little for his evaluation of her art.

He continued. "We were told Matthew and Rory Hornsly had a problem with each other at a faculty party. Could you help us with that?"

Her eyes were on his eyes, studying him as if trying to judge the planes of his face with their lights and shadows. Finally, she said, "There was nothing to it. The man was drunk and acting like a clout. He kept pawing at me, and Matthew told him to stop it."

"The last time I was here I failed to ask *you* about Hornsly," Bramlett said. "Did you know him?"

"No," she said.

"I see. Could you tell us why he was at a faculty affair?"

"He's an alumnus. Frequently, local alumni are invited to functions. That's the way colleges operate. Alumni give money. Lots of money. I don't know whether he gave anything or not. Maybe the president hoped he would."

"I understand Naresse Clouse was catering that night."

"I don't remember."

"I just wondered if you knew her well."

"I didn't know her at all."

"Your husband grew up out there at Hebron, and, I understand, you all still have the property out there."

"We do. But we may sell it. I've only been out there a couple of times. I'm not even sure how to get there."

"Did you know Lydia Gressete?"

"No."

Bramlett smiled again. "Well, I appreciate you helping clear up this matter of you and Hornsly."

She looked questioningly at him. "What's to clear up?"

"I just heard there might be something between you two, that's all."

"What?" Her voice indicated her astonishment at such a ridiculous idea.

Bramlett shrugged. "We have to be going," he said, placing his hands on his knees and pushing. "Mrs. Bramlett should be about ready to put supper on the table."

Once outside and walking back to the car, Curry asked, "Who said anything about her and Hornsly?"

Bramlett chuckled. "I was just doing a little fishing with the bait the Reverend gave us about the party."

Curry scowled. "That was close to a lie, wasn't it?"

Bramlett reached for the car's door handle and said, "You don't catch fish without tricking them, do you? I wasn't lying. I was just fishing." He pulled open the door and gave a low laugh. "And you know how I love to fish."

Chancy Curry set a plate on the table in front of her son H.C. She'd stopped by Kentucky Fried Chicken for a box of wings on the way home from the hospital where she worked. Beside the wings, she'd placed turnip greens, creamed corn, and a biscuit on the plate. She laid a hand on H.C.'s shoulder and, at the same time, looked across the table to her husband Witt, giving him a look which meant for him to close his eyes.

"Thank you for this food, Lord," she prayed, "and for keeping H.C. safe through another day. And bless all our loved ones near and far. Jesus' name, amen." She then returned to the kitchen to dish up her own plate.

Witt Curry picked up a wing, pulled the two bones apart and tore the meat off one piece with his teeth, chewed a couple of bites, then looked at his son and said, "I hear you and the sheriff been after Reverend Doffey pretty hard."

H.C. buttered his biscuit and nodded. "This white man that got killed seems to have known Lizzie's mother. We back now to talking to a lot of people that knew her." He shrugged. "Investigating means mostly talking to people." He looked up at his mother and smiled as she joined them at the table. "Not running around shooting at folks and being shot at all day."

"Your father says they got a opening down at the lumberyard. I wish you'd go down and apply for it," she said.

Witt Curry snorted in a contemptuous manner as he sucked the rest of the meat off a wing. He was about the same height and weight of his son, darker but with light-brown eyes. He was not yet fifty and had raised all seven of his children to be hard workers like himself and Chancy, and most of them went to church, even though he himself wasn't a fanatic about it.

He chewed hard with his mouth open, then, his eyes on his son, he said to her, "This boy's gonna be the first black sheriff of Chakchiuma County one day. What's he want to work at a place toting lumber all day, getting sawdust up his nose and staying out in the cold and heat all the time for?" He chuckled. "Let this boy alone, woman. He on the right track."

H.C. looked at his mother and winked. "You probably won't even vote for me, will you?"

She shook her head and spread her napkin in her lap. "You needs a wife and a regular job. That's all I got to say on it."

"Sure," H.C. said with a grin.

"Except I do want to ask you about the Reverend Doffey and Naresse. What's that you was saying?"

"He was her pastor," H.C. replied.

"That's true. Then way back yonder—I means years ago—I understand they was seeing each other. I may be wrong, of course. Naturally, that was before he got saved at that revival meeting."

"You mean like . . . before she was married?"

Chancy Curry had a peculiar look on her face, as if she'd just tasted something unpleasant. Then she quickly shook her head. "I can't remember just now. Yes . . . I guess that was it. Back 'fore she married Patterson."

They ate in silence for a few moments, as if digesting this, then Chancy said, "I went by to see Adele this afternoon before I left work. She ain't too good." Chancy Curry sometimes spent an hour visiting folks in the hospital, not just patients she knew, but friends of friends. She didn't know Lizzie's grandmother all that well.

"Was Lizzie there?" H.C. asked.

"Just Shamona. She was expecting Lizzie at any time." She laid down her fork and wiped her mouth with the napkin, then said, "It would be a terrible thing to lose a child. God's done taken good care of us." This last she said to her husband. He made no reply. She continued. "I think Naresse was closer to Adele than any of her other childrens. I mean, Naresse was gonna get all that farm and everything. I'm surprised it didn't just kill her when Naresse was taken." She pushed her plate away. "I think I'd just go absolutely crazy if something like that was to happen to one of mines."

H.C. took a long swallow of his iced tea, then set the glass back on the table. "I need to run on to the hospital," he said. "Lizzie's probably there now."

"You ain't eat but one wing," Chancy said.

"Save me a couple. I'll eat them when I get home." He pushed back his chair, stood, and kissed her on the cheek. "Maybe I'll just have chicken and beer for a late snack."

He grinned as he left the room, knowing Chancy Curry was glaring at him.

Adele Winter was on the third floor of County General. H. C. Curry found both Shamona and Lizzie in the room. The old woman's eyes were closed and she was breathing in a labored manner under a clear plastic oxygen mask.

"How is she?" he asked.

Lizzie shook her head sadly as she looked at her grand-mother and answered, "The doctor says it was a slight stroke. She hasn't lost her speech or use of her arms, but she seems confused at times. The doctor says that's natural. It will go away, he said." She paused, then added, "He says her body is just all worn out. She's simply running down."

"What's the weather like outside?" asked Shamona. She was sitting in the recliner chair beside the bed.

"Cold. It was just starting to sleet a little when I was coming in," he answered.

Lizzie was standing beside the bed. She reached out and tucked the blanket around the old woman's neck.

"Can I go get y'all something to eat?" H.C. asked, taking a chair near the end of the bed.

"We took turns going down to the cafeteria here at the hos-pital," said Lizzie. She walked over to the counter beside the sink. "This morning Shamona was going through some old boxes there at the house. She found this." She picked up a small piece of paper and handed it to H.C.

He took it and began to read. "What's this? A land receipt?"

Lizzie nodded, still standing beside her grandmother and looking down at her. "It's from when my grandfather bought the land from Matthew Farris's father."

H.C. studied it, then said, "He bought seventy acres for *ten dollars?*"

Lizzie sighed and turned away from the bed and went to the window. She didn't reply.

"I ain't never known no white person to be that generous," said Shamona. "Maybe they might give you an old dress they ain't never gonna wear again, but they don't give *land* away. No sirree. That's for sure."

H.C. held up the receipt, looking at Lizzie. "What's it mean?"

She shrugged. "We don't have any idea." She turned around, half sitting on the wide windowsill. "No doubt the only one who can answer that question lies right there," she said, look-ing at Adele Winter.

"I had a wild idea today," Shamona said.

"Don't repeat that," Lizzie snapped.

Shamona laughed. "No, I just wondered if maybe there wasn't something between Mama 'Dele and old man Farris."

H.C.'s brow wrinkled. "Matthew's father?"

"That's stupid," Lizzie said. "I asked you not to repeat it."

"Well, things like that happen," Shamona said, looking at her sister. "And they been happening since slavery days. We all knows that."

"Mama 'Dele wasn't that kind of woman," said Lizzie.

Shamona Clouse, unmarried and the mother of three children by three different men, stiffened. "Oh? And what kind of woman would that be exactly?"

Lizzie closed her eyes as if she were very tired, and said, "Let's don't talk about this now. You got your way of living and I got mine."

Shamona jutted out her jaw, then said, "You damn right I got mine. And I'm taking care of my children. Ain't nobody else keeping them. And, besides, can I help it if mens finds me attractive?" She gave her sister a taunting smile.

Adele Winter gave a groan and began shaking her head hard back and forth. Shamona came up out of the chair and Lizzie moved to the side of the bed. "She gets like this sometime," Lizzie said to H.C. "She must be having bad dreams or something."

The woman's face was twisted as if in great pain. "The doctor has given her pain medicine," Shamona said, as if reading H.C.'s mind. "She's not really hurting, he says. Least ways, not physically."

"She's trying to say something," Lizzie said.

Suddenly, the woman's eyes snapped open and she looked up at Lizzie. There was anger in her eyes, flashing and burning. One of her scrawny hands came out from under the blanket and jerked down the oxygen mask. Her eyes were still on Lizzie. "I tried to tell your mama, girl," she said. Her speech was a bit slurred and her voice rose as she spoke. "I tried to tell her. He ain't no Moses. I told her that. She just wouldn't listen." She was pulling her head up as she spoke.

"Please, Mama 'Dele," said Lizzie, her hand gently pressing the woman's shoulders, trying to get her to relax and lie back down.

"What's she talking about?" Shamona asked.

Adele resisted Lizzie's pushing, strained against her hands

with her shoulders, and said, "I told her to quit him. Lord, Lord, how many times I told her. He weren't no Moses." There was a wild look in her eyes as she spoke, then suddenly she collapsed back onto the bed.

"What? What?" asked Shamona, looking at her older sister, waiting for an explanation, an interpretation.

The woman's eyes closed again and she struggled to breathe. Lizzie readjusted the mask. "Something about Uncle Mose," she said. "I think she was trying to tell me something about Mama." Lizzie glanced at her watch. "It's almost eight-thirty," she said to Shamona. "Why don't you go on to the house."

"I can stay a while longer."

Lizzie shook her head. "No. You'd better go check on the kids. I'm going to stay the night. We can't both sleep in that recliner. Here," she said, taking her purse from the counter and opening it. "Take my car. I won't need it." She handed Shamona the car keys. Shamona had come to the hospital with Lizzie. They had dropped the kids off at the Armstrongs' on the way.

"You sure you don't mind?"

Lizzie shook her head hard. "Not at all. And take my coat, for goodness' sake."

Shamona pulled herself up out of the chair and gave a short laugh. "You sure? You gonna let me wear your coat?"

"Take it."

"I just wasn't thinking when I came away from the house with just this sweater. I mean, I just wasn't thinking how cold it was gonna get." She took Lizzie's long black leather coat from the narrow closet and slipped it on. "I'll be back in the morning right after the school bus picks up the kids."

"I don't need to go anywhere," Lizzie said. "Do what you need to do before you come."

Shamona reached down and gave H.C.'s knee a slap. "Be good," she said with a laugh. "As if, with my sister, a man can be anything else." She laughed harder as she closed the door behind her.

Lizzie sank down into the recliner and pulled the lever on the side. The footrest sprang out. She folded her arms across her chest and looked at H.C. "I sometimes feel like I'm supposed to be a mother to her now," she said. She shook her head and continued. "I love her so much, but she drives me absolutely crazy."

H.C. looked at her. She was so beautiful and he wanted to be with her all the time. "Marry me," he said out loud, just like he'd said to her so many times before.

She smiled. "Maybe. Maybe when all this is over."

He sighed. "When is anything ever really over?"

"We'll know," she said, stretching. "We'll know."

Shamona wasn't expecting the cutting force of the winter wind that hurled itself at her when she stepped through the glass doors of County General's main entrance into the night air. She reached down and buttoned the bottom two buttons of the coat and bowed her head into the wind as she hurried across the street and into the hospital's parking lot.

A freezing mist floated down across the glare of the streetlights in the parking lot. She looked quickly at the rows of cars, trying to remember where Lizzie had parked when they came back to the hospital that afternoon. So many cars, and so many looked alike.

If anybody needed a car, she did. Three children to run around. Always having to get her father's pickup or ask Lizzie to carry them places. If she could just get a job.

Lizzie said Wayne Carr would give her a good deal on a car. If she only had a good job she could afford a monthly payment.

She saw Lizzie's turquoise Mitsubishi halfway up the second row. She walked faster and fumbled with Lizzie's keys, looking for the one to open the car. Her exposed hand was freezing.

Another car started and its headlights flicked on. Shamona glanced up and saw a light-colored, probably gray, car pulling out of a parking space. She stood beside the Mitsubishi and looked down, trying to get the key into the lock. The other car was passing. She didn't look up.

The blow felt like a sledgehammer had crashed into her left shoulder. She collapsed onto the edge of the roof of the car, her mouth banging against the metal. She'd broken a tooth. She couldn't believe it. She'd just broken a tooth.

Then a second blow hit her, in the side, and her legs turned to water. She sank to the pavement, vaguely aware of the sounds of an automobile speeding away, and, strangely, only then aware of the crashing noise of the gunshots thundering in her ears.

She lay on her back, floating, and felt the cold mist pricking at her face, and her tongue moved over to touch the broken tooth. Then she slipped beneath a warm blanket of darkness.

# 27

Shamona Clouse was already in surgery before Sheriff Grover Bramlett arrived at the hospital. He came immediately after Curry phoned. The shooting occurred over an hour before. Headquarters didn't disturb the sheriff at home for routine shootings.

Curry explained to him that, in the chaos, no one thought of anything other than getting her inside the hospital. It was only after a doctor came to the emergency room waiting area and told them they were taking her into surgery immediately and that family could wait upstairs in the surgical intensive care waiting room that Curry thought to phone the sheriff.

As Bramlett entered the intensive care waiting room, he spotted Curry with the family at a grouping of couches and chairs in the far corner. Curry saw him coming and hurried over before Bramlett reached the others.

"A security guard heard the shots," Curry told him. "He was around the side of the building, and by the time he got to the parking lot, all he saw was Shamona down. There were at least two vehicles down the street, but he couldn't make out anything about them."

"How bad is she?"

"The doctor said she's been hit at least twice, once in the shoulder and once just above the kidney. He says there's probably a lot of internal bleeding, and they won't know anything about the extent of her injuries until they get in."

Bramlett looked back toward the family. Isaac Clouse was pacing back and forth near the window behind the couch on which his father Patterson, the same father he'd tried to kill once with a baseball bat, sat. Patterson perched on the edge of

205

the couch, leaning forward with his elbows on his knees and his face in his hands. Lizzie was beside him, leaning back with her head resting on the back of the couch.

"How long before they know something?" Bramlett asked.

"The doctor wouldn't say. Said it might be several hours." He turned toward the family. "Cynthia and her husband went to the cafeteria to get some coffee." Cynthia was Lizzie's older sister. "And we haven't found Hugh yet."

Bramlett looked at him questioningly.

"Lizzie's younger brother," Curry explained. "He's fifteen."

Bramlett nodded. He'd forgotten the boy for a moment, big for his age, very quiet. Of course, Bramlett hadn't seen him in three years, not since his mother died.

Bramlett made his way on across the room. "I'm sorry," he said when he reached the couch.

No one was looking at him. Patterson didn't look up, and Lizzie's eyes were closed. Isaac paused in his pacing and gave the sheriff a contemptuous stare. Then he continued pacing.

"Like I said," Curry said to Bramlett in a low voice. "She'd just left Mrs. Winter's room. Lizzie was going to stay the night, so Shamona was taking her car." He paused and shook his head.

Bramlett looked around the large waiting room. There were other clusters of easy chairs and couches, other families camping out, waiting for the next visitation period, waiting to go back and see dying parents or children struggling to breathe, or loved ones unexpectedly slapped down by an act of violence. Someone like Shamona Clouse, mother of three.

"I'm going on down to the office for a while," Bramlett said to the deputy. He glanced at his watch. "I'll probably be home in an hour or so. Call me when you get a report."

Curry nodded.

Bramlett turned to the others and said again, "I'm sorry," but he knew no one was listening.

After the sheriff left, Curry sat down in an armchair adjacent to the couch. He looked at Lizzie. Her eyes were shut tight as if she were hurting. He wasn't sure how long Shamona had been hit before they knew anything about it. In fact, he'd just stepped out from Mrs. Winter's room into the hallway, leaving

206

Lizzie for a moment, and overheard two nurses at the station talking about a shooting that had just occurred.

By the time he got down to the parking lot, paramedics were already putting her into the ambulance for the short ride around to the emergency entrance. No witnesses came forward, if there were any.

Lizzie opened her eyes and sat up. She looked at H.C. "Why?" she asked again, as she had several times over the last hour.

He shook his head again, and mumbled, "I don't know," as he had each time she'd asked, and, as he had each time, he told himself that he was lying, lying, because he was afraid he really did know why but didn't want to say anything yet.

Isaac walked over and sat down heavily beside Lizzie. He'd been drinking at the Log Cabin when they located him. He stared at H.C., then said in a surly tone, "How's the little colored deputy?"

"Stop it," Lizzie said. "Don't even get started."

Isaac made a contemptuous grunt. "Did the fat boy run out to try and catch whoever shot my sister? Or did he just take hisself back to his warm bed?"

Lizzie sighed. "Why don't you go look for Hugh?" she asked.

"This is Friday night, little sister. How am I gonna find that boy on a Friday night?" He looked at H.C. again. "They let you load that gun?" He chuckled.

H.C. looked away, ignoring him.

"Please," Lizzie said. "This isn't the time for all this."

"For all what? If you gonna marry this sucker, hadn't he better find out all about his new family?"

"I'm asking you to please shut up," she said evenly.

"Why? Who's to hear? Your father there?"

H.C. looked briefly at Patterson. The man didn't move, gave no indication he heard a thing, or, if he heard, that any of it bothered him.

Lizzie closed her eyes and said nothing.

Isaac leered at H.C. "I guess you know, man, that this here ain't my father. He may be hers, and Shamona's and them, but he ain't none of mines. That's the deep family secret." He looked at Patterson. "Ain't that right, old man?"

The man gave no reaction.

H.C. sensed the mounting tension. He wasn't sure what to do. After all, it wasn't his family, not yet anyway.

"Stop it," Lizzie said, her eyes still closed. "He is your father, fool."

Isaac shook his head in a slow arc. "No, ma'am. My daddy gave Mama money for me all them years I was growing up, and this old fellow ain't never give me nothing but a hard time. He may be your father, but he ain't mines."

Patterson slowly lowered his hands.

Isaac reached across Lizzie and poked him in the shoulder. "How you doing, old man? Why ain't you out at that college cleaning toilets? Don't you reckon there some toilets out there you need to clean?"

He tried to poke Patterson again, but the man suddenly sprang to his feet. Isaac stood also, swayed slightly and his chest swelled up. He raised his hands as if expecting Patterson to charge.

Patterson, however, hurried away from the couch and moved across the room. Isaac gave another scornful laugh and collapsed back onto the couch.

Lizzie made a low moan.

"I'll be right back," H.C. said, standing up.

He walked to a bank of six pay telephones against the wall. A white woman in a long dress and wearing a black Mennonite cap was talking on one of the phones. H.C. slipped a quarter into the coin slot and dialed. In a moment, Sheriff Bramlett came on the line.

"I thought I'd stay here a while longer," H.C. said.

"Any word on Shamona yet?"

"No, sir."

There was silence on the other end of the line for a moment, then Sheriff Bramlett said, "We don't have anything right now to go on, you know. We don't have any idea who to look for or what kind of car or anything like that."

"I know," H.C. said.

"It doesn't look good. I mean, you say Shamona was wearing Lizzie's black coat and getting into Lizzie's car?"

H.C. swallowed hard. Then he said, "That's why I need to stay right here."

"I understand," Bramlett said. "Keep me posted."

After H.C. hung up the receiver, he turned and looked back

across the room to the couch where Lizzie sat. The only thing on her mind, he knew, was a swelling monster of anxiety for her sister.

She had not yet, H.C. knew, realized the full significance of what had happened.

# 28

Saturday morning at five o'clock, H. C. Curry was asleep on the couch in the intensive care waiting room when Dr. Anderson Sinclair came with news about Shamona. Lizzie pushed H.C.'s shoulder, and he sat up at once. Cynthia and Lizzie were already standing, talking with the surgeon. Isaac was gone.

"She'll be in surgical intensive care for at least forty-eight hours," he explained. "The bullet that entered the shoulder came at such an angle that it ricocheted off the back of the shoulder blade and exited without causing severe damage. The major concern is the wound in the side. I think we've stabilized her. We've stopped the internal bleeding. The bullet passed through the kidney and lodged by the liver in a place hard to get to. We don't know how much damage there is to the kidney. We may have to go back in if it doesn't begin to function. If it puts out urine in forty-eight hours, okay. Otherwise, we may have to go back and take it out."

Both Lizzie and Cynthia stood together with their eyes riveted on the doctor and their arms wrapped around each other. H.C. stood beside them with a hand on Lizzie's shoulder.

"When can we see her?" Lizzie asked.

"She'll be in Recovery another hour or so." He looked at his watch. "There's an eight o'clock visitation time. I think she'll be ready for that." His brow furrowed. "Now bear in mind, she's on a ventilator and highly sedated. We won't try to take her off that ventilator for at least twenty-four hours."

Then he left.

H.C. gave Lizzie a hug and said, "I'm going to have to run on now. You want me to bring y'all some breakfast before I go?"

Lizzie shook her head. "No. We're okay."

He kissed her on the cheek and left.

He went home, cleaned up and put on fresh clothes, ate a bowl of corn flakes, and was at headquarters by six-thirty.

The Tupelo newspaper was on the corner of the reception-ist's desk, still tightly rolled up with a blue rubber band around it. He picked it up and slipped off the rubber band as he walked to his desk.

He sat down and opened the paper. The story about Lydia Gressete was on page three. She was identified as a resident of Sheffield, unemployed. The cause of death was still under in-vestigation, the article stated, and a witness who saw someone leave the body on the logging road had given a description to the sheriff's department.

Curry breathed a small sigh of relief. At least the reporter didn't give Lonsdale's name or repeat that he'd identified the person as a black male. He hated it when the news did that. Suddenly, every black male in northeast Mississippi became a suspect.

He turned to the sports section and scanned the area high school basketball scores. The Sheffield boys had lost to Pontotoc last night. The girls, however, won their game.

The intercom buzzed. Curry picked up the receiver, remem-bering he hadn't been able to attend a single basketball game this year.

It was Sheila Gates, the weekend dispatcher. "Unit six has just reported an abandoned automobile on Tugel Road. That's Deputy Taylor. He says he thinks an investigator ought to look at it. He thinks there are bloodstains on the backseat."

"Okay," Curry said, rising from his chair. "Tell him I'm on my way." He glanced at his watch. The sheriff should be up by now. He picked up the receiver and punched Bramlett's home number.

Grover Bramlett was sitting in his recliner in the den having a second cup of coffee and watching the weather station on tele-vision when Curry phoned. It was already above freezing. At least they wouldn't have to worry about bad road conditions today. Whenever the bridges iced, too many units got tied up all day with fender-benders.

Curry told him first that Shamona Clouse had come through surgery and was doing okay. Then he told him about the abandoned car with what might be bloodstains on the backseat.

"I'll meet you there," Bramlett said.

He hung up the phone and reached for his gun belt on top of the refrigerator. Valeria wasn't up yet. Before leaving, he went into the bedroom and kissed her on the nose and patted her rump.

Tugel Road was only a few miles north of Sheffield right off Highway 45. In fact, it was the turnoff to Sheffield College. Curry was already on the scene when he arrived.

In front of Curry's car was another patrol car. Both vehicles were parked half off the shoulder of the road. Adrian Taylor, a deputy Bramlett didn't know very well yet, stood in the middle of the road with Curry.

Taylor was in his early thirties, and had been in the Marines before joining the department. His father had been a constable out in the county for many years.

Bramlett parked his Corvette behind Curry's car and got out. From the road, an embankment dropped steeply, and in the midst of a cluster of brambles higher than a man's head was an older vehicle. A dark, probably black, Ford. The trunk was badly rusted.

"It definitely looks like blood on the backseat," Curry said.

"I've run a check on the tag," Taylor said. "The vehicle is registered to Toby C. Carson."

"Toby Carson?" Bramlett asked. The name was familiar. Very familiar.

"He's in Parchman," Curry said. "Had a habit of writing bad checks. Went down about a year ago. Second time."

Bramlett smiled, remembering now. "Seems he left his car behind for someone else to keep the battery up."

"The address on the registration is eighteen-ten Howser Street in Sheffield," Curry said.

"Howser Street?" asked Bramlett. That struck a bell of familiarity.

The deputy nodded. "Yes, sir. This is Lydia Gressete's address. I think Toby Carson is her brother."

Bramlett took his foil pouch out of his back pocket. "So what we may have here is the vehicle that interrupted Mr. Lonsdale the other night."

"Possibly."

"Call the crime lab at Tupelo. See if they can get somebody up here to check it out. Do a workup for prints and whatever else. I'll send Baillie out to help you."

He then pulled open the door of the Corvette and lowered himself onto the seat. As he turned the key in the ignition, he gazed at the road ahead. It curved to the left, continuing through this forest of dark gray, leafless hardwoods for a couple of miles or so until it reached Sheffield College. And, at Sheffield College, Patterson Clouse worked as a janitor.

Not long after Bramlett got to his office, the phone rang. It was Valeria.

"Well?" he asked. "What did you think about Sylvia's *person?*"

"I think she's falling in love with him," she said. "And we don't really know much about him. At dinner he had three glasses of wine. And he was driving. That made me uncomfortable."

"Maybe he was just nervous," Bramlett said.

"Nervous? Why?"

"Knowing Sylvia's hypercritical sister was sizing him up," he said with a laugh.

"You don't really care, do you?"

"You know I do," he said, smiling. He was glad for Sylvia. She deserved the warmth.

As he hung up the phone, he glanced at his doorway. Jacob Robertson stood waiting. "You do, too," the sheriff said.

The deputy looked puzzled. "Sir?"

"Warmth, Jacob. Warmth. You deserve some. We all do."

Robertson cocked his head, waiting for the sheriff to explain.

Bramlett gave a wave of his hand, dismissing the line of discussion, then asked, "What you got?"

"I've just been going through Lydia Gressete's place again this morning," he said. He laid a stack of envelopes on the corner of Bramlett's desk. "I found these."

They looked like old letters, the envelopes were of assorted sizes, and the paper was aged.

"And?" Bramlett asked, sitting down in his chair.

"They were in a top drawer in the chifforobe. They're personal letters the woman received over the years. Some go back thirty years or so. Mostly from family, best I can tell."

"Her brother is in Parchman, it seems."

Robertson reached to the stack and ran his fingers down several envelopes. "These," he said, handing them to Bramlett, "are addressed to her when she lived in Mobile for a while. And they are all from Naresse Clouse."

Bramlett looked at the postmarks on each envelope. Four were dated 1960, and two 1961. He arranged them in order. "Have you read them yet?"

Robertson said, "Yes, sir. Apparently, Gressete was working as a maid in Mobile and living with an aunt. The Clouse woman makes a lot of references to someone named Abraham. She doesn't use his last name."

Bramlett laid the letters on his desk blotter. "Where's Baillie?" he asked.

Robertson tilted his head toward the outer office. "At his desk. We just got back a couple of minutes before you came in."

"H.C. is out on Tugel Road. That's the road to the college. There's an abandoned vehicle that was possibly used to transport Gressete's body to the woods. Y'all go out there and help him look it over." He glanced at his watch. "And tell H.C. to meet me here at ten o'clock."

When the deputy was gone, Bramlett slid the first letter out of its envelope. The postmark was Sheffield, Monday, November 7, 1960. The letter was only one page, written on three-holed, lined notebook paper. The handwriting was awkward, labored almost, like that of someone young. He read:

Dear Lydia,

I wish you were here so that I could tell you all that has been happening. Abraham and I can't see each other as much as I want because he is at college again, of course. He does come home on weekends. We meet in the cave. I can't stand him being gone all week. I wish he could just come home more but he says he can't because of all the studying he has to do and he says he loves me more than life itself, more than David loved Bathsheba even. I know you think I'm stupid for continuing to see him, but I can't help how I feel. Abraham is the only man I have ever been

214

with or ever want to be with. I know some people think I been with lots of boys but that is not the truth. When are you coming home? Do you still hate your job? I need to talk to you. I got to hurry. The mailman will be coming in a few minutes and I want to get this out to the box before he come.

Your friend,<br>
Naresse Winter.

Bramlett refolded the sheet of paper and slid it back into the envelope and laid the envelope to the side. He picked up a second letter and read it. It was pretty much the same, as were the next four.

Naresse Clouse wrote of her boyfriend Abraham. He was in college, but came home on weekends. From Naresse's questions and answers, Bramlett judged Lydia Gressete had hated her job as a maid for the family in Mobile. She didn't think the relatives she lived with liked her much, either. She wanted to be back home.

Naresse mentioned that she loved Abraham too much to go out with other boys. In one letter she referred to someplace called Machpelah, where she and Abraham met regularly.

The last letter was postmarked in January 12, 1961.

Dear Lydia,

I sure hate it that you could not come home last weekend. I know you had wanted to. Write and tell me why you did not. I need to talk to you. I don't have anybody I can talk to. Of course, I talk to Abraham about the situation but he don't know what to do either. It's like a nightmare to him he says. He don't blame me. He loves me and he wishes there was some way we could get married but we can't. I don't know what to do. I know Mama will find out soon. I am scared but I already picked out a name. I am going to name him Isaac. I just know its going to be a boy. Please come home. Please please please.

Your friend,<br>
Naresse Winter.

Bramlett set the letter aside. The name Abraham didn't mean anything to him. In 1960 Naresse Clouse would have been about twenty years old, out of high school a couple of years. Would it have been someone she was in school with? At that time, there was only one high school for blacks in Chakchiuma County and it was located in Sheffield.

This Abraham was in college. Did Wayne Carr go to college? Yes. Jackson State. What about James Doffey? He wasn't sure.

Somehow, this Abraham, Naresse's boyfriend of more than thirty years and father of Isaac Clouse, was a substantial key. But how to identify him? Who would know?

Probably Naresse's mother, old Mrs. Winter. She would definitely know. Isaac? Bramlett wasn't sure. Maybe.

He reached for the rest of the envelopes. Perhaps someone else writing Lydia Gressete would have something to say.

All of the letters were old, none more recent than ten years before. Either people stopped writing to her or Lydia Gressete stopped saving the letters. Perhaps a little of both, thought Bramlett. There were no letters from her parents, possibly indicating they couldn't write, a reminder of a time when education for blacks was severely lacking in the state. Lydia and Naresse would have finished school, like Bramlett, long before the desegregation mandates started coming down.

H. C. Curry returned to headquarters just after nine-thirty. "There's an officer from the Tupelo crime lab working with Johnny and Jacob," he said, referring to Baillie and Robertson. "He says it's definitely blood. He's going over the whole vehicle there at the scene."

Bramlett handed him the letters found at Lydia Gressete's house. "Read these six now," the sheriff said. "Then go through the others. Have Lizzie look at them, too. Maybe there's something in them I didn't see."

Curry sat down in a chair in front of the desk and silently read each letter. When he was finished, he looked up at Bramlett. "Abraham? Who's Abraham?"

Bramlett shook his head slowly. "No idea. Obviously, he's Isaac's father."

Curry sighed and leaned back in his chair. "Isaac is all the time throwing this thing up in Mr. Clouse's face, that some other man is his real father. Of course, Lizzie never believed it."

"We'll need to show her these letters her mother wrote."

Curry frowned. "She's going through hell right now. Her

sister has just been shot and her grandmother is out there in the hospital, too."

"I thought maybe the grandmother might know who this Abraham is."

Curry gave a low grunt. "Maybe. But right now she doesn't make much sense half the time. I don't think she's going to pull through."

"What do you make of this cave the letter mentions? Are there any caves around here? And where's this Machpelah? I don't know anyplace named Machpelah. Do you?"

"No. I never heard of it, and I don't know anything about a cave."

"Is Lizzie still out at the hospital? We need to see her."

Curry nodded and laid the letters back in front of the sheriff.

Bramlett and Curry found Lizzie Clouse in Adele Winter's room. The old woman seemed to be resting peacefully, breathing evenly under the oxygen mask.

Lizzie's fifteen-year-old brother Hugh was in the room when they arrived, and, without a word, he left. Bramlett was surprised how much he'd grown since he'd last seen him. He was big, over six feet and probably close to a hundred fifty pounds. He didn't look either Bramlett or Curry in the eye and seemed in a hurry to leave.

Lizzie sat in the armchair beside her grandmother's bed. She had a scarf around her head and her eyes were swollen. "Cynthia and I went in to see her this morning," she said, referring to Shamona. "Seeing that breathing tube running down her throat was horrible. I told her it was all going to be okay. I don't know if she could hear me or not."

Bramlett handed her the three-and-a-half-decade-old letters. "What's this?" she asked.

Bramlett explained that the letters were found at Lydia's house, and these six were written by Lizzie's mother. "Please," he said. "Read these and tell us anything you can about them."

Lizzie sat forward in the chair, her elbows propped on her knees, and read each one. Her shoulders sank a bit more each time she finished a letter.

Finally, after the sixth and final one, the one that alluded to

Naresse's pregnancy and desire to name the child Isaac, Lizzie handed the letters back to Bramlett. "Mama 'Dele was right," she said, reaching out and laying a hand on the bedspread under which was the form of the old woman's arm. "She said for us to let Mama rest in peace. But all we're doing is making things uglier and uglier."

"Does this name Abraham mean anything to you?"

"No."

"What about the place called Machpelah? Or a cave?"

She shook her head. "Not really."

"What that supposed to mean?" asked Bramlett, turning his good ear toward her.

She shrugged a shoulder. "There was something in the woods near the church that we called a cave. It was just a washed-out place in the creek bank. It could hardly be called a cave. And, besides, I hid there once or twice from Mama. She never knew about it."

She looked the sheriff directly in the eye. "I don't like all this trash y'all trying to dredge up."

"Your mama would want us to find out who killed her," Curry said.

She shot a hard look at him. "Is that what y'all doing? Trying to find out who killed Mama? I thought it was that white man's killer y'all wanted."

"Lizzie," Bramlett said softly. "It seems more and more somehow . . ." He paused and shook his head and swallowed, trying to swallow down a knot growing in his throat. "It seems your mother's death and the deaths of these other two are connected. I don't know how, but . . ." He didn't finish.

"What's any of this have to do with these old letters?" Her words carried a bitterness, a resentment, apparently, at the harsh truth about her mother and her brother which the two lawmen had just forced her to face.

"Do you think Isaac knows anything about this Abraham?"

"I wouldn't know. Why don't you ask him."

Bramlett watched her for a moment. Her hand was still resting on her grandmother's arm. She was looking blankly toward the window. She seemed so tired, so angry, so frail. "And you're sure you have no idea who this person is?" he asked.

She shook her head. "No, I don't."

"It may be possible somebody thinks you know."

218

Her eyes narrowed and she slowly turned her head to face him. "What?" She was frowning.

Bramlett swallowed, then said, "Listen. Shamona was wearing your coat and trying to get into your car." He paused, watching her face, watching for a sign of recognition of the facts.

She held the frown for a moment, looking at him questioningly. Then she looked at Curry as if asking for help in understanding. Curry said nothing, merely nodded as if to affirm what the sheriff had said.

Her lips parted slightly, then she asked, "But . . . but why . . . ? Who?"

"We don't know," Bramlett said. "But whoever shot Shamona must know by now he shot the wrong person. And, whoever he is, he must be trying to figure out how he can get to the right one."

Lizzie leaned back in the chair and closed her eyes. She said nothing.

# 29

As they were leaving the hospital, Sheriff Grover Bramlett and Deputy H. C. Curry ran into Patterson Clouse in the lobby. He was wearing a faded denim work coat and a black wool watch cap. Bramlett stepped in front of him and put his hand to the man's arm to stop him.

"We'd like to talk with you a minute," Bramlett said.

Clouse's jaw muscle tightened. "I ain't got time," he said. "I going up to see my girl."

"I understand," the sheriff said softly. "It's a terrible thing, but she's doing okay, Lizzie says. This won't take but just a minute."

"Listen," Clouse said through his teeth, looking the sheriff straight in the eye without blinking. "I done talked to y'all all I want. I ain't got nothing else to say."

"Patterson, something new has come up. We think you need to hear what we got to say."

In a corner of the lobby away from the front door was a vinyl-covered couch and armchair. The three of them sat down, Clouse and Bramlett on the couch, Curry in the chair. Bramlett explained about Shamona wearing Lizzie's coat and starting to get into Lizzie's car.

Clouse's chest expanded and his hands clenched into fists. "Who?" he asked. "Why?"

"Somehow there's a link between Rory Hornsly and Naresse."

"She didn't even know him."

"Maybe not. But there's also this other man and Naresse. You know what I'm talking about."

Clouse stiffened. He glared at Curry, then at Bramlett. He said nothing.

Bramlett continued. "I know this is painful to you, but we've got to find out who he is."

Clouse looked away, his eyes unfocused but directed toward an information desk at the other side of the lobby. "I'm told it wasn't Wayne," he said flatly.

"Who told you?"

"Just someone."

"Addie Carr?" Curry asked.

Clouse looked at the deputy for a moment, then the corners of his mouth hinted at a smile. "You love my little Lizzie, don't you, Son?"

Curry swallowed, then said, "Yes, sir."

"But she don't love you. Is that right?"

"Well . . ."

"Naw," Clouse said, dismissing his last statement. "Maybe she do. How am I to know." He ran his palm roughly across his mouth, then continued. "Peoples do some crazy things for love. I don't know. Addie and me go back a long ways. But it didn't work out for us. I been knowing her 'fore I knowed Naresse." He shrugged. "What does it matter now? Now we just getting old and tired."

Neither Bramlett nor Curry said anything, waiting to let him continue. "I don't know who would want to kill my Naresse," he said. He shot his eyes at Bramlett, as if challenging him to make the accusations the sheriff had before. He didn't speak for a few moments, then he looked back toward the desk and continued in a more meditative tone. "I don't know if there was somebody else or not. Maybe every man suspects at one time or another that there somebody else."

"Why did you have a gun at Wayne Carr's place?" Bramlett asked.

Clouse's shoulders sank slightly as if he were very tired suddenly. "I got it in my mind once it might be him. Addie says she know it weren't. I don't really know. I guess it don't make a lot of difference right now. Right now I got a baby girl up there fighting for her life."

"This is the difference it makes," Bramlett said tersely. "You got another baby girl somebody meant to kill when they shot Shamona. And if we don't find out who that person is and stop him, he's going to try again."

Patterson turned his face and looked at Bramlett. There was a look of indecision as if he were trying to decide whether to work with this white man he'd hated and mistrusted or not.

"Tell me," Bramlett continued, "do you know anybody named Abraham?"

Clouse shook his head. "No. I knowed an old man with that name when I was a boy but he been dead now forty years."

"You know of any place called Machpelah?"

He shook his head again.

"Any caves around here?"

He raised one eyebrow. "Caves?"

Bramlett pulled the packet of letters out of his coat pocket. "There's something I want you to see," he said. He took off the rubber band and separated Naresse's last letter to Lydia Gressete, then stretched the rubber band back over the rest of the letters. He looked up at Curry. The deputy had a disturbed expression on his face. Bramlett continued. "Believe me, Patterson, I don't like having to show you this, but . . ." He paused and handed him the letter. "Please read this."

The two lawmen watched in silence as Patterson Clouse pulled the old letter out of the envelope and read the words his then future wife Naresse Winter wrote to her friend Lydia Gressete about a man named Abraham and their child who she planned to name Isaac.

When he was done, he handed the letter with the envelope back to the sheriff. He stared at the floor for a long moment, then said, "It was all a long, long time ago."

"And you have no idea who this man is?" Bramlett asked.

"No," he said, standing up. "I got to go see my girl." Then he walked away. He didn't hurry. He walked as if he were very tired.

Bramlett and Curry ate hamburgers for lunch at the Eagle Café. In that it was Saturday, the café had fewer customers than usual. Then they met with Johnny Baillie and Jacob Robertson in the sheriff's office. "The vehicle's been placed in the compound," Robertson said. "And we searched the woods all around where it was parked in case a weapon was tossed." He paused, shook his chin slightly and said, "Nothing."

Bramlett turned in his swivel chair enough to look out the window at the gray sky. It was supposed to turn much colder tonight. "So, whoever dumped Lydia Gressete's body out on a logging road, abandoned the car afterward in a ditch on Tugel Road. Then what? Walked away? How close is the nearest house?"

"About two hundred yards," Baillie said. "There aren't many houses, and we've talked to the residents on both sides of the road all the way to the college. Nobody seems to have seen the car being left."

"Whoever did it could have been picked up by someone else if he didn't just walk away," Bramlett said.

"No one we've talked to saw anyone walking along the road," Robertson said. "Of course, it would have been dark, and if he'd seen a car coming he could have gotten off the road until he got wherever he was going."

Bramlett scratched his chin for a moment, then said, "I want you all going through any records available looking for the name Abraham," he said to Robertson and Baillie. "And find out what this Machpelah is." He turned his chair back around to the desk and stood up. "H.C. and I are going to have to talk to a man about his father. 'It's a wise son who knows his own father.' Isn't that what the Book says?"

Baillie gave an exasperated look at the sheriff. "I think it's 'A wise father knows his own son.' " Baillie taught Sunday school at his church and knew Scripture better than any man on the force.

"Whatever," Bramlett said. "Do we have an address for Isaac Clouse?" The question was directed to Curry.

"I know where he lives."

"Wait," Johnny Baillie said. He and Robertson were almost out the door. "You were asking about Abraham. . ."

"Yes," Bramlett said, at the same time blinking in recognition. "Of course. Abraham and Isaac." He turned to look at Curry. "Abraham was Isaac's father."

Curry frowned. "So?"

"Well, it's something anyway." Bramlett looked back at Baillie. "Thanks."

Isaac Clouse lived on Eptin Road in south Sheffield. "This is his girlfriend's house," Curry explained as he drove up a dirt drive into the front yard and stopped the patrol car beneath the twisted limbs of a huge oak tree. "Her name is Chattel Jenkins. She has four kids, I think. They aren't Isaac's. He's only been here a few months."

Two small boys standing on the front porch stared at them for a moment, then hurried inside the house.

A woman who looked to be in her late twenties pushed open the screen door and stepped onto the porch as Bramlett and Curry approached the house. She was thin-faced and light-skinned, wearing a gray sweater, and had her arms crossed and her jaw jutted in a defiant manner. Her cool gaze was directed at Curry, as if, somehow, working for the white sheriff made him a traitor to his people.

"Good afternoon," Bramlett said pleasantly. "We need to see Isaac Clouse."

She looked at him while he spoke, straight into his eyes as if to demonstrate she wasn't afraid of him or his authority.

"He's in bed," she said.

Bramlett placed his foot on the lowest step. "This is important," he said. "Tell him we're here to talk about his father. His *real* father."

She continued to stare at him for a moment longer, then gave a contemptuous sniff and went back into the house. She didn't invite them in.

Bramlett and Curry looked at each other. "Well," Bramlett said with a weak smile, "we sure as hell can't talk to him out here in the cold." He made a motion with his head for the deputy to follow him. He then climbed the steps, walked across the porch, and shoved open the front door, letting both of them into the house.

The air was thick with the smell of the wood-burning stove in the middle of the room. Three small children stood against the side of a tall iron bed across the room, staring at Bramlett and Curry. They huddled together timidly with their eyes riveted on the strangers who'd entered their home.

In a couple of minutes, the woman came back into the room followed by Isaac Clouse. She walked over to the children, shooed them out of the room, and went after them down the hallway.

Clouse leaned against a doorjamb and looked from Curry to Bramlett, and waited for an explanation.

"Sorry to disturb your sleep," Bramlett said. "May we sit down?" He sat down on a short couch without waiting for an answer to his question. Curry took his place beside him. Clouse didn't move from the doorjamb.

"What's this about my father?" he asked.

"I understand you do not believe Patterson is your real father," Bramlett said.

Clouse gave a half-smile and cocked his head. "My *real* father? What's this about my real father?"

Bramlett gave a slight shrug. "Just something we heard, that's all. Probably nothing to it, now that I look at you."

He scowled. "What you mean, now that you *looking* at me?"

The sheriff chuckled. "Ain't no doubt about it," he said. "Patterson Clouse done marked you. You him all over."

Clouse hissed. "The hell. Ain't none of his blood in my veins. Not a damn drop."

"How do you know this?" the sheriff asked, wondering whether to show him Lydia Gressete's letter or not.

"Mama told me."

Bramlett looked at Curry. Curry's eyes were on Isaac Clouse, the older brother of the woman he planned to marry. Curry made no reaction to Clouse's statement. Bramlett wondered if the young man ever thought about how he and Isaac would get along as brothers-in-law.

Bramlett cleared his throat. "What exactly did she say?"

"It was when I was small. She used to say things like, 'You got your daddy's brains. You can do anything you want.' And sometimes, when I was playing ball, after a game when we were home, she'd be all happy and tell me how proud my daddy was of me for doing so good. And I knew she wasn't talking about him." By *him* Bramlett understood him to mean Patterson.

"How could you tell?"

"Because it might be a baseball game in the afternoon and he be off cleaning his toilets at work. And Mama would tell me afterwards that she was watching my daddy during the game and how proud he was of me."

"Then you know who he is?"

"I have a good idea. Don't have no proof yet, but I have a pretty good idea."

"But your mother never told you specifically?"

He shook his head. "Naw."

"Who do you think it is?"

"Why? What's this got to do with anything?"

"We're trying to find out who killed your mother and shot your sister and a man named Rory Hornsly and Lydia Gressete. We don't know if all these are actually related, or if the same person is involved, but there are some links between your mother and these others, even Hornsly."

"I *know* who killed my mother. That bastard husband of hers."

Bramlett noted how the man always avoided mentioning Patterson by name. "Is that why you attacked him with a bat?" he asked.

Clouse ground his teeth, then said, "I wished I'd killed him."

"We worked real hard three years ago trying to prove Patterson killed her, but never could," Bramlett said. "Why are you so sure of it?"

"Because he was jealous of my real father," he said with a twisted smile. "He couldn't stand the fact that she loved somebody else."

Bramlett considered this for a moment, then asked, "Was your real father still around? Or, I guess I mean, is he still around now?"

Isaac nodded. "He gave her money for me the whole time I was growing up. When I was down at Jackson State and called her about needing some money, she'd get some and then say, 'This is from your father.' "

"And she didn't mean Patterson?"

"Hell, no. Where does a janitor get a hundred dollars? I mean, it might be two hundred or three hundred, and she'd always get it." He had a very pleased look on his face. "So, naturally, I knew my real father had some money."

"Then, who is he?"

Clouse smiled broader. "Why? Why do you need to know?" It seemed to please him that he had information the sheriff wanted and that he could or could not at his own pleasure release this information.

Bramlett tried to look pleasant. He wasn't sure what was the best way to get this man to tell him what he needed to know. He didn't know him well enough to know what he wanted bad enough that he could give him. Finally, he said, "We do know the name of your father."

Clouse gave a low chuckle. "Really, now? Then why are you here *asking* me who he is?"

"Like I said, we know his name. At least his first name."

"Sure. I'm sure you do." It was obvious Clouse thought this was incredible.

"We've got evidence of that in your mother's own handwriting."

The sarcastic smile slipped from Clouse's face and he frowned. "What? What you got?" His voice was hurried.

Bramlett was pleased to see the eagerness in the man's response. "Your father's name is Abraham," Bramlett said, his eyes fixed on the man's face watching for a response.

Clouse's eyes squinted slightly and his lips parted, but he didn't speak. He looked at Bramlett. The confusion was apparent in his eyes. Bramlett knew this wasn't what Clouse expected. The sheriff leaned back more in his seat, as if, having just dropped his heaviest bomb, he was waiting to see the results.

Clouse pushed himself off the doorjamb and sat down in an armchair. He looked at Curry as if trying to determine if the deputy knew this, too, in advance, or was this just a name the sheriff had thrown out.

He looked down at the floor, obviously considering this. The arrogance was gone from his demeanor. The name seemed to have not only taken him completely by surprise but started churning within his brain other thoughts.

Finally, he said, "Abraham is not his real name."

"Oh?" Bramlett asked. "Why does she call him that then?"

Clouse half closed his eyes and looked at Bramlett. "What's this written evidence?"

Bramlett took the letter from Lydia to Naresse out of his pocket and handed it to him. He watched the man read the letter, saw the expressionlessness of his face, and wondered who he suspected of being this Abraham.

When he was through, Clouse refolded the letter but held it under his fingers on the arm of the chair. "That wasn't his real name," he said again. "I remember her once telling me that she had once hoped that she and me and my daddy could all go away to California or someplace. But then, she told me, all the other kids came along and she got stuck here."

"When did she tell you this?" Bramlett asked. "I mean, how old were you?"

Clouse looked away for a moment as if thinking, then looked back and said, "Young. I don't know. Grade school, probably. The reason I remember it so much is that she said when we went she was going to change her name."

"Why?"

He shrugged. "I don't know. She said she was going to be called Sarah. That she was really Sarah, not Naresse." He paused and sighed. "But that was all a long time ago. I don't know if we ever talked about it again."

"Strange that you still remember it after all these years," Bramlett said.

"I guess I just thought it was weird, you know? I mean, why Sarah?"

Bramlett rubbed his knee. The damp coldness of the room was beginning to seep into his joints. "Sarah was the name of Abraham's wife," he said.

Isaac Clouse looked confused.

The sheriff continued. "In the Bible. You know, the Old Testament. Abraham and Sarah. And, they had a son named Isaac."

Clouse's mouth twisted. "What?"

Bramlett nodded. "So Abraham wasn't his real name any more than Sarah was your mother's. But now, listen." Bramlett paused and looked Clouse hard in the eye. "We need to talk to this Abraham. We need to know as much about all this as we can. *Who* do you think your real father is?"

"Why? I don't understand why you think you need to know."

Bramlett scratched the back of his neck for a moment, trying to think of what he could say to get this man to tell what he knew. Then it hit him. "Well," he said, "I think your real father may be able to give us evidence that would help us convict Patterson Clouse of killing Naresse." He turned to look at a dumbfounded Curry. "Isn't that right, H.C.?"

Curry stared uncomprehendingly at Bramlett.

Bramlett looked back at Clouse. "So?"

The man's face hardened immediately and he said, "Wayne Carr. Wayne Carr is my real father."

# 30

Deputy H. C. Curry shifted into drive and steered out into the street. "That ain't fishing," he said. "That's just out and out lying."

"All fishing is lying," the sheriff said. "Otherwise you'd never catch anything. And he did give us a name."

Curry nodded. "Lizzie did tell me that Wayne Carr had given money to Isaac," he said. "And it ain't been all that long ago."

Bramlett was silent for a bit as the car gathered speed. Then he said, "Carr had dealings with Hornsly. Hornsly screwed him out of a lot of money. Isaac might be right about Carr being Naresse's longtime lover and his real father. And Lonsdale says it was definitely a black man who dumped Lydia Gressete's body. Who else do we have?" Bramlett didn't want to—couldn't—believe it was James Doffey.

Curry didn't answer. He drove silently back through Sheffield's business district and to the east, to the upscale, predominantly white neighborhood of young professionals and fast-rising businessmen where Wayne Carr had built a home a few years earlier.

Carr's wife, Lucille, met them at the door and then led them into the den where Wayne was wearing a red warm-up suit and stretched out on a long sofa watching a college basketball game on television. He grimaced when he saw them, and sat up when they entered the room. Lucille disappeared.

"Don't you guys ever rest?" he asked, standing up and reaching out his hand to the sheriff. "I mean, even I don't work on Saturday afternoon."

Each lawman shook his hand.

He motioned for them to sit down, and raised the remote

control and muted the volume. "So," he said, after they were all seated. "What else can I tell you?"

"We've been talking with Isaac Clouse," Bramlett said.

Carr smiled and shook his head. "There's a waste for you. The man is what now? Thirty-four? -five? He was a fine athlete and he's done nothing with his life. I tried to get him into selling cars for me. Or burial policies." He paused and put his arm on the back of the sofa and shook his head again. "What a waste."

"We understand you've given money to help him out on occasion," Bramlett said.

Carr shrugged. "A little here and there. Like I told you, I've known the family a long time."

"And you told us you and Naresse were quite close."

"She was one beautiful woman," he said with a smile. He looked toward the ceiling. There was a look of pleasure in his eyes as he remembered the past.

"When was the last time you helped Isaac out a bit?" Bramlett asked.

Carr looked at the sheriff. "There some law against a man giving a little money to folks here and there?"

"No. I'm just curious."

"I can't remember exactly. Some time ago."

"Years? Months?"

"More like months, I suppose."

"And you've been doing this for a long time? I mean, like since Isaac was in college?"

Carr's brow furrowed. "What? College? What are you talking about?"

"When he was at Jackson State and needed a hundred dollars or so. You gave Naresse the money to give to Isaac?"

Carr laughed. "Hell, man. That was how many years ago? Fifteen or so? Naw. I wasn't yet in a position to do something like that. In fact, Naresse never asked me for money. Isaac told you that?"

Bramlett ignored his question. "Are you familiar with someone named Abraham?" He watched closely for a reaction, watched for some slight facial change or something in the eyes to indicate surprise or shock. He saw, however, only puzzlement.

"What? Abraham? Who's he?"

"The name means nothing to you?"

"I don't have any idea what you're talking about."

"Isaac Clouse thinks you're his real father."

Carr's mouth opened slightly. He swallowed, then said, "What? His father? Where the hell did he get an idea like that?"

Bramlett pulled lightly on his ear. Either Carr was a great actor or he was telling the truth. Then again, he sold used cars. Bramlett pressed on. "Let me ask you this. Did you ever sleep with Naresse Clouse?"

Carr dropped his arm from the back of the sofa and shot a look at the doorway through which Lucille had exited after showing the two men into the room. Satisfied that she wasn't there, he looked back at Bramlett. "Now this is a hell of a note. You come into a man's home on Saturday afternoon while he's trying to relax and ask him a question like that. What the hell difference does it make now anyway?"

"It makes a lot of difference if you are indeed Isaac's father and if somehow you killed his mother."

Carr's face turned rigid. "You mean to tell me you think . . ." He paused and the muscles in his cheek drew taut and his breathing became heavier. To Bramlett, he looked more angry than afraid. He said in a lowered voice, "You listen to what I'm telling you. Yes, I loved Naresse Winter even before she met Patterson Clouse. No, I never gave Isaac any money that long ago. No, I never had the wonderful pleasure of sleeping with her before she married Patterson Clouse." He glanced at the doorway once more, then looked back at Bramlett and spoke in an even lower voice. "But a long time ago, we were together some. I think she was just down about a lot of things and I happened to be convenient. It was during my first marriage. I'm telling you this because there may be some people who know. Probably. But then she broke it off after a while. I would have given anything if she would have divorced Patterson and married me. In fact—and you'll probably hear this so I'm telling you now—our being together had a lot to do with my divorce." He paused, cleared his throat, then said wearily, "No, I'm not his father. And I don't think Patterson is, either."

"If Patterson is not his father, who is?"

Carr shrugged one shoulder. "Occasionally, when we were

talking Naresse said some strange things that didn't make a lot of sense. And whenever I tried to get straight what she was talking about, she'd change to talking about something else. But, I remember once she said she wanted to marry a preacher once, but it just couldn't be worked out. She told me she would have made a good preacher's wife."

Bramlett raised an eyebrow and looked at Curry. Curry looked as mystified as he was. "Preacher?" Bramlett asked. "What preacher?"

Carr shook his head. "She never said."

"Do you have any idea who she meant?" Bramlett asked, not wanting to hear the answer.

He nodded. "Yes. I have an idea."

"Who?"

"Well, to tell you the truth, I've always thought she was talking about an old friend of ours from childhood. The Reverend James Doffey himself."

Bramlett and Curry immediately drove to north Sheffield and the home of the Reverend James Doffey. His wife, a heavyset woman with a big smile, told them the pastor was in Corinth for a conference and wouldn't be back till late that evening, but would they care to come inside out of the cold and have some hot chocolate? She was just, she said, getting ready to have some herself.

Bramlett and Curry thanked her kindly and returned to the car. "This is the craziest thing I ever heard of," Curry said as he fastened his safety belt. "There ain't no way James Doffey is Isaac Clouse's father. Besides, where in the world would a preacher have the money to give out a hundred dollars, or two hundred dollars, like Isaac said he got back then? I'm telling you, there ain't no way he's the man."

Bramlett rubbed his palm hard from his forehead down across his nose and to his chin. Then he said, "There's probably only one person who can tell us who this Abraham is for sure. And, even if she was to tell us, I'm not sure what we'll have."

Curry turned the key in the ignition and the engine started. He shifted into gear and moved forward, passing a mail carrier stopped at a mailbox on the street shoving in a handful of letters. "Who you talking about?"

"Adele Winter. Naresse's mother."

Curry snorted. "Ain't no way she's going to tell anybody anything. I don't know how she's still alive."

Bramlett looked out at the small houses they were passing. Most had vinyl siding. The front yards were narrow and few had lawns. Smoke swirled from the chimneys of most of the houses.

You live and then you die, he mused. And then all the suffering is over. How many generations have lived in these houses and suffered and died?

"Sometimes," he said out loud, "I think it's sad that all a person's personal history dies with him. And then in a couple of generations, he's forgotten."

Curry turned at the corner, heading back toward town, and frowned. "What?"

Bramlett sighed. "Just old man's talk, son. Old man's talk. I guess, on the other hand, it's good that all the old secrets keep dying. All the old mysteries. It's kind of like dumping out the blackish water you've been painting with and rinsing out the jar and filling it up again with fresh, clear, clean water. You know what I mean?"

Curry grunted. "I don't have the slightest idea what you're talking about. I mean, I know it's got something to do with painting, but . . ." He paused.

Bramlett turned and looked at him, waiting.

Curry continued. "Hey. The other night when I was with Lizzie and Shamona in Mrs. Winter's room, she was half out of her head and she started talking. Lizzie said she was talking about her mother, about Naresse. Anyway, she was talking about a man. And she said something about he wasn't like her brother."

"Her brother?"

Curry nodded. "He's an old guy who lives out in Hebron. I've met him at Lizzie's house a couple of times. His wife died a few years ago and Mrs. Winter used to have him over for dinner on Sundays after church."

"So?"

Curry shrugged. "I don't know. I just thought maybe he

knows some of the same stuff Mrs. Winter knows—or knew. Maybe he could tell us something."

"You know where he lives?"

Curry nodded.

"Let's go, then," Bramlett said.

It took twenty minutes to drive to the Hebron community. It was shortly after three-thirty in the afternoon.

Mose Martin lived on a dirt road that snaked north of the state highway just beyond Hudnall's Grocery. Martin's house was a small, asbestos-shingled box of a structure, painted white, and with a narrow porch that ran across the width of the front.

Martin invited them in out of the cold, offered to make coffee, which both lawmen politely refused, and asked them to sit down in the cramped front room. Against the wall was a butane stove, sizzling.

Martin was stooped and gaunt, with a face splotched with dark areas against the light skin. His overalls were dark blue, obviously not very old, and pressed, and his face betrayed no apprehension or fear in this unexpected visit by the sheriff and deputy, as if he'd lived long enough to be surprised at little. Bramlett judged him to be in his seventies.

"Shamona is doing better," Curry said, answering the man's unspoken question about his great-niece.

He shook his head. "This family been hit so hard. So very hard."

"We're investigating the shooting," Bramlett said, "and, at the same time, reopening the case of the murder of Naresse. And we don't want to leave any stones unturned."

Martin nodded, and waited for more information.

Bramlett continued. "I understand you're Adele Winter's brother."

"That's right," he answered. "There was eleven of us altogether. Five boys and six girls. There only three of us left. Me and Adele and Cammy. Of course, Cammy's in a nursing home. She's not good."

Bramlett thought of his own mother for an instant, then asked, "Are you the youngest?"

"That's right. I was the baby." He grinned, showing his several gold-capped front teeth. Above me was Adele." The grin faded. "I hear she ain't doing good, either. I'd like to go see her, but that climb up to the hospital, I think, would just be too much."

"She's very sick," said Bramlett. "In fact, there're a lot of answers probably she can give us, but she's too sick to do it. So we thought we'd see what you can tell us."

Martin shook his head sadly. "I couldn't bear to see her like that no way," he said. His lower lip trembled slightly.

Bramlett looked at his deputy, and made a gesture of his hand for Curry to ask the questions. Curry, already known to the man, could get further than the sheriff in a situation like this.

"Mr. Martin," Curry began, "I know some of these family things may not be pleasant to have to talk about, but we need to know as much as possible. Right now, we're trying to see if there is any link in all this to a man Isaac claims is his real father. Can you help us with this?"

Martin was very still, hardly breathing, it seemed to Bramlett, his eyes fixed on the young man, studying him, taking him in. Perhaps he considered him family already, thinking it was only a matter of time before he married his great-niece Lizzie. He didn't say a word, however.

Curry continued. "Do you know anyone named Abraham?"

Martin didn't answer at first, his eyes unblinking and staring at the deputy. Finally, he said, "All that was a long time ago, son. A long time ago. I don't know what good comes of walking around in old garbage pits. You just come out smelling bad."

"Yes, sir. I understand. But we think this may help us."

He shook his head. "No. I don't know any Abraham."

"You're sure?"

Martin's face hardened slightly, obviously interpreting the question as either calling into doubt his memory or truthfulness. "I'm sure," he said coldly.

"Can you tell us who this man Isaac is talking about is?"

"I never knew. Adele never say. I do know it grieved her heart. She told my wife, I think. But they never told me. 'Fact, there was lots they never told me. I really didn't want to know. I really still don't want to know."

Bramlett thought he detected some resentment in the man's tone of voice.

"But there was a man?" pressed Curry.

Martin shrugged. "Maybe."

"You're not sure?"

"Naresse was a very pretty girl. Lots of mens was interested in her, and she in them."

Curry looked at the sheriff. Bramlett understood Curry's look of frustration, indicating he thought he was making little headway with the old man, and, at the same time, inviting the sheriff to jump in anytime he wanted. Bramlett gave a slight nod of his head that he got the message but for the deputy to continue.

Curry cleared his throat, then said, "Last night Mrs. Winter was talking about this man, and she said he wasn't like you."

The man's eyes widened. "What? Not like me?"

"Yessir. That's what she said. She said he wasn't like you."

"I don't know what she talking about."

"She said, 'He ain't no Moses.' "

Martin squinted his eyes. "Come again?"

"She said, 'He ain't no Moses,' " Curry repeated.

"That's what she said?"

Curry nodded. "Yes, sir."

Martin slowly shook his head. "Well, she weren't talking about me then. She must have been talking about somebody else, but it weren't me."

Curry looked surprised. "What do you mean?"

"I mean my name ain't Moses. It's Mose. That's the name my mama give me. And Adele ain't never call me *Moses* a day in her life. It ain't me."

Curry sighed and looked at Bramlett. Bramlett's eyes were still on the man.

Bramlett said, "We know all of this is hard on you, Mr. Martin, and we appreciate you helping us."

The man was looking beyond Curry and didn't respond to the sheriff.

Bramlett continued. "Let me ask you. You said they didn't tell you about this man, and that there were other things they didn't tell you about. What was it they weren't telling you?"

Martin rolled his shoulders as if he were tired, then said, "They never really explained how they bought that land. I mean, I was farming as good as Fraizer Winter was back then, but I ain't never had enough money to buy that kind of land. I did later. Later I bought land. But none of us had that kind of money back then. It just seemed mighty funny to me." He stopped and gave another head shake. "Naw, sir, there ain't nobody who can tell you about that land now and who that Moses fellow is and all that except Adele Winter. That's who can tell you. They never told me nothing." He clamped his jaw shut tight, and looked at Bramlett, then at Curry, as if to say he had nothing else to tell them.

Bramlett and Curry exchanged glances. Mose Martin obviously didn't know about the ten-dollar transaction Lizzie and Shamona had discovered.

The telephone rang. Mose Martin strained as he pulled himself to his feet out of the chair. He moved unhurriedly across the room to a small telephone table.

"Hello?" he said in a loud voice after he lifted the receiver to his ear.

He was silent then, listening, nodding. Then he said, "All right. No, I'm okay."

He hung up the phone and stood beside the table, his hand still touching the receiver, his eyes on his hand. Then he turned and looked at them and said, "That was Lizzie. She was just calling to tell me that Adele died just now. Just stopped breathing, she said."

# 31

It was dark and much colder by the time Bramlett and Curry got back to headquarters. Curry left at once to see if Lizzie was still at the hospital. Bramlett made a quick check of the phone messages on his desk.

One message was from Valeria for him to call before he came home. He dialed the number. She answered. She told him she'd taken some groceries by his mother's place this afternoon and sat with her a while. "I'm worried about her," she said. "They're calling for possible sleet or snow tonight."

He told her he'd leave right away and see how she was doing, then he'd be home.

The lights were already on at the Club Hawaii when he turned off Highway 45 on the Ettawe Road. Several vehicles were parked in front of the honky-tonk. In two hours or so, there wouldn't be a parking spot left. It was, after all, Saturday night.

His mother was more than ready for the cold. She had turned every gas space heater up full blast, and had built a fire in the fireplace. Bramlett moved around the house cutting down each one. He figured it was at least eighty-five degrees in the house.

"You're going to suffocate," he grumbled as he came back into the living room where Regina Bramlett, her legs covered in an afghan, was sitting in an armchair. The television set was tuned to the country music station.

"I'd like to dance one more time before I die," she said, watching the couples on television spin and stomp.

"Have you had supper?" Bramlett asked, standing at the doorway to the kitchen.

239

"The food in that horrible place like to killed me," she said, not taking her eyes off the dancers. "I think they were trying to poison all of us."

"It was good food," Bramlett said with a sigh.

"It didn't have no taste."

"You're supposed to be on a low sodium diet."

"I can't believe you put me in there with all those crazy people." She turned to glare at him. "There was an old man who kept peeing in the hall. They had to have someone watch him, because next thing you know, he'd unzip his pants and pee right in the hall. And then he'd laugh like crazy. Of course, that's what he was. That's what they all were. Did you want me to get like that?"

Bramlett walked over to the couch and sat down heavily. He suddenly felt very tired and old himself. "What do you feel like eating?"

She looked back at the television screen. "There wasn't any privacy there. They'd come in your room anytime they wanted. There weren't no locks on the doors. Did I tell you about that old woman trying to steal my clothes? She said her niece was going out west."

Bramlett stood up. "I'll make you some soup. Soup sound good to you? It's freezing outside."

"I already ate some. What I need is a little whiskey. Your wife didn't bring me anything but food."

"You don't need to be drinking."

"It's good for the heart. I read that in the paper. People who have a little pop once a day live longer. Don't you want me to live longer?"

He sighed again and went into the kitchen. In the garbage can under the sink was an empty Campbell's tomato soup can, and the pot she'd used to warm up the soup was in the sink, filled with water.

He washed the pot and the spoon and the bowl she'd used, then went back into the living room, leaned down and kissed her on the forehead. "I'll come check on you tomorrow," he said. "Don't stay up too late."

Just as he was closing the front door behind him, he heard her call out, "I prefer Jack Daniel's."

At home after supper, Bramlett wanted to do a small water-color of the Murphey barn. He'd painted it so many times he could render a nice quick painting of it without even looking at his sketches. That would be nice, to paint for an hour or so, and let everything else slide off his back.

Valeria walked over to the kitchen table and set down his plate. Two hamburger patties, sweet potatoes, and corn. Then she sat down in her place beside his. There was no plate in front of her.

"You already eaten?" he asked, pulling back his chair.

"I'm not hungry."

He sat down and picked up his napkin and spread it across his lap. "Why?"

"I just got off the phone with Margaret. She's worse, and both kids are running fever. I think I need to run up there again and be with her."

Bramlett lifted his glass of iced tea and took a long swallow. As he set down the glass, he nodded. "Okay. When?"

"In the morning. I told her I'd be there by noon." She looked at his plate. He hadn't taken a bite yet. "Eat," she said. "I've got enough to worry about with your mother and now Margaret without worrying about you not eating."

He picked up his fork. He didn't want to eat, and now he didn't even want to paint. He hated it when he didn't want to do his favorite things.

Bramlett went to bed early but had a hard time falling asleep. His mind kept flitting around. He thought of Naresse's mother, Adele Winter, now dead, too, and of his own mother back home, and Margaret and the kids. And of barns— so many barns he'd painted—but the one that he kept seeing was the one at Hebron where Naresse had died. Finally, sometime after he heard the hall clock strike twelve, he slipped into a fitful sleep.

Then came the jarring ring of the telephone beside his bed. Bramlett fumbled the receiver to his ear and groaned into the mouthpiece. "What?"

"Sorry to bother you, Sheriff," the dispatcher said.

"What?" Bramlett said with a moan. "What time is it anyway?"

"Three o'clock, Sheriff," he said. "Sunday morning. Anyway, I thought you'd like to know. There's a fire out at Palm

Tree Trailer Court. We've just found out it's Gale Lonsdale's place."

Bramlett groaned again. Who the hell was Gale Lonsdale?

As if he'd read his mind, the dispatcher said, "He's the witness who saw the Gressete woman being dumped."

# 32

Sheriff Bramlett rolled out of bed, dressed in the bathroom to avoid awakening Valeria, kissed her good-bye on the side of her sleeping head, and drove to Palm Tree Trailer Court in less than half an hour. He had no idea why it was called Palm Tree. Sheffield was two hundred miles too far north for palm trees to grow. But that was the name the court had had for forty years or more.

Two fire engines were squeezed in the narrow lane leading down between the rows of trailer homes, and three fire hoses still poured water onto the now-smoldering twisted metal that had once been a trailer home.

Bramlett parked his Corvette behind another sheriff's department patrol car and walked along beside the two trucks until he reached the scene. A stream of water flowed along the asphalt pavement from the smoking rubble. Deputy Jacob Robertson stood beside Larry Swain, chief of Sheffield's fire department.

Swain was in his thirties, tall and rugged-looking with a heavy jaw. "The place was gone when we got here," he said to Bramlett. "The neighbors told us who lived here, of course, and we knew if he was inside, he was already dead. We finally got the flames knocked out enough to look for him, and then we noticed the door."

"The door?" asked Bramlett.

Swain arched his back, then said, "Yeah. It had a padlock on it. From the outside."

Bramlett stared at him, trying to follow what the man was saying.

The fire chief continued. "The door had a hasp for a padlock

243

on the outside. And it had a lock on it." He paused, looked back at two firefighters pulling a hose toward the back side of the trailer, then said, "Somebody locked him inside."

Bramlett could feel a definite headache mounting.

"Of course," Swain said, "he was no doubt dead before the flames got to him." He nodded at the sheriff. "Smoke inhalation, you know."

Bramlett reached to his back pocket for his foil pouch and turned to Robertson. "Jacob, I want you doing nothing else right now but finding out everything you can about Gale Lonsdale."

The tall deputy looked at Bramlett and wrinkled his nose. "And is there something in particular I'm looking for?"

"We need to know who was in the car with him the other night. We need to find out if that person saw what Lonsdale now can't tell us he saw."

Robertson nodded. "Yes, sir," he said.

Before Jacob Robertson left the scene of the fire, he asked the resident manager to check the files in his office on Lonsdale. The manager said Lonsdale had moved in six months ago and that he was only renting the trailer. He had no idea who his next of kin was.

Back at headquarters, Robertson ran a check on the computer. The Department of Motor Vehicles gave an address for Gale Lonsdale on Sweetgum Circle, not Palm Tree Trailer Court. Sweetgum Circle was in west Sheffield.

Deputies Jacob Robertson and Johnny Baillie found the pale-yellow house with no difficulty. The houses of the neighborhood were built right after World War II, mostly frame construction with two bedrooms and single-car carports, reflecting a time when few blue-collar families owned more than one vehicle. Now almost every house had one vehicle in the carport and another either directly behind it or parked against the curb in front.

The woman who answered the door had obviously just awakened. She was small, probably in her thirties, and wore a man's white T-shirt. Her hair was uncombed, and she held her hand on the door and shivered against the outside chill. Robertson introduced Baillie and himself.

"Burrrr," she said. "Come in." She stepped from one foot to another as if the floor beneath her feet was cold.

The deputies moved into the house. Baillie closed the door.

Robertson noticed she didn't seem to have anything on under the T-shirt, and that, possibly because she was still half asleep as well as the outside cold, she'd invited two strange law officers into her house without even asking what they wanted.

"We're checking on Gale Lonsdale," Robertson said.

She blinked her eyes rapidly and scowled. "What?"

"Gale Lonsdale," he repeated. "Are you a relative?"

She sighed and shut her eyes hard, then opened them, coming more awake now. "What's wrong?"

Robertson drew a short breath, then said quickly, "He's been killed. We're trying to locate relatives. This is an address that was given . . ."

She staggered backward, then turned around and walked hurriedly to a sofa and sat down. She wasn't looking at them, but toward a doorway to the hall.

"I'm sorry," Robertson said. "Could you tell us your name?"

Johnny Baillie took his notepad out of his shirt pocket.

"Whoa," she said. "Are you sure about this? Gale is *dead*?"

"There was a fire this morning," Robertson said. "Yes, ma'am. He was identified as the resident of the trailer that burned."

She nodded. "He lives in a trailer. At the Palm Tree Court. Yes." She suddenly put both hands over her face. "God! I can't believe it," she said through her fingers.

The deputies sat down in chairs in front of the sofa. After a moment or two, Robertson said again, "We are terribly sorry to have to tell you this, ma'am. Are you a relative?"

She lowered her hands and swallowed. "Yes. I'm his wife."

Robertson noticed she wasn't crying. "I take it you all are separated?"

She nodded, looking toward the hallway again. "We have three little girls . . ." she said. "I don't know how they're going to react." She paused, then looked at Baillie, then to Robertson. "You said something about a fire?"

"Yes, ma'am."

She made a face and asked, "He burned to death?"

"Actually, he died of smoke inhalation."

She looked up at the ceiling and pulled the T-shirt over her knees. "I was going to divorce him. In fact, I have an appointment to talk with an attorney next week."

"We have reason to believe Mr. Lonsdale was seeing another woman," Robertson said. "Could you tell us who she was."

She sneered and gave him a hard look. "Just one? You've got to be kidding?"

"Can you give us the names of whoever he was seeing?"

She shrugged. "He's been fooling around with that whore Maxine Dollar for I don't know how long. She works at the plant with him."

"Does she live here in Sheffield?"

"Yeah. But I don't keep up with trash like that."

"Who else?"

She curled her lip. "I don't know. Ask his buddies. They'll probably lie, though. They always lie."

"Can you give us the names of any other relatives or friends?"

"His mother is Corene Lonsdale. She lives in Pontotoc. He has a brother up at Rienzi. Charlie. I don't know about friends. Except maybe Billy Calder. That's his best friend. He lives in Crumpton." Crumpton was a community a few miles west of town. She looked at Johnny Baillie as he wrote the names down in his notebook, then slowly shook her head and smiled. "Funny, ain't it? I mean, here he burned to death, and now he's burning in hell."

Robertson and Baillie exchanged glances, then Robertson rose to his feet and said, "Thank you, ma'am."

As they walked back to the car, Baillie said, "It doesn't have to be like that, you know."

Robertson turned his head to look at him, confused. "What?"

"Marriage," Baillie said.

"Oh," said Robertson as he reached for the door handle.

There were no automobiles on the Sunday-morning streets of downtown Sheffield when Bramlett pulled into the parking lot at headquarters. At his desk, he opened the file on Rory Hornsly. What the hell did he have to do with any of these others?

246

And Lydia Gressete? And why would somebody try to shoot Lizzie? Would they try again? Probably.

He read down the list of names found in Hornsly's apartment. His eye paused first on the word *Roach*, and then on *Black Snow*. What were these names? A code?

He looked up at the doorway. It was Jacob Robertson.

"Johnny and I talked with Lonsdale's wife," he said. "They were separated. She gave us the names of some others who might know who he was with in the car. In fact, she gave us a woman's name as a likely candidate but we don't have an address yet."

"Excuse me," Johnny Baillie said, putting his hand on Robertson's shoulder and looking around him at the sheriff. "The guys just got back who were searching around the fire scene."

"And?" asked Bramlett.

"They found a two-gallon gas can in the thicket behind the trailer. It doesn't look like it's been there very long."

"Call the lab at Tupelo and see if they can check it out for us as soon as possible," the sheriff said. "Take it down there yourself."

"They work on Sunday?"

"Tell 'em it's an ox-ditch thing," Bramlett said.

Baillie moved away from the doorway.

"Follow up on whatever you got," Bramlett said to Robertson.

The deputy left and Bramlett looked back at the file on Rory Hornsly. He read the record of his bank transactions and then the names of those who'd invested money with him: Wayne and Addie Carr, and James Doffey. There was a lot of money involved here. Who else gave him money for his clay scheme?

He reread the typed notes of the interviews with Wayne Carr. In one interview Carr said Naresse Clouse had said she once considered marrying a preacher. Carr also indicated Naresse and the Reverend James Doffey were very close. Was it possible that there was more to this than just friendship?

Maybe he ought to lean on the reverend a little more, hit him hard and fast for once. Maybe a bit more pressure would break him if he was, in fact, not telling the whole story about himself and Naresse Clouse. Many a time Bramlett had returned a second or even a fourth time to question someone who seemed rock solid until finally, during one session . . .

247

He looked at his watch. Would Doffey already be at his church? Sunday school probably wouldn't start till nine-thirty or so. He could be out at the Hebron community before nine. But he sure wouldn't want Doffey's church members arriving and wondering why the sheriff was talking with their pastor so early on a Sunday morning.

He opened the Chakchiuma County telephone directory and found the pastor's home number. He dialed. Doffey himself answered the phone.

"I'd like to follow up on a few matters," Bramlett said.

There was a long silence on the other end of the line, then, "I really have to leave for church."

"This won't take long," Bramlett said. "I can be at your house in three minutes."

"No," he said. "I'll come there."

"When?"

"I'm on my way," he said. Then the line disconnected.

Fifteen minutes later, the Reverend James Doffey appeared at the doorway of Sheriff Bramlett's office. He was wearing a dress shirt and bright red tie and a black suit. On his face was a look of impatience.

"I really should already be on my way to Hebron," he said.

"Please, sit down," Bramlett said, not rising from his desk.

Doffey sighed and sat down in a chair in front of the desk.

"I'll come straight to the point, Reverend," Bramlett said. "Did you ever at any time have an affair with Naresse Clouse?"

The man's head jerked like he'd been slapped in the face. Then, almost immediately, his eyes hardened into a cold stare. "Why in the world would you ask such a thing?" he asked.

Bramlett placed his elbows on the desk and spread his hands. "Something someone said seemed to indicate that not only were you and Naresse friends but perhaps you were more than friends."

Doffey held the stare for a while longer. Then, gradually, his face relaxed and he dropped his gaze to the top of the sheriff's desk. He swallowed hard, then spoke. "Naresse and I grew up together in Hebron. We dated some early on. To be completely honest, there was even a time when we talked a bit about the two of us getting married. I mean, this is when we'd just got out of high school. It was about the same time the Lord was starting to call me to be a preacher. We used to talk a lot even then." He paused and licked his lips, then continued. "But that's not the way it was to be. Her and me. Then she married Patterson Clouse."

He looked up at Bramlett. "I swear before God Almighty, Sheriff, Naresse and I never . . ." He licked his lips again, then continued. "We were never like that. Never."

"You've told us y'all talked a great deal. I'm talking about up until she died."

He nodded slowly, looking down again. "Naresse was very special to me. We did talk a lot. I don't just mean counseling. But as friends. I shared with her what was going on in my life as much as she shared with me what was happening in her life." He ran his fingers over his mouth. "I loved her like a sister. And our relationship was always honoring to God. I swear it was." He looked back up into Bramlett's eyes as if challenging him to think otherwise.

Bramlett nodded and said, "Okay. That's settled." He tried to give Doffey a look showing he believed him. "I'm sorry I had to pursue this, but . . ." He shrugged and didn't finish.

"Is that it?" Doffey asked, placing his hands on the arms of the chair.

"Just one more thing. Do you know anyone else besides the Carrs and yourself who were investing money with Rory Hornsly?"

He thought for a moment, then said, "Back when I first talked to him—this was after Wayne Carr recommended the venture—he told me a teacher at Sheffield College was in it, too."

"A teacher?"

"Dr. Farris."

"Matthew Farris?"

"That's right."

Bramlett pushed himself up out of the chair. "Thank you for taking time to come by, Reverend," he said. "I hope I haven't made you late for Sunday school."

After the man was gone, Bramlett phoned Margaret's. Valeria had left for Memphis right after he'd returned home from the fire. She hadn't arrived yet, Margaret said. He told her he couldn't see any way he could break away and get up there. She said to try if he could.

"I love you, girl," he said.

"I know that, Daddy," she said. "I love you, too."

Then he drove down to Ettawe to check on his mother. She was frying bacon when he got there and insisted he sit down and eat.

He was back at headquarters by ten. Jacob Robertson told him he'd located the woman named Maxine Dollar. She now lived in Jackson. He talked with her on the phone. She said she hadn't seen Lonsdale in over six months and hadn't been back up to Sheffield since Christmas. Robertson was now trying to locate Lonsdale's brother in Rienzi.

Bramlett took a phone call from the crime lab in Tupelo. It was Johnny Baillie.

"Only one set of prints on the gas can," he said. "And we got a quick match."

"Oh?" asked Bramlett. He could feel his heart speeding up.

"Yessir," said the deputy. "A perfect match, in fact. The prints belong to Patterson Clouse. No doubt about it."

# 33

At noon Deputy H. C. Curry went to the intensive care waiting room at the hospital to see Lizzie, but she'd gone. The sign-out sheet at the reception desk had a note from her that she would be back by two o'clock.

He found her at home. She was alone. Her roommate, Nena Carmack, had gone home to Columbus for the weekend.

Lizzie was wearing a terry-cloth robe and had a towel wrapped around her head. "I just needed to take a hot bath," she told H.C. as he walked into the living room. "I began to feel so yucky, you know. It's like all that sickness and death at the hospital stains you, and you have to soak it out."

He told her about the gasoline can with her father's finger-prints. Units were searching for him now. He wasn't at his house.

Lizzie sat down on the edge of the couch. She closed her eyes and sighed wearily. "This doesn't make any sense," she said. "I mean, do you honestly think my own father would try to kill me? That's what it comes down to, isn't it? Isn't each of these things related?"

H.C. sat down beside her and leaned back. He didn't know what to think. Everything seemed to be flying off in all directions. There was nothing to grab hold of. By *these things* he knew she meant the killings as well as the shooting of her sister Shamona.

She continued. "There must be some mistake about those fingerprints. There's no way my father could have set that fire."

H.C. didn't want to believe it was his future father-in-law, either. But Gale Lonsdale had identified the man pulling Lydia

251

Gressete's body out of the car as a black man. What black man? Wayne Carr? James Doffey? Or Patterson Clouse?

He gave a low groan. "Nobody really fits," he said.

She looked at him with puzzlement on her face.

H.C. shrugged, then said, "We talked with your uncle. He said your grandmother never called him anything but Mose."

Lizzie raised an eyebrow. "Oh?"

He nodded. "Never Moses."

"Then who's Moses?"

"I have no idea."

Lizzie pulled her legs up under herself. "They say Shamona will probably get to go into a private room this afternoon," she said. "If that's the case, then I may go back to class tomorrow."

H.C. frowned. "I wish you wouldn't. Maybe just for a day or two longer. Give us a little more time."

Lizzie's brow wrinkled. "You seriously can't think I'm in danger from my own father."

"No. I don't know what to think." He reached out and put his arm around her shoulder and drew her against him. "And the old man said I could stay right with you all afternoon. Protective custody, in a sense."

She smiled and buried her face into his chest. She didn't say anything. She didn't have to. He understood.

At his desk, Bramlett read through each of the interviews conducted since the murder of Rory Hornsly on Tuesday. Murder cases were often like jigsaw puzzles. You find a couple of pieces that fit together, then you add another piece here and there. Sometimes you get two sections going at the same time and eventually link them up.

Usually you begin by sorting pieces according to color, assuming somehow they go together. Then you begin to match this piece with that piece. The problem with this case was that there were so damn many colors. He had too many one-piece sections. And nothing was linking up.

The only logical assumption was that somebody killed Gale Lonsdale because he could identify whoever dumped Lydia Gressete's body. That somebody presumably killed her. But why?

Could there actually be two separate things going on? Could the murder of Rory Hornsly and Lydia and Lonsdale, not to mention the attempted murder of Shamona Clouse and the killing of her mother Naresse three years ago, all be unrelated?

Bramlett closed the folder and rose from his desk. Every available unit was looking for Patterson Clouse. Maybe somehow he was involved. Maybe, as Bramlett suspected before, he really did kill his wife. But shoot his daughter? It didn't make sense.

He walked to the halltree and got his hat and overcoat. It was a sick world.

Before leaving town, he went through the drive-through at Captain D's and got two three-piece dinners, then left town and in fifteen minutes pulled up the graveled driveway to the old place in Ettawe. His mother was not in the house. He went from room to room looking for her until he got back to the kitchen. The back door was wide open and gusts of cold air sucked into the house.

He set the two fish dinner boxes on the table and quickly stepped outside, closing the door behind him. "Mother!" he shouted.

He heard a muffled answer. Could she have fallen? He hurried across the yard.

Then he saw her through the doorway to the chicken house. He stepped inside. She was wearing pink bedroom slippers and a bathrobe. She had the egg basket in her hand.

"What are you doing?" he asked.

There was a perplexed look in her eyes. She said nothing.

He reached out and took her hand. "There aren't any eggs, Mother," he said gently. "There aren't any chickens anymore."

She snatched her hand away. "Of course there ain't any eggs. You sold all my chickens when I was in that damn loony bin."

"Then why are you out here?"

"I'm going to get more chickens. I was just thinking how many biddies I need."

"Okay, okay," he said. "I'll get the biddies. Now let's go inside and get warm."

She put her hand on her hip. "That reminds me. I bet you didn't bring me that bottle like I asked you, did you? Am I going to have to go get it myself?"

He sighed. "I'll get it," he said. "Now come inside."

He escorted her back into the house, and she sat down at the kitchen table.

"You eaten?" she asked. "You want me to fix you something to eat?"

"Here," he said, opening a box and sliding it over to her. "I've brought you some dinner." He then got down two glasses from the cabinet and took the carton of buttermilk out of the refrigerator.

"I love fish," she said, picking up a piece and biting into it.

He poured the milk, then sat down and opened his own box.

"You look tired, Son," she said, chewing a bit of fish. "What's wrong?"

He smiled. "Chasing killers is hard work," he said. "And right now I'm trying to find a man who may have killed his wife. That kind is the most tiring of all."

"Who?"

"Patterson Clouse."

She frowned and took another bit of chicken. "Do I know him?"

He smiled. "No, ma'am. I don't think so. The family lived down in the Hebron community. They lived across the road from the Farrises."

"I knew John Farris and his wife Marie."

"Yes," Bramlett said. The french fries needed more salt. He picked up the shaker. "You were telling me about their son Matthew and the honky-tonk woman."

She giggled. "Ain't that something? And, I'll tell you something else. Marie told me once—now this was a long time ago, of course—that she thought God was calling that boy into the ministry." She paused and smiled. "Too bad he didn't make it. Think of the stories he could've told about his wicked life before he got converted. Now that's the kind of preaching I like to hear."

Bramlett stuffed a large piece of fish into his mouth.

"And," she said, "at least two cows."

He swallowed. "What?"

"While you're getting the biddies for me, get two good cows. Heifers."

254

Jacob Robertson glanced at his watch. Five twenty-eight. Johnny Baillie stopped the car in front of Higgins Funeral Home. They got out of the car and walked to the front door. A short man in a dark-gray suit, one of the employees at the funeral home, held open the door for them to enter. Another young man, also in a dark suit, ushered them to a back room where Jimmie Lonsdale was just talking with a director about making arrangements for his brother's funeral.

Robertson had phoned Lonsdale's house in Rienzi and had been told by his wife that Jimmie was already down in Sheffield.

Jimmie Lonsdale nodded as the deputies introduced themselves and offered their sympathy. Then he said, "We can't do anything until they release the body."

Gates Higgins, a skinny man in his mid-sixties who owned the funeral home and wore a dark suit identical to his employees, explained, "They will have to do an autopsy. We never know for sure when we'll get the body."

Higgins offered the two deputies use of the room to talk with Jimmie Lonsdale, and excused himself. He closed the door quietly as he left, and the three men sat down at the round conference table.

Lonsdale looked to be in his mid-thirties, was thin with a large head, and wore his light-brown hair shoulder length. He looked up at Robertson with his gray eyes and said, "They say he was dead before he started burning."

Robertson nodded in agreement and assurance, then said, "Your brother saw someone leave the body of a murder victim on a deserted road the other night. We think there's a good possibility whoever he saw did this."

Lonsdale had a blank look on his face. "What?"

Robertson continued. "To keep him from identifying that person."

Lonsdale fingered the funeral arrangement brochures on the table in front of him. "Gale was a good boy. A little wild, liked to have a good time, but was good at heart, if you know what I mean. He'd give you the shirt off his back."

"He was apparently with someone when he was on that road," Robertson continued. "A woman."

Lonsdale's eyes were on the brochures. He didn't respond for a moment, then he looked up, first at Robertson, then at Baillie, then back to Robertson. "I was hoping he and Janet could work things out," he said. "For the girls' sake if nothing else."

"You have any idea who that woman might have been?"

His eyes fell back onto the brochures. There were tears in his eyes. "I had to call my mother this morning to tell her about it. It's killing her." He sniffed, then said, "I can't stand the thought of them taking his body all apart now."

"I'm afraid that's the law," Robertson said softly. "Now, about this woman . . ." He paused, waiting for an answer.

Lonsdale nodded. "We talked about a week ago. He was up at Rienzi. He said he was seeing someone. It wasn't any good. I told him that. In fact, I told him it stunk like shit. Pure and simple. Stunk like shit. You see, he and Billy Calder been friends for years. Since high school. I mean, best buddies." He nodded at each of the deputies in turn as if seeking confirmation, then continued. "And he's been seeing Christine. That's Billy's wife. She's got three little kids. It stunk like shit and I told him. I mean, it would've just broke Mama's heart if she'd found out." He pulled a handkerchief out of his back trouser pocket and nosily blew his nose. He refolded the handkerchief and then said, "And this is what it comes to."

Both Robertson and Baillie thanked him and told him again how sorry they were about his brother. Then they rose and left the room.

In the sheriff's office, Johnny Baillie placed the notepad on the desk blotter. The name Christine Calder was heavily circled. "That seemed to be who was with him," the deputy said to Bramlett.

Bramlett looked at the name on the notepad for a moment. It rang no bells of recognition. Then he took the county telephone directory out of a desk drawer and opened it. There were six Calders listed for Chakchiuma County, but only two in Sheffield, and one was William.

He dialed the number.

A woman answered. The sheriff identified himself, then said, "We'd like to come talk with you."

"What?" she whispered. "No. No, I can't talk now." Bramlett could hear the fright in her voice.

"I'm afraid this is necessary, Mrs. Calder."

"I can't today. You can't come here. Oh, Lord . . ."

"I think you know what this is all about."

"Listen, I'll come down there tomorrow."

"We need to see you now," Bramlett pressed.

"I don't have anyone to keep the kids."

"Is your husband there now?"

"He's just gone, he'll be back any minute. I can get somebody to keep the kids in the morning—"

"This is a homicide investigation, Mrs. Calder," Bramlett said coldly. "Every hour counts."

"Damn!" she said tersely. "Billy just pulled into the driveway."

"You coming here or do we come there?"

"No, no. Listen. I'll come there. Don't come here. I'll come."

"When?"

"Just as soon as—" Then the line buzzed dead. She'd hung up.

Bramlett placed the receiver back into the phone cradle, then said, "We give her fifteen minutes. Then we go visit her house."

"Any word on Patterson Clouse?" Johnny Baillie asked.

"No," Bramlett answered. "And while we're waiting, Johnny, see if we've got a photo of Clouse on file. Maybe Mrs. Calder can give a look and see if he looks like the man they saw pull Lydia Gressete out of the car."

Baillie nodded, and left the office.

Robertson looked at the sheriff. "I can't believe a man would try to kill his own daughter," he said.

Bramlett took his foil pouch out of his rear pocket, lifted his feet up to the corner of his desk and placed one on top of the other, then opened the pouch on his stomach. He didn't reply.

Christine Calder arrived at headquarters in less than fifteen minutes. She was sitting at the table in the conference room with Robertson and Baillic when Bramlett entered the room. He introduced himself and pulled back a chair and sat down across the table from her.

She was a blonde, small and trim, and looked to be about thirty or so. Her face was drawn in anxiety. "Listen," she said, her eyes darting about the room. "I told Billy I had to run out to the store for something. I said I'd only be gone a minute or two. I really don't know anything. I have to get back."

Bramlett tried to smile pleasantly to help put her at ease. "Would you like a cup of coffee?"

She gave a quick head shake, and said, "I don't think you understand what kind of trouble I'll be in if Billy finds out I'm down here. I need to go." She put her hands on the table as if to push herself up.

"Now, you listen," Bramlett said. The smile was gone. "I'm terribly sorry about your domestic problems, but we're talking murder here. Not only the murder of Gale Lonsdale, but of a woman named Lydia Gressete."

She sighed. "I'm trying to tell you I know absolutely nothing. I never heard of that woman."

"I want you to look at some pictures," Bramlett said, nodding at Johnny Baillie.

The deputy stood quickly and walked to the side of Christine Calder's chair. In front of her, he dealt out like a hand of playing cards faceup seven mug shots of black men. Patterson Clouse was one of the seven. Then Baillie stepped back.

"You recognize any of these men?" Bramlett asked her.

Her eyes had been on the photos since they had been placed in front of her. She frowned, shook her head, and looked up at the sheriff. "What am I supposed to be looking for?"

"For the man you and Lonsdale saw out on that logging road," Bramlett said impatiently. "Lonsdale told us it was a black man and he'd recognize him if he ever saw him again."

She gave a contemptuous laugh and leaned back in her chair. "I don't hardly see how that would be possible," she said.

"What?" asked Bramlett.

She had a thin smile on her face. "I pulled his head down when the other car was coming. As soon as I saw the lights, I pulled him down. And we were both down until the car started leaving. He was lying. He never saw whoever was there. And neither did I."

Bramlett raised his hand and gave a quick squeeze of his forehead between his thumb and forefinger. Then he asked, "You're positive about this?"

She nodded. "I'm positive. We didn't even know what had happened until we were leaving and saw that colored woman's body lying on the road. And I never saw her before, either."

"Then why did he say it was a black man?" asked Bramlett.

She gave a shrug. "He just assumed," she said. "The woman was black. And, besides. . ." She paused a moment, then said, "He didn't like blacks." She looked at each man in turn as if seeking some sort of understanding. None gave it.

Bramlett stood up. "Thank you, Mrs. Calder," he said coldly. "We'll let you get back to your family now."

He showed her to the door.

Moments later both Baillie and Robertson joined Bramlett in his office. "So," Robertson asked after the deputies had taken chairs in front of the desk. "Where does this leave us?"

Bramlett didn't answer for a long moment. Then he opened the file on Rory Hornsly again and stared at the sheets of typing paper. "It leaves us back at the beginning," he said, "We may be looking for a black man. Or we may be looking for a black woman."

"Or," said Johnny Baillie, "we may be looking for a white man or a white woman."

Bramlett nodded and tapped the sheets of paper with the back of his fingers. "Any one of these people we've talked to could be our killer. Any one of them."

# 34

Lizzie replaced the telephone receiver. Another call expressing sympathy and wanting to know about the arrangements.

H.C. had gone with her earlier in the afternoon to Wayne Carr's funeral home to select a casket for Adele Winter. She'd given Carr all the information needed for the newspaper obituary. The service wouldn't be held till Saturday in order to give the relatives in Chicago a chance to get down.

The doorbell rang.

It was Keesa Hudnall. His arms held several brown paper sacks and he rushed right past Lizzie as she stood at the open door. "I brought this stuff from the restaurant," he said. "Nothing fancy. Potato salad, bar-be-que, baked beans, peach cobbler, garden salad."

He went into the kitchen and set the bags on the table, then opened the refrigerator door and started putting containers away.

Lizzie stood watching him. She couldn't help the mixed feelings in her mind toward Keesa. On the one hand, she recognized and appreciated the friendship he and her mother had. On the other hand, she resented the fact that he'd been named manager of the Wisteria Inn when the job should have gone to her mother.

He closed the refrigerator door, and turned to look at her. There was distress in his eyes. "I thought the world of Aunt Adele," he said. "You know that." He shook his head with sadness. "And, your mother . . . Dammit all! This has been a hell of a week."

It really wasn't his fault, she suddenly said to herself. Getting the job. If it hadn't been him, it would have been somebody else. And he did love her mother.

She made a motion with her hand toward the table. "Would you like to sit down, Keesa?" she asked.

He smiled and pulled back a chair for her, then sat down himself. He looked at her, waiting for her to speak.

"You knew Mama very well," she said. She paused, saw him nod, then continued. "You've probably heard some rumors . . . You know." She looked at him.

There was only confusion in Hudnall's eyes. "What rumors?" he asked.

"About Mama and another man."

He shrugged his shoulders. "I don't pay any mind to rumors."

Lizzie looked down at her hands on the table. "The sheriff thinks she was going out to the barn that day to meet someone."

"Horseshit on the sheriff," he said.

She smiled. She was really glad he'd come by. Then she shuddered. "That barn," she said. "It's like it's always there in my mind. You know?"

He gave a quick shake of his head. "I never go down that road. I couldn't bear driving by that place."

"But I can't avoid it. That's no way to get to church except to drive by there."

"Then go to another church."

She gave a low laugh. "I don't think I could do that." She looked at him. "You know, there's something else." She paused for a moment. "I have these flashes in my mind." She gave a slight shake of her head. "I don't know. It's like something from long ago. I do know I always thought of the barn as having snakes. I think Mama told me when I was little that there were snakes in there."

Hudnall smiled. "She wanted you to stay out of it. She was afraid you'd get hurt."

"Yes. That's true. But it seems somehow I see Mama in the barn. Standing there and yelling at me. I was real small," Again she paused and slowly shook her head.

Hudnall smiled sympathetically. "The mind can play lots of tricks on us, taking an image here and there and putting it in

261

another setting. Maybe Naresse yelling at you happened some-place else and then you put it into the barn."

Lizzie looked into his eyes and said, "Keesa, I really do appreciate you coming by."

He grinned as he stood up. "Hey," he said. "I'm at the restaurant all the time. Drop in whenever you can."

She saw him out the front door, and as she walked back toward the kitchen, an image flashed in her mind again: her mother standing in the middle of the barn, yelling at her to go home, go home.

Lizzie's head ached. Right dead center between her eyes. She took two aspirin, then wet a washcloth. She lay down on the couch on her back, closed her eyes and placed the cool washcloth across her forehead and folded her hands together on her chest.

She was falling into a restive state just as the doorbell rang again. It was H.C. He stepped inside, closed the door, and slipped his arms around her, squeezing her against his chest. Then he kissed her and pressed her to himself again.

"People keep phoning about the arrangements, wanting to know," she said, moving back to the couch.

Curry sat down in an armchair. He unzipped his leather jacket, pulled it off, and laid it across the arm of the chair.

"It makes absolutely no sense," she said.

"What?"

"Daddy's fingerprints on that gas can. Why would Daddy kill that man? He didn't even know him?"

H.C. didn't answer.

Then Lizzie said, "We have to go tell Aunt Cammy." Cammy was Adele Winter's older sister. She was at Still Waters Nursing Home.

H.C. had gone with Lizzie one Sunday afternoon several months before to visit the old woman. They'd taken Mama 'Dele. Cammy didn't seem to recognize either Lizzie or her sister.

"Maybe she won't understand what has happened," he said.

Lizzie gave a slight sigh. "I guess that's one of the blessings of getting old and losing your mind. You don't have to understand what can't be understood."

The telephone rang.

"I'll get it," H.C. rose and crossed the room to the telephone table.

"Hello?" he said.

He waited a moment, then said, "Okay," and hung up. "It was a man. Wrong number, he said." H.C. smiled. "Maybe he wasn't expecting a man to answer."

"Maybe he wanted Nena."

H.C. gave a nod. "Maybe."

"What time is it?" she asked.

He glanced at his watch. "A little after nine."

She stood up. "Come," she said. "We need to go see Aunt Cammy."

H.C. held the front door of Still Waters Nursing Home open for Lizzie. She scurried inside out of the cold.

As they moved through the wide central foyer, Curry smelled the smell of aging and death again. He hated places like this. He could understand why the sheriff didn't like having to bring his mother here.

He followed Lizzie down a hallway until she came to a room and went inside. There were two beds in the room and bright yellow curtains on the window. In the bed near the far wall was a white woman with pale, translucent skin and white hair sprayed out over her pillow. She was asleep on her back and her mouth sagged open.

On the other bed was Cammy Ward, ninety-year-old sister of Lizzie's grandmother. Cammy was the oldest of the eleven Martin children. Mose was the youngest. Now, with the death of Lizzie's grandmother Adele Winter, only Cammy and Mose survived.

She was skeletal thin with sunken cheeks and skin the color of pale ashes. She looked nothing like the beauty she had been seventy some odd years before. Lizzie once showed Curry a photograph of Cammy when she was a young woman. He thought she was movie-star pretty.

Her husband farmed and preached and died young. She raised four children who all lived in Detroit now. She'd been in Still Waters four years.

She looked up with bright, shiny eyes at Lizzie and Curry

when they entered and grinned. Amazingly, she still had her teeth.

"Lord, my Lord," she said, stretching out her arm toward Lizzie. "Come here, child, and let me hug you."

Lizzie moved to the bed and the old woman wrapped her thin arms around her.

"Thank you, thank you, thank you for coming," she said against Lizzie's ear. "I gets so lonesome."

Lizzie stepped back, holding one of her aunt's hands, and said, "Auntie Cammy, you know H.C., don't you? He was with me the last time I came."

The old woman nodded and looked at him. "Yes, yes," she said. "He's a fine-looking man. Who your parents, Son?"

"Witt and Chancy Curry, ma'am," he said.

She looked back up at Lizzie without bothering to say whether she knew them or not. "You marry this man, honey. You marry him and settle down and have childrens."

Curry grinned. "That sounds fine with me."

Lizzie gave a soft laugh and said, "Someday I might do that, Auntie Cammy." She shot a quick, teased look at Curry.

"I'm serious now," the woman said. "You do what I say. Enough of this foolish business."

Lizzie's brow furrowed and she looked at Curry. She obviously had no idea what her great-aunt meant. But then again, Cammy Ward often didn't make sense. Usually when Lizzie was there, the old woman talked about her husband as if he were still alive.

Then Lizzie looked back at her and said, "Auntie Cammy, we've come to tell you some sad news."

The woman's eyes widened. She waited as one who has received much sad news in her life. And the news was usually about the death of a loved one.

"It's Mama 'Dele," Lizzie said. "She's gone."

The old woman continued to look at Lizzie as if trying to understand exactly what she had said. Then tears came to her eyes. "We have to all be strong now, girl. We have to be strong." She breathed deeply, exhaled, and said, "You know I'm here whenever you needs me."

Lizzie smiled and said, "I know that, Auntie Cammy."

The woman took Lizzie's hand in both of her own hands and squeezed tightly and looked up at her. "Now, listen to me child. You got to forget all this other foolishness. It's killing your mama."

"Ma'am?" asked Lizzie.

"You know what I'm talking about. I don't like to say much in front of him . . ." She paused, gave a slight nod of her head toward Curry, then continued. "This thing is killing your mama. She 'fraid if your daddy find out, no telling what he gonna do to you. Frazier Winter is a fine man but not one to rile."

Lizzie smiled then and looked at Curry. He understood also. Fraizer Winter was the long-deceased husband of Lizzie's grandmother Adele. Cammy obviously thought Lizzie was Naresse. "Don't you worry, Auntie Cammy," Lizzie said. "Everything is going to be all right."

"No, no, child," the woman said. She was pulling herself forward as if trying to sit up. "I knows you think you love that boy, but this thing ain't no good. You forget him and I means right now. You forget him good and quick."

Lizzie took her hand out of Cammy's grasp and put her hand on her shoulders, gently pushing her back to the bed. "Relax now, Auntie Cammy," she said. "Everything is going to be all right."

The woman strained forward and grabbed both of Lizzie's arms. "No, no, child," she said. "Everything ain't gonna be all right until you stay away from him. That's nothing but fire that's gonna burn you bad."

Lizzie looked at Curry again. There was fright in her eyes. She knew as Curry knew that Auntie Cammy not only thought she was Naresse but was talking now about Naresse and some man.

"You marry this man," Cammy gasped, jerking her head toward Curry. "Do it now 'fore you get yourself and all of us killed, you hear? I means it." Then she collapsed back onto the pillow. Curry, for a split second, wondered if she just died. Then he saw her breathing.

Lizzie pulled away, and the woman's hands fell limply onto the bed covers.

Lizzie looked at Curry in bewilderment.

H.C. reached out and took Lizzie by the hand. "Come," he said softly. "Let's go."

# 35

Monday morning Grover Bramlett was up early. He made coffee, but decided he'd wait on breakfast. This was a good morning with Valeria being out of town for him to stop by the Eagle Café again. He was so tired of the bran cereals she put out for him each morning. She'd decided to stay the night in Memphis. In fact, when he'd phoned her last night, she said she might have to stay till Friday.

He sat in his recliner, sipped his coffee, and watched the weather channel on television. Locally, the current temperature was twenty-five degrees. The chill factor was fifteen. It was every bit this cold, he remembered, when they were first at the crime scene after Naresse Clouse was killed.

After talking to Valeria last night, he'd looked through a few photographs of barns, thinking he might paint a quick one. He came to a photo he'd made of the Farris barn before Naresse was killed, and wondered if maybe in the morning he ought to visit it again. Perhaps he would hear something there—maybe the voice of Naresse Clouse?—telling him what he was looking for.

He finished his coffee, stood up and looked out the window. The blackness of night was quickly dissolving into a gray dawn. It would be full light by the time he got to the Hebron community. Then he'd come back to town and get that breakfast and still be at the office by eight o'clock.

Twenty minutes later, he rounded a long curve on Hebron Road, and Hudnall's Grocery came into view on the left just ahead. He slowed and then turned to the left just past the grocery store onto the graveled road that led to the old farm where the barn was located.

In less than a minute, he passed the Clouse farm on the right. No smoke from the chimney. No activity. No vehicle in the yard. No one there, as far as he knew. He wondered where the teenage boy was staying.

Not far beyond the Clouse place lay the barn on the left side of the road. He crossed the old drive over a concrete drainage culvert and stopped the Corvette in the tall, brown grasses just off the road and took his flashlight out of the glove compartment.

The yard in front of the place where the farmhouse had been was filling in with saplings now. Brambles tangled across the site of the house itself, hiding the blackened fire rubble. Only the two chimneys that had stood at either side of the house rose in testimony that once there had been life here.

As he walked toward the barn, he rubbed his butt, thinking as he did so that pride goeth before a sore butt. Ice glazed over the deep washed-out places in the trail. Bramlett hunched his shoulders and felt the sting of the wind on his face.

He looked up at the barn as he moved toward it. It was typical in style of barns built from the last century until twenty years ago or so when metal buildings came into full use. And, like all these old barns, it was slowly disintegrating. Yet, the roof was so new the tin was still pale blue with only a few streaks of reddish rust.

Bramlett stepped inside through the open front doorway. He looked around, again noticing the daylight in the cracks between the dark, wide boards. A quick wisp of a vision of the woman with eyes bulged out and tongue protruding hanging from the loft floated darkly across his mind. He shook his head and closed his eyes for a moment as if to clear his head, then clicked on his flashlight.

He played the oval of the beam along the ceiling. He didn't see any bats or owls. They were probably up there, though, he suspected.

There was a steep stairway on the right leading to the loft. He examined the steps. Unpainted wood, boards quite thick. He stepped up onto the first step, then the second. He dipped a little with his knees like he was on a diving board. Everything seemed sturdy enough. When you're a large person, you can't be too careful.

He shined the light up through the darkness. Did he come

up here when they went over the crime scene three years ago? Probably not. He probably had let Johnny Baillie and Robertson handle it. Robertson, especially, would have recognized anything peculiar.

He eased his way up the stairs, pausing each time a board creaked. What would happen if these old timbers gave way? Hell, he could be laying out here in the freezing cold with a broken back, unable to move, and nobody in the world would ever know. He could starve to death. Bramlett ranked starving to death right up there with burning to death as his least favorite ways to die.

He reached the loft and took one step onto the floor. He certainly wasn't going to chance walking across the loft floor any more than he'd have walked out on a frozen cattle pond when he didn't know how thick the ice was. A musty smell rose into his nostrils.

He slowly moved the flashlight beam over the floor and into the corners. He really couldn't see too well into the corners. Should he chance the floor and investigate closer? He wasn't sure.

He took one more step. The floor didn't even creak. Maybe with the roof being kept in good shape, the floor wasn't rotten. Maybe there was nothing to worry about. "Sure," he mumbled out loud. "And, maybe they won't find my starved-to-death skeleton till next winter when some hunter comes in to get out of a cold wind."

He turned back toward the stairs, and the light swept across a four-by-four post running from the floor beside the stairway up to the rafters.

What was that? He brought the beam back to the post.

There was writing on the post. About a foot from the floor. Almost as if someone had been sitting on the floor when writing. He squatted down.

It was printing, actually, and in pencil. The letters had been retraced again and again to make them dark. Two names. And something else.

Abraham and Sarah<br>Our Cave<br>Love is as strong as death

Bramlett reached out his fingers and touched the wood, touched the graphite, now—what?—thirty-five years old or so? His knees suddenly ached. He held on to the post as he pulled himself up.

They were here. Naresse and the man she loved, the father of Isaac. Which one wrote this? Perhaps they were together. Perhaps . . .

He looked down the stairs. He thought he'd heard a sound.

He began slowly descending the stairs, the fingers of his right hand on the holding strap of his revolver. The daylight brightened as he neared the ground. He saw nothing unusual.

Then he walked out of the barn into the open. He pulled the cold air deep into his lungs as if he'd been holding his breath inside, possibly avoiding the smell of death.

He walked quickly toward his car.

As Bramlett neared town, he decided against breakfast at the Eagle Café. Maybe later. He walked through the outer office at headquarters and nodded good morning to Jacob Robertson, who was already at his desk. Neither Curry nor Baillie seemed to be at work yet. He glanced at his watch. It was almost seven-thirty.

He hung his overcoat on the halltree and his hat on a hook, then sat down at his desk. The writing on the wall was printed, but maybe an expert could compare it to handwriting anyway. He could have a photographer make shots of it, then they could fax copies of the pictures to a crime lab for a comparison with the handwriting on Naresse's letters to Lydia. Could have been her. Or. . . it could have been him . . .

Bramlett walked back out to Robertson's desk. "Tell me what you know about Abraham and Sarah," he said to the deputy.

"Who?"

"Never mind," said Bramlett. "Listen. As soon as Johnny Baillie gets here, I want y'all to go back to Tupelo to that plant where Hornsly worked. I want you to talk to that friend of his again. And his boss and the woman he used to run around with. Ask them to let you look at his correspondence. See if you can review any files he was working on. And see if you can find that application form Shamona Clouse filled out. It was missing before."

Robertson looked confused. "What are we looking for?"

Bramlett rubbed his fingers across his chin, then said, "There has got to be a strong connection between Hornsly and Naresse Clouse. There's something we aren't seeing. I want us to look at everything again, hoping this time, knowing all we know, something will fall into place."

The deputy nodded and said, "Yes, sir."

Bramlett glanced at his watch again. It was just after eight. He wondered if David William, his pastor, had gotten to the church office yet. He pulled out the phone directory to look up the number.

Dr. David William was not only pastor of the First Baptist Church of Sheffield but chaplain of the Chakchiuma County sheriff's department. Bramlett could never look at the pastor, even when he was preaching, without remembering a much younger David William pitching for Sheffield College. He was good. Very good.

After graduation, William had done a year of graduate work in England, then gone to seminary in New Orleans, then from there to California where he pastored a small church and soon married a young woman in the congregation. Things went well for a few years. They had a baby girl and the church was growing. Then there was an automobile accident and both the wife and child were killed.

It was not long afterward that William returned to Sheffield, first to the college where he taught Greek to the ministerial students, then a couple of years later, the church called him as pastor. He had never remarried.

William's secretary, Flossie Gwaltney, smiled at Bramlett as he entered the church office. Flossie now had two boys at Mississippi State and had been the church secretary twenty years or better, Bramlett supposed. It was well known around the churchhouse that Flossie Gwaltney kept the ecclesiastical machinery smoothly running and, if she were to leave First Baptist, utter chaos would result.

"Grover," she greeted. "Harvey Johnson and I were just talking about you. He's going to give you a call."

"What?" Bramlett said, wondering what in the world the church's music director would want with him.

"He wants you to sing in the Easter musical. Rehearsal starts next month," she said.

Bramlett snorted. "Forget it," he mumbled. Then, "The preacher told me to come on down."

"He's waiting for you in his study," she said. "Go right on in."

Bramlett knocked at the paneled door, then pushed it open when the pastor's voice called out, "Come in."

Reverend William greeted the sheriff warmly as they shook hands. They then sat down in two sturdy armchairs in front of the claw-footed oak desk. The walls of the study were lined from floor to ceiling with books.

The pastor looked to Bramlett fit enough to take the mound for Sheffield College again as he'd done years before. "I need some Bible information," Bramlett said.

The pastor's eyebrows rose. "*Bible* information?" A grin spread across his face. He obviously didn't expect Grover Bramlett to come to see his pastor about a biblical matter.

Bramlett cleared his throat. "It's a case we're working on. I need to know something about Abraham and Sarah."

"Oh, really?" William said, leaning back in his chair. He placed one elbow on the arm of the chair and touched his chin, as if pondering the matter. "Well, there's so much that can be said."

"How about just the highlights." Bramlett started to glance at his watch again, then caught himself.

The pastor nodded, then looked toward the ceiling and said, "Let's see. Where to start." He gave a quick nod, as if having found the place, and said, "Originally, his name was Abram and hers was Sarai. Later they were called Abraham and Sarah. They first moved up from Ur and eventually came to Palestine, or, Canaan, as the Bible refers to it." He paused. "There's so much . . . Is there a specific area about Abraham's life you're interested in?"

"You're doing fine."

He nodded again, then continued. "He was the father of the Hebrew people. God promised him a land for his people and told him he would have a son and his descendants would be as numerous as the stars of the sky. This son of the promise was named Isaac."

"Yes," Bramlett said. "That makes sense."

The pastor gave the sheriff a bemused look, then continued. "He had a nephew named Lot. That was the Sodom and Gomorrah episode, you remember."

"What about a cave?" Bramlett asked.

"Cave?"

"Yes. The Cave of Machpelah."

"Oh, yes, of course. Actually, that was the only piece of the land of promise Abraham ever owned. He bought it from the local people as a place to bury Sarah after she died."

"I see," Bramlett said. He rolled his head slightly. There was a stiffness in his neck.

"One thing not mentioned much by preachers that's really interesting, I think," William said, "is their relationship."

"Relationship?"

Reverend William gave a wry smile, then said, "They were not only husband and wife, they were also brother and sister. At least, half-brother and -sister. They had the same father even though they had different mothers."

"You're kidding."

William nodded. "No, that's the truth. Folks seemed to have married rather close in those days. In fact, Abraham would tell people she was his sister when it was convenient." He paused and the smile faded. "I wish I knew what you needed to know."

Bramlett nodded and stood up. "The cave thing helps," he said. "Maybe I just need to think in terms of lovers."

"Lovers?" William asked, standing also.

"I assume Abraham and Sarah were lovers."

"Why, surely. Most happily married people are."

Bramlett thanked the pastor, then left the study, said goodbye to Flossie Gwaltney, and bowed his head against a slapping winter wind as he hurried to his car.

272

# 36

Deputies Jacob Robertson and Johnny Baillie arrived at Adamstown Furniture shortly after nine-thirty. "We wanted to follow up on a few things," Robertson told the company's president Daniel Koph.

Koph met them just outside his office. He seemed to be in a hurry and didn't ask them to be seated. "I can't imagine what else you might find here," he said.

"We thought we might talk with Elsie Kimble," Robertson said, referring to the married design artist who had been seeing Rory Hornsly.

Koph shook his head. "No, she's no longer with us."

Robertson raised an eyebrow. "Oh?"

"She hasn't been back to work. Things are a bit confused right now since we don't have a personnel manager, but someone is filling in. Anyway, we finally got her on the phone and she said she isn't coming back."

"I wonder if we could look at any records or files that Hornsly was working on."

The man shook his head wearily and asked, "What is it you want to see?"

"Perhaps he left something personal behind," Robertson said. "You know. A phone number or something. It shouldn't take but a minute or two. You don't mind, do you?" The deputies had been well-trained by Bramlett to always obtain permission for a search if they didn't have a warrant.

Koph led them to a small office at the other end of the hallway. It was Rory Hornsly's office. He checked the filing cabinet drawers. They weren't locked. He pulled out one particular drawer, then pulled out a file folder.

"This is a copy of the file on former employees and why they terminated," he said. "The sheriff had asked about it. I had to make the entries about Hornsly and Elsie Kimble myself. The reason for termination is given in each case." He handed the folder to Baillie and said to them both, "Please don't take anything. And I would appreciate it if you would check with me before you go." Then he left them.

"I'll take the desk," Robertson said, sitting down in the swivel chair.

He slid open the middle drawer. It seemed to be a catch-all for memos, bulletins, paper clips, and pens. In one corner was a stack of Polaroid photographs. "A clay pit, looks like," he said.

"What?" asked Baillie.

"He had photos of his operation—or some operation—in Union County."

He put the photographs back and pulled out the sheets of papers and began scanning them one by one.

Baillie stood at the side of the desk examining each form in the terminated employees folder. He took out his notepad to list any who had been laid off for any reason whatever.

Robertson saw nothing of any interest. He slid the papers back into the drawer and took out a small address book.

He turned through the pages. There weren't many entries: Hornsly's son in California, the names of those individuals already known to have invested in his Union County clay thing: Matthew Farris, James Doffey, and Wayne Carr. And the names of women: Elsie Kimble, Alice Fielder, Kattie Ruth Davis, and Beryl Calhoun. And a Tommy West in Ripley, Clarence McDonald in Gulfport, and Jerry Dowdle in Memphis.

Robertson wrote down the names and phone numbers and closed the drawer. Then he pulled open a side drawer. On the very top of several small boxes of computer floppy disks was a single sheet of paper folded in half. He took it out and held it with both hands..

Printed across the top were the words "Job Application." In the space for a name was written in a clear, steady hand "Shamona Clouse."

"This is what the sheriff told us to find," he said to Baillie.

Baillie looked up. "What?"

274

Robertson held up the sheet of paper. "Shamona Clouse's job application."

Baillie walked around and looked at it over Robertson's shoulder. Both quickly read down the page to the list of references. The form asked for four. Shamona had filled in the lines with the names of two black men and two white. The black men were Reverend James Doffey and Wayne Carr. The white men were Keesa Hudnall and Dr. Matthew Farris.

When Deputy Robertson appeared at his office door, Sheriff Bramlett was talking with Robert Whitehead, the sheriff's department's administrator. Whitehead stood erect and tall, his bearing the same as it had been through a twenty-five-year career in the Air Force. He'd retired with the rank of full colonel. On his face was a very concerned look as he listened to the sheriff.

"I don't know what's wrong with it," Bramlett said. "It just doesn't seem to run right. I want you to get me another car while y'all check it out."

"Yes, sir," Whitehead responded. "But the last time we had it serviced, it seemed to be running perfectly."

"I have to have a dependable car," Bramlett said tersely. "If you can't get it to operate satisfactory, then we'll just have to assign it to someone else. I really enjoy it, but . . ." He didn't finish, but made a gesture indicating how unhappy he'd be to have to give up his vehicle.

Whitehead left, and Robertson stepped into the office. He handed Bramlett a photo copy of Shamona Clouse's job application from Adamstown Furniture. He then showed him the names from the address book that were new.

"Check them out," Bramlett said. "See if they can tell us anything about Rory Hornsly."

As Robertson walked out, H. C. Curry walked in. He was scowling.

"What?" asked Bramlett.

"I went with Lizzie last night to tell her aunt about Mrs. Winter," he said. "She didn't make much sense, but—"

The buzz of Bramlett's intercom interrupted. It was Ella Mae. "Sheriff Bramlett," she said, "we've just had a call from the police department at Corinth," she said. "They've picked up Patterson Clouse."

"Good," Bramlett said. "We'll send somebody up to get him." Corinth was only twenty miles away. They should have Clouse here within the hour.

Curry cleared his throat, then said, "You mind if I call Lizzie? I mean, and let her know?"

Bramlett tried to stretch the muscles in his back. "No," he said softly. "Go ahead. Curry left at once.

Bramlett stood up and looked out the window. The wind was picking up. The chill factor was probably below zero already. He held up his arms and stretched his back again. Then he returned to his desk and shuttled through the Rory Hornsly file. Too much of all this simply didn't make any sense.

Ten minutes later, he walked out of his office. Lizzie Clouse had already arrived and was standing beside H. C. Curry's desk. She didn't live very far away. Only a few blocks. He started walking toward them.

Lizzie noticed him and turned her back as if she didn't want to see him. He halted and went to the water fountain, drank, and returned to his office and to the Hornsly folder. No, too much of this didn't make any sense. Not at all.

Ella Mae buzzed when the unit called in that it was arriving in the parking lot. Bramlett stepped to his doorway to wait.

He didn't have to wait long. In moments, a deputy led a handcuffed Patterson Clouse inside the office suite.

Lizzie ran to her father. She threw her arms around his neck and began crying. Her face was pressed into his shoulder. With cuffed hands he couldn't hold her, but he pressed the side of his head against her head and smiled.

Bramlett moved toward them. He indicated with a slight nod to the deputy to take Clouse to the conference room. Curry stepped to Lizzie's side and put his arm around her.

"I want to go with him," she said.

"Not now," he whispered. "He's going to be okay."

Bramlett and Jacob Robertson followed Clouse and the escorting deputy into the conference room. Once inside, the handcuffs were removed, and Clouse, Bramlett, and Robertson sat down at the table. The deputy stood against the wall.

Bramlett crossed his arms and looked at the man for a long

time. Clouse's gaze was directed at the wall to the right. He didn't meet the sheriff's look.

"Innocent men don't usually run away, Patterson," Bramlett began. He waited for a response. There was none.

Bramlett continued. "There was a fire and a man is dead. A trailer fire. Do you know anything about that?"

Clouse looked back at the sheriff. There was a blankness in his eyes. He said nothing.

"Gale Lonsdale? Did you know him?"

Clouse made a face, then shook his head. "Never heard of him."

"He was the man who found the body of Lydia Gressete out on a logging road."

"I said I never heard of him."

"Lonsdale died when his trailer burned. We found a gas can at the scene of the fire. The gas can has only one set of prints on it. Your prints, Patterson." Bramlett watched the man's face closely for the slightest reaction. He saw only a confused look.

"Maybe it would refresh your memory to see this can," Bramlett said. He looked at Robertson and gave a nod.

The deputy rose from the table and left the room. Bramlett said nothing until he returned. In his hand was a two-gallon metal gasoline can painted red. Robertson set the can down in the middle of the table.

"Now," Bramlett said. "Do you recognize this can?"

Clouse squinted at the gas can for a moment, then cocked his head slightly. "Yes, sir," he said slowly. "I believe I do . . ."

"Oh?" asked Bramlett. "Is it yours?"

Clouse pouted his lower lip and shook his head. Then he said, "No, sir, it ain't mine. That be Mr. Matthew's gas can."

Bramlett swallowed the sudden thickness in his throat. "Matthew Farris?" he asked.

Clouse grunted, then said, "I do yard work for him and Miz Esther. I do their grass."

Bramlett stared at the can. Of course. A man wearing latex gloves could easily handle a can like this one and never leave a print. And that same man could know all along that whoever's prints were already on the can would fall under suspicion.

"Tell me, Patterson," Bramlett then said. "After your wife was killed, wasn't it Matthew Farris who arranged an attorney for you? Seems like he was around your family all the time then."

Clouse nodded. "Yes, sir. He's always been a friend of our family."

Bramlett took a deep, even breath, exhaled slowly, then forced a smile. "Thank you, Patterson," he said.

The sheriff then rose and left the room. Lizzie Clouse was sitting at H. C. Curry's desk. Curry sat in a folding metal chair beside her. Bramlett walked over to them. "You can go in to him now," he said to her. "Then you might want to take him home."

Lizzie stood quickly and hurried toward the conference room.

Bramlett turned to Curry. "Find out what unit is closest to Sheffield College," he said. "Have them pick up Dr. Matthew Farris."

"Yes, sir," the deputy replied, and turned toward the dispatcher's desk.

# 37

"Sheriff," Ella Mae called to him. "Deputy Robertson is on line two for you."

Bramlett made a gesture with his hand in acknowledgment that he heard her and returned to his office. Robertson had gone to Ripley to talk to a man whose name had been in Rory Hornsly's address book. He was a insurance agent named Tommy West.

"What you got, Jacob?" Bramlett asked.

"I'm here with Mr. West in Ripley," Robertson said. "He's been telling me that he and Hornsly were at Sheffield College together. Hornsly had tried to interest him in the clay deal, but Mr. West didn't go for it. Anyway, he was telling me how none of his old college crowd was around now except Hornsly and Roach. And you'll never guess who Roach—"

"Matthew Farris, by any chance?" interrupted Bramlett.

There was a moment of silence on the other end of the line, then Robertson said softly, "Yes, sir."

"Let me speak to Mr. West."

"This is Tommy West," said a deep voice.

"Mr. West, this is Sheriff Bramlett. We appreciate your help." As he spoke, the sheriff flipped the pages in Hornsly's file until he came to the sheet he was looking for. It was the list of names originally found in Rory Hornsly's apartment. In the margin beside the word Roach was written "Black Snow."

"What can you tell me about Black Snow?"

"Black Snow?" West repeated the phrase as if wondering what the sheriff was asking. Then he said, "Ah, damn. That's does go back. Hell, I'd forgotten all about that. It had to do with Roach's girl."

279

"Girl?"

"We were all drunk one night and he told us he saw this gal whenever he went home. Of course, he didn't live but a few miles from the college and he went home just about every weekend. They'd meet in some barn, I think he said. Anyway, we were drunk and he told us. So we teased him a lot, called her the Snow Queen at first, because he was so snowed by her. Of course, as you can imagine, once we were sober, he denied there was anything to it."

"Do you know her name?"

"Naw. If he ever said, I forgot. Then, later, we started calling her the Black Snow." There was a pause, then, "Say. I do remember something now. About her name. It was a funny first name, but the last name was Winter. That's where the snow came from, I guess."

"Why *black* snow?" Bramlett asked, although he already knew the answer.

West gave a quick laugh. "Because she was colored, of course. And that was back in the early sixties, Sheriff. Do you remember what Mississippi was like then?"

Bramlett thanked Tommy West, spoke to Robertson again, then hung up the phone.

He walked down to the dispatcher's desk. "Any word on whether they've got Matthew Farris yet?" he asked Deputy Thompson.

"Unit three is on the campus," Thompson said.

"Let me know as soon as they've got him."

"Yes, sir."

Bramlett returned to his office and paced the floor in front of his desk until Deputy Thompson called him on the intercom that unit three was on its way back to town with the professor.

The sheriff walked out of his office and to the doorway leading to the parking lot. Curry joined him, and together they stood looking through the glass door as a patrol car parked. Two deputies took Matthew Farris out of the car and began walking him toward the building.

"Did you know Moses married a black woman?" Curry asked him.

"What?" mumbled Bramlett.

"Moses. You know, in the Bible."

The sheriff smiled. "So Farris was no Moses, the old woman

said," he said. Then he added, "Tell them to bring him into the conference room." Bramlett turned and walked away.

Bramlett was already sitting at the table when Matthew Farris was escorted inside the room. The sheriff did not look up at the man, but rather studied the open file folder in front of him.

The deputies pushed Farris down into a chair, then stepped back and stood by the wall. Robertson and Curry took their places at the table also. Johnny Baillie positioned a tape recorder on the table and pressed down the Record button.

"Please state your name and address," Bramlett said to him.

Farris's eyes had a glazed, almost drunken look. "What?" he asked.

Bramlett repeated the question, and this time the man stated his name and address in a low voice. "The deputies have already informed you of your rights," the sheriff continued. "Is this not so?"

"Why am I here?" Farris asked.

"Please answer."

"Yes, yes. But what is it you think I've done?"

Bramlett looked down at a form in front of him and read, " 'We have decided that it suits our purposes to merely record our conversation rather than to go into a written statement. Is that agreeable with you?' "

"Please," Farris said. "I haven't done anything wrong."

"Would you answer the question," Bramlett said coldly, looking up at Farris over his reading glasses.

Farris made a gesture with his hand and said, "Sure. But I haven't done anything wrong. Why am I here?"

"We want to talk to you about Rory Hornsly, for one thing," said Bramlett, sliding the form to Robertson. The deputy took a pen out of his shirt pocket.

"I need to call my wife," Farris said.

"There's a telephone on the counter over there," Bramlett said, motioning with his hand toward the far wall. "Just press nine for an outside line."

Farris rose unsteadily from his chair and moved to the counter. He punched the number on the phone. Then he turned his back to Bramlett.

After a few moments, he replaced the receiver. His hand was shaking. "She . . . she's not at home."

"You can try again later," said Bramlett. "Please sit down."

Farris returned to the table. He sank back down into his chair. "I don't want to say anything without Esther," he said.

"Fine," said Bramlett. "But while we wait for her to get home, why don't we just talk a little about Naresse."

His mouth sagged open. "What?" he asked.

"You were friends for many years."

"Yes," he said. "We were."

"Like brother and sister," Bramlett said, his eyes not missing the slightest movement of the man's face.

"W-what?"

"Like Abraham and Sarah," Bramlett said, smiling knowingly at the man.

Farris was hardly breathing. "I . . . I . . ." He closed his mouth and looked down at the top of the table.

"We know all about that," the sheriff continued. "And we know about Isaac and the fact your father sold Naresse's father his farmland for ten dollars." Bramlett paused, watching to see if these hammer-blow statements were having the desired effect on the man.

Farris's shoulders sagged all the more. He was silent for a long time. Bramlett waited. Finally, the man opened his mouth and spoke slowly, haltingly. "Yes. We loved each other since we were children." He paused. There was a heavy resignation in his voice. Then he continued. "Neither of us could ever remember a time when we weren't together." He paused again and shook his head. "We should have run off together thirty years ago, to California or someplace. *Any*place but here."

"Does your wife know?"

Farris sighed. "Yes. I've always told her everything. We have a completely honest relationship. It like to have killed her. She was so hurt. I swore before God it was over, but somehow it was always there. Neither Naresse or I could stop . . ." He paused, took several deep breaths, then continued. "And Esther was afraid if it became known, I'd lose my position. Then we never talked about it any more until . . ." He paused and shook his head slowly. He suddenly looked very tired.

"Until when?" Bramlett asked.

"Until this thing with Rory."

"You mean when Naresse was killed, y'all didn't talk about it?"

He shook his head. "There was nothing more to say."

"Okay," said Bramlett, leaning back in his chair. "Now tell me about Rory Hornsly."

Farris wiped his mouth with the back of his hand, then spoke. "Rory and I went to Sheffield College together. After he came back here a few years ago, he got me to invest in a business deal. He swindled me, actually, and I wanted my money back. I kept pressing him about it, then . . . Well, he'd known about Naresse and he said he was going to go to the college president or whoever would listen. It was very unpleasant. He said he was going to talk with Lizzie."

"How does she fit in?"

Farris closed his eyes and drew a jerky breath, swallowed, released the breath, then said, "It was a long time ago. She was just a child. Naresse and I were together in the barn . . . and she walked in on us. I don't think she really remembers . . ."

"But she possibly could identify you as her mother's lover."

Farris nodded.

"How did Hornsly know something like that?"

"Years ago I ran into him in New Orleans. We had a few drinks together. There was never anyone—not anyone, you see—that I could talk with about Naresse. And Rory already knew. He was my friend." He paused as if the ironic bitterness of that word describing their relationship just struck him.

"So Lizzie had to be eliminated before she would remember who she saw with her mother," said Bramlett.

"No, no. That's not the way it was."

"Did you try to kill Lizzie Clouse and shoot her sister Shamona instead?"

Farris's face glistened with perspiration. "No, I'm telling you the truth." He swallowed hard.

Bramlett grunted, looked down at his notes, and asked, "And Rory? He had to be silenced, too?"

Farris was panting. "What? What are you saying?"

"Did you kill Rory Hornsly?" Bramlett asked bluntly.

"No! Of course not! I never killed anyone. Surely you don't think . . ." He put his hands on the table. "Is that why I'm here? You think I killed Rory? You think I shot Shamona?"

"What about Naresse? Don't you want to tell us about her? Was she threatening you as well?"

"Naresse?" There was a confused look on his face.

"Let's take it from the beginning," said the sheriff. "Was she threatening you with exposure?"

Farris's shoulders sagged even more. "Why . . . yes," he said. "I suppose. She always wanted money. She always wanted more money . . ." He gave his head a hard shake. "Listen to me. I would never have harmed Naresse. I *loved* her. Can't you understand that?"

Bramlett pulled four photos from the folder and stood up. He walked around the table and leaned over Farris's shoulder and placed each photo on the table in front of the man. "Look at the woman you loved so much, Matthew," he said, tapping his finger on the photograph of Naresse Clouse hanging by her neck from the loft in the barn. "You loved her so much you killed her and hung her up in y'all's Cave of Machpelah."

"No . . ." said Farris. "I . . . I loved her . . ."

"I know," Bramlett said, "*Love is as strong as death.*"

"*. . . and jealousy as cruel as the grave,*" muttered Deputy Johnny Baillie.

"What?" snapped Bramlett, glaring at the deputy. He didn't like interruptions when he was interrogating.

Baillie shrugged and looked away. "Sorry," he said. "Just finishing the quote."

Bramlett glared at the deputy for a moment, then looked back at Farris. "Look, dammit," he said, tapping the picture of Rory Hornsly lying beside his car on the wet parking lot. "You've told me this man was threatening you. So you shot him. I can understand that. Now he wasn't going to tell anybody anything."

"No, please," Farris said, shutting his eyes tight and turning his face away. "It wasn't me."

"Look!" Bramlett said through his teeth. "Look at this woman on the road in the woods where you dumped her. Lydia Gressete knew, didn't she? Naresse had told her about the two of you and she knew. What did she want? Money? Is that why you killed her?"

Farris's face was very pale. "Stop it!" he said, refusing to look at the picture. "Stop it!" He began gagging.

"And this is the body of Gale Lonsdale. Do you remember him?"

Bramlett looked at the photo taken after the fire. Then he

looked back at the picture of the Gressete woman lying beside the road where she'd been dumped.

The body was lying beside a small tree with twisted limbs, and beside the tree was a much larger tree, like an oak. The small tree had no leaves, but . . . could it be a dogwood?

He squinted at the picture, and tried to remember another one.

Then he looked up at Curry, then at Robertson. "Shit!" he said. "Throw him in a cell and hold him."

He snatched up the photograph of the Lydia Gressete crime scene and picked up his folder. "H.C.," he said, "come with me." Then he hurried through the door.

Just outside the room, Bramlett stopped and looked at Curry. He started to explain what he'd just understood, then shook his head. There wasn't time. "Come on," he said.

He hurried toward the door to the parking lot. In his brain now thundered the phrase, *and jealousy as cruel as the grave.*

# 38

Sheriff Grover Bramlett turned the steering wheel hard at the corner, and the tires squealed as he drove through the turn.

Curry braced himself against the dashboard. "I don't understand . . ." he said.

Bramlett reached down and flipped the switch to the warning lights. He certainly didn't want to wreck this car and have to go back to driving that damn butt-pinching little Corvette. "Listen," he said tersely. "I've got to check something at my house."

In less than three minutes the car bounced up into the driveway of his house and screeched to a halt. With the photograph in hand, he rushed inside. Curry followed.

In the den he stood in front of the framed photograph on the wall. The photograph was of a woods scene in early spring. The center of interest was a dogwood, the sunlight dancing on the white petals, the hardwoods of the forest just coming into leaf, and at the base of the tree, peeking through the leaves, was a rusty bucket, a bucket discarded no doubt by a farmer many years before and now slowly dissolving into the earth.

He looked down at the crime scene photo in his hand. Curry stood beside him, looking from one photo to the other also.

The picture in the sheriff's hand was a winter scene. A woman's body laying on the side of a logging road. But the tree, without the leaves, was very possibly the same. The angle was different. He couldn't tell for—

Then he looked up at Esther Farris's photo again. The bucket. "Damn!" he said.

"What?" Curry asked.

"That bucket."

The deputy looked again from one picture to the other, then he looked at the sheriff, his eyes widening in sudden comprehension. "Out at the crime scene, you like to broke your neck on a . . ." Curry took a step back. "Oh, shit!" he said.

"Where's Lizzie?"

"She's still with her father."

"Phone her."

"They don't have a phone."

"Damn!" said Bramlett. He turned and hurried toward the outside door. "Let's move!" he said.

With H. C. Curry now at the wheel of the patrol car, they raced down the state highway toward the Hebron community. "She knew that place," Bramlett said, referring to Esther Farris. "She knew that was a place where she could get rid of Lydia Gressete's body."

"But why?" Curry asked, pulling into the left lane to pass a battered pickup.

"Farris said he told his wife everything. She knew about Naresse and her requests for money. She wanted to protect him, probably. And then there's jealousy. Cruel as the grave." Bramlett remembered what Keesa Hudnall had said about Esther and Matthew getting into a spat at the Wisteria Inn. And Naresse had just been to their table, he said.

"But why Lizzie? Why now?"

"She's still trying to protect him," he said, referring to Esther again. "He must have told her about Lizzie walking in on him and Naresse when she was a girl. Lizzie can identify him as the lover."

"This is crazy."

"Can't you go faster?" Bramlett said, pushing his hand against the dashboard. "Hell. I should have driven myself."

Esther Farris slowed down as she rounded the curve, and the shack of a house came into view. Her eyes fell at once on the turquoise Mitsubishi parked in front of the house. Esther smiled. Good. Very good. She's here. Esther had figured she would be with Patterson.

She stared at the house as she passed. Smoke from the chimney. A pickup truck parked on the side. Probably just her and Patterson inside.

Not far past the house on the opposite side of the road began a pine thicket. As she drove by, Esther looked at the trees. There. She saw an opening, an old road it looked like, into the trees.

She drove a little farther, then stopped and carefully turned around in the middle of the road and drove back. She stopped beside the opening. Yes, a road, somewhat overgrown with shag grass and small bushes, but she could get in. She was glad the Buick had front wheel drive in case the ground was muddy. It wouldn't do to get stuck right now.

She slowly backed into the opening, then stopped and turned off the engine. The nose of the car was only a few feet from the road. And through the trees she could watch the house.

She took a deep breath, and placed her hand on the 9 mm semiautomatic on the seat beside her.

Now what? Well, she'd just wait. If nothing happened, then she'd just have to go to the house. She liked Patterson, felt a certain strange kinship with him in that they were both wronged by their spouses, but . . . well, if the only way to take care of her was to take care of him, then that's just how it would have to be . . .

# 39

Lizzie looked at her watch. It was just after two o'clock. Her father was lying on top of the covers in his bedroom, fully dressed in clean clothes after his hot bath. He'd eaten the lunch she prepared quickly and with obvious pleasure. As he ate she watched him, wondering what was going on in his mind.

She wished she could say something about Mama, say something about the fact that in spite of what Sheriff Bramlett was saying about Matthew and Naresse, she knew Naresse truly loved her husband in her own way. She was convinced this was so. Was it possible to love two men at the same time?

She'd never had much time for love herself. She supposed she loved H.C. He was a good man, and, no doubt, would one day achieve his ambition to be elected sheriff. And Sheriff Bramlett could retire in a couple of years and the way would be open for him.

But did she love him enough to marry him? She wasn't sure. It seemed her mind had been so fastened on doing well at Ole Miss, graduating, then succeeding as a high school teacher, that she'd had little time to think about love.

Before leaving town, they'd gone to the hospital to see Shamona. She was asleep and the nurse said she was doing great. Patterson Clouse and Lizzie stood holding hands looking down at her for a few minutes before leaving.

They stopped by the florist's on the way home. This was her mother's birthday, and ever since she'd awakened that morning she knew if she did nothing else today, she had to take flowers to the cemetery. She bought a nice bunch of daisies. White. Her mother's favorite.

She stepped into the bedroom and stood beside the bed. His eyes were closed but she knew he wasn't asleep. "I'm going on to take the flowers to the graveyard now," she said. "You want to come?"

"No," he said in a choked voice. He didn't open his eyes.

"I won't be long." She leaned down and kissed him on the forehead. "I love you, Daddy."

"I love you, too, baby girl," he said.

She slipped on the dark-blue wool coat Cynthia had loaned her. The sheriff's folks still had her leather coat. She really wasn't sure if she wanted it back. She went out onto the front porch. Across the road crows perched high in a dead tree with most of its limbs fallen off and shouted at each other.

Lizzie buttoned her coat all the way to the neck and walked to her car. She got in, started the engine, backed around in the front yard, and drove onto the road.

As she passed the woods on the left, she thought she saw a car. A gray car parked on the old road the pulpwood cutters used. Some hunter, she supposed. Was it still deer season? Probably.

A bit farther on the left, the tight forest of hardwoods rolled past and the barn was approaching. The thought of snakes immediately popped into her mind. She pressed her lips together. There were no snakes there. Her mother hadn't wanted her to go there for fear she'd stumble on to something. From a dark corner of her mind Lizzie could clearly see her mother standing over her, yelling at her. And someone else was there, standing near by.

She pressed the accelerator, kept her eyes straight ahead, and in moments she was by the barn, speeding onward. Then she was past it, and she realized she hadn't been breathing.

Her eye caught a dead possum on the left side of the road, probably hit the night before, and then she came out of a curve and the white church appeared.

As she slowed to turn off the road, she glanced in the rearview mirror and saw the gray car behind her, not close, but coming.

She parked in the graveled parking lot. The other vehicle went on past. She hadn't seen many deer around lately anyway. She assumed the hunter hadn't gotten one.

She walked across the cemetery to her mother's grave. Her

little brother's plastic flowers had blown over again. She straightened them, then lay the daisies in front of the headstone and stepped back, still looking at the stone. Her legs were cold, and she shoved her hands deeper into the pockets of the coat.

"Happy birthday, Mama," she said out loud. "I miss you. I love you."

She heard a vehicle approaching and looked up. The gray car was back and was parking near her car.

Someone got out, looked in her direction, then looked around toward the church, then back at Lizzie. There was something familiar . . .

Lizzie first recognized it was a woman, and, a split second later, that it was Matthew's wife, Esther. What in the world? She never comes to Hebron.

The woman started toward the cemetery. Lizzie recalled seeing her at Hudnall's that day rushing around, dropping the gas pump nozzle. Her eyes had such a look of fright, of terror almost. And she was wearing a heavy jacket. And—now that she thought about it—that day when she saw Esther Farris in such a tizzy at Hudnall's was the same day her mother had died.

She watched the woman now walking slowly toward her. She was almost halfway and she carried her right arm down at her side in an odd manner and . . .

Lizzie saw the gun in the woman's hand.

"Oh, my—?" she gasped.

Lizzie looked around quickly. The woods were only a few yards away. She looked back at the woman. She was walking faster, and now raising her arm.

Lizzie turned and broke into a run. At once there was an explosion like a clap of thunder against the side of her ear. Sharp. Loud.

Her heart likewise exploded in her chest. And she ran for the trees. There was a second shot, and she wasn't sure whether she was hit or not.

She reached the first large tree and ducked behind, her eyes jumping about, looking for a place to hide. She pushed a twisted vine aside with the back of her hand and rushed through some brush and scrambled down the embankment of the creek where she and Shamona had played so many times

with the other children of the church when they were children.

She jumped into the water and the icy wetness wrapped
around her legs. She paused for a moment and heard the crack-
ling of brush and knew the woman was coming. Lizzie surged
forward through the water and around a little bend.

She stepped into a deeper place and the water folded around
her waist. She quickly moved to the side and put her hand to a
gnarled and exposed root of a tree on the bank to steady herself, and tried to remember where the cave cupped out of the
creek bank was. It had been so many years . . .

No time. She scrambled up out of the creek on the opposite
bank and *bang!* Another shot. This one thudding into a large
tree to her right. She fell through a matted cluster of vines and
scooted behind the trunk of a large sweetgum.

She waited. At first she heard nothing. No doubt the woman
was listening for her. She strained to hear. Her breathing was
jerky. Then a limb cracked. She could hear her moving slowly,
obviously not far away. She pressed her body against the tree,
trying to squeeze herself into it, if she could.

The woman was probably standing on the other side of the
creek, looking in her direction. She held her breath. The wind
whistled through the leafless trees.

Then she heard a splash, and she knew the woman must
have noticed where she'd slid down the embankment into the
creek. She must have seen her tracks in the mud.

Lizzie slowly turned her head. Could she rush off farther
away? Now? Her legs were jelly.

Carefully, she looked around the tree. The woman was in
the middle of the creek, slowly wading upstream in Lizzie's
direction. She was holding the pistol up and looking from one
side of the bank to the other. In a minute or two she would be
right beside the tree Lizzie was hiding behind.

Lizzie waited. Why was this woman trying to kill her? What
had Lizzie ever done—

Then she understood. She understood why Esther Farris was
in such a panic at Hudnall's that day. She had just left the
barn. She had left the barn where she'd killed Naresse Clouse
and . . .

Lizzie took several deep breaths. She clenched her fists and
looked around the tree. The woman was parallel to her.

Lizzie whirled around the tree and dived right at the woman in the creek.

Esther Farris turned her head just as Lizzie came crashing into her. Together, locked in each other's arms, they plunged into the freezing creek.

Lizzie gulped a mouthful of water and choked and at the same time dug her fingers into the woman's face. She felt the woman grasping her by the hair and the neck, and, in that instant, realized she'd dropped the gun.

The two of them rolled through the shallow water.

Lizzie was pounding at her and the woman was punching at her and both were choking and hissing and snorting. They clawed and slashed with their hands. Lizzie thought she heard a shout. And another.

Suddenly, the woman was on top of her, holding her head below the water. Lizzie reached down, trying to push against the bottom. Her hand fumbled at a stone, a heavy stone about the size of a baseball, and her fingers clutched it. At the same time, she jerked her head to one side and sank her teeth into the hand.

The woman released her, and Lizzie surged up out of the water and swung her arm, crashing the stone against the side of the woman's jaw.

Esther Farris fell backward and her head landed on the side of the creek bank. Lizzie was immediately on her, clutching the front of her blouse with her left hand and raising the stone with the other, holding it high, looking down at the face and eyes of the woman who had killed her mother. She wanted to crush that face, to pound it until it was no longer a face.

She held her hand hovering in the air with the stone. Esther Farris's eyes were locked with her eyes. She was breathing heavily and suddenly was struggling no more, but rather, waiting for Lizzie to strike. There was a resignation in her eyes as if the final death blow would be welcomed, that somehow it would end the hurt.

"Lizzie!" a voice said, and she was aware that she'd heard it a couple of times already. It was H.C.

She released the woman's blouse and lowered her hand. She looked up onto the creek bank. Sheriff Bramlett, his chest heaving, was standing beside H.C.

She looked back to the face of Esther Farris. The woman's

eyes were closed and her mouth distorted as she gave an agonized sob.

Lizzie slammed the stone down into the water. She then pushed herself up and climbed the bank. H.C. reached out his hands and helped her up.

All three of them stood looking down at Esther Farris. Her head rested in the mud of the bank and the swirling water of the creek washed over her. She made no attempt to get up. She was crying.

Bramlett looked at Deputy Curry. "I guess you'll have to go down and pull her out," he said. "Then let's get out of here. This wind is tough." He looked at Lizzie. "We've got blankets in the car."

She nodded at him and turned away and walked back toward the cemetery. She couldn't feel the cold of the wet clothes and the wind. She couldn't feel anything.